NO SAFE HARBOR

A Novel

by

Robert Shemeld

The final approval for this literary material is granted by the author

First printing

This is a work of fiction. Names, characters, businesses, places, events, and incidents are either the products of the author's imagination or used in a fictitious manner. Any resemblance to actual persons, living or dead, or actual events is purely coincidental.

PUBLISHED BY
Robert Shemeld

Printed in the United States of America

'Desperate Affairs Require Desperate Measures.'
Vice Admiral Lord Horatio Nelson

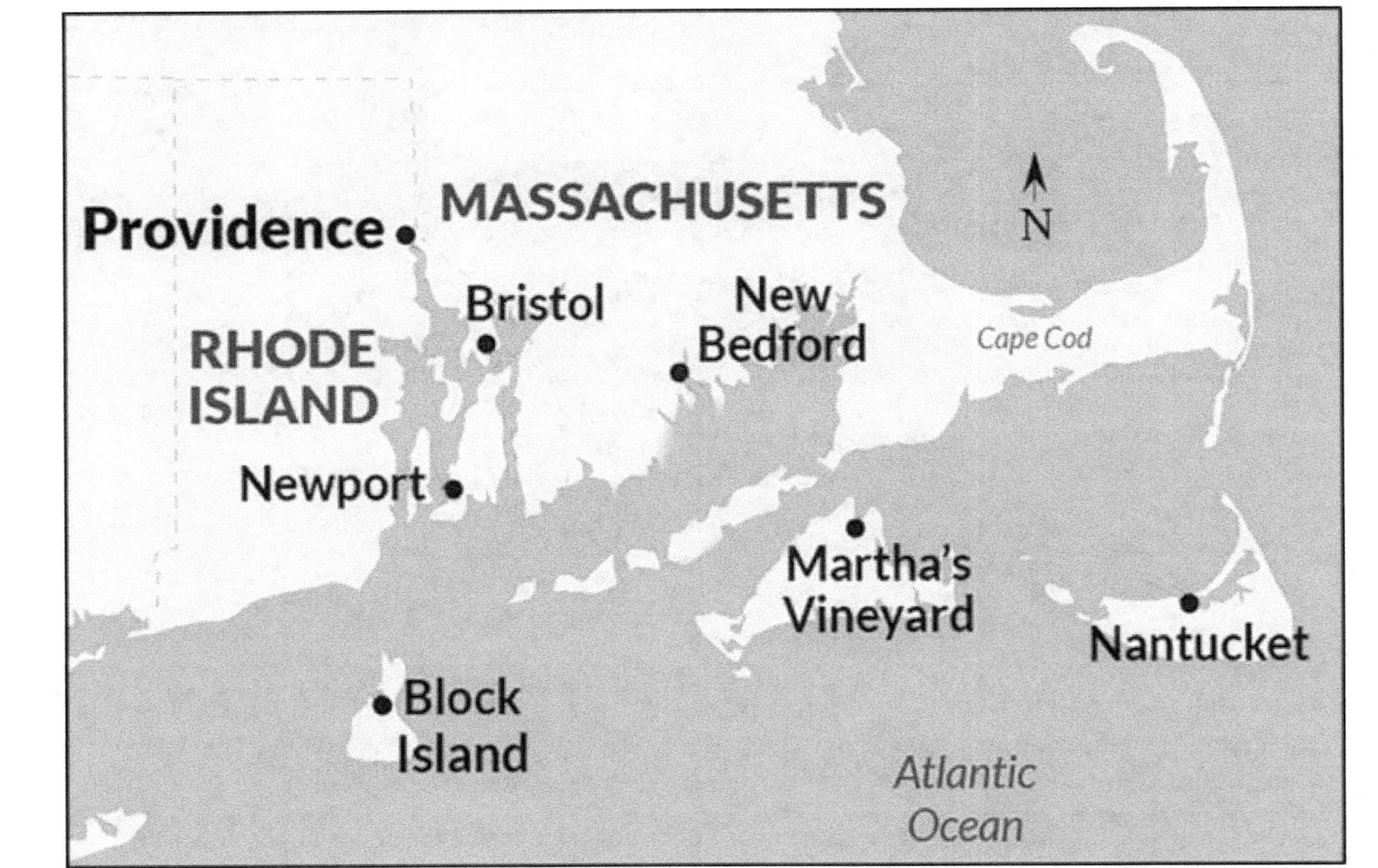
Providence
MASSACHUSETTS
N
Bristol
New
Bedford
Cape Cod
RHODE
ISLAND
Newport
Martha's
Vineyard
Nantucket
Block
Island
Atlantic
Ocean

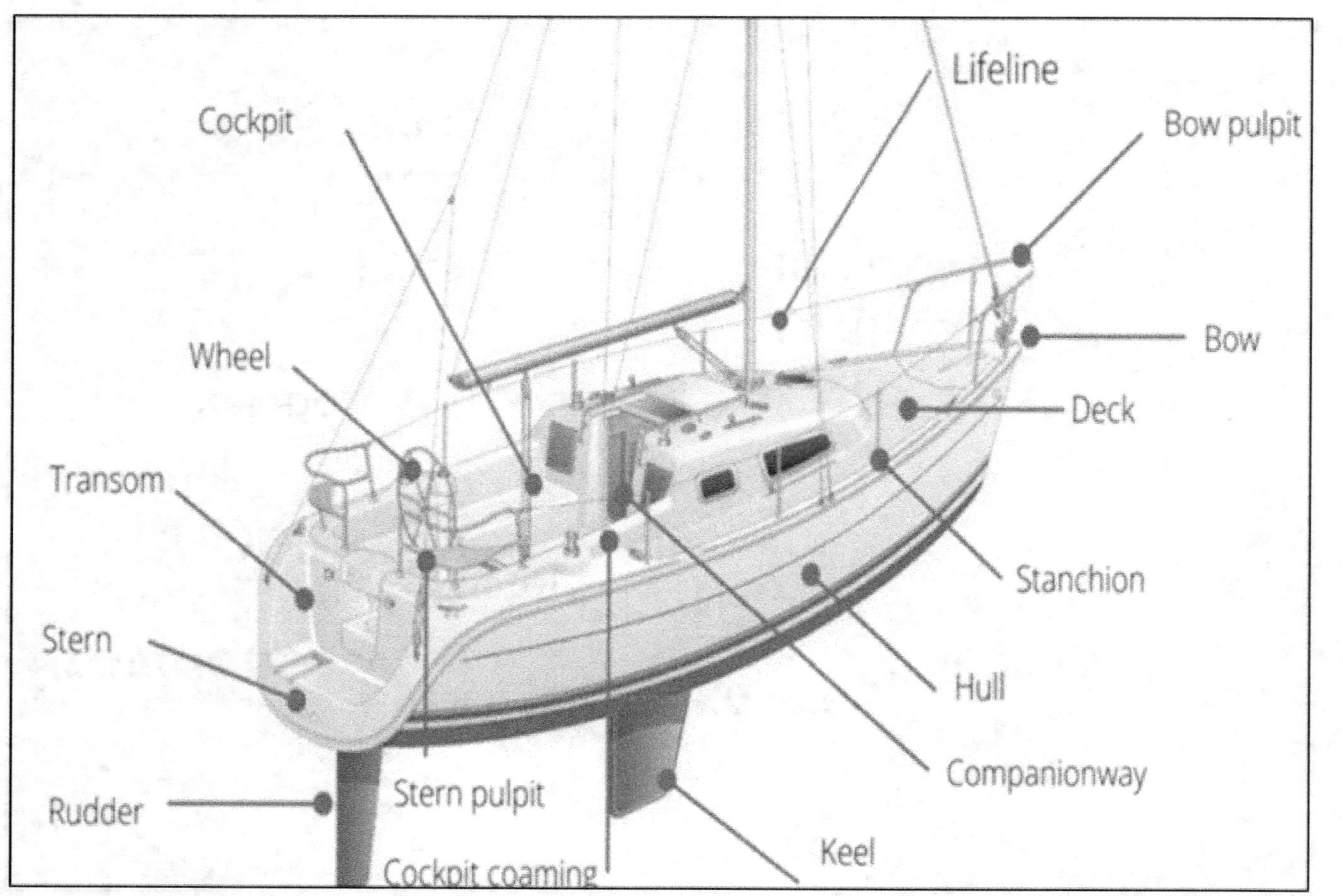

Cockpit
Lifeline
Bow pulpit
Wheel
Bow
Deck
Transom
Stanchion
Stern
Hull
Companionway
Rudder
Stern pulpit
Cockpit coaming
Keel

Prologue

He looked again at the lifeless heap on the deck, the dead eyes still watching, frozen in disbelief, as blood and urine drained into the scuppers. Killing had been easy. Disposing of the body was the hard part.

It wasn't premeditated. He'd wanted information, not a corpse, but a struggle and gun had cheated him out of the information he desperately sought. And now, like the proverbial albatross, he had this corpse. He laughed at the metaphor—*albatross*. How appropriate.

He was tired, wet, and frustrated; the entire affair had been a fiasco. On the positive side, it was a dark, moonless night, with plenty of seclusion, and the rain was a plus. He guessed the boat was providential, too. It was a good place and a good time to kill.

He was not handy with boats, not that he disliked them. He hadn't been around many, and none this large. Yes, it was a simple matter to turn on the engine and put it in gear. The problem was with all the ropes and lines that obstinately held the damn boat in place. What really riled him, as he manhandled the thing out of the dock, was the open steering area that offered no protection from the incessant rain. The thing must have cost a fortune. Why not spend a couple of extra bucks on a roof?

Navigation was another matter. He knew about GPS and radar, and fortunately, the boat had both. It had been an hour or more since he had extracted himself from the dock and there had been nothing on the radar except some *sea return*. Some five miles out, he could still see lights to the west from Fort Lauderdale. Freeport was somewhere to the northeast but too far away to see, as was Bimini to the southeast.

His biggest worry was running into the Coast Guard before he could dump the body. His goal was to get well into the Gulf Stream, which he calculated to be another ten miles from his present position. At the boat's current speed, the whole trip would take eight hours and get him back to the dock at about five in the morning. That might cut it a little thin. There were a lot of people out at five in the morning. If he could just get the damn boat to move faster.

It started with a quiet dinner at his favorite restaurant: grilled swordfish, mashed sweet potatoes, and broccoli, with a pleasant Riesling. Over dessert, he saw him—sitting next to the window, four tables away, the man he had been hunting for three years. Long thought to be in South America, some said dead, others said in a Cuban prison, Alberto Pérez was sitting in Fort Lauderdale, drinking a glass of wine. The older and grayer image belied decades of international intrigue, espionage, assassination, and, finally, drugs and murder.

Discreetly as possible, he paid his bill and walked to the front door and out of the restaurant. The early evening had turned to late evening. The darkness brought with it a light, steady summer rain that cooled and cleaned the air, a welcome relief from the hot and humid Florida summer.

At the rear of the restaurant, he found his car, then drove back to the street. He parked at the curb, staying far enough up the street to be unobtrusive but close enough to see customers passing through the front door of the restaurant. He waited and watched, periodically using the wipers to clear rain from the windshield. About forty-five minutes later, Alberto came out through the front door, turned right, walked down the sidewalk about half a block, and got into a silver Lincoln.

For the next several days, it was a game of cat and mouse until the last day, the day Alberto died.

The rain flattened what little sea chop there was, reducing the likelihood of *mal de mer*, but he was chilled from the constant wet. He assumed there was some type of automatic pilot, but its operation had eluded him and, not wanting to risk going below to look for a jacket, he remained wet and cold. Perhaps a jacket or a raincoat should have been a prior consideration, but when you are killing someone, most other things seem secondary. In addition, the gunshot could easily have attracted attention, so getting away from the dock took precedence.

When the GPS said he was fifteen miles from shore, he slid the transmission into neutral. The boat lost its way and drifted in the light air. He calculated that shortening his trip to fifteen miles would cut two hours off his running time. That would get him back to Fort Lauderdale closer to three o'clock. Much better than five, he thought.

Shutting off the engine, he listened. Other than the rain and the gentle slap of water against the hull, there were no sounds. Seeing nothing on the radar, he lifted the body to the side of the boat. He double-checked the man's pockets for anything that could identify the corpse. With any luck, if it didn't sink, the Gulf Stream would have the body in Ireland before it was discovered.

Fatigue and cold had sapped his strength, so lifting the dead weight was difficult, more difficult than he had imagined, and there were the extraneous legs and arms to contend with. Eventually, he stuffed everything through the stanchions, then, after a final push—a satisfying splash as the body hit the water. It briefly sank, then floated to the surface, air in the clothing still providing buoyancy. Well, there was nothing he could do about it. Presumably, the body would eventually sink as air bled out of the clothing.

He turned on the engine, pushed the gearshift forward, and steered the boat back toward land. He still had to clean up the blood, but first he had to get back to the dock without being noticed and before the boat was missed.

CHAPTER ONE

Army Navy Country Club - Arlington, Virginia

I was in the Grille of the Army Navy Country Club, just south of Washington, D.C., in Arlington, Virginia. Looking over the menu, I was trying to decide between the angus burger and cob salad when I felt a tap on my shoulder. I looked up.

"Bob! Bob Osborne," I said.

"It is you! How the hell are you?" Osborne said.

"I'm great! Last I heard, you were playing James Bond in the far east. Please, sit down."

Bob Osborne was an old friend from years gone by when we were both working for the government.

"Okay, for a minute." Bob sat in one of the three reaming chairs at the table. "Yeah, I was station chief in Bangkok. But I pulled the pin. Amy and I bought a place in Great Falls."

"How is Amy? She know you're wearing that ugly shirt?" I said.

"Says the arbiter of fashion. I'll bet your polo shirt collection must exceed several thousand by now—" He laughed. "She's fine, she's still working, says if she has to live with me for more than two days in a row we'll be divorced in a month. How's Elizabeth?"

"Liz is fine. I think she's a little sad the kids are out on their own."

"I see her around some. So, did they ever get you to join the company?"

"No, I played cops and robbers for a while, then when Liz and I got married, I started a commercial real estate business."

"Remember when the suits approached us in that scruffy bar, told us how innovative and resourceful we were . . . just the people they wanted for the job—"

"I remember. Baghdad, right? But it wasn't for me, for a lot of reasons. You did Okay."

"No complaints. Almost got waxed in Kosovo, but I'm out now."

"Listen, how about the four of us throw some steaks on the grill sometime soon?"

"You got it. Look, I have to run, but I'll call you. Great seeing you. Give my best to Liz."

Bob stood, we shook hands, and he walked out of the grill.

CHAPTER TWO

By anyone's definition, Newport, Rhode Island, is the naissance of yachting. I savored the 160 years of history each time I literally and figuratively ghosted into the harbor. I could almost see Charlie Barr at the helm of the largest sloop ever built, his 200-foot *Reliance* with its ninety-foot mast and 17,000 square feet of sail battling against Lipton's *Shamrock III*.

On September 3, 1903, a cannon crashed, starting the historic sea battle between the United States and the Tea King. Sailors on each side yelled, strained, and cursed as they fought to bring the two goliaths into the fight, each trying for early dominance in one of the greatest match races of all time. One hundred years later, the boats and the men that sailed that race are still venerated.

This latest visit to Newport was special because now I was aboard my aquatic leviathan, *Pinafore*. Although it didn't approach the stature of my predecessors, I thought of our entrance into the harbor as sharing the heritage with the great captains, Vanderbilt, Sopwith, and Lipton, who drove the equally famous yachts *Valkyrie* and *Rainbow* in colossal battles for the Auld Mug. I was *sharing* history with the contemporary captains such as Ted Turner and Dennis Conner, skippers of the smaller, but no less famous, *Courageous* and *Stars & Stripes*. *Pinafore* and I were part of the history and the tradition, or so I imagined for a few wonderful moments.

I couldn't have imagined my sea battle was days away and I would be fighting for my life.

The dock master looked to be about twenty. I guessed college help for the summer. Cute, tan with short blond hair and sunglasses, she was dressed in khaki shorts and a khaki short-sleeve safari shirt with obligatory boat shoes. I received a polite smile presumably reserved for us old harmless guys. She snagged my bowlines and secured them to the dock with an experienced flourish, then waited while I wrestled with the stern lines.

All secured, I used the shrouds to swing to the dock in my best Tarzan impression, just to prove I could. I signed her registration book with a promise to show up at the office with my credit card. Another smile, a "thank-you," and she was off to help a boat two slips away. I rigged a spring line, shut off the engine, and then connected the shore power.

Getting to late afternoon, the shadows had started their evening stretch and the stark white of daylight was warming to yellow. Bone tired and crusted with salt from days of sea spray, I was ready for a shower, then dinner on good old dry land. Nonetheless, I dutifully spent the next forty-five minutes washing down the boat with fresh water to remove the salt that had coated the deck, hull, and equipment.

I usually enjoyed washing the boat. It was a cooldown for both of us and an opportunity for me to look over the rigging and fittings for signs of stress, tears, and fraying. Sixteen tons of fiberglass and teak could get away from you in a hurry, especially single-handed. Better to do repairs at the dock instead of at sea in a thirty-knot wind.

The combination of shoeless feet and sailboats usually results in cuts or broken toes. When washing down the boat, I ignored the precaution of shoes because I liked the feel of the wet deck under my bare feet. It gave me a tactile connection with the boat as she gently moved with the water and wind. It sometimes felt like walking on the back of a huge, tethered marine beast as it waited impatiently to make a break for the open sea.

Pinafore is my most prized possession, and I am very proud of her. I have owned other boats, but *Pinafore* is my first and probably only "big boat." I bought her in Fort Lauderdale from a dentist's widow. She is a fifty-foot, aft cockpit, keel/centerboard. A mongrel one-off design reminiscent of the Niels Helleberg–designed *Alden* but with a shorter stick and a slightly deeper draft. Her bow and stern have that graceful overhang missing in the short, chopped bows now popular. The gleaming teak interior was copied from an older Bob Perry design with the head forward where the V berth is usually located. The main stateroom is immediately aft, with a Pullman bunk set into the portside parallel to the teak-lined hull. A built-in chest of drawers, vanity, and hanging locker is opposite the bunk. The design combines ample room with an old nautical look. I often imagine Sir Thomas Lipton or Harold Vanderbilt sleeping in a cabin of very much the same design. The main cabin includes a settee with a folding table, the galley, the navigation station, then, farthest aft, another guest cabin and a small head.

After I received an enthusiastic phone call from my best friend, Ed Colombo, I flew to Fort Lauderdale where the *Pinafore* was docked. I made a preliminary inspection of the boat and its equipment. The seller agreed to pay for the survey, so we made a deal. Aside from the rather dated electronics, there wasn't much I didn't like about the boat. Her moniker, *Pinafore,* was not first on my list of lusty, seafaring names. I had envisioned something similar to John MacDonald's *Busted Flush* or Garland Roark's *Red Witch*, but *Pinafore* was already emblazoned in gold leaf on her gleaming reverse transom, so *Pinafore* she remains. I installed the standard flat-panel TV and state-of-the-art entertainment system. (In this instance, "state-of-the-art" refers to equipment that fits the boat and my budget.) I also updated most of the electronic gear with a nod toward quality, at least the best I could afford. A fax machine/printer combination and a computer were already built into the navigation station. The computer was "last year's model" but serviceable. The diesel engine was new, as were the inverter and the generator. She had heat and air conditioning, though the latter didn't work. Best of all, she had electric primary winches and a bow thruster, which is like having another crewmember without having to feed him. Though if one had to amortize the cost of a bow thruster and two electric winches, it was probably about the same, but I didn't, so I was delighted.

Stories have been published in the cruising magazines, some true, some not, about encounters with the modern pirate. Real incidents have been frequent enough to rate a warning from the International Maritime Bureau that says in part "... there's nothing romantic about piracy. Contemporary pirates are ruthless, heavily armed and prey on people that are weaker than they—waters off Somalia and Indonesia are considered the most active for modern pirates."

I had no intention of sailing to Indonesia, but the IMB added, "the incidence of piracy has also increased in areas of Caribbean," and I was certainly planning cruises to the Caribbean. This brings me to a custom-built feature on the boat I call my "repel boarders locker." It is built into a void in one of the bulkheads and cleverly accessed from behind a framed print of the *Bonhomie Richard*. At the bottom of the print is a quote from Captain John Paul Jones: "*I wish to have no connection with any ship that does not sail fast, for I intend to go in harm's way.*" Going in harm's way was furthest from my thoughts, but the locker holds a Smith & Wesson Model 19, sometimes described as a .38-caliber pistol on steroids, a Model 1911A1 Colt Automatic, a Beretta TX4 shotgun, and an M14. The M14 is a Vietnam-era rifle still used in competition. A military version with a selector can fire seven 750 rounds of 7.62 ammunition in a minute if you can load it fast enough. I never hoped to see a pirate, but I owned the weapons, so why leave them at home?

Pinafore and I were now soaking wet but desalted. I turned off the water, coiled the hose, and went below. I showered, using all the hot water, dried off, then sat behind the navigation desk with a cold beer from the icebox. Pulling out the charts, I went over the trip *Pinafore* and I had just completed. We had covered over 350 nautical miles, counting a stop at Cape May, New Jersey. Except for a thunderstorm off Atlantic City and catching a small but tasty grouper, the trip had been uneventful.

The sail from Annapolis, Maryland, was the first leg of our summer vacation that would take us from Newport to Block Island, Martha's Vineyard, and Nantucket, back to Block Island, and then the blue water sail back to Annapolis.

Elizabeth, my wife of fifteen years, had stayed at our home in northern Virginia to play in a series of summer concerts produced by the semiprofessional symphony orchestra in which she plays violin. In two days, she was flying into Providence, where she would rent a car and meet me at the boat. Thus far, it had been a lonely trip, and I was counting the hours until she arrived.

I grew up in rural Fairfax and Loudoun County, Virginia, in the days you could carry your favorite .22 rifle defending the countryside from the ever-present menace of crows. Later in high school, my brothers and I shot competitively, and when I had a few bucks, I bought rifles from the Division of Civilian Marksmanship and soon had a sizable collection. The years passed, and when firearms became my portfolio of office and tools of the trade, my interests turned to cars, then to sailing.

Like many other guys with similar backgrounds, I reached majority in a sordid region of oppressing heat, talcum like dust, unrelenting flies, and the dank smell of mold, cooking pots, and diesel fuel. I and other pubescent boys saw and experienced things that no man should be subjected to, regardless of age. However, like so many before and since, we fulfilled our destiny as child warriors. I went to college on the G.I. Bill, spent some time as a county police officer and detective, then later worked as a private investigator for a large corporation. The prospect of providing for a wife and two small children required more practical employment and, by luck rather than design, I parlayed a real estate broker's license into a moderately successful real estate business. The children, now in their twenties, have finished college and, except for the occasional financial and motivational aid, they are on their own. I miss them, but time and inclination do not lend their lifestyles to sailing, so I settle for seeing them for the occasional holiday and birthday, on or off the boat.

Elizabeth, "Liz" usually or "Lizzie" in moments of extreme ardor or irritation, was also raised in northern Virginia. As in my case, she is the offspring of a Marine Corps officer, whose career spanned the Korean and Vietnam wars. My father was older and a veteran of World War II and Korea. When not serving, he was a civil engineer. Dad died when I was in high school, but Liz's father is alive and well. Coincidently, our mothers were businesswomen in a time when women were expected to stay at home. Now retired, my mother pursues her passions for travel and oil painting. Elizabeth's mom prefers golf and volunteering at the local library. Liz's passion is music. She is a fine violinist and plays part-time for a large community orchestra. Liz has a penchant for languages and did a stint in China as an interpreter for the Department of Defense. A senior partner and computer specialist for a private contractor, Elizabeth's company provides support for agencies with initials that she will not share, even with me. As for sailing, Liz does not fit the definition of "ardent fan," but she seems to enjoy trips on the boat and never complains unless we run out of water, or, more precisely, hot water.

The visit to Newport would include attendance at a gala given for the local symphony. Joyce Freemont, a Newport resident, fellow musician, and Liz's college roommate, had some months prior extracted a pledge of financial and personal support, earning us two of the "hard to get" tickets for the gala.

Our vacation was also an opportunity for a reunion with an old friend Ed Colombo. Ed and I met in college when I copied his phone number from a bulletin board advertisement for private pilot instructions. He became my flight instructor and eventually my best friend. Ed and I chased women, sometimes the same one, caroused, and spent too many late nights playing chess over too much scotch. Ed has probably been flying an airplane since the third grade. During the years I was in the Marine Corps, he was flying in and out of South and Central America. He said he was delivering cantaloupes, but I later surmised the "fruit express" was ferrying guns to infamous places and people about whom I did not ask. Ed earned an Airline Transport Certificate and later went to work for the FAA as an instructor slash inspector. He has traveled all over the world, presumably inspecting slash instructing. I never asked about that either.

Ed was the first of us to marry. His job took him to another state and as will happen, family and distance diluted our friendship. I had not seen him in about five years, staying in touch by email and the occasional phone call. Unfortunately, Ed recently lost his high school sweetheart and wife to cancer. For a year, he had been almost inconsolable, so I was pleasantly surprised when he phoned, suggesting we get together. He said he was "ready to get some downtime" and asked whether he could hitch a ride on the boat for a week or more and maybe stop and see his daughter Stacie, now grown and staying on Martha's Vineyard.

It promised to be a couple of enjoyable weeks, and I was looking forward to the sailing and the good company.

Finishing some entries in my logbook, I stretched some sore muscles, then put on some khaki slacks, pulled on a yellow polo shirt, and slipped into my old comfortable boat shoes, then climbed the steps through the companionway. Locking the hatch, I remembered I wanted to replace the old original lock with a new one.

The dock master's office was open. A room about twelve by fifteen feet, it held two desks and some file cabinets set against the back wall. The front third of the office was divided from the back by a waist-high counter that ran across the width of the office. The cute blonde had been replaced by a surly, pimple-faced kid perched on a stool behind the counter. He was playing with an electronic gizmo that produced an incessant, annoying beep. I paid my slip fee anyway, then asked Pimple Face, "Do you have any locks?"

"Yeah, we got locks."
"Okay, may I have one?"
"You have to pay for it," still *beeping*.
"No kidding. How much?"
"Five dollars plus tax," Pimple Face said.

I put the cash on the counter. Pimple Face put the gizmo down, got a lock from under the counter, and set it in front of me, still in its factory box. I thanked Pimple Face for his gracious service and took the lock back to the boat, pulled the old one off the hasp, and replaced it with the new lock. I was now ready for a large dinner and a large drink, maybe two large drinks.

Before going to dinner, I took time to stroll along the dock to admire the eclectic boats and picturesque waterfront. The backdrop was reminiscent of a Fitz Hugh Lane painting. Shades of blue and gold, backlit by the gauzy light from a waning day, sparkled like broken pieces of colored glass in the inky water. The salty air was cool and fresh. A distant hail for a water taxi and the tinkle of halyards striking idle masts were the only interruptions of the onset of a glorious summer evening. I never tired of the water and the kindred sights and smells.

Hunger overcame my reverie, so I left the dock and walked onto Bannister's Wharf and into a mood-killing throng of people. I wondered what Fitz Hugh would have thought of flip-flops and T-shirts.

CHAPTER THREE

Newport, Rhode Island

Newport was a hardscrabble waterfront town well into the 1960s. The current rendition is the result of one of those rare occurrences when city planning, and an informed community join with developers to create something better.

The renovated brick warehouses and buildings and the few leftover lobster and fishing operations, mixed with the sea air and boats from all over the world, make Newport hard to beat, particularly for "old salts" like me. Bannister's Wharf is the heart of the action.

I walked through the crowd to my favorite restaurant, the Black Pearl. Because it is easy to find and the food is terrific, the Black Pearl has for years been a favorite place for crews to rendezvous with incoming boats and captains. I first came here in 1987 as one of those crew members and never tired of visiting.

I hadn't thought to make a reservation, so while waiting for a table I watched the tourists, marveling that every man, woman, and child seemed dressed in a T-shirt, shorts, and flip-flops as if they were all members of some vast vacation club or army dressed in uniform. Tiring of the parade, I went into the Pearl and sat at the bar and ordered a Blanton's. There was a TV over the bar tuned to the news, so I watched.

A full screen image of President Harriet Jackson as she looks out from her podium in the White House Rose Garden. *"I ask all Americans to help me continue our fight against illegal drugs and their crushing assault on our citizens and our economy." Applause can be heard. "I will conclude with a warning to one of the most prolific hucksters of these drugs. If President Escudero of Venezuelan does not help abolish the manufacture and exportation of illicit drugs and cease his persistent and unfair trade practices, particularly with the exportation of oil, I will remind him of the oil refineries and the network of gas stations Venezuelan owns in the United States and suggest President Escudero consider the probability of tariffs imposed on both Venezuelan oil and gasoline. Need I say more."*

The newscast flipped back to the local blow-dried expert, Chase Anderson, who expounded on what everyone had just heard:

"President Jackson imposed sanctions against a Venezuelan official after U.S. authorities found Mauricio Rojas facilitated shipments of narcotics to the U.S. through Venezuela . . . Sandra, that's a wrap from the White House. Back to you."

"Thanks, Chase. In an effort to ease relations with the U.S., President Escudero's son will attend a series of concert benefits he is funding in the name of his mother, a world-renowned pianist. The first is our own Newport Symphony Gala this weekend. Should be quite the event. Hope you have your tickets."

Sandra laughed, *"I'll check my dance card."*

As she continued with her dribble, a weathered bartender with deep laugh lines and a large veiny nose turned from the TV to me. "Wow, the President's wound up today. How about another?"

I slid my glass toward him. "I suspect she's doing a little campaigning, but she has a point."

"Blanton's, right?"

"Please."

"From the look of you, I'd guess you're just off a boat." The bartender poured Blanton's over a glass of ice.

"You mean I have that burned-to-a-crisp look?"

The bartender dutifully laughed at my joke. "And well salted. Here you go, this one's on me. How long you in town?"

"A couple of days. My wife is flying in tomorrow, so we can attend that gala they were just talking about. Then off for a vacation on our new boat."

"Sounds like fun. The symphony is a big deal around here, even for the great unwashed like me."

"My wife is the musician in the family, but we're here as guests."

"Anyway, if you have the time, stop at Block Island."

"That's our first stop."

"Guess you've been here before?"

"Yep. Though this will be my wife's first time."

The bartender walked down the bar to attend to a new patron. The hostess finally found a table, so I threw a fifty on the bar and went with her to a booth next to the far wall across from the main entrance. My waitress was a thin, dark brunette who spoke with a European accent. She said she was from the Balkans and in the States for the summer. Pleasant and efficient, she was not overly chatty. Fine with me. I ordered a Blanton's and soda.

Advertised as single-barrel bourbon, Blanton's is my favorite. I admit a certain kinship to the brand because the distillery also owns Bowman's, once located near my home in Virginia. At the age of fifteen, Bowman's Virginia Gentleman was my initiation into the manly art of libation when I was taught to enjoy the aromas and sweet charcoal flavors of bourbon. The old distillery and the Bowman farm are now the community of Reston, Virginia.

The waitress brought me a bowl of clam chowder and a mixed green salad. I had lobster for my main course with iced tea and, for dessert, Key lime pie.

The restaurant gave off the comfortable feeling you get from visiting with an old friend, and I caught myself looking for some of my old "shipmates." I reminisced about those I had met over the years in the Black Pearl, the good meals, the laughs, and the adventures we had here in the New England waters, as well as in the Caribbean and the Chesapeake.

A friend had introduced me to sailing and, in turn, I introduced my friends to the wonderful sport. Several of them took to it, and a few, blessed with more discretionary capital than I, expressed their enthusiasm with larger and larger boats. I was always welcome on their trips, perhaps because of my good company, but as I seemed to draw mostly the blue water trips, perhaps it was because I was an experienced hand. In the winter, we would band together on bareboat charters in the Caribbean, usually in the Virgin Islands. A vocabulary more erudite than mine is required to describe the pure enjoyment of eighteen days on a sailboat in the Caribbean. Illustrative of the point is my friend who flew to the Caribbean for a five-day charter and stayed five years. Including wives and girlfriends, there were a dozen or so in the "core" group, and we always started or ended our "Newport cruises" at the Black Pearl. Realizing I would not see those faces, at least not now, perhaps never, loneliness seeped into my already melancholy consciousness.

I had another Blanton's to buttress me for the walk back to the boat. I paid my bill, then my wounded psyche and I ambled off to a warm bunk and a good night's sleep. Despite the season, or because of it, the perfect summer evening had become a night, cold-soaked by the infamous New England fog so impervious you need GPS to find your wallet. Demon rum—bourbon, actually—had impaired my usual catlike dexterity, so the labyrinth of dock lines that raised and lowered with the anomalies of the water hindered my progress. Any misstep would result in an unintentional late-night swim.

Gratefully, I found my slip. As I was carefully navigating the last ten feet of the finger pier, I looked up in time to see a small light on the *Pinafore*. It flickered for a moment, then it was gone. The fog was heavier now. I squeezed my eyes shut for a moment and looked again. I was sure I had seen a light. It was possible Liz had arrived early, but no, she would have called. Maybe it was Ed, but he wasn't due for another three days, and he would have called. I took another step and yelled, "Hey, you on the boat!" No points for originality—nothing happened.

I felt the pier shudder and turned in time to see an arm swing out of the murk. I stepped inside the swing, taking the brunt of the impact on my shoulder and back. I drove my right fist up into the assailant's solar plexus. He grunted and stepped back. Keeping my left arm up, I followed through with another right-hand punch to his groin. He screamed. A second person grabbed my arm as I drew back to throw my next punch. I turned to meet him, but I was sent reeling from a crushing blow to my head. I stumbled, falling backward over the first assailant. As I tried to get to my knees, I was hit again. A light flashed behind my eyes, then I neither felt nor saw anything.

I woke lying face down on the dock. My head was throbbing with pain, and there was an incessant ringing in my ears. Picking up a splinter or two from the dock, I rolled over carefully so as not to compound matters with a nocturnal swim. My jaw and ribs hurt, and there was a bloody lump behind my right ear. Moving slowly, I propped myself against one of the wooden piles. I had no sense of how long I had been unconscious. It was still dark, and

I had been out long enough for the fog to soak my clothes. My cell phone was still in the pants pocket where I left it. I dialed 911.

A protracted exchange with the officious police dispatcher did little to alleviate my mood or the throbbing in my head. After I declined an ambulance for the third time, the dispatcher finally assured me she would send an officer when the next shift change was completed. I said I would wait.

A uniformed officer arrived about twenty minutes later. He was young and had large ears that protruded unabashedly from under his hat. I gathered he was rather tall, but from my position on the dock, it was hard to judge heights. His name was Palmer.

Officer Palmer had a notebook in which he recorded all pertinent information, opening and closing the notebook as if to punctuate sentences. He took my information, looked in and around the boat, and noted the boat's name and registration number, conceding that the broken lock might be a crucial piece of evidence. He was most sympathetic to my plight but said he could find no other corroboration of a crime. That I had greeted him from a prostrate position was apparently irrelevant. He surveyed the crime scene further, furrowed his brow several times, and I could swear he wiggled his ears.

Finished with his extensive examination, he loomed over me and opened his notebook.

"Sir, what time was it when you were assaulted?"

"I don't know. About nine thirty, I guess."

"Is there anything missing?"

"I don't know. I haven't looked yet."

"Did you see anyone?"

"No," I said. "But there were at least two people, maybe three. Men, I assume. One on the boat, and probably two behind me."

"But you didn't see anyone?"

"No, I got a glance at the one, but not enough to make identification."

"You said you saw a light on your boat?"

"Yes."

"You said someone walked up behind you. When did you first notice him?"

"When he tried to hit me with his fist. When I got him down, his friend clubbed me over the head. I guess he could have been the one I saw on the boat."

"But you didn't see anyone's face?"

"No."

"Did they leave by boat or on foot?"

"I don't know. As they say in the movies, I was out cold."

"Sir, are you sure you don't need medical attention?"

"No, thanks. I think I just want to go to bed."

"Can you get on your feet?"

"Maybe—in a minute."

Officer Palmer closed his notebook, flicked his flashlight around some more, then told me he would file a report. I could get a copy at the police station between nine and four thirty the next day. Officer Palmer said goodbye, then he and his notebook left.

Mostly ambulatory, I staggered the few remaining feet to the boat, climbed into the cockpit, then into the cabin. I turned on the lights, which didn't help the head situation, and looked around the boat.

The cabin floor, or "sole," is mostly solid construction, but it has some removable sections enabling access to the bilge where tanks, plumbing, valves and like equipment are located. Several of these boards were removed. My uninvited guests were looking in the bilge, but for what? The "repel boarders locker" is well hidden, but I checked anyway. As far as I could tell, it was untouched. While it was open, I pulled out the Smith & Wesson, then replaced the concealment panel. Until daylight, it would be hard to see anything more, and I was not seeing too well anyway. I got a bag of frozen peas from the icebox, striped off my clothes, and crawled into bed. I put the peas on the lump behind my ear and my pistol under my pillow. Not the same as a Teddy Bear, but comforting, nonetheless.

Trying to sleep, I went over what led up to this absurdity. It was a Saturday. We were at home in Alexandria. I was flipping burgers on the grill when the phone rang. It was my best friend, Ed Columbo, calling from Florida.

"Hey, bud, what's up?" I turned toward the house and the screen door and yelled at Liz in the kitchen. "Honey! These burgers are almost ready."

"I'm ready when you are!" she replied.

"I found your boat," Ed said.

"I didn't know I lost one."

"Bullshit, that's all you talk about . . . Seriously, it's a sexy boat. It's got one of those stick things in the middle and everything. I just sent you a picture."

I moved the burgers off of the heat, put the spatula down, and looked at the phone. I casually glanced at the pictures, then paid closer attention.

Ed said, "So?"

I had to agree with him, at least from the pictures. "You're right, It's a nice boat."

"Everyone wants it," Ed said. "The owner will sell for a price even Liz will go for. But you need to get here soon—like tomorrow!"

I looked at the pictures again. Ed has been flying airplanes his whole life. As much as he knows about planes, he knows equally nothing about boats.

"Well?"

"Okay," I said, "meet me at the airport. I'll send you the time and gate."

The next day, I was winging my way to Florida, killing time by scrolling through the photos Ed sent me the day before. The flight attendant told us to prepare for landing and we began our descent.

Miami was warm and humid. Ed was on time and seemed more excited than I was. Once at the marina, we met with Ben Hancock, who was in his mid-forties, fat, dressed in khaki shorts and a golf shirt embroidered with the name of his company, Hancock's Marine Survey. He huffed and puffed as he led us down the down the dock. "Mrs. Vasquez will join us for the sea trial. The original owner died. I believe she's his wife or sister . . . I don't know. Anyway, she has the title, so I guess it doesn't make any difference."

I pulled up short. "You don't know who she is? How do you know she owns the boat?"

"I checked with the county and the coast guard. The title is in her name, and it's good."

"Look, I don't want that title to bite me in the ass. Maybe we should look at something else."

Ed chimed in, "Hey, bud, she's an old lady. She doesn't speak English very well. Ben says the title is good, so let's go for a boat ride."

"She's not old, and she's a knockout. Walks with a limp, though. Said she was in an auto accident down in Caracas," Ben corrected.

"Any glaring issues with the boat?" I asked.

"Overall, she's in great condition. It's really been taken care of. Some superficial things, a few blisters, and the AC doesn't work." Ben pointed to the end of the dock. A glistening, trim sailboat gently rocking in its slip. "There she is." Ben pulled out his clipboard and looked at some notes as we walked to the boat.

"She's pretty, no doubt about it."

"If you look here, you can see a couple of blisters." Ben pointed to a few small bubbles in the hull's gel coat. "As you can see, minor repair. As for the AC, we can get it fixed before you take delivery."

The boat, it was a fifty-foot aft cockpit, a one-off design, her bow and stern had that graceful overhang missing in the short, chopped bows now popular. The gleaming teak interior was copied from an older Bob Perry design. Two guest cabins and heads were on either side of the companionway.

I stepped back into the cockpit just in time to see a woman in her early forties, slim build and dark shoulder-length hair, approach. Dressed in a yellow T-shirt and white shorts, she was a site, if slightly marred by a limp and rosy scar on her left leg. She carried a pink pastry box.

Ben said, "*Hola, Señora* Vasquez! We were just finishing up the inspection. A few minor problems."

"*Maravilloso*! I bring some empanadas as picnic. It's how you say, yes?" I shook hands with Mrs. Vasquez, introduced myself, and suggested we go for a sea trial.

Once we had cast off the dock lines and were all aboard, we slowly motored into the calm waters of the Intercostal Waterway and then the long and narrow Lake Mabel. Once in the lake, I took the helm from Ben. A light breeze came up, so we raised the main and unfurled the jib. The boat leaned into our course.

"Wow! Ben put the board down. Let's see how close we can get her to the wind."

Ben lowered the centerboard, and I eased into the wind until the sails started to luff. "Pull in the sails, please." Ben winched the jib and main sheets tighter. The boat heeled over, taking the new trim and course. I steered her until the sails were as tight as a drum and the sheets were like steel cables. The beautiful boat charged forward like a thoroughbred.

"Damn, she can sail!" Yelling over the sound of wind and water, "Mrs. Vasquez, I love your boat!"

The sail was over too soon. While Ed and Ben were tying up, Mrs. Vasquez and I walked to the bow.

"My husband, he was a dentist for thirty years. This boat is his only escape till his death."

"My condolences, ma'am. If you would like to sell, this seems to be the boat I've been looking for. I promise I'll take care of her."

"Yes, I believe you will."

"Will you be staying in the area?"

"No, I am from Spain and will return home. My family, they manufacture automobiles and want my son to enter the business."

"Oh, I assumed you were from one of the Americas."

"No, my husband and I met in Spain when he was there on business for the Cuban government."

"I thought he was a dentist?"

"You are not local, no? I include the survey and transport if you can pay the deposit in cash. But I am leaving to visit my son and have to sell soon."

I was getting mixed signals from this woman, but if the title was okay, then I was in.

"You have a deal, ma'am."

CHAPTER FOUR

Pinafore, Bannister's Wharf, Newport, Rhode Island

The next morning, I was sore, though not frothing at the mouth or seeing double, so I opted for a day of light duty instead of a trip to the doctor's office.

I had looked around the boat, but other than the dislodged bilge covers, there were no other obvious indications that intruders had been in the boat. More puzzling, there was no sign of anything missing. Maybe I interrupted them before they could cart away their loot. Theft of marine electronics is not unheard of, and in some areas, it has been a genuine problem, but there was no evidence of tool marks around the electronics or, God forbid, my state-of-the-art entertainment system.

I went up into the cockpit, bent over—carefully, so my head wouldn't fall off—and picked up the lock. I turned it over and looked at it closely. It wasn't broken, as I originally thought. I looked at the bottom. There were some shiny marks where someone might have scraped it with a tool. Could the lock have been picked?

The cute blonde walked up and from the dock said, "Good morning, just stopped by to see if everything is Okay."

I looked up at her, wincing as my head complained about the movement. "Good morning to you," I replied, more cheerfully than I felt.

She was still dressed in the requisite khaki shorts, short-sleeve safari shirt, and boat shoes. Putting the lock away, I invited her aboard. I offered her a cold drink. She accepted, sat down on the cockpit bench, and told me her name was Charlene. I told her about the break-in and asked her if there had been a theft problem in the area. She looked bewildered for a moment, as if it were a personal affront, then assured me there had been no problems, at least during her sixty-day tenure. She asked me if the police had been called, and I told her of my visit with Officer Palmer. Laughing, she said she knew Palmer, that he was a reserve officer taken on for the summer. "He's a little green, but his heart is in the right place."

We eventually talked about other things. Confirming my suspicions, she told me that her employment as the assistant dock master was a summer job and that she lived with her parents in Newport. In the fall, she would go back to the University of Virginia for her senior year. I told her my brothers and daughter had graduated from UVA, so we talked about the beautiful campus, about Jefferson, Monticello, and Charlottesville. As she told me about her major in theater arts, an incoming boat caught her attention. She thanked me for the drink and ran off to help with the new arrival, assuring me she would tell the dock master of the break-in.

I spent the day eating aspirin and working around the boat. In my vertical moments, I inspected the drum and lines for the jib furling gear, checked the lifelines and standing rigging for signs of stress and made sure each clevis pin was secured and taped so the sharp edges wouldn't catch on expensive sails or soft body parts. I inspected the halyards, sheets, and lines needed to operate the boat, then disassembled, lubricated, and reassembled two of the winches.

A mode of transportation that probably dates from the fifth millennium BC, sailboats are now primarily designed for recreation. As with most things, their quality runs from poor to bulletproof. And, as with most things, poor quality equals high failure, but unlike your vacuum cleaner, a failure on a boat could easily lead to injury or even fatality.

Pinafore is a sloop. Sloops have only one mast. The mainsail is attached so it can travel up and down the mast by using a halyard. The headsail or the jib is fastened to the forestay and also raised and lowered by a halyard. Ropes or lines that control the right to left movement of the sails are called sheets. Collectively, the sheets and halyards are called the running rigging.

Pinafore's mast is held in the boat with eight steel cables, one forward, the forestay, which also carries the jib, one at the rear, the backstay, and three cables to either side of the mast, called the shrouds. These cables or shrouds are the standing rigging.

If any part of the standing or running rigging breaks, one could lose a sail or the mast. Embarrassing anytime, in a heavy sea and high winds, failure is potentially lethal. The prudent sailor always checks the rigging, lifelines, winches, and the hundreds of other things that he and his crew's lives depend.

My head still throbbed, and I didn't feel like fixing dinner, so I headed back to the Pearl. On the way to the restaurant, I looked into the dock master's office, intending to buy another lock, but no one was around.

The hostess at the Pearl seated me on the patio at a table facing the wharf and the tourists. Halfway through my lobster roll, I noticed a man watching me. He changed locations occasionally, pretending to window-shop. Even from a distance, it was clear he wasn't shopping or taking in the ambiance. In days gone by, I was a pretty good detective, but it didn't take Sherlock Holmes to pick this guy out of the crowd. Virtually all the people on the wharf were dressed in standard tourist attire, bright colors, and flip-flops. My admirer was dressed in black clothing and black cowboy boots. He stood out like the proverbial sore thumb.

I finished eating, paid the bill, and then strolled up the wharf assuming my best nonchalant, obtuse look—not much of a stretch. Trying to close the distance between my friend in black, I felt like the sheriff in a western movie, moseying up the street lookin' fur Black-Bart. I thought about buying a white hat. Each time I got noticeably closer, he would move farther up the wharf toward America's Cup Avenue. Trying to get closer, I occasionally used his trick and pretended to window-shop using the reflection of the window to watch him watch me. When Black-Bart reached the end of the wharf, he turned right, presumably walking south on America's Cup Avenue, but when I reached the street moments later—subtly turning the corner after him—he had disappeared. I waited a few minutes, hoping he might reemerge. When he didn't show, I walked back to the boat, stopping sporadically to look over my shoulder, but Black-Bart never reappeared.

I slept late the next day. I was feeling better, so while the coffee was being made, I treated myself to a shower. After coffee and some more aspirin,

I went to the dock master's office and found Charlene sitting behind the counter. Happy not to be dealing with Pimple Face and his gizmo, I said good morning and bought another lock. We talked for a few minutes. She told me she had asked her boss, but there had been no other reported incidents of thefts or break-ins. I thanked her, took my lock, and left. I installed the new lock on the companionway hatch, then started organizing the sail lockers.

About noon, I was on all fours, upside down in the lazarette straightening some spare dock lines, when I heard a voice, "Hey, sailor boy!"

Startled, I popped up, bashing my pre-tenderized head. Trying to massage the pain away, I turned slowly and looked up. A tallish, pretty woman with shoulder-length blond hair was standing on the dock. She was dressed in a white silky blouse, black linen slacks, and black heels. Next to her was a piece of roll-along luggage, a garment bag, and her ever-present violin case.

Rubbing my head some more, I grinned, "Hi, honey, I didn't expect you until tomorrow."

She arched her brows. "I can come back later if it is not convenient. Do you need to empty the boat of errant boat bunnies?"

"No, no boat bunnies, errant or otherwise, but my libido thanks you for the compliment."

She slipped off her heels, gave me her hand, and stepped on the boat. We hugged and enjoyed a long kiss.

"Damn, it is good to see you," I said.

"Was my sailor lonely?"

"That's not the only thing I was—"

"Well, we may have to do something about that. I don't want my sailor grumpy," she said, laughing. "I went AWOL before our last performance, unprofessional I know, but I missed you so much. How have you been?"

I didn't mention the incident or my irrepressible headache.

"I was good, now I'm great."

"Well, let me change my clothes and let's get something to eat. I'm starved."

"So am I," with as much leer as I could manage.

"Food first or I'll be the grumpy one."

"I'm not grumpy, just famished," I grinned.

"Food first." She gave me a smoking hot kiss, then looked over the boat.

"The boat looks great. I love the name. We should name the dingy *Gilbert and Sullivan*.

"I was thinking about *Josephine*."

She laughed, "Cute, but too subtle." She gave me another passionate kiss, then went below.

I had no idea where I was going to put the wheeled suitcase. Liz was impervious to my pleas for soft, boat-friendly luggage.

CHAPTER FIVE

Newport, Rhode Island

Dressed in shorts, a polo shirt, and boat shoes, her hair pulled back in a ponytail, Liz was her typical, coordinated self, but she looked a little wilted from her trip. I decided to stay close, so we went back to the Pearl and had lunch on the patio. We each had a lobster roll, coleslaw, and french fries. Liz never ate french fries, and I could never understand why she ordered them. I had iced tea, and Liz had a gin and tonic. She chatted happily about the kids, the symphony, projects at work, her friends, and our large fluffy cat, Sable, who kept the home fires warm with the help of a neighbor.

"Aren't you excited about the gala?"

"Ecstatic."

She leaned over and in a conspiratorial whisper said, "I know it's not your thing. But if you're a good boy, I'll make it worth your while."

"In that case, I'll wear my tux."

"You brought it! Thank you, sweetie." She sipped from her glass. "So, what's our schedule?"

"Well, the gala first and, as I mentioned, Ed will be here tomorrow, very early if I'm any judge. Then off to Block Island, then Martha's Vineyard, then probably Nantucket."

"I'm not crazy about Ed encroaching on our vacation, especially at the last minute, but it will be nice to see him. What's it been, two or three years since they were in D.C. with Stacie?"

"I've seen Ed a couple of times."

"I hate that we've all been so distant since Caroline passed away. At least the kids stay in touch."

At that moment, my phone rang. "Damn, it's the alarm company. Hello."

"This is Shield Home Security. We've detected a breach in your residence. We have sent the police."

Elizabeth's phone dinged with a FaceTime call. "It's Brad. You want to bet the calls are related?"

Brad, our handsome son of twenty-two, fiddled with his phone before it settled on an unflattering angle of his half-in, half-out position in our kitchen window. The house alarm blared in the background.

"Mom, it's me. Don't call the cops!"

"I can see it's you. What on earth are you doing?"

Still on the phone with the security company, I said, "Hello."

The security guy said, "Password, please."

"Throckmorton," I said.

The security guy said, "I beg your pardon. Will you spell that, please?"

"T-H-R-O-C-K-M-O-R-T-O-N."

Holding her hand over the phone, Elizabeth said, "I told you to change that stupid password. It's Brad. He forgot his keys again. He's climbing in the kitchen window."

I said to the security guy, "Never mind, it's one of my kids."

"Sorry, I forgot my keys. Glad to see you got to Newport safely!" Brad said.

I took Liz's phone. "I see you're almost in the house. Will you be hanging around long?"

"That's funny, dad." With banging coming over the phone, I gave the phone back to Liz and took a long pull on Liz's gin and tonic.

"Are you planning to answer the front door?" Liz said to Brad.

"It's just Emily." Brad wiggled out of the window, then ran to the front door with the phone in hand. The image on the phone was of the ceiling. We could hear Brad open the door for Emily.

"Brad! You set off the alarm. The alarm company is going to call mom and dad and they'll be pissed."

"Hi, honey. The alarm company called," Liz said.

We could hear Brad talking with some men. Emily, our beautiful twenty-four-year-old picked up the phone. She turned the camera toward Brad. Liz and I could see two police officers with guns drawn.

"Uh, mom, we have a problem."

A man's voice says, "Ma'am, please put the phone down."

Elizabeth turned to me. "Now what do we do?"

I picked up my phone and dialed the security company. "You just called. The police are at my home and have detained my children. Yes, the password is THROCKMORTON. No! I will not spell it!"

"Dear God, not again," Liz said.

Emily got back on the FaceTime call, "Mom, the nice police officer wants to talk with you."

"Good afternoon, ma'am. I'm Corporal Johnson with the Fairfax County Police Department. I assume these two belong to you?"

Sighing, "What happens if I say no?"

Chuckling, "We could arrange a night in jail."

"Mom! That's not funny."

"Yes, they are my darling children. And, officer, thank you for watching over our home. My husband and I appreciate it very much."

"You're welcome, ma'am. Have a good day."

"Emily, I want you two to find the house keys before you leave. No more alarm calls. Are we clear?"

"Yes, ma'am."

"Your father wants to talk with Brad."

Liz handed me the phone. "Brad, we've talked about this key thing before. They charge for false alarms. Next time you're paying."

"Yes, sir, I'm sorry."

I handed the phone back to Liz, and she disconnected. "I hate it when they act like airheads, especially when we're away."

"Okay, we're on vacation. Let's eat, drink, and have lots of sex."

"That last part will be a little difficult after you invited Ed."

"He called and invited himself. I couldn't say no."

"Sometimes I'm ready to retire and just stay on vacation," Liz said.

"And have sex?"

"That too."

"So, we take a couple of months off. Take the boat down to the Caribbean and drink piña coladas."

"Tempting, but I can't take that much time."

"Liz, you own the company. Put someone in charge and run it remotely."

"Sometimes we need a warm body with my clearances to take in projects."

"Okay, I'm not going to argue. Are you ever going to tell me what the hell you guys do?" I asked.

"In the most basic terms, we analyze data for government agencies. Other than that, you know I can't say."

"Okay, sweetie, we'll take it as it comes. We're on vacation!"

"Yes, we are. Finally."

After lunch, we walked up Bannister's Wharf holding hands, looking into the shops, talking, and laughing, buying the obligatory "perfect" gift and souvenir.

We were also being followed. He was not very good; I spotted him twice. It looked like the same person, or at least the same wardrobe, as yesterday. He was dressed in black. I wasn't complaining, but you think he would try to blend in with the crowd.

Liz and I walked the length of Bannister's Wharf, turned left onto America's Cup Avenue, then left again on Bowen's Landing, and walked back toward the water.

I said, "Honey, I know you're tired, so why don't we go back to the boat so you can take a nap?"

"I am tired, but I didn't want to be a stick-in-the-mud. You don't mind?"

"No, of course not," I assured her.

I suspected my visitors didn't break and enter in broad daylight, but once at the boat, I went down into the cabin and made a quick inspection. Liz came down behind me, shed her shoes and shorts, went forward, and crawled into the bunk. She was asleep almost immediately.

I went up to the cockpit and called Officer Palmer. The dispatcher said he was "on days off." I asked for an investigator and was put through to Detective Lieutenant James Gallagher. Gallagher was puzzled by my request, but as it was a "slow day for crime fighting," he agreed to meet me on the wharf for coffee.

I asked that he meet me at the food court because it was a few hundred feet from the dock, and I could keep an eye on the entrance from my seat. Still, no sign of my friend in black. It was probably too much to hope he would appear after the detective arrived.

Gallagher was about five feet, eight inches, sandy hair that might have been red in his youth. He looked to be about fifty and spoke with an accent that betrayed a South Boston lineage. He was dressed in gray slacks, an open-neck white shirt, and a dark gray blazer. In the current fashion, his gold badge was clipped on his belt, and there was a bulge on his right hip.

We introduced ourselves. Keeping an eye on the dock entrance, I mentioned I had been a public and private cop. He gave me an unimpressed grunt and said, "So, what can I do for you?"

I told him about the incident two nights ago, the guy I saw yesterday at lunch and the one who just followed Liz and me.

"What makes you think this person, or persons were following you?" he asked.

"Because every time I turn around, he's behind me doing a poor job trying to look like the landscape. Look, my boat has been broken into, I have been knocked over the head, and I have only been in town three days. When my friend arrives, we will be out of here. Meanwhile, I am afraid for my wife's safety."

"What business you in?" Gallagher asked.

"Real estate."

"You sell someone a house with a leaky roof?" he grinned.

"Commercial real estate. I develop mixed-use projects, and I haven't done that in a while. And customarily, any complaints would be handled by litigation, not by banging me over the head."

"Maybe. You say you're leaving in a day or so?"

"Yes, we're waiting for a friend, then we're leaving, probably tomorrow."

Gallagher pulls out his phone.

"The marina and the wharf have surveillance cameras. After you called, I pulled this footage off the cameras." He played some footage that led up to the attack. In the video, the men on the boat are meticulously going through the cockpit lockers and cabin interior. When I approached, they attacked me, until I lay unconscious. One assailant dropped into a Zodiac, pulled his partner out of the water, then motored away.

"You pretty much just lay there until you call Palmer."

"Everyone's a critic. That was my first live performance."

"Funny. Lucky you didn't get a knife in your gizzard." Gallagher puts his phone away.

"I'll email you a copy of the video. Unfortunately, you can't see their faces, so pursuing criminal charges is going to be tough."

"I get that locking them up is too much to hope for, but I have to stay here until tomorrow, and I wouldn't care for a repeat performance."

"Performance—you're quite the wit. I'll bet you knock them dead at the VFW."

"Elks Club."

"Okay, I'll put a uniformed officer on the dock to watch your boat. They will be there during the night and early morning shift. If you have any other problems or think someone is following you, call me. That fair?"

"Very fair, and I appreciate your understanding. As I said, if it were just me, I wouldn't be so worried, but with my wife on board . . ."

"Don't worry about it. Glad I could help."

Gallagher gave me his business card. We shook hands, and he walked back up the wharf toward the avenue. I went back to the boat. Liz was still asleep, so I walked to the harbor master's office. Charlene was at her desk. "Hi, what can I do for you?"

"I was wondering if you recognized these guys." Using my phone, I played the video, zooming in on the first assailant, freezing the frame.

Pointing, "You know, I've seen him around. Matter of fact, he and another guy came by the day you arrived. It was odd because they were both wearing suits. You don't see many suits around here. I would have said they were detectives, but I know all the local cops. They could have been federal guys. Anyway, they wanted a key card to get out on the dock. Wouldn't tell me who they were or why, so I said no."

"Okay, thanks. If you see them again, will you let me know?"

"Sure."

As I walked back to the boat, I was wondering if I should call Gallagher, but I didn't really have anything to tell him. Nothing he could use anyway. When I got to our slip, there was no police officer. Worried, I ran to the boat and down into the cabin. There was no sign of Liz. I went up the companionway and looked forward. There on the bow was Elizabeth in a bikini, motionless and face down on the deck. I ran to her side in three steps. She was still. I grabbed her shoulder.

"What! Oh, hi. Guess I fell asleep. It got so hot in the cabin, so I came up here. I tried to turn on the AC, but I couldn't make it work. You'll have to show me the secret."

I sat slumped on the deck, breathing a sigh of relief. "Jesus, Liz, you scared me to death."

"Why, what did I do?"

"Nothing." I pulled her close, hugging and kissing at the same time.

"I don't know what I did, but I like this part."

I sat back. "The secret to the AC is that it doesn't work. The surveyor offered to have it fixed, but I foolishly told him no. Now, of course, New England is having a heatwave."

"Please see what you can do. It's really stuffy down there."

I climbed below to see if I could fix the air-conditioner.

Liz called after me, "Do you want a sandwich or anything?"

"No thanks. Are all the ports open?" After checking to see if the ports and hatches were open, I removed the cushions and disassembled the settee. I wedged myself into the space behind the settee and pulled off the cover to the box containing the AC compressor. Pushing the cover aside, I looked into the void. "What the hell?"

There was no compressor, no condenser, or anything resembling AC components. The box was filled with $100 bills! Stacks of $100 bills were packed tightly in every square inch. I backed out of the compartment and sat on the deck, staring at the open space.

I called out. "Liz, will you come down here, please?"

Liz climbed down the stairs and moved around me and sat on the floor. "Did you find the problem?"

"No, but I found another one." I pointed to the space under the settee. "Look in there."

"If there is a dead animal in there, I'll brain you."

"Just look and tell me what you see."

Liz got on all fours and peered into the open cavity. "Good grief! Is that what I think it is?"

"If you think it's about a million dollars in U.S. currency, then that's what it is."

"Where did it come from?"

"My suspicion: the previous owner, a guy named Pérez. There's been no crime. For now, let's keep it between us."

"Should we count it?"

"No. Let's leave it alone. Though you will have to do without air conditioning."

"For a million dollars, I can do without. What if the people who left it send like thugs or somebody to take it?"

"I'll get it sorted out. No one knows we found it, or that it's even on the boat. The prior owner probably hid it before he died."

"Didn't you say he had a wife? What about her?"

"I'm not sure I can still get in touch with her. I'm not even sure who she is, but I'll try calling."

"Maybe we could keep enough for that red Jag I was telling you about."

I laughed. As I reassembled the AC cabinet and settee, I was thinking things were starting to make sense. The break-in, the attack on the dock. The money had to be what those guys were looking for.

After I finished, I went up to the cockpit, where Liz was reading a magazine.

"You, Okay?"

"Yep, still trying to stay cool."

"I'm going to run out and get some groceries and ice. Will you be all right for a while?"

"Sure, but don't be too long."

I walked up and down the wharf for about thirty minutes, looking into alleys and stores, trying to find the guy in black or even anyone suspicious. No luck. Perhaps it *had* been my imagination.

I returned to the boat at about four in the afternoon. Not to be empty-handed, I bought some groceries and two bags of ice. True to Gallagher's promise, there was a uniformed policeman, or I should say policewoman, at the entrance to the dock. She was about five-four, thick in the middle, and wore her dark hair short. She was a tad truculent, but we exchanged pleasantries without getting into a fistfight.

I wrangled the ice and groceries on board, then stored everything in the cabinet and icebox. I could hear Liz was in the shower.

Like all consumables on a boat, water has to be brought aboard and stored. Fresh water is stored in three large tanks under the cabin sole until it's used cold or converted to hot water via the heat exchanger or with a small electric heater powered by electricity from the dock. In some places, water is expensive, and on a boat, it is always in short supply. For those reasons, there is the sailor's universal three-step rule about showers: wet, soap, rinse, then dry. Liz has never recognized the value of this rule, and though she has never said as much, I think she believes water, hot water to be precise, is her birthright. Because I'm the one who has to fill the tanks, I believe it is my duty to conserve water at any opportunity. So, I try to abide by another old saying—"shower with a friend."

I threw my clothes on the bunk. "Hey, I'm home. Want some company?"

"Sure. Will you wash my hair?"

Not what I was hoping, but I went with another old saying—"Any port in a storm." I was chockfull of old sayings. I should probably write a book.

I stepped into the small shower compartment, which is also the forward head. The late afternoon sunlight funneled through the small overhead hatch and bored through the thick steam. Reflected by the mirror, the sunlight took another run into the steam, illuminating the compartment as if the light came from within. The salt air mixed with the fragrances from Liz's body wash and shampoo complemented the effect until it was something close to sensual perfection.

Liz gave me a wet soapy hug, a sweet kiss, then turned, leaning her back against my chest.

"Wash my hair, please."

I poured too much shampoo over her hair and as I messaged the semi liquid into her blond curls. She made little, contented purring sounds.

Moving her hands behind her back and between us, she gently took hold of me. "Sailor boy has been at sea for a long time, hasn't he?"

She moved my hands to her chest. The soap squeezed through my fingers as I gently kneaded her breasts until they were firm, and her nipples hardened. I slid my hands down her flat stomach, slowly moving them lower and lower. In a hoarse whisper, she said, "I've already washed there." Bending over the sink, she pushed her soapy bottom toward me, and with the same husky voice said, "Fill me up, sailor."

CHAPTER SIX

Pinafore, Bannister's Wharf

With the shower and ablutions, I knew Liz would be in the head and forward compartment for another hour or more, so I jumped into the aft head and turned on the shower in time to get the last thirty seconds of hot water. I shaved, washed behind my ears, rinsed, and toweled off.

The shower wasn't draining properly, leaving an inch of water in the shower pan. I made a mental note to check it later.

My tuxedo, shirt, and accessories were laid out on the bunk in the aft stateroom. Dried, deodorized, and talced, I put on the freshly starched shirt, pressed slacks, and cummerbund. A tuxedo is not standard gear aboard my boat, but as a surprise for Liz, I had brought mine for the gala, and even I had to admit I looked devilishly handsome. I discarded my boat shoes for a pair of black shoes normally associated with formal wear. As a further concession to convention, I wore socks.

Liz walked into the aft stateroom, wrapped in a towel, carrying her makeup bag. She sat down on the bunk. She started applying her makeup. "Hot water's out. I was thinking we might visit some of the homes and museums tomorrow, you know before Ed gets here."

"Okay with me, but he's liable to get here early, especially if he rents a plane."

"Well, it's just a thought, it would be nice to do something together as a couple." Finished with her makeup, she stood, the towel slid to the floor. Her damp body glistened in the sunlight as she walked back to the forward stateroom.

"Maybe you could wear that," I said.

"Not after all the money I spent on my gown. But just to keep you interested, perhaps I'll go commando."

"Count me among the very interested," I chuckled. After she closed the door, I walked over and took my S&W from the 'repel boarders locker'. I couldn't wear a holster, so I was counting on my ever-expanding waistline and cummerbund to substitute. To check for fit, I stuck the thing in my waist. The weapon was big, but in theory, with its two-and-a-half-inch barrel and round butt, it was designed for concealment. It was a bit slippery, so I found some rubber bands in the chart table, twisted them around the grip and put the gun back in my waist over my right hip. I was long over the novelty of wearing a concealed gun but given what had transpired during the last several days, it felt good to have my old friend along for the ride.

I was building two gin and tonics when Liz came out of the forward compartment and twirled.

"Well, sailor boy, what do you think?"

She was dressed in a strapless, floor-length gown that seemed made of gold, iridescent foil. Emphasizing her beautiful cleavage and small waist, the gown flowed out from the waist down to a gentle fold onto the floor. The gold necklace around her neck was my first anniversary gift, and her gold dangling earrings were antiques we found on a visit to New Orleans. Her hair, almost the color of the dress, was combed in a soft flip just touching her shoulders.

"Well, how do I look?" she asked again.

Liz's face is the product of fortunate genetic design, but her figure is the result of hard work. Forty-five or not, she is a stunning woman and a sight I never tire of. I was having trouble getting my breath. I croaked a totally inadequate "You look great!"

She smiled, walked over, and kissed me on the cheek. "Thank you, sweetie. That's the best compliment a girl could ever have. You may breathe now. You look *very* pretty too." Carefully wiping the lipstick off with her thumb. "Thank you again for bringing your tux. That was very sweet."

Back on oxygen, I pulled her toward me. "Maybe we could go to the party later?"

"Behave yourself. We are leaving now, so let's get it together or we are going to be late." She added with a grin, "But keep the thought. It's not every night a girl gets to come home with a big, strong sailor."

She handed me her heels, a green and gold silk shawl, and a purse that reminded me of a large, gold Tylenol capsule. Gathering her dress, she climbed the steps to the cockpit and out into the pleasant summer evening.

I climbed after her, set all the accessories down, pulled the hatch closed, and secured it with my new lock.

Getting off the boat with clouds of dress, Liz's accouterments, and my gun without anything falling into the water was an achievement of some proportion. Liz steadied herself on my arm, slipped on her heels, made sure everything was in its right place, then with a "good evening" to the policeman that had replaced the female officer, we were off for an evening of glitter, dancing, and libation.

There was a parting of the seas among the diminished tourists still roaming the wharf, probably from our incongruous attire, but Liz turned heads no matter what she was wearing. As we waited for our car, I pretended not to notice the man watching us. I gave some thought to calling Gallagher, but I wasn't ready to tell Liz. Seeking some reassurance, I touched the gun on my hip.

CHAPTER SEVEN

Rosecliff Mansion, Newport, Rhode Island

Our town car rolled through what appeared to be a demonstration, and a gaggle of press. Then our driver stopped at the gate to Rosecliff Mansion. He showed a police officer Elizabeth's invitation, then continued up the driveway to the mansion. A valet opened the car door, and Liz and I stepped out. Liz took my arm, and we walked toward the entrance.

"Rosecliff is one of the half dozen or so 'cottages' built by late-nineteenth-century robber barons, before the income tax, when a million dollars was real money. A Nevada silver heiress built this. These so-called cottages were retreats to escape the summer heat. The owners tried to outdo each other, and over the years they got more outlandish."

"My, you are a font of information."

"You may remember, I minored in architectural history."

"I remember you minored in a professor of architectural history."

"Well, she was quite inspirational, architecturally speaking."

"Very amusing."

We entered the opulent vestibule where people were greeting each other and receiving name tags. If possible, the inside of Rosecliff was more impressive than the exterior. Like most Newport mansions, the Historic Trust owned Rosecliff and often rented the mansions for functions such as the gala or even a movie. In fact, the ballroom scenes for the movie *True Lies* were filmed in Rosecliff, as were scenes for *The Great Gatsby.*

We signed in, received our stick-on name cards, which I thought was a bit tacky, and walked into the main hall, which was overflowing with chandeliers, black ties, gowns, and cleavage. An orchestra was on the far side of the ballroom and a fair number of the crowd were waltzing to Strauss's *Blue Danube.* The promised open bar was still eluding me when Joyce Freemont bounded over and gave Liz a kiss on either cheek, then planted one on me. I had met Joyce before at several similar events. She was short, pale, with a round face and straight mousy hair, tending to slightly plump. She was apparently a brilliant flutist, Liz's college roommate, and the reason for our attendance.

As Liz and Joyce chatted amiably, I went in search of a Blanton's and two champagnes. Discovering the bar, I waited patiently while several people ordered champagne cocktails. I ordered my drink on the rocks with a splash of soda and champagnes for Liz and Joyce. Drinks in hand, I returned to find Liz minus Joyce but in the company of a handsome man in his mid-forties. He was about six feet and dressed in a tuxedo that probably cost more than our daughter's first year of college. He was dark in complexion, hair, and eyes. His longish hair, slathered in hair tonic, hair gel, or whatever substitutes these days, was slicked back into one of those little pigtails you see in films but never in actual life. I looked into his eyes. They seemed to lack light, as if they were artificial or reptilian. His mouth was thin with an indolent sneer.

"Hi, handsome." Liz took the two champagnes, offering one to the man with the eyes. "Honey, this is our host, Reynaldo Vicente."

"A pleasure, *señor*," he oiled, extending a firm, confident handshake. "May I compliment you on your most good fortune and exquisite taste in woman? Your wife is very beautiful and quite charming."

He'd need another box of adjectives if he knew her underwear was back on the boat. Two could play this game. "You are very gracious, sir. Yes, I am indeed fortunate. And thank you for your kind invitation. The party is most enjoyable."

"*Gracias*, it is my pleasure, a small contribution to help the *comunidad* for how to say—payback for my many blessings."

Liz interjected, "Honey, Mr. Vicente is from Venezuela, and guess what? I met his mother once when she was in New York. She is a very well-known concert pianist."

I started to say something gratuitous, but Liz interrupted.

"Mr. Vicente—"

"Please, call me Reynaldo," he oozed.

"Please tell me, is your mother well?" Liz asked.

"Yes, thank you. Regrettably, arthritis has claimed her talent, so I'm afraid she plays little."

"Oh, I am so sorry to hear that. She won't remember me, but when you next speak to her, please tell your mother I asked about her."

The orchestra started another waltz. Reynaldo turned to me, "Sir, may I be so impetuous to ask for a dance with your lovely wife?"

Oh, brother, I thought, "If it's okay with Liz—" They were off in a swirl of gold fabric and hair gel.

I went looking for another Blanton's, taking time to walk through the room, admiring the parquet floors, paintings, architectural friezes, and plunging necklines. I imagined myself dancing the tango with Juno Skinner, the sultry vixen in *True Lies* played by the sultry Tia Carrere. Arnold Schwarzenegger, I was not, but I was in my tuxedo. The night was young, so anything was possible.

Then I saw him. The man that had been following us. I was sure of it. I followed him through some immense glazed French doors that led to the top of a marble staircase overlooking a massive green lawn. An ornate fountain the size of a swimming pool was adorned with a fountain lit with muted colored lights. The backyard was big enough for a polo match. Within stood two open-air tents covering about a dozen candlelit tables. Another dozen tables were arranged in the open around the manicured lawn. My prey entered one of the tents. I took a sip from my drink and strolled down the stairs onto the lawn. The booze must have been catching up to me: *Warily, James Bond follows his arch-rival into the throngs of beautiful people . . . nothing like a snoot full and a .357 to make you delusional.* In the tent I found a smattering of attendees, seated and standing, enjoying drinks and conversation. Still looking for Juno Skinner, I made the few steps to the bar and ordered a Blanton's.

"Excuse me, *señor*, do you have a light?"

I turned, "No, I'm sorry—"

The voice and cigarette belonged to a woman about five-eight, olive complexion, perhaps thirty-five, with long, straight, black hair that fell to her waist and shimmered in the light. She wasn't Juno Skinner, but just as exotic. She was even dressed in a floor-length black gown. The gown was held in place by two thin straps overtaxed by her ample breasts. I couldn't tell whether she was pretty or beautiful. Her face was attractive, but there was something disconcerting, almost cold, about the eyes—as if I had seen them before.

"You were saying," she said with a slight, perceptive smile.

"I'm sorry," trying not to stutter, "I don't smoke, but let me see if I can find—" turning back to the bar, "bartender, may I have some matches, please?"

The bartender handed me a book of matches. She stood closer, so I could light her cigarette, giving me a spectacular view of her spectacular breasts. The cigarette lit. She blew a long string of smoke over my left shoulder.

"Do you like them? They are real."

"Ahh, yes, very much. I understand real is all the rage now."

Piano wire must be the secret. The straps were probably made from piano wire. Desperately trying to concentrate on her eyes, I remembered where I had seen them before.

"Hello, my name is Adel Vicente. Please call me Adel," she said in what could only be described as a sultry voice.

"Are you related to Reynaldo Vicente?"

"He is my brother. We are in Newport for holiday."

"How do you do? I am—"

"I know who you are, may I please have champagne?"

Turning back to the bar, "Bartender, champagne and another Blanton's, please." A couple more whiskeys and I would be in the pool, but I would be well dressed.

"How do you know who I am?"

"My brother said you would be here with your wife. She is a famous musician, si?"

"She is an amateur musician. I guess in amateur circles she is pretty well known."

"I see you come into garden, so I come to keep you company, do you mind?"

"No, not at all. You are very kind."

I would have thought it was impossible, but she moved closer.

"Perhaps we could go upstairs. I have a room available to me." She slid her index finger down the front of my shirt, stopping for a moment at each stud, "I like studs, it is how you say it, *studs*?"

"Thank you. I am flattered, but my wife would not approve."

"Pity," she cooed.

"Have you been in town long?" I asked, trying to change the subject.

"No, we arrive yesterday."

"There you are, and of course with the most beautiful woman at the party," Liz said, floating to the rescue in a cloud of gold.

I made introductions, the women measured claws, and then Liz and I retreated to the dance floor.

"So, flirting with the hostess?"

"More like fending off a tiger."

"Jaguar, dear. There are no tigers in South America."

"So, did you and Reynaldo have a pleasant dance?" I asked, determined to keep the conversation about anything but Adel.

"Yes, very pleasant, thank you. He is extremely charming."

"I'll bet," I mumbled. We started dancing.

"Sweetie, are you jealous?"

"Maybe a little," I replied.

Liz smiled and kissed me lightly. "That's cute, but no need," she said as we danced.

"You seemed to be enjoying yourself," she continued. "She's very attractive. I didn't know you went for the slinky, Latin types. Was she having wardrobe problems?"

"Yes, I mean no—what do you mean 'wardrobe problems'? And I go for American blonds, one in particular."

She kissed me again, "You smooth talker, I only meant that it appeared that perhaps one of her straps had broken and you were trying to help her," she said a tad too sweetly.

Enough with the straps. We swung into another waltz. This time Lou Handman's 'Are You Lonesome Tonight?' Not prophetic, I hoped. "Is there any reason that Reynaldo would know who we are or, more specifically, who you are?"

"No, why do you ask?"
"Adel seemed to know a lot about us."

"You two are on a first-name basis. My, that was fast," Liz said, with an arched brow.

"A little too fast, if you ask me," I said.

Liz looked at me funny but didn't say anything. Soon we were enjoying the rest of the evening, and to my surprise, it *was* enjoyable. The shrimp and lobster patties were exceptional, as was the champagne. I enjoyed meeting new faces and was particularly pleased to find some old friends from D. C., also 'boat people'. We made plans to meet at Nantucket. We chatted with Joyce and her husband, a writer for one of the boat magazines headquartered in Newport.

I wasn't ready to leave, but the evening eventually wound down, and soon we were saying goodnight. Liz and I tried without success to find Reynaldo, so we could pay our respects. Just as well, I didn't like the guy.

Our driver took us back to the wharf, then we walked back to the boat. The police were still on duty, a new officer. We introduced ourselves and wished him a good evening. Standing guard duty was never my idea of a good evening, but I was glad to have him at his post. Before we boarded the boat, I pulled Liz close to kiss her. Through sweeps of blond hair, I spotted Bad-Bart on the dock just before he slinked behind a boat. Liz removed her heels. I helped her aboard, then we both went below to the main cabin.

Liz started to take off her gown. Turning her back to me, she said, "Undo the hook, please. I'm going to get ready for bed. Will you make me a nightcap?" I unhooked the gown and she let it slide to the floor, revealing only some tan lines. Admiring my wife's beautiful figure as she walked into the forward cabin, I tried to concentrate on making her gin and tonic—glasses, there were no bar glasses? *What happened to the glasses?* I know I had made two gin and tonics just before we left.

"Hey Liz, did you put the bar glasses away before we left?"

"No, why?"

"No reason, I guess I put them away." I got two more glasses from the cupboard and mixed a drink for each of us.

How could anyone get on the boat without breaking the lock? Moreover, why take two bar glasses? I went back up the stairs, found the padlock and looked at the keyhole. Holding it up to the dim light, I could see no signs that it had been tampered with or picked, but I knew someone had been on the boat. Possibly, I could get him to come to me if he were still around. A snoot full of booze and a .357 revolver also make you stupid brave, mostly stupid.

"Hey, Honey, I have to get some ice, okay? Your drink is right here."

Liz walked back into the main cabin wearing only her earrings. She removed one of them.

"Now? Perhaps you failed to notice I kept my promise—no lingerie."

I didn't know what to say, so I stared.

Annoyed, Liz pointed at the drinks. "Very well. Is one of those mine?"

I was now in the monster of all doghouses. But this creep was on our boat. I could not allow him to be anywhere near Liz. Exasperated, Elizabeth took her drink to the stateroom and slammed the door. Wincing, I adjusted the pistol in my cummerbund and climbed out of the boat.

Back on the dock, I greeted the police officer again, walked past the closed harbor master's office, then began walking up the wharf. Fog coming in from the water folded over the land, giving the wharf and the buildings an ethereal look and feel. Maybe the diminished visibility would help. Three or four minutes later, I was on the deserted wharf about halfway between the water and America's Cup Avenue. I stopped and quickly sidestepped to my left into an alley and flattened myself against the wall nearest the water. I waited.

I heard him first, rapid footsteps on the moist pavement. He went by in a hurried walk. I stepped out of the alley behind him.

"Stop right there." He stopped, not turning. "Keep your hands where I can see them and walk backward into the alley." He didn't move. I drew the hammer back on the revolver, the fog amplified the ominous click. "Move!" I said. He slowly stepped back into the alley, his hands at his side, but away from his pockets.

"Now, carefully, and I mean very carefully, turn and put your hands on the wall." He turned and put his hands on the wall.

"Step back and put all your weight on your hands. Step back some more," I demanded.

I carefully leaned in and checked for a weapon. I ran my free hand around his waist and his back, finding a Glock 19 concealed under his shirt. I stuck the Glock in my cummerbund and stepped away from him. From what I could tell in the dim light, it was Black-Bart from the other day.

"All right, why are you following me?"

"I wasn't following anybody."

"You fucked up getting near my wife. If we were anywhere else, I'd kill you where you stand."

"You have no right to hold me at gunpoint," he said. His English was perfect, educated perfect with a slight Spanish accent. He was about five-ten, in his late forties, I guess you would say swarthy looking with long black hair pulled over his ears. He was dressed in black pants, a black T-shirt, a black windbreaker, and black cowboy boots with silver toes. No doubt, the arbiter of fashion for the thug set, a real Beau Brummell. I backed away a few more steps and dialed 911 on my cell phone. The fog momentarily thickened, almost eliminating visibility. "Detective Gallagher, this is . . .

Not interested in talking to the police, my new friend turned and started crabbing sideways for the open end of the alley, then Black-Bart made a break for the fog—

BANG!

I fired my pistol, putting a round in the brick next to his right ear. He stopped. His hand shot to his ear. Then, showing me his bloody hand, he hissed, "You shot me!"

"Brick splinters," I said. "But if you move again, I'll put one *in* your ear."

Modesty usually forbids me to mention that I am very good with firearms, and at this distance I could have stitched my initials across his chest.

"Now, get on your stomach and spread your arms and legs as wide as you can spread them. Do it!"

Once he was on the ground, spread-eagled, I dialed 911 again and asked for Detective Gallagher. The dispatcher told me he was off duty but after listening to the circumstances said she would find him. Meanwhile, she would send a uniformed officer.

The officer assigned to watch our boat showed up first with his gun drawn. He recognized me and said, "I thought I heard a shot!"

"Yeah, I just called for Detective Gallagher," I replied.

Shortly, two more uniformed police officers arrived, their car's red and blue strobe lights bouncing off the buildings and fog. The first thing they did was tell me to put my gun down on the pavement and step back while placing my hands behind my head. Two of the officers spoke with Black Bart aka Beau Brummell, the third asked for my identification. I took my wallet out of my pocket, removed my driver's license, and handed it to the officer.

As the police officer was examining my identification, Gallagher arrived. The small emergency light in the windshield of his car looping through the fog and mist. He got out of the car and ambled over to the officer and me. He looked over at Black Bart, nodded hello to the other officers, and turned his attention to me.

"Put your hands down. I thought you were going to call me if anything happened," he said.

"I did."

"Yeah, after the fact. What's the story with the cowboy over there?" Nodding his head at Black-Bart.

"He's the one who followed Elizabeth and me this afternoon. I spotted him this evening in the parking lot at a gala we were attending and again when we were coming home after the party."

I gave him the entire story, starting with our trip to the gala, the missing bar glasses, finishing with the scene in the alley, carefully glossing over the shot I fired into the wall.

"All right, give him his gun," Gallagher said to the uniformed officers. Then to me, "Stick around until I find what the cowboy has to say. Then I want you back on your boat."

Black Bart's answers to Gallagher's questions were predictable for their vivid imagination and lack of information. He said he was very frightened. He told Gallagher I pointed a gun at him, and he was sure I was about to "rob" him until the police arrived and prevented the robbery.

"Let me get this straight. The man has a four-hundred-thousand-dollar boat tied up at the dock, but he's a little short of cash, so he gets dressed in a tuxedo to go out and commit armed robbery. Is that about it?" Gallagher said.

"*Si, estoy muy asustada.* I *muy* scared."

"Why were you carrying a gun?"

"*Estoy muy asustada.*"

"Where is your identification?"

"*Lo pierdo.*"

"You what?"

"I think I lose it."

"Uh-huh," Gallagher turned to the two officers with the patrol cars, "Lock him up and we'll talk to him in the morning." He looked at me. "You have anything else?"

"Only that he gave the impression of being well educated, fluent in English until you got here, then he started the *no habla* routine."

"Okay, call me about ten tomorrow morning, then I want you out of here. By that, I mean out of town, and leave the sleuthing to us. And I don't want to see that gun anymore."

"Thanks, lieutenant."

I walked back to the boat with the duty officer. Neither of us said much, other than goodnight. By the time I climbed back on the boat, Liz was asleep. I drank my watered-down gin and tonic, pulled my clothes off, put the gun away and crawled in beside Liz, and went to sleep.

CHAPTER EIGHT

Ed arrived about nine-thirty the next morning, thankfully with soft luggage. There was much hugging and kissing on Liz's part. Ed and I are too manly, so we skipped the kissing part. We stored his gear, and I put him in what we euphemistically call the guest stateroom.

Leaving Liz to do some shopping, Ed and I walked to the dock master's office and stepped inside. Charlene was sitting at a desk behind the counter. Whoever the dock master was, he had a great gig. He never worked. Charlene looked up and smiled, "Hi there, you leaving today?"

"No, first thing tomorrow morning. You may remember I bought a lock from you the other day."

"Yes."

"May I see the box the lock came from?"

"You took it with you."

"No, the box or carton the locks are packed in from the factory. It should be about twice or three times the size of a pack of cigarettes."

She paused for a moment. "I guess so." She stood and walked over to us, pulled a cardboard box from under the counter, and placed it on the countertop.

"Is there something wrong?"

"No, I just wanted to look at the box for a minute."

The box was a factory six-pack, which, when originally opened, held six individually boxed padlocks, each box contained two keys. I looked at the end of the box. The label was partially worn, but it was obvious from the remaining portion that it had once been printed with *KEYED ALIKE*. I took two of the individual boxes from the carton and emptied them on the counter. All four keys opened both locks. I repackaged the boxes.

I looked at Charlene. "Someone mistakenly bought a carton of keyed-alike padlocks. Every time you sell one of these locks, you are also selling keys to all the other locks. It probably doesn't make too much difference in a transient area like this, but you may want to tell your boss not to sell anymore, at least out of this carton." I pointed to the end of the carton. "You see, it's marked on the label. I don't suppose you keep records of lock purchases?"

She looked at me, then the label, "No. I'm so sorry, I don't think any of us realized. I can refund your money."

"Thank you, but no, I suspect the dock master bought them to secure the gas pumps and other equipment. Just be sure not to sell anymore."

We found the rental car where Liz said she left it and while driving to the police station, I filled Ed in on the events leading up to last night. "Does Liz know about any of this?"

"No, but I think she smells a rat. I got that look last night when I went looking for the tail."

"Well, do what you please, but my suggestion is to tell her. For one thing, another set of eyes could prove useful."

"I didn't want to ruin her vacation. Now that this guy is locked up, I suspect this thing is all over. Hopefully, we won't need another set of eyes."

"What was all the stuff with the locks?"

"I think there are two sets of people, or two groups involved in the burglaries. The ones who hit me over the head bypassed the lock somehow, conceivably they picked it, but I think the second bunch had a key they got by buying a lock from the dock master."

"It had to be another boat owner or certainly someone who knew about the screw-up with the locks," Ed said.

"Perhaps, but maybe it was dumb luck. Maybe they bought a lock to replace the one they were going to break and discovered the keys were the same." I thought for a moment. "That doesn't make any sense, does it?"

"No, but none of it makes any sense to me," Ed said.

We parked along the street and walked into the brick and glass edifice that was Newport police headquarters. A young woman sat behind a waist-high counter at a desk with several multi-buttoned telephones, a computer screen, and a keyboard.

"May I help you?" she asked.

I asked for Detective Lieutenant Gallagher. She made a call, then directed us to his office. A few minutes later, Gallagher came in with a cup of coffee and walked around the desk to his chair. He offered us some coffee, but we declined. I introduced Ed. They shook hands, and then we sat around Gallagher's desk.

"Who's your friend? Ed, is it?"

"The friend I told you about. He arrived this morning."

"I'm here for moral support—have been since college," Ed said.

"You guys roommates? I still lift a few with my college roommate."

"No, night classes. We were on the G.I. Bill and worked full time."

"Mostly, we chased women," Ed said.

"Ha. Help yourselves to coffee and donuts."

"So, what do you have on the cowboy?" I asked.

Gallagher drank from his coffee cup, then set the cup on the blotter. "I don't know. He's totally off our radar, so we tried the Feds and INTERPOL. INTERPOL thinks he might be Victor Fuentes, who used to work for the DGI, the Cuban CIA. Trouble is, he got bailed out early this morning." Gallagher turned his computer screen toward me, and Ed. Victor Fuentes's profile and mug shot were on the screen.

"Yep, that's him."

Ed took a bite out of a donut. "DGI. What's he doing up here?"

"Bailed by whom?"

"An attorney from Boston, and he's not saying who he's working for."

"Great, just perfect," I said. "That's the last we will ever see of him."

"Yeah, that's my opinion too," Gallagher said.

"Perhaps that's a good thing. What the hell does a Cuban intelligence guy want with me? The closest I've been to Cuba was Guantanamo Bay, but I was with a thousand other marines, and we only stayed three days, though we did tear up the E Club."

"I don't think he's seeking damages for the E Club. Truthfully, I thought you were full of shit, but this DGI thing has me reconsidering. You two work for the Feds by any chance?" Gallagher asked.

"I assure you, lieutenant, I'm just trying to enjoy a vacation, and Ed is an instructor and check pilot for the FAA."

"Check pilot—that makes you the best of the best. Used to do a little flying myself." He looked at me, "You say you were in the Corps?"

"Six years, couple tours, but that was long ago. Do you think there is a connection between Fuentes, or whatever his name is, and Reynaldo Vicente? As I told you, I'm pretty sure I saw him at the gala."

"I don't know much about Vicente; he spends some time here during summer, but he's Venezuelan, not Cuban," Gallagher said.

"That's what he told us too, or that's what he told my wife. He didn't say much of anything to me."

"Any chance of getting the name of the law firm this attorney works for?" Ed popped the last bite of a donut into his mouth.

"I have a couple of connections. Possibly I can learn a thing or two, but even if I find the attorney, what will that do for you?"

"I don't know, but it's more than we have now. Might be useful later," Ed said.

I interjected, "If you get the name of the firm, shoot us an email, but as far as I'm concerned, there isn't going to be any 'later,' we're out of here tomorrow."

I handed Gallagher my card. "That's got my email on it. We have a computer on the boat, access should be pretty good. I appreciate your posting the guard at the boat and helping the other night, probably saved me from a night in your jail. Unless you have anything else, I think we would like to get the hell out of your lovely town."

"No, nothing else. Remember what I told you about that gun," Gallagher warned.

Ed and I thanked the lieutenant again and went back to the car.

"Ed, you once told me you flew produce out of South America. I always suspected you were flying more than cantaloupes."

"What makes you bring that up?"

"You knew about the DGI."

"Even if I did, I couldn't tell you about it. Besides, that was a long time ago and everyone knows about the DGI."

"I didn't."

We spent about an hour shopping for stuff I needed, and that Ed forgot. After returning the car to the rental agency, we caught a cab back to the boat.

Liz was already aboard and helped us put away our purchases. Then she showed us her newest 'finds,' a pair of shorts and a black cocktail dress. I understood the shorts but didn't grasp the value of a cocktail dress on a sailboat, but in such instances, I had learned long ago to keep logical thought to myself.

CHAPTER NINE

I stood in the cockpit, cleared my throat, and yelled, "Make all preparations to get underway!"

Ed and Liz stared at me. I grinned. "I always wanted to say that."

"Do we address you as *captain* or *sir*?" Liz asked.

"I prefer *captain*, but *skipper* or *sir* will be acceptable."

She threw a wet sponge at me. Ed laughed, "Where we headed, skipper?"

"For high adventure on the bounding main." I had no idea how literal that statement was going to be.

A brief stop at the fuel dock to top off for what I was sure would be the first of many water stops, then we motored into the harbor. Our departure brought with it a glorious sunny morning. The sky was a Matisse blue with a few wisps of white clouds. The wind was warm and light out of the east, promising to swing to the southeast, perfect for our trip to Block Island. Steering to the northeast, we motored around Goat Island. Once past Fort Adams and well into the East Passage, we turned southwest. After skirting a ferryboat, we hoisted the mainsail. One always hoists, never pulls sails. You can *raise*, but I like *hoist,* and it was my boat, so we hoisted.

We set and locked a course of 221 degrees into the Autohelm. Ed and Liz unfurled the jib and trimmed the sails for the thirteen-mile sail to Block Island. I shut off the engine and felt, as I always do when the engine stops, the built-up tension from my back, arms, and legs drain into the deck. All was right with the world. Sailing on a sunny day with a blue sky and about fifteen knots of wind is truly heaven on Earth.

I turned the wheel over to Ed and joined Liz, already forward, stretched out on a towel, sunning herself. She was wearing a black and white one-piece swimsuit with a huge white floppy hat and oversized sunglasses. Sitting in the bow pulpit, I watched the heavy summer boat traffic, both power and sail, ply the shining waters. A momentary glint of polished teak focused my attention on a picnic boat several hundred yards away. A man was standing at the rear of the boat looking at *Pinafore* with a pair of binoculars. He looked familiar. It was Fuentes. The powerful picnic boat leaped ahead on a parallel course. I watched until it was out of sight. Then, forgetting about the picnic boat, Liz and I enjoyed the warm sun and the fresh breeze across the bow with the occasional spray of sun-kissed saltwater. We chatted, napped, and read. Later, I fixed some crackers and cheese, then later still fixed some ham sandwiches and lemonade.

Ed called out, "Hey, bud, you better look at this!"

It took me a moment to get up and walk aft to the helm. "Look at what?"

"This big blob on the radar. I think it's what us pilots call a big effing thunderstorm. If I were in an airplane, I would get the hell out of the way."

I looked at the radar, then over at the ominous clouds hanging over the close horizon. "That, my friend, is what us sailors call a big effing squall. And we can't get out of the way. Start the engine and get the sails down. Liz! Get all your stuff below and get your life jacket on!"

I dove below as Liz gathered up all her paraphernalia and shoved it down the forward hatch. She followed, closing the hatch behind her and bolting it down. I jumped into my rain gear and life jacket and started back up the companionway, then turned to Liz. "Get the hatch boards, then you and Ed install them."

On deck once more, I furled the jib until it was about the size of a handkerchief, then double-checked that the mainsail was tied down. I jumped behind the wheel. "Ed, get your life jacket on, then help Liz with the hatch boards."

"Gotcha. And I thought sailing would be boring." He ran below.

"Ed! Whatever happens, do not open that companionway to the sea. Okay! Here it comes!"

The wind slammed into *Pinafore* causing her to heel over, then suddenly pitch up as a roller of water followed the wind—then she dropped into a chasm. Wind shrieked through the boat's rigging as it climbed, then suddenly plunged again. Mountains of dark green water crashed over *Pinafore,* driving the bow deep into the sea. *Pinafore* rolled on her side until the mast was parallel to the water. Righting to the vertical, the boat plunged into another trough. Another knock-down, the masthead caught the sea again. This time, the boat refused to right itself. Now on its side, *Pinafore* took tons of water into the cockpit. Arms sheathed in yellow, the attached gloved hands held on as the boat, still on its side, eventually pivoted into the wind.

Through screaming wind, I pleaded, "Come on, girl, stand up! Stand up!" The boat started to stand, then suddenly another mountain of green water crashed over the transom and a jumble of yellow legs and arms were swept overboard only to be brought short by a black harness tethered to the boat.

Dragging behind the boat, it felt as if my left arm was broken. I knew I had to get back aboard before she completely righted, or I would have no chance. Struggling, aided by another crash of seawater, I finally climbed back aboard. Regaining my stance behind the big wheel, I yelled through the screaming wind, "Son of a bitch! You didn't have to throw me overboard! I damn near broke my arm."

As suddenly as it started, the wind diminished. Only the rail and winches were submerged.

"Good girl! Damn, what a sailor!"

Shortly, the sun returned and started to streak through the storm clouds. Off to starboard, a right whale breached.

Speaking to *Pinafore*, "Wow! Girl, look at that." I watched the massive ocean creature soar for a moment, then crash into the water disappearing in the ocean troughs. I watched for another breach, but the behemoth was gone.

The boat stood a little taller, so I turned on the autopilot, unhooked my harness, then maneuvered carefully to the companionway, my boots squishing and squeaking on the deck. I banged on the hatch.

"Olly olly oxen free!" I went back to the wheel.

The hatch cover slid back several inches. A set of fingers removed the top hatch board. Both Liz and Ed peered through the narrow opening.

"Fun, huh?" I said.

"Fun! I have bruises all over my body!" Liz said indignantly.

Ed grinned.

"You guys can come out and play now. You missed the whale!"

"Whale?" Liz said.

Arriving at Great Salt Pond at about three-thirty in the afternoon, we picked up a mooring without too much drama, secured the boat, and made dinner plans. Liz is a superb cook, and I am a fair hand around the stove but, when possible, we have dinner ashore, saving galley duty for lunches, intimate dinners, and those times when, because of either distance or weather, no restaurant is accessible. This evening, we opted for Dead Eye Dick's, a quintessential landmark of Block Island and a good place for food. During dinner, I did as Ed suggested and told Liz about the problems, we, that is I, was having.

"Liz, I've been meaning to tell you something. I've been putting it off so as not to affect our vacation."

"What? Can't be any worse than this afternoon. I look like I've gone five rounds with the Energizer bunny."

I told her about the break-in, the assault, and Fuentes, leaving out the shooting part. She was quiet for a long time. Ed and I stole glances at each other, neither saying anything. Finally, she said. "I wondered why the police were around all the time. Are you okay?"

"I'm fine."

"What about this Fuentes character?"

"I cornered him and had him arrested. No one seems to know who he is, but I think it's all over now. I didn't want to worry you."

"I wondered what tore you away from my bed. So, it wasn't another woman."

I thought she was joking, but I wasn't sure. "No, of course not, Lizzy. First and foremost, I want this to be the vacation we have tried to have for years. I didn't want to worry you."

"Yeah, you said that. Well, I don't want to embarrass you in front of Ed, but this is not acceptable. I am your wife and the mother of your children, and I am plenty damned worried! We're a thousand miles from home with no resources and you're running around playing Dick Tracy. You should have told me about all of this right away. From now on, there will be no more secrets between us. You are my husband, and we should not have secrets. Frankly, I'm pissed as hell!"

"I'm sorry," I said.

"Okay, let's forget it and enjoy our vacation."

The early morning was thick with fog that threatened to last all day. Cold and damp penetrated the boat, so I turned on the heater, a small central heating system that uses a fan and a diesel fuel burner. By late morning, the sun bled through the high scud, giving us a reprieve from a grimy afternoon. We had lunch at the Harborside Hotel, then walked around the town. Mostly, Ed and I looked in the windows while Liz shopped, but I bought a wool sweater at a small store specializing in goods made in Scotland. By the time we worked our way uptown near the ferry dock, we were hungry again, so we found a little place that had good pizza. Things were a little tense between Liz and me, and I looked forward to a thaw. Hopefully soon.

CHAPTER TEN

Great Salt Pond, Block Island

To my surprise, we still had half our fresh water on board, so at about six-thirty the next morning we slipped our mooring, left Great Salt Pond, and turned north headed for our next port of call on Martha's Vineyard.

Reminiscent of a huge, vacant soundstage I had once visited, the seascape was devoid of color or perspective, the ocean and sky blended perfectly so there was no horizon. Flattened by the oppressive steel-gray sky, the sea was smooth and pond-like.

About fifty minutes out of Great Salt Pond, we made a right turn at Bell G1 to a new course of 086 degrees or, to the uninitiated, more or less east. Off the starboard bow, a half dozen gulls floated on the water, quietly rising, and falling with the gentle swells coming in from the Atlantic. Their color was almost an iridescent white against the oppressive grayness.

With no wind, the engine had been running most of the morning, but when a slight breeze came up, we turned it off. Leaving the centerboard up, we set the sails. *Pinafore* was on a beam reach, port tack making about three knots. With the two knots of current it gave us a speed over ground of about five knots. The depth showed to be ninety-five feet. For an hour or more, or since we turned at the G1 Bell, there had been a powerboat at the edge of our visibility, abaft our port beam, paralleling our course.

I sat behind the wheel idly contemplating the word *abaft*. It has a manly sound, and I thought us manly, seafaring types should use it more often in conversation. The trouble was, *abaft* is hard to work into conversations unless maybe it's at the abaft end of a cocktail party when no one cares what you say. I decided to think more on the subject but after breakfast.

Liz had prepared a breakfast of bacon, pancakes with real maple syrup, and lots of hot coffee. Seated around the cockpit table, the three of us had a pleasant time eating and chatting while enjoying the excellent breakfast.

Pinafore, on autopilot, was still sailing east. After breakfast, I was on watch seated behind the wheel enjoying my coffee. Ed was on KP helping Liz put away the dishes. I could hear them talking, laughing, and bantering good-naturedly. Ed probably has the best sense of humor of anyone I know, and it was good to hear his off-color jokes again, perhaps a sign his heart was healing after the death of his wife.

Some five miles east of Block Island and about ten miles south of Point Judith, our powerboat companion was no longer abaft, but now about a mile off our port beam. It looked like one of those *picnic boats* sailboat manufacturers currently build. My guess is they use old sailboat molds because the things look like sailboats without the mast. The boat was about forty feet with a forward cutty cabin that left the back two-thirds of the boat open. Our companions were keeping pace with our speed, which for a boat that could probably due thirty knots had to be boring. Maybe they were fishing. I couldn't tell and lost interest.

Liz climbed into the cockpit and handed me another cup of coffee, then curled up with her coffee and a copy of *Vogue*. Ed followed shortly and took charge of the helm. I grabbed my cup and went below to make some entries on the chart.

With automatic helms and electronic charts that interface with the onboard GPS and radar systems, navigation, even with small yachts, is now mostly pushing buttons. The GPS uses a network of thirty satellites. Civilian units are accurate to about ten feet and can give you vertical or horizontal positions anywhere in the world. In short, they are amazing, but if the boat experiences a power outage, one is literally and metaphorically in the dark. For that reason, I like to keep track of my course the old-fashioned way, on a paper chart.

I penciled in our position on the chart every hour or so trying to verify it with some dead reckoning. I was usually close, but with the wonders of GPS, it was never a real contest.

"Ahoy, Pinafore, this *eese* Coast Guard Auxiliary. We come aboard for a safety inspection. You will heave to!"

"Who the hell is that?" I yelled up to Ed.

"Some guys off the portside," Ed said.

I looked out a portside window and saw the picnic boat now only about 400 yards away, still keeping station with us.

"Should we stop?" Ed asked.

"No!"

"Why?" Liz asked.

"Coast Guard Auxiliary inspections are strictly voluntary, usually on weekends, and they would call us over the radio, not on a hailer. Plus, they would be flying a Coast Guard Auxiliary flag."

"Well, captain, what are your orders?" Ed said, a bit amused.

"Ahoy, Pinafore, this is the Coast Guard Auxiliary. We are coming aboard!"

Back at the nav station, I switched the radio to hailer and keyed the mike, "Unidentified boat, you are not welcome aboard. Stand off or we will call the Coast Guard!"

I climbed topside and looked to port. They backed off some, and we could see what looked to be heated discussion and gesticulation among the five or six men aboard the picnic boat.

"Pinafore, this is Coast Guard Auxiliary. We are coming aboard for safety inspection!" said a voice I seemed to recognize.

I pulled out the binoculars and looked over at the picnic boat again. "Hey, Ed, I think I see our friend Fuentes."

"This can't be good," he replied, no longer amused. "Let's hope he doesn't have any artillery."

I spoke into the mike again, "Unidentified boat, stand off! You do not have permission to come aboard!"

In the confusion, we had fallen off course, so I turned my attention to trim the jib, which had started to luff—

POP! POP! POP!

Three geysers of water plumed just in front of our bow! The distinct sound of an AK-47 dredged back memories I thought had been stuffed in a seabag long ago.

"Jesus, they're shooting at us!" Liz yelled.

"Pinafore, stop your boat, or we shoot into you," the amplified voice said.

I yelled, "Okay, guys, take it easy! They want something on this boat, so they are not going to sink us before they look for it. Ed! Get on the hailer and stall them. While you're doing that start the engine but keep it in neutral! When I tell you, I want you to drop the mainsail. Whatever you do, do not change course, we need the wind off the starboard bow! Okay?"

"Got it!" Ed turned the key on the instrument panel and pushed the button that brought the diesel to life.

"Liz! Go below and start calling the Coast Guard! Our position is on the GPS, and it's marked on the chart. Ask them to get their asses out here, like now! When the shooting starts, lie on the cabin floor. That will put you below the waterline. Bullets don't do well in water!"

"What do you mean, when the shooting starts?"

"Please just do as I ask. We don't have much time!" I followed her below.

Liz jumped behind the nav station. Just then her phone rang. It was a FaceTime call from Brad. She answered. Brad had a phone in one hand and a spatula in the other. There was a crash in the background as a small box fell and Brad turned face forward.

"Mom! There's a squirrel in our kitchen. What do I do?" Just then, the squirrel flew across the room behind Brad.

"Not now, Brad!" She threw the phone down and started calling the Coast Guard.

I knew our friends in the picnic boat would monitor the radio, but maybe an SOS call to the Coast Guard would scare them off. I quickly yanked the M14 and the shotgun out of the special hidey-hole along with a box of ammo for the shotgun and three magazines for the rifle, one wrapped with electrical tape. *Where was Horatio Hornblower when I needed him? This was supposed to be a fucking vacation!* I passed the shotgun and ammo up to Ed, "Ed! Take this. If they get close enough to use this thing, we're in trouble but take it anyway!"

"Thanks for the encouraging words," Ed said.

I took the magazine wrapped in the electrical tape and inserted it in the rifle, cycling the action, chambering a round. Liz was talking to the Coast Guard. No surprise, she was calm and articulate.

"Pinafore, this is your last warning. Stop *zee* boat."

From the bottom of the companionway, I yelled, "Okay, Ed, drop the main!"

Ed let the main halyard run, allowing the mainsail to thunder down the mast. The wind coming across the starboard side of the boat caused the sail to fall just port of the main hatch, forming an enormous pile of Dacron from the cockpit to the mast. I ran up the companionway stairs and using the lowered mainsail as cover, crawled forward lying down on top of the cabin. The sail wouldn't protect me from gunfire, but it would hide me from the picnic boat until I could set up to shoot.

Magazines for the M14 hold twenty rounds of *ball* ammunition. The infamous *full metal jacket* ball ammo is made with a lead bullet that for "humanitarian reasons" is copper clad. *Tracer* ammunition is essentially hollow and contains phosphorus or magnesium that burns at about five thousand degrees. Armor-piercing is self-explanatory. The magazine marked with the electrical tape contained my "pirate recipe," the first three rounds were armor piercing, the next five were tracers, the next three were ball, the next three tracers, and so on. If the improbable happened and fending off pirates became a reality, the idea was to destroy their engine and fuel tanks with the armor-piercing rounds, then ignite the fuel with the tracers. The ball ammo was to irritate them.

"Ed, warn them again to stay away from our boat!" I yelled.

Ed's amplified, almost mechanical, voice boomed over the water, "Stay away from our boat. You are not welcome aboard!"

They were at 150 yards now, and one of them was holding an AK-47.

Mikhail Kalashnikov, poet, tank commander, and Ph.D., designed the AK-47. His design, an impressive mix of features from Garand, Williams, Browning, and Sturgewehr is the most widely used weapon in the world. Oddly, I met the famous Kalashnikov at a cocktail party. Not speaking Russian, I didn't get to try *abaft*. My introduction to the wrong end of his infamous weapon was particularly unpleasant, and I had no wish to repeat the experience, especially with my wife and best friend fifteen feet away.

"Pinafore, have everyone on board stand in the rear of the boat with their hands behind their heads."

"Hey, bud, they're still coming!" Ed yelled.

"No, they're not," I said to more to myself than to Ed and slipped the barrel of the rifle through the folds of the sail, snugged it into my shoulder, aimed at a place on their hull where I assumed the fuel tanks would be, and fired three quick rounds, *BAM! BAM! BAM!* Then three more, *BAM! BAM! BAM!* The engine hatch blew off and I could see splinters of fiberglass flying off the boat—

The rifle thumped against my shoulder spewing tracers through the moonless night into the far tree line. I yelled to the mortar pit, "Put some rounds right there!"

"On the way, Sarge!"

The 60mm HE rounds left the tubes with a flash, trailing sparks of burnt powder like big fireworks on the Fourth of July. When they reached their pinnacle, the rounds arced over, descending into a series of thumps across the sunbaked dirt, each thump flashing like an enormous flashbulb. Finding their range, more and more HE rounds hammered into the tree line. Orange flashes from secondary explosions reflected off the low cloud cover putting the tree line in silhouette.

—Ed was yelling, "Hit them again, bud. They're mad as hornets!"
Except for the irksome ringing in my ears, it seemed my six rounds had done little but created a lot of confusion. I fired again.
BAM! BAM! BAM!
Three rounds punched into the side of the picnic boat's hull. The men on the picnic boat dove for cover as fiberglass splinters skewered the air.
BAM! BAM! BAM!
Three trails of white-hot phosphorus streaked across the water. The tracers drove into the punctured fuel tanks, igniting the fuel with molten phosphorus. The fuel tanks exploded, blowing out a section of the picnic boat's hull.
"And three rounds to piss them off."
BAM! BAM! BAM!
Round after round slammed into the picnic boat, ripping gaping holes in the hull, tearing into the fuel tanks and engine. The engine hatch buckled, then blew off in pieces that were thrown yards away. Pieces of the engine

and superstructure blew through the deck, severing a man's foot. His screams cloaked by the fusillade from the M14.

I repositioned my aim. "For those slow learners, the rest of the magazine."

BAM! BAM! BAM! BAM! BAM!

An explosion and ball of fire engulfed the picnic boat. The men remaining on the rear of the boat were hurled into the water, some like rag dolls, were launched into the air. A loan man on the bow of the sinking boat aimed his AK-47—

I yelled, "Ed! Get down!" I fired.

BAM!

The shooter pirouetted into the water. I continued firing into the boat until the second magazine was empty, then inserted another, and fired until it was empty. I looked up after inserting the fourth magazine. The picnic boat was demolished. Flames and thick oily smoke rose from the wreckage. I lowered the rifle.

Ed rose and peered out at what was left of the picnic boat. "Goddamn, bud. Remind me to never piss you off."

"Ed, get us out of here, try to keep our portside to them until we're out of range of that AK!"

Ed put *Pinafore* in gear and brought her up to full speed. I kept my rifle trained on the picnic boat, but by then the rear two-thirds of the boat was sinking and the remaining occupants were jumping in the water trying to get away from the fire.

We were about a mile away when we stopped. Liz yelled from the cabin and said the Coast Guard was on the way.

Shortly, an H-65 helicopter arrived overhead. Like a huge orange bee between two flowers, it hovered back and forth between the burning boat and us. The crew chief hung out the side door watching with binoculars.

Liz called from the nav station again, "The Coast Guard helicopter says to remain on station until one of their boats arrives."

"Thanks. Keep monitoring in case they have more instructions. Are you okay?"

"I'm fine. I'm sorry, I forgot to lie on the deck. Is it over?"

"It's over, but I'd like you to monitor the radio in case the Coast Guard wants to talk with us."

"OK!"

We could monitor the radio from the cockpit, but I thought she would be safer below.

After plucking three survivors from the water, the chopper headed to the west. About fifteen minutes later, a Coast Guard RB-M boat arrived on the scene. The RB-M circled where the picnic boat sank, fished another person out of the water, circled the area again, then came over to us. The four crew members were dressed in body armor with sidearms and carried M-4s. The Coast Guard's new RB-Ms are forty-five-foot jet boats, and though probably not intentionally, they look like small tugboats. They are very fast, have a long range, and carry loads of electronics.

Petty Officer First Class Jim Davis, the boat commander, was about six feet, pleasant looking with a good smile, and spoke with a southern accent. He was probably about thirty with the demeanor and confidence of someone much older. The guardsmen asked if they could tie up alongside our starboard side in a manner that suggested they would do so with or without permission. I said "Sure" and invited them on board. Davis climbed into *Pinafore* followed by two of his men, both kids that looked as if they could play nose tackle in the NFL. One went forward to the bow, and the other stood on the transom, each holding his M-4 at the ready.

I had already stored my M14. Automatic weapons are legal to own, provided they were made before 1986 and you purchased a tax stamp, but I was not about to get in a discussion on the nuances of the law, especially with the Coast Guard. These guys deal with particularly bad people and have very little patience with nuance. More importantly, they have my sincerest respect.

PO1 Davis and his nose tackles looked around the boat, then Davis walked forward and saw the forty or so spent cartridge cases lying around the mast. Liz climbed up from below and stood in the cockpit. PO1 Davis gave her a little salute, "Ma'am," then turned to me and said, "Hear you all had some excitement this mornin'. Mind if we look around your boat?"

"No. Please help yourself," I replied.

Liz said, "Would you gentlemen like something to drink?"

"No, ma'am, thank you just the same. We'll just look around a bit. If you all don't mind staying up here while I go below—you all don't have anybody else on board, do you?"

"No," I said.

"You all carrying any contraband?"

Liz looked at me. I looked at Ed questioningly, then he mouthed the word *drugs*. The guardsmen were paying close attention, and they were very edgy.

"Guys, please relax. We are not carrying any drugs, if that's what you mean. We have firearms on board, but other than the shotgun there, they are now locked away. My wife and I are on vacation. This man is my best friend and is traveling with us.

"Uh-huh." Davis spoke to Ed, "Sir, you mind handin' Petty Officer Milan that shotgun. Carefully, please. Don't want any accidents."

Ed handed the Beretta to the nose tackle, "It's not loaded."

"Uh-huh. Your radio call said that men were tryin' to board your boat and had fired at you with an automatic weapon."

"Yes, they said they were Coast Guard Auxiliary and wanted to board our boat for a safety inspection. I told them no and we repeatedly asked them to stand off. They refused, then shot three rounds across our bow. We asked them to stand off again. They told us to put our hands up and threatened to fire into our boat. I believed them and shot into their engine compartment. We called you immediately."

"What do you suppose is so all-fired interesting about your boat that made them that insistent on coming aboard?"

I was wondering the same thing myself. I was reasonably sure Fuentes, probably now deceased, was key to the answer, the attack, the earlier break-in, and the whack on my head. I kept coming back to the money in the AC. Was it enough for all this mayhem? Probably, but I had a feeling there was something more.

"I don't know. They started following us just north of Block Island. Picked us up at the G1 Bell, staying well off our beam. Suddenly they were right next to us. Did the guys you picked up by chopper say anything?"

"They said they were just fishin' and you all opened up on them for no reason."

"What's the guy in your boat say?" I asked.

"He's not saying much of anything. He tried the *no habla* routine, but PO2 Carlos over there," nodding at the RB-M, "speaks fluent Spanish, so when he realized we *habla'ed* he stopped talking. It doesn't look much like he was dressed for fishin'."

"There should be another one floating around," I said.

"Dead?"

"Pretty sure. He aimed an AK at us, so I shot him," I replied.

"He probably got hung up in the boat when it went down—from the amount of brass lying around, looks like you hit him more than once."

I shook my head, "No, I was trying to disable the boat. He had already fired three rounds at us, then aimed that AK at us again, so I shot at him—once."

"Guess you know an AK when you see one?" PO1 Davis framed it as a question.

"I've had some prior experience with them."

"Well, you sure enough disabled the boat. Be nice to know what was on it. You said it was a picnic boat, right?"

Not waiting for an answer, PO1 Davis went below while the nose tackles watched the three of us. In a few minutes, he came back up to the cockpit, made some notations in a notebook, pushed his hat back revealing some close-cropped, sandy blond hair.

"All right, you all stand by for a few minutes." He crossed back to the RB-M while the nose tackles continued to watch us.

Ed walked to the side and asked Davis if he could come aboard.

Davis replied, "Sure, watch your step."

Liz moved next to me, "Are we going to be arrested?" she whispered.

"Probably. We just blew up somebody's boat and killed at least one man, probably more. If they find that money, we'll be in real trouble."

"What's Ed doing?"

"I have no idea."

About ten minutes later, Ed came back aboard *Pinafore*, gave me a wink, and then sat behind the wheel.

PO1 Davis walked to the side of his boat and handed me a business card and then looked over at Petty Officer Milan, "Milan, you two can come on back." He then looked at me, "If you and your crew are okay, you all can go. You have my card and number if you need anything, I can be reached at Coast Guard Station, Point Judith. If we need to reach you, we will try to raise you on the radio, then your cell phone. You all try to enjoy the rest of your trip."

I was dumbfounded. All I could do was stare. I was sure the boat would be impounded and all three of us would be thrown in jail pending some kind of hearing. I looked over at Ed as he started the engine, but he didn't say anything. I regained my wits, thanked Davis, cast off the lines securing the RB-M, and watched as they backed away and motored off to the northwest.

Ed shifted the transmission forward and brought *Pinafore* into the wind. We raised the mainsail, secured the halyard, and trimmed the sheet for a port tack. Once the jib was unfurled and trimmed, we shut off the engine. I went forward, collected all the brass, and threw it overboard. I couldn't understand why the Coast Guard would, or for that matter could, let us go. Yes, it was self-defense against attempted piracy, but certainly the incident rated more than a cursory stop. More like a formal inquiry with all the trimmings. More importantly, at least to me, what *did* our friends on the picnic boat want with us or, more likely, the *Pinafore*?

"Ed, what did you say to the Coast Guard?"

"I told them I was with the State Department, and I was on some more or less official business and they could contact my boss to verify."

"Did they?"

"Yep."

"Why would your boss do that for us? He doesn't know me."

"No, but he knows me, and he does know you, or at least he knows Liz. Actually, he knows *of* Liz, because of the work she does for State. I told him what happened, and he vouched for us and assured Davis that we would be available anytime he wanted us for further questions."

"Well, that was nice of him. Fast thinking on your part, thanks."

"You're welcome. Anytime you get in a gunfight, give me a call."

"Yeah, that will be never. This is supposed to be a vacation, so let's vacation. Liz, please sit down. You're white as a sheet. How about a drink?"

Liz replaced a cockpit cushion pushed aside in all the excitement and sat down. I went below, retrieved the Blanton's, and filled three shot glasses. *A gun battle on the open sea, for Christ's sake! This wasn't some third-world country, this was the United States.* I handed the glasses up to Liz and climbed from the cockpit.

The ordeal was too much to wash away with a shot of bourbon, and contrary to the forecast, the fog turned into a cold, dreary, mist matching my mood. Liz and Ed didn't look much better.

"Hey, crew, let's head for Menemsha. By the time we get there it will be five or six. We can pick up a mooring and have a quiet dinner."

All of a sudden, Liz jumped up, spilling her drink. "Oh, damn! The squirrel in the kitchen!" Liz ran below, leaving Ed and me staring after her.

Some five hours later, just outside the Menemsha Bite, we raised the centerboard, dropped the sails, and turned on the engine. Liz climbed below, slid behind the nav desk, and picked up the radio.

"Menemsha harbor master, Menemsha harbor master. This is Pinafore."

"Pinafore, this Menemsha harbor master. Over."

"Menemsha harbor master, this Pinafore. We are a fifty-foot sailing vessel and would like to come inside for fuel and water."

"Pinafore, come ahead, tie up at the fuel dock left of the entrance."

"Roger. Pinafore out."

Liz turned and yelled up to the cockpit, "Honey, we have permission to go inside the basin!"

"Okay, thanks!"

With the narrow entrance, a sharp left turn, and the shallow water, navigating *inside* the basin called for some diligence, but we moved the big boat gently against the dock and, after securing the lines, turned off the engine.

Liz jumped off the boat to meet the dock master, who was walking toward us. She was a woman of about thirty-five, who wore the ubiquitous khaki safari shirt with jeans and boat shoes. She and Liz chatted amiably while Ed and I filled the water tanks and hosed off the salted boat.

Liz walked to where I was coiling the water hose. "Jennifer said we could stay tied up at the dock, provided we move if someone needs fuel."

"Jennifer?"

"Yeah, the dock master, nice lady, even complimented our landing."

"I was rather adroit, wasn't I?"

"Adroit?"

"It means—"

"I know what it means. It means you're full of you know what. So, captain, we're staying, right." It wasn't a question.

I had moored *outside* before, and it could get bouncy if the wind veered and came out of the north or northwest. And as a captain, it was always good to know your limitations, like who was really in charge. "We're staying," I said in my best captain speak.

"Good, because that's what I told Jennifer," Liz said.

Menemsha is a small commercial fishing community in the town of Chilmark on the western tip of Martha's Vineyard and is famous for its seafood and dazzling sunsets. We would be missing the dazzling sunset on this cool and drizzly day that turned into a cool and drizzly night. Cold, damp, and generally subdued after the terrible morning, the three of us walked the kinks out by touring the small town. Enthusiasm waned quickly, so after poking into a shop or two we decided against eating in town and went back to the boat to make dinner.

Liz worked on the computer at the nav station while Ed, acting as chef, prepared a spaghetti dinner. The boiling water and steam added some welcome warmth to the chilled cabin, and the smell of garlic, tomato sauce, and browning ground beef bolstered our spirits. I was in the engine compartment catering to a habit developed after a particularly exciting night on a friend's boat off Cape May, New Jersey. The throttle linkage had broken, leaving us with no engine control, off a lee shore, in twelve-foot seas and thirty-five-knot winds. I now habitually checked for loose wires and fittings anytime I had the chance.

As I puttered, I was again, unsuccessfully, trying to determine how we had become embroiled in something not of our making. What was so intriguing about this boat? Another question, how did these people, whoever they were, know where to find the boat? From a distance, *Pinafore* looks like hundreds of other sailboats. To find us in the right place at the right time in a thousand square miles of ocean wasn't chance. For the hundredth time, I came back to the money we found in the air-conditioner? Was this just about money? Maybe. Maybe with the demise of Fuentes our problems were over, but I had assumed that before. Another thing rattled around in my brain. Why was Ed's boss so magnanimous? If he or she were a political animal like most upper-level government functionaries, he wouldn't have touched this incident or one like it with a proverbial ten-foot pole. How would they know about the money? The only thing that made sense was that Ed knew something about this whole affair that he wasn't telling us.

We quietly ate Ed's surprisingly good spaghetti dinner, sharing a bottle of cold Lambrusco and a loaf of Italian bread we had picked up at the Menemsha Market.

After dinner, I tried calling Detective Gallagher. The detective answering phones told me Gallagher had gone home for the evening and would be off the next day, so I left a message, asking him to return my call.

I took a warm shower and tried to remove the tangible and emotional chill. Liz and Ed soon followed my lead. Feeling better after the meal and shower, I was sitting on the settee glancing through some of my new sailing magazines when Ed, dripping water and soap, stuck his head out of the aft shower.

"Hey, bud, the damn shower won't drain."

I looked up from my magazine and replied, "Okay, when Liz is finished, use the one in the forward head and I'll look at it tomorrow."

"Okay."

Showered and dressed in warm sweats, the three of us watched an old movie on the state-of-the-art entertainment system. I angled to watch my favorite John Wayne movie, the *Horse Soldiers*, but Liz threatened to mutiny, so in keeping with the nautical theme we chose *The Big Country*. It's an old western, but the main character played by Gregory Peck is a sea captain. Close enough. After the two-plus-hour movie, Liz and I went to bed, leaving Ed searching for another movie.

CHAPTER ELEVEN

Pinafore, Vineyard Sound

The day was bright and blustery. The temperature hovered in the seventy-five-degree range, twenty-knot winds out of the northwest made it feel colder. Bound for Edgartown we sailed up Vineyard Sound on a beam reach, starboard tack, steering about eighty degrees with probably too much sail. An opposing one-knot current added some drama. Ensconced in harnesses and foul-weather gear, the Autohelm turned off, we took turns at the wheel driving the big boat through the four- and five-foot seas. We laughed and yelled as *Pinafore* raced down troughs and shouldered through crests shoving the sea aside, sending great spumes of water over the gunwales creating rainbows in the soaring spray. At times, the bow dove deep into the swells, tons of green water crashed on the decks only to cascade over the sides as the bow lifted majestically into the sunlight. The noise from wind and water, the sting and the taste of the cold salt spray, the motion of the boat pounding through the sea created such joy that we all grinned from ear to ear—exhilaration, distance, and time separating us from the past day.

About noon, we turned to one hundred twenty degrees on a broad reach, starboard tack. The winds had diminished—ten to fifteen knots—the seas were running about three feet. Passing to the north of the R2 Bell, we started dropping into the Edgartown Harbor. We raised the centerboard, turned on the engine, and furled the jib. Lowering the main, we turned around N8, squeezing between Edgartown and Chappaquiddick Point. Inside the anchorage, we picked up our reserved mooring on the first try. Practice makes perfect.

Moored, we raised the sails for about forty-five minutes to dry them in the fresh breeze. When they were furled and covered, and the boat was squared away, the three of us took a water taxi into town. We had a late lunch at the Seafood Shanty, then walked around town looking into the shops. By seven o'clock, we were back on board. I tried reading some Patrick O'Brien but gave up during the first battle.

Waiting for Liz to get out of the shower, I thumbed through my copy of *Eldridge Tide and Pilot Book*, a real page-turner. Ed and I still had not spoken about the day of the gun battle, specifically why the State Department intervened on our behalf with the Coast Guard. Perhaps I was making too much of his visit to the Coast Guard boat. Maybe they let us go because, after all, it was self-defense.

Ed hollered, "Hey, bud, I forgot. The drain in this closet you call a shower is clogged!"

"It's called a head, and I forgot to look at it." I put down *Eldridge,* got on my knees, pulled up a couple of deck boards, and found the pump that drains the aft shower. My head stuck in the bilge, I yelled, "Turn off the pump, will you!"

Ed wrapped a towel around his waist and tracked water and soap over the cabin sole to the electric panel and turned off the switch. The pumps—there are many on a boat—all come with filters, and they often become clogged. I unscrewed the cup that holds the filter in place and removed the filter that, in this case, looks like a small rolled-up piece of window screen.

"Ed, look at this!" Inside the roll of screen was a small flash drive.

Ed took it from my hands, "I wonder how long that's been in there?"

"I don't know. I didn't put it in there, and I usually don't use this shower, so I have never cleaned the filter."

Liz came out of the forward cabin dressed in a robe, her wet hair wrapped in a towel. "What's up?"

Ed handed her the flash drive. "We found this in the sump filter," he said.

She looked at the flash drive, turning it over in her hands.

"Well, no news to you guys, it's a flash drive. I think it's one of the newer generation 512-gigabyte drives. They can hold a lot of information. Assuming water didn't get to it, you want me to see what's on it?"

"Yes, please," I said.

Cinching the belt on her robe, Liz sat at the nav station, then plugged the flash drive into the USB port of the computer. We waited for a few minutes while her fingers danced over the keyboard.

"Well, it's in Spanish. I don't read Spanish as well as I should. As far as I can tell, it's a list of people and companies with corresponding numbers that could be bank accounts." She pointed to the screen, "These look like ledgers in U.S. Dollars. Looks as if there are also a dozen or so sets of financial records. It's going to take a forensic accountant to interpret all this information, but if that's what they are, financial records, I mean, from what I can see there is—wow! There may be about eighty million dollars just in this one account, probably more."

"Can you make a copy of everything on the drive?" I asked.

"Better than that, I can send a copy to Gery at my South American desk. He can take a look and give us an analysis. You want me to do that?"

"You have a South American desk?"

"Sure, doesn't everyone?"

"Ed, what do you think?"

"Sure, if you can recover it when we need it later. It should be safe there."

"Okay, do it. Ed, finish taking your shower, and while you guys put on some clothes, I'll make a pot of coffee."

With Liz and Ed out of the main cabin, I jumped behind the nav desk and opened the chart table.

I prefer to keep my electronic charts stored on flash drives because they don't get scratched or damaged. I picked up a flash drive labeled *Narragansett,* peeled off the label, then pasted it on the flash drive we found in the sump. I made sure the label was tight and smooth, then threw it in the drawer with the others. I quickly went back to the sump, taking care not to obstruct the water flow, stuck one of my spare flash drives in the strainer. If anyone found the drive, presumably they would leave the boat to read it. The keywords being "leave the boat." They would be disappointed because all it contained was some real estate contracts, but if it ever came to it, perhaps it would buy us some time.

"So, what's happening out there? I'm getting itchy from the soap," Ed yelled.

"Sorry, I had to find a screwdriver, just another minute."

I screwed the cap back on the filter, went to the master panel, and switched on the sump.

"Okay, try it now," I yelled. I replaced the deck boards, then started making the coffee.

Liz came back to the main cabin wearing fleece warm-up clothes. When he finished his shower, Ed came in wearing jeans and a sweatshirt with

MIAMI stenciled across the front. We sat around the table set with mugs of steaming coffee. Ed added some sugar to his coffee and took a sip.

I jumped in the deep end. "Look, Ed, I don't buy you working for the FAA." I plunged on, "I think you work for the CIA or another batch of initials, and I think you know more about all of this than you're saying. You said something to those Coast Guard guys yesterday, so they would let us go."

Ed and Liz studied me. Ed replied with a question, "You told Gallagher that you met Reynaldo Vicente, that true?"

"Yeah, I met him. Liz thought he was charming, I thought he was an obsequious prig. What's he got to do with this?"

"He is charming, he is good looking, educated at Cambridge, well connected politically, and very wealthy. He is also the money behind the Estéban Morales drug cartel."

"You mean he's in the drug business?" Liz asked.

"Yep, and another thing—he is also the son of Victor Escudero."

"President Escudero of Venezuela," Liz said.

"The same," Ed replied.

Liz asked, "Why would drug guys need financing? I thought they 'printed' money?"

Ed took another sip of his coffee, "Two reasons. First, they were the new guys on the block, so they needed seed capital, pun intended. Second, I think it's a kind of reverse money-laundering scheme for money coming out of the oil industry. Reynaldo is the director of *Petróleos de Nacional.* Nothing gets done without his say, and you have to pay to play."

I got up, walked to the galley, and pulled a package of cookies out of the pantry, "Reverse money laundering?"

"Yeah, if dad gets hinky about the graft, Reynaldo lays it off as profits from the drug business and plays dumb about the true source."

I sat down munching on a chocolate chip cookie, "And dad is okay with the drug business, but not graft?"

"Sure, the drug business is the poor man's war against the Yankee menace. But the graft can be dropped on his doorstep, and he wants to remain president."

"I met his sister," I said.

"Adelaida is with him?"

"I guess so. She introduced herself as Adel, she came up to me when Liz was dancing with Mr. Charming. She almost climbed in my lap."

"Yeah," he chuckled, "she's a pistol, married to Venezuela's cultural attaché, lives in D.C. She has the morals of a mink, but as far as I know she's harmless."

Liz's face colored slightly, "She didn't look harmless to me."

"Ed, what is this all about?" I asked, taking another cookie.

Liz slid past me, then walked over to the galley, got a carton of cream out of the icebox, walked back, pushed me over, and sat next to me again.

"I can't tell you. What did you do with the flash drive?"

"It's in a safe place. Don't tell me you can't tell me, and don't tell me you were giving Mr. Charming flying lessons! Jesus, Ed, I've been mugged, and we've been shot at. We could have been killed. I think Liz and I have earned the right to know what this is all about."

Ed got up from the table, poured more coffee into his mug. He turned around to face us, hesitated, then sat down, then added some sugar to his coffee, and stirred.

"Okay, you're right. But I don't work for the CIA. I work for a special committee inside the State Department called SPEOPS."

"I've heard of you guys," Liz said. "Allegedly, you report directly to the president, not even the secretary of state can intervene in your operations."

"Yeah, we try to keep an eye on what State or, of course, the president considers target areas. We're a small group, which means not much red tape. Our goal is to get information to the president on special matters, sometimes in hours, instead of months."

Taking a cookie, Liz said, "It sounds very James Bondish."

"Nothing so glamorous. We are just a few guys that act as a special set of eyes and ears. We deal in information only, can be very precise and move fast, but we act informally, usually dealing with second- or third-tier sources, both government and private. The key is, we report directly to the president, so our information isn't filtered, which I guess, can be good and bad. It doesn't work in every area, but that's what the CIA is supposed to be for."

"So, you have been assigned to talk to Mr. Charming?" I asked.

"Not exactly," Ed continued, "In 1989 a guy named Dr. Alberto Pérez turned up in Miami. The story is that he worked for the Cuban *Dirección General de Inteligencia,* or DGI, possibly as an interrogation specialist, but he lost favor and got himself thrown out of Cuba in the 1989 shake-up. Over the years, he dropped in and out of sight, eventually turning up in Venezuela.

"That's the outfit Fuentes supposedly worked for," I said.

"About five years ago, we got a report that he, that is Pérez, was working for Reynaldo Vicente's buddy Estéban Morales as his chief of security. The thing is, he was totally off the radar, except Morales and some of our CIA people, nobody, including Vicente, knew what the guy looked like or who he was. Pretty soon, even our guys who had known him or at least knew what he looked like, died, or retired."

"What do you mean *was*?" I interrupted.

"Let me finish. Pérez was ruthless, but presumably because he was also well educated and well connected, he went from chief enforcer to become Morales's second-in-command and bookkeeper. Pérez controlled all the bank accounts, political payoffs, investments, laundering schemes, partners, associates, the whole works."

"You keep saying 'was,' so where is Pérez?"

"Wait, the story gets better. Estéban Morales got himself killed in an automobile accident.

"Morales was killed?"

"Yeah, can you believe it, a traffic accident right in downtown Caracas? He got broadsided by a bus and was DOA."

"And we think Mrs. Vasquez was with him—"

"The Mrs. Vasquez, Pérez's sister that sold us this boat. The one we met on the dock?"

"The same. We think she was with Estéban Morales when he died in the accident."

"She did walk with a limp, and she told the boat broker she had been hurt in a car accident in Caracas."

"There is some noise about the accident being a hit ordered by Reynaldo. If true and Pérez found out, Reynaldo's life would be over."

"So, what happened to Pérez?"

"That's the question. He just disappeared about ten months ago!"

"That's it, he disappeared. So how do Liz and I fit into this melodrama?" I said.

"We think when Estéban was killed, from either panic or greed, Pérez came back to the states and hunkered down. Maybe he's dead. His wife was already living in Fort Lauderdale under the name of Vasquez, the Mrs. Vasquez you met."

"The Mrs. Vasquez, which was really his sister?"

"Right."

This is all extremely fascinating, not to mention confusing, but again, how do Liz and I fit into this?"

"We think Reynaldo Vicente is terrified Pérez will show up one day with information that could blow up in his face or worse, in his daddy's face. The problem is Vicente doesn't know who Pérez is or what he looks like. For all he knew, you were Pérez."

"Me! I'm fair and blond. Okay, fair and gray, but do I look Cuban?"

"I think you're very handsome, even with a little gray," Liz interjected.

"Pérez isn't Cuban, he's Spanish. His mother was American, so yeah, you could be Pérez. Say, maybe you are Pérez."

"Funny."

"Anyway, he used the boat as a kind of mobile office—"

"That's why the boat was loaded up with the computer, fax, and satellite phone," I interrupted.

"And you're right. I don't think Vicente believes you are Pérez, at least not after the going-over he and his sister gave you, but I'm sure he still thinks the boat is the place to look for the records. I thought so too, and I guess we were right."

"Ed, before I bought this boat, the surveyor was all over the thing, and I've been all over the boat. There is nothing on Pinafore that shouldn't be here except my 'repel boarders locker,' which I installed."

"Well, now we know there was a flash drive hidden in the sump."

"So, they broke into the boat looking for some of Pérez's files. And they are still following me or the boat—I suppose the missing bar glasses could have been taken to determine my identity through fingerprints."

"What bar glasses?" Liz asked.

"Remember the night we went to the gala. If you recall, I mixed us some G&Ts just before we left, and when we came back the glasses were gone."

"You mean the night I was—" Liz said.

"Yes, that night."

"How did they get into the boat? It was locked, wasn't it?" Liz asked.

"Yeah, I wondered about that, too, so I went back and spoke to the dock master and asked to see the carton the locks came from. It seems someone screwed up and bought a bunch of keyed-alike locks."

"What does that mean?" Liz asked.

"It means in a carton of twelve locks, each of the twenty-four keys open all twelve locks," I replied.

"So, all anyone had to do was buy a lock from the dock master and they had a key that would fit our boat," Liz said.

"But how did they know where the boat was going or where it would be docked? I never filed a sail plan," I said.

"You can do that?" Ed asked.

"Sure, with the Coast Guard. Few people do, but the service is available," I said.

What had Adel Vicente said? "I know who you are . . ." and that line about Liz being well known—maybe in D.C. circles, but not in Venezuela. But Adel lives in D.C. Perhaps that's how she knew Liz. But she couldn't know me. Hell, my mother barely recognizes me. She said, "My brother said you would be here with your wife," so she probably didn't know us. It had to be her brother who knew us, and he was waiting when we walked in the door at Rosecliff. But how did he know we would be attending? Of course, if Fuentes was watching the boat, he would have followed us to Rosecliff, then called Reynaldo, who was the gala's sponsor. It would have been natural for him to greet us.

"Ed, I keep coming back to the same question. How did Reynaldo know the boat was going to be in Newport?" I said.

"They probably followed the boat. They could get information on the sales contract, title search, lien docs, canceled checks, that sort of thing. You were only in Annapolis for a few days, so there was no time there. They had to follow you to Newport. Then your first night at the dock, they watched the boat until you left for dinner."

"Okay, so he somehow got my name from the purchase agreement. I guess that would be easy enough, maybe he even got it from Mrs. Vasquez. And he had the guestlist for the gala, so if he found my name, our names, on the guest list, all he had to do was wait for us to show. He would know my arrival time within a day or two, and there are only so many places to dock, so he just waited. Once we were at the party, he checked us out the same time Fuentes gave the boat the once-over. It seems pretty thin, though."

"If that's the case, who were the people that attacked you on the first night?" Liz asked. "And how did he connect us to the guest list?"

"I don't know the answer to either question," I said. "But it's pretty clear he used the gala to see if I was Pérez and have someone look in the boat. I'll bet they weren't expecting the cop at the end of the pier. He would have been easy enough to get around from the water side, but the cop probably scared him off before he could get a good look, so all he ended up with were some bar glasses."

"So, you were incidental, or you were Pérez," Ed said.

"Incidental. Ed, I just killed one guy and possibly some others, and what about Liz, is she incidental?"

"Look guys, the missing cartel records are only part of the picture," Ed said.

"What do you mean, part of the picture?" Liz asked.

Ed got up from the table again and helped himself to more coffee. He sat down, added some sugar to the coffee, and took another cookie.

"It's mostly about an opportunity to smoke out a guy who could help make an unfriendly government our ally."

"Ed, what the hell are you talking about?" I asked.

"We have an opportunity to influence a government that controls one of the largest gas and oil reserves in the world and do it without firing a shot. And because they are a member of OPEC, that means we can control the oil reserves in the Middle East."

"As our kids say, 'What have you been smoking?' And you keep saying *us*. Who is *us*?"

"The state department," Ed said. "And I don't smoke."

"You mean that alphabet outfit you work for?"

"You weren't listening. That alphabet group is the president."

"Last I heard, there was a thing called 'advise and consent' in our government."

"You're right, but if all goes as planned, we are going to watch while all the work is done for us."

"Well, I never had much luck with things 'going as planned' and I still don't understand how anything on this boat is going to impact the international oil markets? And I thought you said Pérez was dead?"

"I said maybe, and I'm not talking about Pérez, I'm talking about Reynaldo Vicente."

"Okay, aside from being the director of *Petróleos de Nacional*, what does Reynaldo Vicente have to do with the international oil markets? Besides, you said he was in the drug business."

"Look, every Arab in the world is pissed off at us because we stood with Israel when they bombed Iran," Ed replied.

I countered with a snappy, "So?" I was getting tired.

"So, the OPEC conference is coming up in ninety days. They plan to cut or withhold oil production as punishment for our support of the Israelis. If we can't get the members to back off or soften their stand, oil prices are going to skyrocket. The administration believes the shortest route to that end is to get Venezuela to be our seat at the table."

"It always comes down to oil, doesn't it?" I sighed.

"Nobody wants a repeat of the 1973 oil crisis, including the Arabs. We think Saudi Arabia will hold the line, but if we can get another vote in that meeting—namely, Venezuela—it will give us a huge advantage in the overall outcome of the vote."

"Again, what does Reynaldo Vicente have to do with the international oil markets?"

"If we can get Reynaldo involved with the recovery of Pérez's records, preferably find him with the records in his hands, we can use that with the additional information we have to indict him for drug trafficking, at the least," Ed said.

"But now we have the records. Why can't we just give them to the FBI?" Liz asked.

"Because, even if there is direct information on the flash drive tying Reynaldo to those files, which I doubt, the evidence could still be interpreted as hearsay. We have to get the files and Reynaldo together, preferably in an overt action to take or destroy them, both would be better. Then we have something to trade with."

"Trade with who—or is it *whom*," I asked.

"The whom is Reynaldo's father, Victor Escudero, the president of Venezuela. Remember, I said Reynaldo is terrified Pérez will show up one day. That's the key. Now *we* have the information that blows up in daddy's face."

"Aaah, you leverage dad, you leverage his administration, and you leverage OPEC," I said.

"Right," Ed said.

"That's called blackmail," I retorted.

"My people call it diplomacy," replied Ed.

"I suppose by 'overt action' you mean something illegal like killing me and Liz and blowing up our boat?"

Ed laughed, "Yeah, that would do it."

"Well, he already tried that. The faster we get rid of these files, the safer we are. And I guess this means your appearance on the family vacation was no coincidence. You snookered me into buying this boat, knowing all the while that it probably contained the Pérez documents. Then you conned your way into our vacation."

"In your last email, you said you were looking for a boat. When I learned that Pérez's boat was for sale, it became the perfect opportunity."

Ed drank some coffee and took another cookie.

"Truthfully, that's only part of the reason. I wanted to get away, get some sun, see you guys again, and visit with Stacie. She's taking her mom's death very hard. We haven't talked much, and I wanted to spend some time with her. I guess you could say I'm on a working vacation."

"I don't understand how Reynaldo was ahead of the curve," I said.

"He wasn't. When he learned, you were headed to Newport and the gala, he bought into the gala with a large contribution. Plus, it's not unusual for him to summer up here, even Lieutenant Gallagher said as much. Look, guys, I need your help with this. All we need to do is let Reynaldo make his move, snatch him up, and hand him to the Feds."

"Ed, he's already made his move, at least twice. I've been assaulted, and we are lucky we weren't all killed in his last 'move.' And if the past is any indicator, Reynaldo won't come near the boat. He'll send more goons."

"So, honey—this vacation everything you had hoped for?" Liz asked with a smirk.

"Maybe we should have bought an RV."

"Do they have hot water?" she replied.

"Your right," Ed said, "but this time we'll follow the goons back to the source."

"Yeah, Liz and I are the bait with all the risk. Ed, I have kids and several bartenders that depend on me. I've done my bit for good old U.S.A., and Liz was in the wrong place at the wrong time. She doesn't even like the boat."

"I like the boat, just not for more than a week at a time, maybe two weeks," Liz said defensively.

"I'll bet Venezuela sells 50 percent of their oil to us, so why don't we just threaten them with a boycott?" I asked.

"Sixty-five percent, but the idea is to maintain or increase the oil supply, not decrease it," Ed replied.

"I think you had a lot of nerve bringing this mess into our lives. If we didn't go back so far, I'd ask you to leave."

"Honey, I think Ed is just trying to do what's right," Liz said, as she poured me the last of the coffee.

I got up from the table, found some more cookies, and started to make another pot of coffee. It gave me a few minutes to think. *Damn, all I want to do is go on a sailing trip! Sail, eat good food, have long showers with my wife, then do it again. I just want a vacation.* I turned to Ed, who was watching me over his coffee cup.

"Ed, I'm sorry, but Liz and I are out of this."

"Okay, okay, forget it." Ed got up and paced back and forth for a few minutes. "I don't blame you. You guys have already done more than people being paid to do this work. Being bashed on the head, and that shoot-out was too much. Hell, our people aren't even authorized to carry weapons. We are just professional busy bodies who try to pick up international gossip." He sat down, finished his coffee, and polished off another cookie.

Our water consumption was nothing compared to the hit *my* cookie supply was taking.

I took another crack at O'Brien, this time getting through a couple of chapters. Tired, I said good night and went to bed. A short time later, Liz crawled in beside me, and we went to sleep.

"Sarge, they're in the wire at the bottom of the hill!"

"Okay, listen up guys! Everyone that has a Claymore, make sure you have the clackers ready. Last time we were shooting high, so keep your fire down. Watch for that grunt unit coming out of the ville on the left flank. You start shooting at them, they'll get pissed off and shoot back!

"Jesse, go tell those tank guys to swing the tube around so it points at the crest of the ridge. That'll scare the shit out of them—wait! Tell them not to fire the main gun, the muzzle blast will blow us all off this hill. Tell them just to use the coax and the fifty."

"Okay, Sarge—."

"Honey, wake up! Wake up, you're talking in your sleep."

I opened my eyes. In the small light of the morning, I could see Liz's face a few inches away, "Sorry, just a bad dream."

I'd had one flashback in thirty years, and now I'd had two in as many days.

CHAPTER TWELVE

Edgartown Harbor, Martha's Vineyard

The following day, Liz and I were planning another trip ashore for lunch and shopping. I was mostly planning for the lunch part. Ed left early, saying he was going to meet his daughter for the day, so I was surprised to see him in the water taxi as it pulled up to the boat.

"Hi, guy," Ed said.

"Hi, yourself, what happened to your day with Stacie?"

"She got called in to work. How about some lunch—my treat?"

Liz poked her head up from below: "Someone mention lunch?"

"No, somebody mentioned *free* lunch," I said.

"I'm ready," Liz said.

"I thought you were all atwitter to go shopping?"

"Atwitter?"

"Yes, you know, all ahead full, let's shop."

"As you are fond to point out, I am always 'atwitter' to go shopping, but a girl has to eat."

I asked the water taxi to wait for a moment. I locked the boat, reminding myself to buy another lock, while Ed helped Liz board the taxi. All secure, I climbed in the taxi, and we left in a smell of diesel fuel and saltwater.

Another perfect day, the sky was an amazing—well, an amazing sky blue with no clouds. The sun was bright and warm, and the water sparkled. Sometimes the taxi would catch a small wave or wake at just the right angle and a spray of water would catch the sunlight before it landed in the boat. Ed was in his tourist attire, a multicolor island shirt and shorts, and I had on a variation of my uniform, a blue polo shirt and khakis. The distaff part of our threesome was dressed in a pink sherbet sundress, sandals, and white floppy hat. We all wore the obligatory sunglasses.

Ed suggested we lunch at the Atlantic Fish & Chop House. I had eaten there in the past. It was a good restaurant with a better view.

The dining rooms were enclosed on three sides by glass windows overlooking a large deck and the harbor. Before we got to the entrance, the door was opened by a big guy dressed in a dark suit that was too tight across the shoulders. I didn't pay much attention to him until I noticed he was wearing one of those earplug things for a two-way radio. Another similarly attired gent at the opposite end of the room was trying unsuccessfully to blend into the woodwork.

I would have bet a hundred dollars the bookends were Secret Service. Not counting the bruisers, the section of the restaurant we were escorted to was almost vacant. Two other men in suits were already sitting at a round table set for six. Their suits looked more expensive, and they weren't wearing earplugs. Ed walked to their table, so Liz and I followed. Ed turned to Liz and me.

"I would like you to meet the undersecretary of state, Richard Silvers, and this is Jonathan Collins."

The two men stood.

"How do you do?" I said shaking hands with both men. "This is my wife, Elizabeth."

Each, in turn, shook hands with her. I had never seen Silvers, but Jonathan Collins was almost a household name, partly because in a former administration he had been the attorney general, but mostly because he was now, in a peculiar turn of events, the current president's chief of staff. From what I had read and seen, he was a tough guy with a tough job. He was wearing a blue suit with gray pinstripes and a red and gray tie. Probably about fifty, he had a brown, thinning haircut like a drill sergeant. He had an expensive tan. People like Collins didn't drive convertibles or lie on the beach, so he got it on the golf course, maybe a boat. Maybe we were going to be sailing pals. My philosophy is you can never have enough friends.

"Please, everyone take a seat," Collins said.

"You gentlemen up here on vacation?" I asked wryly.

Collins sat and placed his napkin on his lap, smiled warmly but insincerely, a feat I previously thought impossible.

"No, we are here to see you."

"Me!"

"Yes, and of course Elizabeth. Mr. Colombo said you were not particularly keen about the idea of helping us with our, shall we say, situation?"

"It seems Mr. Colombo has been very busy," I said, looking over at Ed, "but Mr. Colombo is correct. My wife and I are on vacation. We invited Mr. Colombo to accompany us because he is an old friend and, I thought, in need of some time off, not because he is a secret agent. As I reminded Mr. Colombo, my wife and I are just private citizens trying to enjoy a few weeks with each other before we go back to work at our very unsecret jobs."

I stopped and chuckled. "Well, at least me anyway, I have no idea what Elizabeth does, but I'm pretty sure she's not a secret agent."

The waitress, a tall thin young woman of about twenty, with long red hair, put glasses of water in front of each of us and took our drink orders. I ordered a well-deserved Blanton's and soda and a backup, which I thought was also well deserved. Liz had a Belvedere martini. Ed ordered a beer. The two suits ordered iced tea.

As a rule, I like iced tea. In fact, it is probably my favorite beverage, but not in New England. You just can't get a decent glass of iced tea north of the Mason–Dixon Line. I could never figure out why—I mean what is so hard about making iced tea? It's tea, water, and sugar, for Gods' sake, and maybe a lemon. South Carolina has the best iced tea, great shrimp and grits, too. I was thinking Liz, and I should have gone to Myrtle Beach for vacation—seedy hotel rooms, blazing hot sun, sand, and screaming kids . . . sounded idyllic.

Silvers spoke for the first time. He was also wearing a blue suit, but with a slight red pinstripe, blue shirt, and gray tie. He was thinner than Collins, but about the same age, with a lot of combed-back silver hair, appropriate to his name, I thought.

"Perhaps I could interject for a moment. With all due respect to you and Elizabeth, I work directly for the secretary of state. You know who Johnny works for. But just so we're clear—"

He stopped talking when the waitress walked to the table with our drinks. She placed one in front of each of us and walked away. Silvers took a sip of his iced tea, shifted his weight, and leaned forward to emphasize the point he was about to make.

"We are here at the behest of the president."

Anytime someone starts with "With all due respect," I always assume the rest of the statement is 100 percent bullshit.

"You guys flew up here to see us, on behalf of *the* President of the United States?"

"Technically, we are on a golf outing," Collins said.

"You guys always play golf in suits?" I took a sip from my drink, "Technically speaking, I mean."

"Hey, bud," interrupted Ed, "listen to what they have to say. Worst case, you get a free lunch."

"Okay, speak." Too soon for the booze. I was just being a smart ass. Hunger made me grumpy.

The waitress came back to take our lunch orders. I hadn't even looked at the menu, but I ordered a lobster salad and another Blanton's. Liz had the Cobb salad, Ed had a club sandwich, and the two suits had BLTs, each also ordering more iced tea. The bookends were evidently going to do without. I thought about sending them a basket of breadsticks, then I remembered they had guns. They could get their own breadsticks.

Silvers continued, "Well, I think Ed here gave you most of it. We have a bad situation. The OPEC people are pissed as hell. Excuse me, ma'am. The OPEC people are angry as hell because we sided with the Israelis when they bombed the Fordow enrichment site and the Arak heavy water plant. I mean what did they think we were going to do? Frankly, they are probably pleased. All any of us needs is a nuke in the hands of a maniac, but they can't say as much. Anyway, our intel guys think there is going to be a major move to shut down oil production—"

"–and we know how accurate our intel guys have been at sorting out the Middle East," I said glibly. If I didn't get some food soon, I'd probably be arrested for sassing the undersecretary of state. I'm sure there was a law against it.

"Excuse my husband, gentlemen, he tends to be very direct when he's been drinking on an empty stomach, especially when he's right."

Collins picked up the baton, "Yes, we know we have been snookered more than a few times, but some of this latest information comes out of the Saudi embassy. They say they don't want to cut production, but they will have to go along, at least for a while, and that could add twenty-five, maybe fifty, percent to the cost of a barrel of oil."

"Gas prices at six dollars a gallon would probably make for a tough time in this November's election." My mouth runnith over again.

Finally, lunch arrived. The waitress served everyone, then took more drink orders. She removed my two empty glasses and left.

"Yes, it would, and frankly it's a concern," Collins said, "but the real issue here is the availability of oil. Politically motivated manipulation of production and prices is not unprecedented. In retaliation for our support of Israel during the Yom Kippur War, OPEC raised the price of oil from three dollars per barrel to twelve dollars per barrel and stopped selling oil to the United States."

"How about the Bakken oil fields? I hear they are pumping a million gallons a day out of those fields in North Dakota and Montana, oil and natural gas. Some say it will make the United States oil independent, maybe an exporter."

"Yes, Bakken and Three Forks have proven reserves of some two billion gallons and ultimately may reach as much as seven billion. The fracking technology is getting better, but the infrastructure is limited, and transportation to bring the oil out of the region is limited to rail and trucks. Until a pipeline is built, we won't be able to fully exploit the region's potential."

"So, why Venezuela?" Liz asked.

Silvers expounded, "Venezuela was one of the first members of OPEC, and it is said Venezuela may have initially proposed the idea of OPEC to the Saudis in 1959. OPEC controls some eighty percent of the world's proven reserves, and Venezuela owns about twenty-five percent of that. If you include the Saudis share, it's almost fifty percent of OPEC's production. This could make our idea into a strategy that could manage oil prices not only at the next OPEC meeting but possibly for the foreseeable future."

"Or at least for the duration of the next presidential term," I said.

Not to be deterred, Collins picked up the thread, "If Venezuela will object to the proposed production cuts, the Saudis have promised to put their substantial clout behind it, but without the Venezuelans there is nothing they can do or at least nothing they will do to help us."

"At least until after the election," I interjected. I was thinking perhaps I should order some iced tea. I finished my lobster salad but was still hungry, so I foraged around the table for more to eat. I found some crackers and started nibbling.

Undeterred, Silvers continued, "Perhaps, but more likely this could change the way oil prices are set for years to come, regardless of the administration. It gets us back in the driver's seat. Or to use the same analogy, at least back in the car. You will recall, most oil fields in Saudi Arabia were developed by U.S. companies."

"I thought the British developed those fields," Liz said.

"Not in Saudi Arabia. We bought our first lease in 1933 from King Ibn Saud for two-hundred-seventy-five-thousand dollars," Silvers said.

"I'll bet he was pissed later," I said.

"Probably. He thought he was selling sand, so did the Brits. But of course, we found the huge oil reserve.

"You are right about the Brits and Venezuela, though, just before the First World War, when Shell started developing the oil fields in Venezuela, the Brits owned about forty percent of Shell Oil. Standard Oil was also active there, but to a lesser extent," Silvers said.

"Anyway," Collins said, "if we can control, or I should say persuade, Venezuela to see our point of view, we then have a seat at the table and can influence decisions within OPEC, as Dick said, for years to come. The best part is we exert this influence covertly, completely behind the scenes, by applying pressure on the Venezuelan administration, which is President Escudero."

"Okay, I'm sold on the why, but how come you are so sure President Escudero is going to submit to your, not to put too fine a point on it, blackmail?"

"Blackmail is rather a harsh word, but your argument is well taken," said Silvers. "Victor Escudero is not a very popular president. Yes, he has brought some prosperity to his country by taking over the oil production, but Venezuela now finds itself in much the same situation it was in after the Second World War. The administration sacrificed the rest of the economy for the sake of oil production. Escudero is losing support, and if he were to be the subject of a scandal, particularly if it were tied to his son, who runs the *Petróleos de Nacional*, it would mean trouble he can ill afford."

"What if this blows up in your face?" I asked.

"What do you mean?"

"I mean what if this scheme of yours comes unraveled and you find yourself on the front page of the *Post* or *Times*? You may recall the Iran-Contra mess."

"I believe my husband is trying to determine your thoughts on the possibility of someone, like a member of the press, publishing the administration's plans to blackmail a sovereign power on the front page of their newspaper."

"Well, we don't see it as blackmail. We can remove a significant threat to our country, and we believe we should use this opportunity. If you viewed it more as economic terrorism, I think you would agree. In addition, we believe the Venezuelan vice president, a man named Sabas, is a good person. He's from one of the old ruling families and has good connections in the *Asamblea Nacional*, which is their parliament. We think we can probably count on his support if he thinks it will benefit his country," Silvers said.

"What if this guy Sabas steps up to the plate but decides not to play ball with you guys and wants to start his own team?" I try to keep my metaphors to one sport at a time.

"He could be worse than this Escudero character."

"We never said this wasn't complicated and perhaps risky," answered Collins.

"Yeah, so far, all the risk has been ours. Which brings us back to why me? I'm neither in the State Department nor am I some kind of government professional operative." I said.

"Mostly due to coincidence, you appear to be the right man at the right time and particularly in the right place. But also, because Mr. Colombo says you are smart, can think on your feet, and if comes to it, are very handy with a weapon," replied Collins.

"How kind of him," I said looking over at Ed, who apparently just found something terribly fascinating in his lap. "You may have noticed it's already, as you said, 'come to that' and, yes, I have a knack with weapons. I'm an excellent shot, so for fun I shoot competitively. As a matter of fact, Liz and I shoot competitively, but neither of us is an assassin."

"But you were in the Marine Corps, and you were a police officer," Collins said.

"Collins, I'm sorry, Mr. Collins"—maybe I should have called him Johnny—"that was different, and you know it. Another thing, you all need to realize because of this 'coincidence' as you call it, a bunch of punks tried to pirate our boat. Had we not been armed, I doubt if the three of us would be sitting at this table. Those men were very persistent and particularly unpleasant. I have no wish to expose my wife or myself to them, or others like them, again."

"Which is another reason we have to get these people off the street," Collins said.

"You want them off the street, call a cop," I said.

Silvers interjected, "Mr. Colombo said you trounced those punks, as you call them, hands down in a fair fight."

I leaned forward and lowered my voice, trying to keep my anger in check, "Gentlemen, we are talking about six or seven street punks that by definition are callous and mean but not very smart. They were unorganized and most likely seasick. They probably thought they were taking on some retired insurance agent or the like. Instead, they got a snoot full of military-grade munitions that nothing much short of a tank could have withstood. With forethought and with as much malice as I could muster, I killed a man because he was foolish enough to aim a weapon at my wife. Then I turned their boat, which was about the length of this room, into splinters, small splinters. What was left was burned to cinders. If that's your definition of trounced then, yes, I trounced them, but to use my word, I could have slaughtered everyone on that boat in as much time as it takes to say it.

"Mr. Silvers, it was anything but a fair fight. You gentlemen, being politicians, should know all about that—no one wins a fair fight."

We sat quietly pushing food around our plates, pretending to eat. I wanted to be out of the restaurant away from these stuffed suits. I wanted to be on my boat sailing anywhere.

Collins finally spoke, "Sir, we are not asking you to be an assassin. We just want you to sail your boat around like you had planned," he pleaded. "Ed will do the rest."

"To reiterate, Mr. Silvers's statement, your president is asking for your help. You are a citizen and a former Marine. I don't see how you can turn her down."

"If I said no, I guess someone like the Coast Guard would impound our boat and drop me in a cell somewhere. Is that it?"

"Well, I think that's being somewhat melodramatic, but, yes, I believe we could make things somewhat unpleasant," he said with a smirk.

"So, I guess that's how we got away from the Coast Guard the other day," I said, making it more a statement than a question.

"Yes," Silvers replied.

The waitress came back with another—to my credit—unsolicited drink and dessert menus, which were really the back of the lunch menus. Maybe these guys were Russians, and the waitress was a secret Russian agent instructed to ply me with liquor? I desperately needed coffee.

"Okay," I said, "let's say I'm considering it, but my wife will not be involved. I don't want her anywhere near this fiasco."

"Why don't you let your wife decide for herself?" Liz said, giving me that arched eyebrow thing she does.

"Liz, I don't want you mixed up in this."

"As we said, this is not espionage. And I think your wife would be good cover," Silvers said.

"If this isn't espionage, why do we need a cover?" I replied.

"A figure of speech," Silvers said. "Look, you enjoy your vacation, and the State Department will pick up the tab. Alternatively, we will charter your boat and you can sail it around for us while Mr. Colombo watches our quarry and feeds us information. Then we will contact the FBI and the local police, and they can do the rest."

I looked at the dessert menu. I didn't feel like dessert. I could get Liz out, but it was becoming clear I was screwed and would be in this deal for the duration.

I sighed "So, what now? Are we sure Reynaldo is here for the purpose you assume? Maybe he is here on vacation, the police lieutenant in Newport said he comes up here for the summer."

Jonathan Collins replied, "We have it on good authority that Reynaldo is here for precisely the reason that we suspect. He has as much or more to lose than his father. The *Petróleos de Nacional* is his base of power and, probably more importantly, it is his legitimacy. Without *Petróleos de Nacional*, he is just another thug peddling drugs and maybe not even that. No, he's here to get the documents he believes to be on your boat or to prove to himself that they are not on the boat."

We have it on good authority. Jesus, that came right out of a movie, a bad one. Okay, now I am a secret agent.

The five of us went over several scenarios and settled on the simplest, which was to do what we have been doing and wait for Reynaldo to make the next move. I thought the CIA, FBI, DEA, and all the other alphabets could have come up with a better plan, then I remembered something my grandfather told me: "Keep it simple, stupid." So, for now, we were waiting for Reynaldo. We wouldn't have long to wait.

Collins paid the bill, then I watched as Silvers, Ed, and the bookends followed Silvers out of the restaurant, presumably to play golf. Ed looked over at us and said he would meet us at the boat.

After Ed and the golfers left, Liz and I ordered some coffee. As we waited, we both sat with our own thoughts. I hated getting in this mess with Liz in tow. She was doing it for the right reasons, but she was a soccer mom at heart. She was accomplished and smart, smarter than me, as she often pointed out, but a sinking, foreboding told me that smarts wasn't going to be enough. When I later asked Ed what transpired after our meeting with the golfers, he told me they were less than pleased with my enthusiasm, and Collins was insistent that he report to the boss. "I have to tell her something. The problem is we don't know anything."

"Tell her he has agreed to help with our plan and leave it at that," Silvers had said.

"Okay, let's get her on the phone."

Silvers dialed a number on his cell. "Hello. Good afternoon, ma'am. You're on speaker with Johnny and Ed."

President Jackson said, "Well, does he have the documents?"

The three men looked at each other. Collins shrugged. "Ma'am, all we know is he found a memory stick, and it contains some bank records."

"Dick, Ed, what do you think?"

"He found something. The important thing is he has agreed to help us find Vicente. And though he doesn't know it, he will be our early warning system if Pérez shows up," said Silvers.

"Madam president, this is Ed. He bought the boat from Pérez's wife and found bank records with Spanish footnotes. We have the right boat."

"So, you're convinced?"

"Yes, ma'am," replied Ed.

"I'll bet a gallon of my aunt Jeanie's cider you're right. So, he agreed to work for us?" President Jackson asked.

"I didn't give him much choice," Collins said.

"Johnny, from what I've heard, you probably don't want to get too smart with this guy. We don't want to find you washed up on a beach somewhere." President Jackson said.

Ed and Silvers stifled a laugh.

"Yes, ma'am, I'll keep that in mind."

"Okay, I'll see you tomorrow." The president hung up with an electronic click.

Collins looked at Ed, "So, is this guy going to work for us or not?"

"They're both going to work for us, and for reasons you wouldn't suspect."

"What're those?"

"Patriotism. Another thing, the president is only partly right. You get his wife hurt and he will kill you— only they'll never find your body."

CHAPTER THIRTEEN

Atlantic Fish & Chop House, Martha's Vineyard

The waitress brought our coffee. "What do you think?" Liz asked.

I snapped out of my partially alcohol-induced musings. "I think the president is trying to get reelected and using us to do her grunt work. I think the golfers and Ed are out in that black SUV we saw in the parking lot hatching a scathingly brilliant plan. And if it isn't quite as brilliant as they think it is, and something goes wrong, we will be the fall guys. I also think I don't like her. I'd just as soon she did lose the election."

"Does that really make a difference? Maybe this is a chance to do something that counts?"

"Lizzy, I did something that counted, at least that's what we were told. They said, 'Go to the armpit of the world and do us proud. Do it for your country. Stop the menace before it spreads.' Only the menace, like the communism of the last war, mostly self-destructed. All those boys killed, for what—oil? These guys are big on pissing away lives for noble causes, but very few of them have ever offered their lives or their son's lives. Why should I do this again and, of all people, why should you?"

Liz put her coffee cup down and faced me, "As I said, I'd like to say I made a difference, I want to do something that counts. And no matter how much you dislike the woman, she is the president of our country, and as Mr. Collins said, as a marine or as a citizen, you can't say no to the president, and neither can I, and I think you know that."

"Perhaps, but it doesn't mean I won't take his charter money. Plus, there is something else going on here," I said.

Liz looked at me, "What do you mean?"

"I don't know, but those guys on the boat, as I said at lunch, are ham-fisted street thugs. The people who broke into the boat when I first arrived were careful."

"Careful?"

"Yeah, too careful for street thugs. Come on, let's get out of here and walk around and see the town. At least pretend to be on vacation." I put a $10 bill on the table. We got up and walked out of the air-conditioned restaurant into the warm day. Eighty-five degrees with a slight breeze, it was one of those afternoons that made you feel guilty unless you were doing something outdoors. We walked into town stopping to look into the occasional window. I had a good buzz on but managed to walk without tripping over my feet.

"So, what did you mean when you said they were too careful?" Liz asked.

"I mean, they didn't tear anything up. Instead of prying the lock off with a crowbar or screwdriver, they opened it without damaging it. Maybe they picked it or used a bump key. There *were* tool marks on the lock. Then when they were inside, they were careful. The boat wasn't trashed. They just looked and moved things around, again careful not to break anything.

"The second group, the ones we think stole the bar glasses, used a key they got from the dock master. I think they bought several locks in case they had to break or cut the lock on the companionway. Then they could replace it so I wouldn't know anybody had been in the boat."

"Which means, they had to know you replaced the lock on the day you arrived, and they had to know about the screwup with the keyed-alike locks," Liz said.

"Right, plus they must have been watching me, or at least the boat, probably from some distance with binoculars."

We stopped and looked in a store window filled with the latest fall fashions festooned with signs reminding potential customers that all summer fashions were 50 percent off.

"If the men that attacked me on the first night and the men who attacked us off Block Island were the same, they would have stuck a knife in me on the first night and thrown me in the water. The only thing that makes sense is the men that got into the boat the first night are not the same guys that tried to stop us off Block Island."

"They couldn't have been too careful. You found them before they had finished with their search," Liz said.

"Yeah, they screwed up there. Either they got started late or the lookout missed me leaving the Black Pearl. The fog was so bad I could barely see where I was going."

"You couldn't see where you were going because you were plastered," she said with a hint of irritation.

"Well, there's that too."

Liz turned to me, "So we're dealing with two groups of people. If they are both looking for the records, do you think they are both working for Reynaldo? Which group did the man you arrested belong to?"

"You mean Fuentes?"

"I guess."

"We never did learn his name. INTERPOL thinks he may have been Victor Fuentes. They thought he is or was employed by DGI," I said.

"DGI—that used to be the name of the Cuban CIA, right?"

"Right, perhaps the first guys were working for the Venezuelan government. If Fuentes was on the picnic boat, it's a safe bet everyone on the boat belonged to his team. In addition, all the men we have had contact with are Hispanic. You remember Davis, the skipper of the Coast Guard boat, he said the guy they picked up only spoke Spanish or at least said he only spoke Spanish. Cuba and Venezuela are very cozy, so if there is a DGI connection, I think it's reasonable to assume Fuentes worked for Reynaldo, who probably imported him for the job. Could be he was an employee of the cartel. We may never know. The others were probably locals hired for the job, or maybe the cartel has a branch office up here, who knows. The Coast Guard will probably get a lead from the ones they have in custody."

"So, when the other group, the 'official Venezuelan government guys,' failed to find anything and screwed up by letting you come up behind them, Reynaldo imported an enforcer from the cartel, then hired some street thugs to help take the documents by force."

"Yep, I think that's what happened. Not to say the government agents wouldn't be more than capable of using lethal tactics, but if a Venezuelan agent was caught killing a U.S. citizen, it would be very embarrassing for Reynaldo and his father."

"Our new friends from the administration would have loved that. It would save them a lot of fuss," Liz said.

"Yeah, unfortunately, that's exactly what I was thinking. In fact, I was having darker thoughts. What if our golfing buddies are feeding Reynaldo information? The other group–"

"Give them a name so I can follow you. It's getting confusing," Liz pleaded.

"Okay, we have two groups, team one were the Venezuelan agents that first broke into the boat and knocked me on my ass. team two were Fuentes's guys, who attacked us off Block Island."

"Better," Liz said.

"Team one knew where the boat was docked, so they must have had inside information from someone. But who would have inside information on my or our travel plans? You haven't been talking to anybody, have you?" I asked mostly joking.

"I told some friends and people at work I was going on vacation. I mentioned Newport, but never the wharf. I said I was meeting you, but never anything about your arrival date. I'm not sure I knew when you were arriving, only that I was to meet you on Wednesday, and as it was, I was a day early, and even you didn't know that until I arrived."

"The team one guys that broke into the boat on the first night didn't need to follow me. They knew exactly when I arrived and exactly where the boat was docked, down to the correct slip number. Suppose it was our golfing friends. They didn't find anything and thought it was too risky to try again, so they passed on the location of the boat to the Fuentes team, team two. Then all our golfing buddies had to do was keep tabs on them and pick them up for burglary. Arresting them is not only lawful but expected. If I got hurt or killed, that would just sweeten the deal."

"You're saying you think government agents, *our* government agents, were accessories to, or committed, burglary and assaulted a U.S. citizen."

"It's been done before," I replied.

"And they all received prison terms," Liz countered.

"The ones we know about, anyway. As I said, it's just a thought. I don't think it's a stretch to think these guys could get overzealous."

"My head hurts just thinking about this," Liz said.

"Yeah, me, too."

"Your head hurts because you had too much to drink at lunch."

We started walking toward the harbor again.

"Can you call your office and get someone to translate and interpret those files, including the financial records, and summarize their findings?"

"I guess so. Why? What are we looking for?"

"I don't know. It just seems too much significance has been given to our boat for what we have been told."

"Well, the U.S. economy is pretty important, don't you think?"

"Maybe, but I think there is more to it, like deposing the president of Venezuela. We need a closer look at those files. Can your South American guy look at them? I think the answer is most likely in those records."

Liz pulled her cell phone from her purse.

As she was dialing, I added, "Please tell them to keep a lid on it, okay."

She nodded, holding up her left hand, signaling me to be quiet. "Hi, Susan, it's Elizabeth, is Gery around? Sure, I'll wait. Hi, Gery, it's Elizabeth—yes, we're having a wonderful time. Will you do me a favor and go to my computer and remove a file labeled *Narragansett*—yes, *Narragansett*. You want me to spell it?"

Liz could spell anything. I was never much of a speller, even the spellchecker on my computer laughed at me. Three or four minutes passed.

"That's it. I need you to do a full analysis of all the documents in that file. Yes, that's right, and use the administrative billing code, at least for now. I'll re-bill it when I get back. Great, please call me when you have an abstract. Gery, please see to this as soon as you can. And for now, classify the name and all the contents, top secret. Okay, talk to you soon—Thanks, Gery, goodbye."

Liz turned to me: "What did you mean 'depose the president of Venezuela'?"

"Suppose Victor Escudero is involved somehow with the Morales drug cartel. Suppose there was an argument and Escudero had Morales killed. Suppose Pérez was really loyal and now he's really pissed—"

"And really wants revenge," Liz finished my thought. "Or maybe he just wants to retire. Besides, I thought Estéban Morales was killed in an automobile accident."

"Maybe he was, but suppose he wasn't. Suppose someone in our government suspects or knows Victor Escudero or maybe Reynaldo Vicente is guilty of murder. Hard to imagine the head of a government maintaining a standing in the international community once he or his son slash director of oil production has been exposed as a murderer and drug trafficker, no matter how he sells it at home. And if Escudero had a hand in any of it, I think it would be the end of his administration."

"I don't know. That's a lot of supposes, and there have been a lot of corrupt politicians who killed their citizens in the name of some cause. Unfortunately, more than a few have been in South and Central America."

"True, but they hid behind suppressed or controlled press and the guise of democratic fervor. Even then, most were eventually thrown out or imprisoned. I'm talking about exposure in the world media, particularly the U.S. media. If the right facts came out, I think both of them would be finished."

"Well, if your theory is correct, it would explain the brute force they have used to date. And if Victor Escudero's power and freedom are on the line, what we have seen so far could be the warmup for something more desperate, make that more *deadly*."

"*Deadlier*—that's why I think we need to be more proactive and ascertain what everybody is so wound up about."

"Ascertain?"

"Yeah, that's a technical word leftover from my detecting days."

"Right, well, it's hard to imagine being more proactive than we've already been, so you had better get your ass entertaining some ideas."

"You stretched for that. For now, my plan is to get nosier. Can you say *nosier*?"

"Only on the liquid lunch you just had. How about *more inquisitive*?"

"Works for me. You're the one with the South American desk. I'm just a sailor. You're sure you're not a spook?"

We stopped, and I followed Liz into a lingerie store. Oh boy, just like James Bond, a beautiful spook and lingerie!

CHAPTER FOURTEEN

Edgartown Harbor, Martha's Vineyard

Our departure for Nantucket was delayed by a stop at the water dock to top off, as one might guess, the water tanks which were much depleted by the inability of some to adhere to the sailor's rule for the use and conservation of freshwater. Edgartown has a floating water dock moored mid-channel, which simplifies the process. Ed turned on the water while I held the hose to the filler pipe. Shortly, water could be heard running into the tanks.

"Hey, Ed, maybe we should take the water dock with us."

"I heard that, smarty pants," Liz hollered from below.

Ed laughed. About thirty minutes later, we were watered, clear of the dock, and set a course through the cut, leaving Chappaquiddick Point to our right and then through Edgartown Harbor. A large motor yacht was anchored on the east side of the harbor. She looked to be about one-hundred feet or more, maybe Italian design. Curious, I looked at the yacht through my binoculars. The *Montauk Express*. I couldn't see any sign of activity. Still early morning and with heavily tinted windows, it was difficult to see if anyone was aboard. *Great looking boat.*

Ed made breakfast, so Liz and I cleaned up while Ed had the watch. Gulls and terns swooped and dove for the small fish brought up by *Pinafore*'s wake.

True to the weather report, it was a cold, rainy day with some light fog, but for me any day on a boat was a good day. We worked our way out into Nantucket Sound staying well clear of Bell 7, turning southeast toward the "Gong," which sat atop Cross Rip Shoal. We turned to about 130 degrees to G17, then dropped almost due south to Nantucket, skirting Tuckernuck Shoal to the east.

The water in this part of the sound was full of shallows and shoals. The current coming down the sound and the one from the Muskeget Channel could each hit four knots. If those currents clashed with big swells coming off the Atlantic, it got very interesting.

An hour shy of Nantucket, we were on a broad reach, starboard tack. The fog was thicker than advertised and getting worse. Forty-five minutes later, we were getting close to our destination and on course for the Bell that marked the entrance to the Nantucket Harbor channel. The channel is about the width of a ten-pin lane in a bowling alley. If you miss, you go aground.

Early in my sailing career, an old salt told me, "If a sailor hasn't run aground, he hasn't sailed very far." True, but running your boat on the sands or mud bottom in the Virgin Islands or the Chesapeake Bay differs from running aground in New England waters that are strewn with unforgiving rock.

"Okay, guys, let's get the sails in and the centerboard up." I started the engine. Ed dropped and furled the mainsail with Liz's help. Then I furled the jib, and Liz cranked up the centerboard. By now, the fog was so thick we could barely see the bow. *Thick as pea soup* was an apt description. "Ed, you mind taking the wheel."

Ed took over the helm while I went below and looked at the electronic chart. We had a repeater at the helm, but I preferred the larger screen at the nav desk, and it was easier to see out of the glare of the overcast. Seated at the navigation desk, I looked at the electronic chart on the large screen. I scrolled to the entrance of Nantucket Harbor. Elizabeth walked up to the navigation desk.

"Whatcha doing?"

"When the fog is this bad, I like to overlay the chart and the radar. It gives us a real-time bird's-eye view. Most electronic charts are as the geeks say 'interfaced' with GPS, so there is always an accurate fix, even in poor or no visibility."

"That little boat on the chart that's moving— is that us?"

"Yep, pretty cool right."

"Very. What's the big dot behind us?"

Ed called down, "Hey, bud, look at your radar."

Absorbed with the chart, I hadn't been watching the radar. Adjusting the range and sea control, I saw a very big target trailing us. I crawled out from behind the nav desk and climbed partway up the companionway stairs.

"What's up?" I asked.

"I hear some heavy engines coming behind us, which I assume is that blip at about half a mile," pointing to the radar repeater screen.

I went back to the nav desk and looked at the radar screen. I watched as the target passed the Bell and into the channel.

"Probably a ferry," I yelled. "Let's keep an eye on it and stay well to starboard so it can get past."

"Ferries are slow, right?" Ed asked.

"They can do fourteen knots. The most we can do is eight, and that's downhill."

"So, they're faster."

"You flyboys are really good with math."

Ed concentrated on keeping *Pinafore* straight and in the channel. He periodically checked the radar. The large blip following was still there.

Liz went up to the cockpit and picked up a magazine. I casually followed our progress on the chart. Minutes later, I was in the galley searching for chocolate chip cookies when Ed called down to the cabin.

"Hey, I've changed course twice, and this guy is still coming, I'm afraid to move over anymore."

Clutching a cookie, I went back to the nav desk and looked at the radar. The blip was coming straight at us, though there was sea room on the left side of the channel. I ran up to the cockpit. "Liz, I have a bad feeling. Get our life jackets and get back to the cockpit fast!"

Liz jumped up—"Jesus, not again"—and hurried down to get the life jackets.

"Ed, let me have the helm. You start blasting him with that air horn." Ed pulled the canned air horn from the locker and started three-second blasts. Between blasts, he asked,

"Any chance he can't see us?"

I moved *Pinafore* even farther to the right side of the channel, praying we wouldn't hit bottom, I looked over my shoulder, but the only thing I could see was the fog. "I don't think so. We have our radar reflector up." I looked to the top of the mast to reassure myself. Yep, rather forlorn looking, but the reflector was hanging there.

Liz came up from below, already in her vest. She gave one to Ed. When he had it buckled, he took the wheel while I shrugged into mine. Liz grabbed the horn, triggering the piercing blasts again. I checked to make sure the centerboard was up as high as it could go, then took the wheel from Ed. I tried to inch closer to the starboard side of the channel.

"Listen, guys. if we go in the water, swim perpendicular to the channel, then stand up, the water is only about two or three feet deep once you're out of the channel."

"If we don't end up as fish chum, we'll be lucky to tell up from down, let alone perpendicular," Ed said with noticeable sarcasm.

"Ed, use those aviator eyes of yours and tell me if you can see him." I looked down at the radar screen. The blip had almost merged with us.

"There he is!" Ed yelled.

I looked over my shoulder—A white, gleaming hull as big as a building and taller than *Pinafore*'s mast materialized from the fog. Pushing a six-foot bow-wave of gray water and foam, it crashed closer and closer. We could feel the rumble of its engines through the deck of the boat. The noise pounded in our ears. I pushed the throttle to full power and turned the wheel hard right. The mammoth white crushing machine continued straight for *Pinafore*—it was almost on top of us.

THUD! Pinafore hit the bottom. We were all pitched to the deck. I regained my footing and quickly grabbed the wheel– instantly, I turned the boat to port, swinging the stern out of the way of certain impact.

Liz screamed, "You're turning the wrong way, you're turning into him!"

Scarcely three feet away, the massive wall of white aluminum hissed past. Its huge thrashing prop flooded the cockpit with tons of foamy water. *Pinafore* pitched in the wake like a giant hobbyhorse.

I yanked the throttle to idle and turned the boat toward the channel.

BUMP! Pinafore's keel hit the bottom again with a bone-rattling thump. We were thrown off our feet again. The boat slowed to a stop, then slid off the obstruction and moved back into the channel.

Seagulls floated quietly at the edge of visibility. I regained my feet, my hands were trembling. Liz got off the deck and sat on the cockpit bench.

Ed still sitting on the deck, "That was exciting. You guys do this every summer?"

I sat down and tried to get my hands to stop shaking. "Anyone get the number of that bus?"

"*The Montauk Express*," said Ed.

CHAPTER FIFTEEN

Nantucket Harbor, Nantucket Island

The three of us were sunning ourselves in the cockpit. I was mixing natural vitamin D with some Blanton's, trying to rid myself of the pallor I acquired from our close encounter with the *Montauk Express*. Liz was stretched out on one of the long cockpit cushions, though not much sun was getting through her sunscreen, because the PF rating was analogous to lead paint. Ed always looked tan. Our repose was interrupted by what I assumed was a passing water taxi but proved to be a fourteen-foot Zodiac Pro. It pulled next to *Pinafore* and stopped. The sole occupant of the rigid deck inflatable was a raven-haired beauty of about thirty. She was almost wearing a white, two-piece bathing suit that contrasted with her smooth olive skin.

Flashing a perfect smile, she said, "Good morning, I am Isabella," and handed me an envelope. "Senor Reynaldo Vicente would like you to attend a cocktail party aboard the *Montauk Express* at five o'clock this evening. I hope we see you there." She gave Ed a megawatt smile, put the Zodiac in gear, and roared away trailing a foamy wake.

"Well," Ed said, "I guess he made his move."

"You mean other than trying to run us over? We should have known it was him," I replied.

"Should have known it was *he*," Liz corrected. She took the envelope, removing a vellum card, "It's engraved, no less."

"He probably has his own print shop on that boat. It's big enough," I said.

Liz read the card, "Well, it seems we are all invited for cocktails, dress casual. What are you going to say to him about yesterday?"

"Nothing," I said, "he would just deny it, say something like he 'had a qualified captain driving the boat, it was foggy, nobody saw us, very sorry' etcetera, etcetera."

The *Montauk Express* was an all-white, 130-foot aluminum yacht complete with a helicopter pad. Built in Italy by CRN, the beam was about twenty-five feet, and the draft was probably eight feet or more. It closely resembled the helmets worn by Darth Vader's soldiers, except bigger. Good for Reynaldo.

About sixty people were already on board. The men were wearing blazers or jackets, some wore ties; the women were dressed in pastel cocktail dresses or flowered sundresses. Quantities of sunglasses and big hats complemented the ensemble. Liz was in a white sundress with black trim and straps, a white floppy hat, leather and cork ankle-strap sandals, and sunglasses. Ed, unusually fashionable, wore a wheat-colored linen jacket and dark-brown slacks. I was in a yellow polo shirt, blue blazer, khakis, and boat shoes. Always the consummate trendsetter, I wore the boat shoes without socks.

The three of us took a minute to take in the ambiance and festivities. The salon was decorated as what I imagined a Mediterranean villa would look like, but as I had never been in a villa, Mediterranean or otherwise, I had to stick with conjecture. Waitresses dressed in little black skirts and starched, white tailored shirts carried trays of fluted champagne from guest to guest. Glass-top tables were loaded with shrimp, appetizers, and iced bottles of wine.

"Okay, time to split up. Liz don't get too far afield. Reynaldo seems to have a thing for you, so use it to advantage but under no circumstances leave the solon alone with him. Ed, while you're discussing the merits of Zodiac inflatables with the *invitation* girl from this morning, try to remember we need information. Good luck."

Liz spotted Joyce and her husband—I always forget his name—so with wine in hand she walked across the salon to chat. Ed spotted Isabella and took off in her direction. I spotted the open bar, elbowed my way within striking distance, and asked the bartender for a Blanton's on the rocks.

"Do you have a light?"

I turned around and found Adel Vicente standing well within my comfort zone.

"Hello, Adel. Sorry, still no matches." I found a bowl of matches on the bar and lit her cigarette.

"Nice to see you again," I said.

That was an understatement. She was wearing a strapless, black, and white striped, satin dress, the wide stripes running horizontally. Her hair was still dark, shiny, and long to her waist. She was definitely "nice" on the eyes.

She took a long time to blow out some inhaled smoke, then said, "Are you enjoying your holiday?"

"Well, it's been interesting. I'm still hopeful for enjoyable. May I get you a drink?"

"Cuba Libre, please"

I ordered a Cuba Libre. The Blanton's was sitting on the bar waiting for me, so I took a sip. I was wondering whether Liz would rescue me again when I recalled my agreement with the president's golfing buddies. Time to be a good spy and elicit some information. I took a long drink of my Blanton's and plunged ahead.

"Is your brother on board?"

"Oh, yes. He mingles with the guests. Is your wife with you?"

"Yes, she's standing over there with some friends," I nodded in Liz's direction.

"Pity," she said.

If you're going to speak a second language, I guess it's good to stick with words you've assimilated. The bartender handed me the Cuba Libra. Taking a bar napkin from the stack in front of me, I handed it and the Cuba Libra to Adel, "How long will you be in Nantucket?"

"I do not know. My brother, he makes those decisions. I am just company.

"And may I say very beautiful company."

"You are most kind." She gave me a smile that could have recharged a car battery. "I was most disappointed you had not noticed before now. Perhaps we could meet later?"

The spy stuff was not going well. While learning nothing, I managed to make a pass at the enemy, which could be dangerous. With Liz around, it could be deadly.

"Will you be staying in harbor for long?" she cooed.

Perhaps I could move things along if I told her we were leaving—it might tempt Reynaldo into our trap, if only we could stay alive long enough to spring the trap.

"No, I think we will be leaving the day after tomorrow. What's your next port of call?"

"I am not sure. Maybe we go to Cuttyhunk. There is not much excitement, but very pretty and very relaxing. Perhaps you shall go there also?"

"I'm not sure of our schedule. We kind of go where the mood strikes and, of course, we go much slower than this boat, but I think probably to Vineyard Haven," I said.

"*Si*, yes, this boat she is *muy* fast. Maybe the mood strikes you to go to Cuttyhunk."

Adel and I chatted for a while longer. She thrusted with provocative innuendo, and I parried with sparkling repartee. Mid-spar, Reynaldo walked up with a cigar in one hand, a drink in the other. Sticking the cigar in his mouth and shifting the drink to his left hand, he extended his right so we could shake hands.

"How have you been? I was just talking to your wife. You are very lucky man."

For some reason, it irritated me that the guy was always delighted with my good fortune. "Thank you, Reynaldo, I was just talking to your lovely sister. She mentioned you might be going to Cuttyhunk for a couple of days."

"I think perhaps, then we depart for Newport. I *regresar*—return—to Venezuela by end of week. It is too bad, I enjoy cruising in this most agreeable weather. Will you stay long in Nantucket? Maybe we see you in Cuttyhunk?"

"No, as I was telling Adel, we will probably move on to Vineyard Haven in the next day or two. But before we leave, I promised to show Liz the whaling museum and, of course, there will be shopping."

"So, your next port of call is Vineyard Haven, then? Well, I wish you much pleasantness with your trip. You will excuse me, I must see to my other guests. I'm sure I will see you again before you leave, *si*?"

"Certainly and thank you for the invitation. The party is very enjoyable."

Trailing cigar smoke, he went off to his other guests. Adel had drifted away, no doubt to plot new conquests. Ed appeared at my arm.

"How did it go?" he asked.

"I don't know. I told them we were leaving in a day or two and heading for Vineyard Haven."

"What's in Vineyard Haven? Ed asked.

"People. I think they were trying to get us to go to Cuttyhunk."

"Why, what's there?

"Nothing."

"Gotcha, well, wherever we go he's not coming after us alone. He'll send some of his goons. We dodge them, then follow the goons back to the nest."

"Yeah, well, so far that hasn't worked out too well." I drank some of my Blanton's, "And you're thinking of loons, which is an apt description."

"How's that?"

"Loony," I said.

"Yeah, I guess it's a little thin. That's what you get for making it up as you go."

"Don't lay this off on me, this is your plan. You and your golfing buddies came up with this, remember? What did you find out?"

"Nothing, but I got her phone number."

"Great. Want another drink?"

"Sure."

We went back to the bar. Ed ordered a Grey Goose with a twist on the rocks. I leaned close to Ed. "I'm going to steal away to explore the boat. I'd like to return the favor for the once over they gave Pinafore."

"Okay, I'll keep an eye on Reynaldo."

I walked toward the stern, exiting the salon, then down to what appeared to be the crew's mess. I quickly stepped through a door and closed it behind me. In a corner of the room there was a desk and a computer. The wall in front of the desk was covered with corkboard pinned with pictures. A long lens camera was sitting on the desk next to the computer. I removed one of the photographs from the wall. It was a photo of Liz sunbathing on the deck of *Pinafore*. Pictures of Liz—this was very creepy. I looked up at the corkboard. All the photos were of me, Liz, and Ed sailing the boat and, mostly, reading or sunbathing on the deck. There were a number of close-ups with the faces enhanced. Maybe they were trying to identify us. I heard footsteps coming down the hall. I quickly exited through an escape hatch to the stern. On the other side was a double-deck balcony arrangement. The bottom deck had a Sea-Doo lashed to a cradle. I climbed up on the Sea-Doo, then pulled myself to the second balcony. There was another door. It was unlocked, so I stepped through. The room was an empty stateroom. Just then, Adele walked out of an adjoining compartment. Startled, she put her hand to her chest.

"This is most forward of you."

"Your room, I presume?"

"Si, you interrupted me while I was touching up my make-up, but of course, I forgive you."

"I was looking for the Sea-Doos. Always wanted one. Are they on this level?"

"I do not believe you look for Sea-Doos. Perhaps you look for me." She walked up to me and started playing with the buttons on my shirt, all three of them. "You have taken me up on my offer, yes?"

"No, but I'm sure my friend Ed would be interested."

She stepped back and pouted. "I do not like your friend Edward. He can be most horrid."

"You know Ed?"

Adel looked up quickly, then lowered her eyes. "No, I do not know him."

I walked back topside and reentered the salon. Several dozen people with drinks in hand were standing quietly around a baby grand piano, listening to Liz playing *Nocturne* by Chopin. Ed was still at the bar, so I walked over to him.

"Did you find anything?"

"Yeah, I found Adel."

"And?"

"I found some very creepy long-range pictures of the three of us on the boat."

"What do you suppose that's about?"

"I don't know. Have you ever met Adel before?"

"Not that I recall."

I turned to the bartender. "Blanton's on the rocks, please."

CHAPTER SIXTEEN

The next morning, we were not in the mood to fix breakfast, so we took our hangovers ashore for eggs and Bloody Mary's. Skipping the Bloody Mary's, the three of us had eggs, bacon, and several pots of coffee. Over a last cup of coffee, I listened a tad impatiently as Liz told me about all the money she was going to save with the end-of-season sales. I went into full cringe when I heard about the $200 bra, she had seen but would no doubt resist.

The next two days were spent walking the town, visiting restaurants and the whaling museum. Dinner at Topper's and the whaling museum were the highlights.

The *Montauk Express* left the day after the party with no further contact from Adel, Reynaldo, or, much to Ed's disappointment, Isabella.

On the morning of the third day, we slipped our mooring and headed for Vineyard Haven on the northernmost part of Martha's Vineyard, about a two-hour sail northwest of Edgartown and most of a day's sail from Nantucket. The weather was warm and clear, the wind blowing about twenty knots out of the northwest giving us a hard beat all the way to the harbor mouth until we turned south on a broad reach, starboard tack.

Once inside the breakwater, we found a place to drop the anchor and secure the boat. Tired, salty, and windburned, we showered, then caught a water taxi into town.

Vineyard Haven is actually in Tisbury, one of the many towns erected to support the sailing trade of the mid- to late 1800s. It's now primarily a tourist attraction. Tisbury will always be Vineyard Haven to boat people. We ate dinner at the Blue Canoe, found a place for ice cream, walked around town some, then, tired, went back to the boat for some welcome sleep.

We woke early the next morning. I fixed scrambled eggs, bacon, and grits with orange juice and coffee. When the dishes were cleaned and put away, I worked around the boat while Ed went ashore to meet with Stacie before she went to work. Surprise, Liz wanted to go shopping.

We agreed to meet in front of Black Dog Tavern at eleven o'clock. Liz wanted to show me some things she had seen in a store. Then lunch would be at the Black Dog at about noon. Ed was going to ask Stacie to join us if she could get away from work.

I finished puttering around the boat at about nine-thirty, washed up, put on some clean clothes, and took the water taxi into town. Ed was on the dock. He and Stacie had visited for a few minutes, but she couldn't join us for lunch until one o'clock, which was okay with me. Ed and I walked around town sticking our noses into one shop and the next, mostly to get out of the sun and into some air conditioning. It was abnormally hot, especially for early in the day. We tried to figure a way to get Reynaldo and the flash drive together, but because we didn't know where he was, it was futile. For all we knew, he was in Venezuela. We walked into a hardware store. I looked down the aisle of the cramped mom-and-pop store. A man in his sixties approached.

"Can I help you find something?"
"I need to patch a few holes in my boat."
"What kind of holes?"
"Bullet holes."
Without a moment's hesitation, he asked, "Wood or fiberglass?"
"Fiberglass."
"Aisle four."

After we left the hardware store, we ducked into the Stop and Shop on Water Street to buy a Coke, then went next door to wait for Liz in front of the Black Dog Tavern. When Liz hadn't shown by eleven-fifteen, I called her cell phone, but there was no answer. Ed and I walked across the street to see if she was in the Black Dog General Store. Black Dog has taken over this part of the world. Liz wasn't in the store, so we went back to the tavern and went inside, but no luck. About five minutes later, my phone rang, I was relieved to see the call was from Liz.

"Hey, honey, where are you?"

A female voice replied, "Senor, your wife has been taken and will be flown to Central America in few hours. She is at the airport, you must act *muy rápido*."

"Who is this?"

"You must hurry. She is in old building at south of airport."

"Who has her and why?"

"She is to be traded for Dr. Pérez's files." The phone went dead.

"Who was that?" Ed asked.

"Damn and hell! Reynaldo just made his move! I am pretty sure that was Adel. She said Elizabeth has been snatched and will be flown out of the country if we don't get to her first. She's at the airport."

"Well, it's a trap."

"Sure, it is, but what choice do I have?"

"None."

"Ed, try to round up some police. Hell, I don't even know if they have police in this berg. I'm going back to the boat to get that flash drive."

"Okay, I'll meet you at the airport."

Starting toward the taxi dock, I yelled over my shoulder, "She said Liz was in an old building at the south end of the airport!"

I ran back to the dock and nearly went crazy waiting for the water taxi. Once aboard, I ignored complaints from the few others on the taxi and gave the driver fifty dollars to take me to *Pinafore* first. During the interminable trip, I ran through one scenario after the other trying to think of a plan to save Liz. They all ended badly. I jumped off the taxi telling the driver there would be another fifty bucks for him if he waited for me. I went below, took the *Narragansett* flash drive out of the chart table, and stuck it in my pocket. In the master stateroom I went to my "repel boarders locker." Except for the Colt and M14, I stuffed the contents of the compartment into a canvas bag. I took the Colt, checked the magazine, and slipped the gun in my waistband, concealing it with my shirt. I disassembled the M14 and put that in the bag.

I got topside just as the water taxi was about to leave. I closed the boat, threw the bag in the taxi, and followed the bag.

"I need you to go right back to the dock."

"Sir, I have to deliver these people and pick up other passengers," he protested. The "captain" of the water taxi was a nice college kid, but I had no time or patience.

"Let me put it this way: you get me to the dock now or there is no fifty dollars."

"But, sir," he whined.

"Let me put it another way: you start heading for the dock now or I throw you overboard and you can swim back. Now move this fucking boat!"

The other passengers in the taxi realized I was in no mood for polite discussion and stopped complaining.

When we got to the town dock, I gave the nice college kid a hundred-dollar bill and ran to find a taxi. The driver was a native of the island, a woman in her late forties or early fifties, gray hair, pleasant smile, and more than willing to break a few traffic laws for a hundred dollars. Ten minutes later, we were at the airport, about 300 feet from the building where I figured Liz was being held. I thanked the taxi lady and stepped out into the hot noon sun.

Ed was already standing in the shadow of another building. When he saw me, he walked over, "That's the one," he pointed.

We walked slowly toward the hangar, looking around. The building looked like it had been a maintenance hangar, old oil drums, engine parts, and a wash rack were next to the building. There was a small, high window facing us. Belly down in some thick grass, I looked through my binoculars. Various types of private planes were parked around the airfield. An airplane was taxiing down a runway. A small jet plane sat in front of an open hangar. A mechanic was working on one of the engines, and a man in black walked back and forth watching the area.

"No cops?" I asked.

"None I could find. Our nose tweaking the other night worked. I called Silvers, but he can't get anyone here fast enough, so we're on our own."

"I'm shocked. That was probably always the plan. Let us get our hands dirty—oh, and probably killed."

"Speaking of a plan? We can't go in there like a bull in a china shop."

"That's exactly what I plan to do."

"Oh, good, the direct approach. Great idea."

"Trust me, while you were running guns for God and country, I was killing bad guys for the same outfit."

"I resent the term *gun running*," said Ed.

I handed the binoculars to Ed. He looked for a while, then dropped the binoculars, whipping sweat from his forehead. "That's a Falcon 10. Must be the right hangar. That thing has a 2,000-mile range. If they get her on that, she's gone."

Great, if I screwed up, Liz would be in South America before dinner time and the chances of seeing her again would be about zero. I had no time to wait, no time to investigate, no time to plan.

"No time like the present. There are an M14 and a shotgun in the bag. Watch my back."

The Marine Corps *Warfighting* manual is comprehensive, but it essentially boils down to the premise that "warfare is born of ruthless opportunism. [In a fight one must] paralyze and confound [the enemy] by quickly and aggressively exploiting his vulnerabilities and strike him in a way that will hurt the most." In short, strike your enemy with such ferocity and lethality that he is dead before he even knows you're on the field of battle.

The people holding Elizabeth, like other enemies I had fought, were faceless and nameless, but this time was different. These nameless had threatened my family. This would not be an impersonal fight. Ferocity and lethality were the plan, my only plan.

I maneuvered toward the side of the hangar and peered around the corner. A guard was by the door just turning to walk toward me. I pulled the Colt from my waistband. As he rounded the corner, I hit him in the face with the big pistol. I caught him as he went down, and quietly lowered him to the ground.

I clicked off the pistol's safety, thumbed back the hammer, inched the slide back to confirm there was a cartridge in the chamber, then let the big gun hang behind my right leg.

Despite its name, John Browning designed the Model 1911 Colt to kill Moro guerrillas during the American–Philippine War. Contrary to its recent press, in the right hands, it is an effective weapon and true to its designer's intent: one is not wounded by a 1911 Colt, one is shattered or killed.

An old metal door in an old tin building in daylight was not a recipe for anything stealthy, so my entry had to be direct and violent. I was wearing sunglasses, but I also closed my right eye to preserve some additional "night vision," which I would need in the building. Standing in front of the door, I counted to twenty, willing my heart to beat somewhere close to normal. I waited, waited more, and then walked into the hangar.

I pulled off the sunglasses with my left hand, "Hi, guys, what's happin'!" Visually, I quickly broke the room into thirds, starting from right to left. Three men were in the building. To my right, about fifteen feet away, under the window, was a man in a green John Deere baseball hat. He was seated in a chair tilted against the corrugated steel wall picking at his fingernails with a knife. About twenty feet to my front, standing in front of an old, oil-soaked workbench, was a kid in a white T-shirt and baggy pants. He was pouring coffee from a small coffeepot into a ceramic mug. Liz was sitting in a folding chair opposite and about twenty feet from the man in the John Deere hat. To the left and behind Liz, a third guy was sitting in an old metal desk chair. Older than the other two, he was dressed in black pants, cowboy boots, and a blue shirt with cutoff sleeves displaying the array of tattoos that covered his arms. His long black hair was pulled back in a ponytail. Someone had gone to a lot of trouble to set this up, and I was gambling they wouldn't harm Liz unless they thought it necessary. For a long five or six seconds, they stared at me, not moving.

I shot the man in the John Deere hat. I missed center mass, hitting him in the throat. He started to stand, blood spurting from the gaping wound in his neck. He gurgled, then sat down and fell over, the chair tipping with him. Baggy Pants was hit in the chest, he crumpled the coffee cup still in his hand. I swung to my left, but Ponytail had already yanked Liz out of sight. I carefully walked into the interior of the building.

CRACK!

I turned just in time to see a man with a shotgun collapse. I glanced toward the hangar entrance— Ed gave me a small wave.

Crouching, I hurried further into the hangar. I found Ponytail. He held Liz by the throat with his left arm. In his right hand was a Glock 19 pressed to her head.

"Put gun down or I kill her!" he yelled.

"Okay, okay, I'm putting it down!" I bent down slowly to place the Colt on the floor—Liz smashed her right heel down on Ponytail's pretty boot and wheeled to the left. Still bent over, I flipped the gun up and pulled the trigger. The round hit Ponytail under the left eyebrow and passed through the back of his head in a spray of red gore. He looked surprised, fell over backward onto the floor, his arms and legs splayed like a kid making a snow angel. The Glock rattled as it slid across the concrete.

Suddenly it was deathly quiet. The smell of Cordite hung in the airless space mixing with the smells of coffee, hydraulic fluid, and jet fuel. My ears rang from the noise of the exploding .45 cartridges.

In three steps Liz and I were holding each other.

"What took you so long?"

"Stopped for lunch."

We hugged and kissed. She had never felt so good. It had never felt so good to be alive. One of us said, "Let's get out of here." So, we did. We walked over to Ed standing by the door.

"I love the smell of Cordite in the morning. You two, okay?"

"Yes, I'm fine," said Liz.

"I will be as soon as some adrenalin burns off. Thanks, I never saw that guy."

Liz hugged and kissed Ed, then turned and kissed me again.

"Damn, it's nice to be a hero," Ed said. "Damn, bud you're one hell of a *pistolero*."

"I prefer *gunny*."

Slinging the rifle, Ed walked across the Tarmac to the Falcon, and approached two men in uniforms.

"Did we hear some shooting?" The taller one asked.

"Yeah. I was sighting in my rifle. I have some sandbags in that deserted hangar. You guys flying this bird?"

Holding hands, Liz and I watched as Ed and the two men talked, punctuating their discussion with flying hands, as pilots do. Ed walked back to us. The two pilots walked away.

"Those guys are the pilots for the Falcon."

"Yeah, the uniforms gave it away. Any sign of police?"

"No."

"We made a hell of a mess in there. Maybe I should call Gallagher?"

"We'll be okay. What were we supposed to do, let them kidnap Liz?"

"We were supposed to call the police."

"Well, it's done now, and we have work to do. If there is a problem, Silvers will take care of it."

"What work?"

"The plane is out of Miami. The pilots said they don't know Reynaldo. They only know they were hired to pick up three or four passengers here and fly them to a little airport near Puerto Cabezas, Nicaragua. Then back to Miami."

"Where the hell is Puerto Cabezas?"

"It's a little town on the east coast of Nicaragua, about seventy-five miles south of the Honduras border. I figure Reynaldo squirreled it away for his drug business."

"The pilots said they are not supposed to arrive at the strip until about four this afternoon. Feel like a ride?"

"To Nicaragua, in that jet?"

"Yeah, it's an old plane, but the things are built like tanks, and this one has some good avionics. If we leave now, we can be early. Fuel is already on board, but we'll have to stop, probably Cancun, I got an old friend that has an FBO there. That will give us enough gas to get back without stopping. You game?"

"If we take the plane, what do we do with the pilots? That's got to be a million-dollar airplane. They're not going to just watch while we fly away."

"I flashed my credentials and persuaded them to take a couple of days off, you know, enjoy the beaches and water. Told them they would have probably been killed had they continued the flight. Or if they preferred, I said they could wait for us in the local jail for aiding a kidnapping. I gave them some shit about this being a secret operation. Told them not to call their FBO until tomorrow and told them we would bring the plane back tonight, tomorrow latest. I think they're good guys, they just lucked into this charter."

"And they went for it?"

"Well, as I said, I told them I was a fed, and I said you would pay for their hotel. Plus, the kidnapping thing is no joke."

"You're such a silver-tongued devil, especially with my money. The State Department will pay the bill."

"Yeah, that's what I meant."

"You guys can't be serious!" Liz said.

"This might be our one chance to get the upper hand and grab Reynaldo," I said.

"You two are nuts."

"Liz, this isn't over until we get Reynaldo and the Narragansett Files together and in custody. And to do that we need to get him and the files back to the U.S. and turn him over to the authorities."

"We said we would help by cruising around New England, not by flying off to God knows where."

"Oh, we know where."
"We do?" I said.

"Yep, a dirt strip north of a little town called Puerto Cabezas on the east coast of Nicaragua."

"I suspect this is not a tourist destination, so how do we find it?"

"Puerto Cabezas has an airport with an ICAO code. We home in on that, and when we get there, we fly a course of zero, three, three off the east end of the airport for seven and a half nautical miles and land. Easy-peasy."

"Did you really just say *easy-peasy*?" Liz asked.

"Yeah, it's an old flying expression rarely used except among us professionals."

"Well, I have serious doubts about flying with somebody who says easy-peasy," Liz said.

"That's good, because you're not going," I said.

Liz looked at me as if I had two heads.

"The hell I'm not! Are you going to leave me here to get snatched by some of those creeps again? Where you go, I go," Liz looked at Ed, "Besides, Reynaldo is expecting to see me get off that plane, right?"

"Well, yeah, but—"

I jumped in again, "This could be dangerous. Scratch that, this *will* be dangerous, and more than likely as soon we leave the pilots will call their FBO and we will have a bunch of F-16s shooting our ass off."

"You mean it's going to be more dangerous than being kidnapped by three grease balls and held at gunpoint while you fire live ammunition twelve inches from my head? You mean more dangerous than that? And who's to say there won't be more of these delightful people waiting for me on the boat, only this time I'll be alone while you're winging your way to the sunny Caribbean. I'm going!"

I knew a losing battle. "Okay, I give up. Plus, you have a good point, there could be more of these guys around. While Ed and I do the preflight, how about going over to the restaurant and grabbing some sandwiches and whatever else you think we'll need?"

"You're not leaving me on that boat!"

"I promise. Besides, I could use a ham sandwich, maybe two. Saving damsels in distress makes me hungry."

"Well, *Gunny*, if you leave me here, you're going to get that *pistolero* shoved up you know where. Your stomach will be the least of your problems." She turned and headed off toward the airport restaurant.

"Ed, the more I think about it, the less I like the idea of taking that airplane. I think we should call Collins or Silvers, and probably Gallagher, and get them involved. We have an attempted kidnapping. That ought to be enough to hang Reynaldo."

"I'll call Silvers, but we don't have Reynaldo. The pilots said they were to meet the guy that's paying for the charter at that airstrip. That has to be Reynaldo, so he is probably already there. We need his warm body in our custody, or we have nothing. This is the chance we have been waiting for—the opportunity to nab him with his hand in the cookie jar."

"How about the flight plan and weather?"
"Filed to Miami and good weather all the way."

"I'm not too sure about this, but okay, we've come this far," I said. "Ed, while you preflight, I need to do something with that maintenance hangar, maybe lock it until I can get to Gallagher. I know he's a Newport cop, but I feel I should tell him what's going on."

"Okay, I'll get the pilots on their way, finish the preflight, then call Dick Silvers and fill him in. I should be done in about twenty minutes."

CHAPTER SEVENTEEN

Martha's Vineyard Airport

Vineyard tower, this is Falcon November three, niner, two, two, November ready for takeoff at runway two-four."

"Falcon November three, niner, Vineyard tower, fly runway heading, climb and maintain, ten thousand, contact cape departure 119.7, winds variable at four, altimeter 62.7, clear for takeoff."

"Vineyard tower, November three, niner, fly runway heading, climb and maintain, ten thousand, cape departure 119.7."

At takeoff speed, Ed rotated the aircraft, and then when we reached positive climb he called for, "Gear up."

"Gear up," I replied from the right seat, moving the lever until it hit the stop. The lights on the panel went out indicating all the wheels were in their wells.

"Flaps."

"Flaps," I answered, moving the lever forward.

According to the flight computer, flying time to Puerto Cabezas was about three hours forty minutes. Add another hour for the refueling stop; we could still be on the ground before the scheduled rendezvous. At least according to the pilots. I hoped they were right. Ed and I took turns catnapping and walking back into the cabin to stretch out the kinks. Liz alternated roles between pampered princess and flight attendant. When she wasn't consuming the caviar and champagne, she found in the galley, she was supplying us with coffee and ham sandwiches. For the sake of "our health," the ham sandwiches were actually turkey and cheese on rye, no mayo. In addition, there were apples. I hate turkey. Apparently, Ed would eat anything. He even ate the apples.

Thanks mostly to Ed, I got my instrument and multiengine ratings before I gave up my "ticket," but it had been a long time since I had done any flying. I initially enjoyed the fun and freedom of flying. I scared a few farmers, popping over tree lines playing fighter pilot, but the more hours I accumulated the more flying became a chore. Difficult to pursue part-time, flying is a precision skill. It's sort of like surgery with a view, except you die from your mistakes along with the patient. I took up sailing with no regrets.

Ed was rated as an Airline Transport Pilot and probably had 8,000 hours or more as an aircraft commander (or, as they say, "in the left seat"), so I was determined to take full advantage of his tutelage and get some much needed updating in the cockpit. I was relishing the "kerosene" time and for the moment forgot why we were all together in a luxury jet winging our way over the blue Caribbean.

With the occasional analog backup, the cockpit of the Falcon and most modern aircraft is electronic. By using the flight computer, a combination of GPS and autopilot, planes can essentially fly themselves. I suspect more than one crew has fallen asleep in the cockpit. I reflected on the similarities between sailing and flying. A sail is no more than a vertical wing using the Venturi effect: low and high pressures over the respective surfaces working in concert to produce lift. In a boat, the lift pulls the boat through the water.

We landed in Cancun at an FBO, one of Ed's old haunts, and topped off the tanks using my credit card. Ed assured me I would be reimbursed. I was finding the secret agent business to be expensive. I figured I could be a spy another ten days before I was bankrupt.

Refueled, we continued flying southwest. We had to be early, so we remained conscious of our arrival time. Ed and I talked about the "old days" when we were in college and did a lot of "Hey, I wonder happened to him or her," told some old jokes and a few new ones. He briefly spoke about his wife, Caroline, when she came up in one of the stories. His mood changed appreciably, so I tried to steer the conversation in another direction. Liz brought us some cold drinks, stayed to listen to one of Ed's jokes, then went back to her pampered princess persona.

Ed pointed to the electronic chart, "We're getting pretty close, maybe another thirty minutes. Looks as if we picked up some time with a tailwind."

"Okay, captain, before things get exciting, I'm going to the head, then I'll take over, so you can take a break."

"Roger that," he said in a mock tone of formality.

The airplane in Ed's capable hands, I slid my seat back, climbed out, walked into the cabin, and sat next to Liz, who was reading a copy of *Palm Beach Illustrated* magazine. She looked up, "How's everything going?"

"Any more sandwiches?" I asked.

"Sure," she got up and walked to the galley, pulled a sandwich from a paper bag, took a can of ginger ale from the cooler, and handed me both with a napkin. She sat down and turned to me. "How do you do it?" she asked.

"Do what?"

"You killed those men without so much as a thought. One was probably no older than nineteen or twenty. You didn't give them a chance to surrender or put their hands up or anything."

"Lizzy, I thought a lot about it, but you heard me tell Silvers and Collins, there is no such thing as a fair fight. Those men would have killed us in an instant, and I couldn't allow that. They were soldiers in an army of professional thugs. That's what they do, put themselves out for hire. This time they were working for Reynaldo. I gave them the same chance they would have given me. Okay, maybe less because there was no way I was going to allow them to hurt you."

"Other than the other day on the boat, have you killed before?"

"Yes," I said.

"On the police department?"

"No, I think I only took my gun out of the holster twice."

"In the war? She asked"

"Yes, I killed in the war. Mostly it's pretty impersonal. You pull the trigger, and they fall down. Usually, it looks as if they just tripped and fell. If you're lucky, they don't get up. Most of the time, with the horrendous noise, the dirt, and the chaos, you're kind of numb, and don't know whether you hit anyone or not."

Liz asked in a small voice, "Do you like it?"

"Of course not, and I try not to think much about it. It's what I had to do at the time and it's not something I want to do again, but if I have to protect us, I will."

"Without thinking about it?"

"Without hesitation. Probably not the same thing."

"You seem, I don't know, so efficient."

"I was part of a small group that did special missions."

"I thought you were in recon; you did reconnaissance."

"We did other stuff, too."

"I don't like it," she said.

"I'm glad you don't like it. You're not supposed to like it. No sane person does, and I would be concerned if you did like it." We sat together each with our thoughts. I finished my sandwich and wadded up the napkin. "We'll be landing in about a half hour, Liz, I need you to do something, but I need you to trust me and not ask too many questions, at least for now. It has to do with what we were talking about."

"You mean killing?"

"If necessary, yes."

"Okay."

I pulled my duffel bag out of the storage compartment and set it on the carpet between us, then pulled the weapons out of the bag. First, I reassembled the M14 and made sure there were at least four loaded magazines. Then I loaded the shotgun, reloaded the magazines for the Colt, and put two more magazines to the side. The S&W was loaded and ready, I put it on the sofa next to me.

"Liz, this airport is not going to be much more than a dirt strip, no taxiways, no terminal, perhaps some shacks, but more likely just a dirt runway. During our downwind leg, we will try to decide where we want this meeting."

"How are you going to do that?"

"We will be looking for access roads, buildings, vehicles, that sort of thing, by parking the plane in a place of our choice, we force the location of the meeting, preferably at one end of the strip so we can get the plane back in the air quickly. When Ed finishes his rollout, he will turn the plane to the right. That will hide the cabin door from anyone at the far end of the strip. At that instant, I want you to take the M14 and the magazines, get out of the airplane as fast as you can, and hide at the side of the strip. Hopefully, there will be some brush or weeds you can use."

She swallowed and asked, "Why?"

"You're our safety valve. I don't trust much of what's going on. This thing smells, and I need you to watch our backs. You are a very good shot, and I need that skill in somebody I trust. I need you to be calm, organized, and clearheaded. How much of the champagne have you had?"

"Only about half a glass. It was awful."

"Good, after we drop you off, wait until the plane gets moving and raises some dust, then work your way toward us, hiding as much as you can. If possible, come down on the right side of the runway. We will try to park on the left side. Ed will be taxing slowly. If anyone is on the strip, they will be watching the plane, not looking for you, but you will need to move quickly. Remember, stay low and stay out of sight."

"Then what?"

"If possible, the plane will stop on the far left side of the runway, which will pull Reynaldo to the plane and cause the 'meeting' to take place in your full view. When you get about two hundred yards away from where the plane is parked, set up a shooting position just as we did it at the range, but stay still and stay hidden. Make sure no one can see you."

Except for shotguns that are pointed, all firearms are aimed with sights that are usually adjustable. To hit a target, each firearm must be adjusted to the correct sight picture for the person shooting. These adjustments vary with the weapon and range to target. Knobs or screws in the rear sight adjust these variations, which are known as "dope." Over the years, Liz and I spent many hours on the range, even competing with rifle and shotgun. Unlike me, Elizabeth was a natural athlete and an aggressive competitor. She is an expert marksman.

"Do you remember your dope for the M14?"

"Yes, two clicks elevation, and three clicks right windage."

"Good, remember that was for three hundred yards, so adjust accordingly. See if you can find a cap or dark scarf to tie over all that blond hair."

"You mean I'm going to be a sniper."

"You're going to be our cavalry—only without the horse."

"How about a trumpet?"

"No trumpet, but here are the binoculars from the boat." I pulled them out of the bag and handed them to her. "Use these to watch what's going on. I don't think Reynaldo is expecting anyone on the plane except you and his henchmen but watch the tree line for movement. Lizzy, you have to be resolute. I don't want any unnecessary killing, but if you see things going bad, shoot first, and ask questions later. Shoot center mass, shoot to kill. Ed and I would prefer that you not shoot us. Can you do it?"

She was very quiet, the color gone from her face, "I can do it. Shoot center mass and don't shoot you or Ed." Then with a slight grin, she added, "Just to ensure there are no accidents, you might want to rethink that red Jaguar."

"Good girl. If we get through this, I'll buy you the red Jag and some red Louboutin's to go with it. Okay, when the time comes, I'll be back to help with the door. You may want to find a bag or something to carry the binoculars and ammo."

I stopped and used the head, then went forward so Ed could take his break.

"We still good?" I asked.

"Yep, should see Puerto Cabezas pretty soon."

"You want to make a head call first?"

"No, I'm Okay. Let's get this thing on the ground."

We flew over the coastline, then turned northwest, and with the help of the flight computer found the airstrip. Ed added flaps, retarded the throttles, taking the plane down to about a thousand feet, and then made a pass over the airstrip for a look. The strip looked to be paved. There was a small shack at one end.

"Looks okay to me," Ed said. "You see anything that makes you nervous?"

"No, looks deserted."

On the downwind leg, we looked again but saw nothing that would prevent us from landing. The only thing I could see was jungle, but at 175 knots, we could have missed plenty. We turned crosswind, then turned to our final approach. Flaps extended, Ed pulled the power some more and asked for the gear.

"Gear down," I replied.

The plane flared and settled on the strip with a modest thump. Ed pulled the throttles all the way back to reverse. The clamshells at the rear of the engines opened, reversing the thrust in a roar. He applied the brakes, moved the throttles to idle, and about two-thirds of the way down the strip the plane slowed to a stop.

"Nice—you've done that before," I said.

"Yeah, well the trick will be getting out of here. This is a real short runway."

"Ed, take this thing down to the end of the runway, make a turn to the right, then stop for a moment, I'm going to kick Liz out."

"Why?"

"I don't want her near that guy and the goons he is sure to bring with him. And she's going to be our backup."

"Backup?"

"Yeah, she'll have the rifle. She's a great shot."

Ed moved the throttles forward. "You guys do anything normal?"

"What do you mean *normal*?"

"Golf, tennis, contract bridge, you know, normal stuff."

"I hate golf and I wouldn't know a contract bridge if I fell off one."

"Okay, coming up on the turn." Ed brought the starboard engine to idle and eased the port engine throttle forward. He stood on the starboard brake swinging the plane right.

I slid out of the seat and went back to the cabin. Liz was ready, her hair was pinned and covered with a small, dark-blue apron she found in the galley. The plane turned slightly to the right and stopped. I opened the door.

She looked at me "I don't care about the red Jaguar, just be safe. I love you." We hugged and kissed passionately.

"I love you, too." I said.

She stroked my cheek, then climbed down the airstairs and moved out of sight. I pulled the door closed.

"Okay, go!" I yelled.

CHAPTER EIGHTEEN

Jungle Landing Strip, Nicaragua

Slowly taxiing the plane back down the strip, Ed stood on the brakes while spooling up the engines trying to raise as much dust as possible to give Liz some cover in case anyone *was* watching. "Ed, when you get to the far end, pull to the left side of the runway. That will force Reynaldo to come in on the right side, giving Liz a good view."

"Okay."

Five minutes later, we were at the end of the runway and coasting to the left side of the strip. Ed pulled the nose to the right, stopped, pulled the throttles to idle, shut down the engines, and started through the checklist.

I went back to the cabin, reopened the door, and climbed out into the steamy heat. The jungle crept close to the strip, which looked to be little used. Made from packed dirt and gravel, weeds sprouted periodically down its length. A berm formed by the excess overburden from clearing and leveling of the strip ran down each side of the runway. The Gulf of Mexico, off the end of the runway a mile or so to the east, was hidden by the brush and low jungle. At each end of the strip, there had been some effort to keep the trees from impeding the aircraft. I couldn't help but wonder if jets had ever flown out of this place, but I moved the thought to the back of my mind.

The airplane was pointing at two old shacks about fifty yards distant. They looked to be made of rusted corrugated steel, plywood, and old sheets of aluminum originally intended to make soda cans, the Coca-Cola logos still legible. A narrow dirt road led away from the end of the strip, bending around the buildings, turning left, disappearing into the jungle. The silence was uncanny, no birds, no wind, no noise, just the stifling heat and foreboding desolation. The good news was the place was deserted so Liz would have time to set up in good cover.

In the thirty minutes or more since we landed, tension had become palpable. My jaw hurt from clenching my teeth, a bad habit when under stress. Squadrons of flies were doing touch-and-goes on the back of my neck.

This was not a pleasant place. I looked down the strip trying to see Liz, but she was well hidden. I hoped she was faring better with the flies. For the second or third time, Ed looked over the aircraft getting everything ready for our eventual takeoff. He looked preoccupied, but he was probably feeling the tension, too.

I sat and leaned against the starboard landing gear—.

"Sarge, do you think these guys are coming?"
"Shsssh, not if they hear us, keep quiet and quit moving around."
"Jesus, these fucking flies are biting the crap out of me."
"You and everyone else. Lie still. This is an ambush, not a beer run."
"Sarge—here they come."
"I see them. Remember, let them get to this side of the stream."

"Hey, bud, wake up, I said I think I hear them."

I jerked awake, "Okay—help an old man up."

Ed helped me to my feet, then he took up a position by the nose wheel. I stood next to the leading edge of the starboard wing, where I could get to the shotgun hidden behind the starboard main gear. My Colt was in my waist at the small of my back. Ed had the Smith under his shirt.

Two black Mercedes SELs, one behind the other, drove into the clearing. They stopped about halfway between the shacks and the airplane. Our old friend Reynaldo got out of the right rear of the lead car, two bruisers got out from the front seat, four more got out of the car in the rear. Ignoring Ed, Reynaldo walked toward me until he was about seven or eight feet away. The goons fanned out about twenty feet behind him, I could see Ed in my periphery, his arms crossed in front of him, the Smith revolver in his right hand under his left arm. Reynaldo looked like a Panama Jack advertisement with sunglasses. His thugs were all dressed in dark suits, probably the reason they all looked irritable. Heat prostration.

"Good afternoon, gentlemen," said Reynaldo.

"Howdy," I said. "I see you travel with your own football team."

"Yes, I find it comforting. There are so many unpleasant people in this part of the world."

"Well, here we are—what can we do for you?"

"Actually, I was expecting your wife."

"Yeah, she had to re-wax her bowling ball, so Ed and I came instead."

"Most regrettable. And my employees, did they come with you?"

"No, but the good news is they won't be collecting on their retirement plan."

"I see. Well, you know what they say about good help. Perhaps you gentlemen would care to join me for dinner tonight? There is a friendly cantina down the road."

"Thanks, but no. We have to run. As you can see, our chariot awaits. Thanks for the deluxe ride, by the way."

"Well, perhaps some other time."

"As a matter of fact, we were hoping you would join us."

"Amusing, but now, sir, I think you have something that belongs to me. As soon as you hand it over, we can both get on with our business."

"What do you think we have?"

"You know very well that you possess documents and private information that belong to me!"

"Okay, let's say I have these documents. What do we get in return?"

"You get to live. Now, if you please, hand them to me."

I pulled the flash drive out of my left pocket and turned my palm up, showing it to

Reynaldo, who looked surprised.

"Ah, no wonder they could not be found. Throw it over here to me!" He commanded.

"No, I don't think so. You come and get it and be very careful to stay between me and your bozos."

He glared at me, then laughed and walked toward me, "This changes nothing, and you will never leave this hellhole unless I permit it."

I lifted my hand to give him the flash drive. As he reached out, I dropped the drive and grabbed his hand, yanking him toward me. At the same time, I pulled the Colt out of my waist and shoved it under his chin.

"Now, you tell those guys to lie down, or I'll blow your fucking head off."

"They will kill you," he hissed.

"Maybe, but you won't live long enough to see it. Now, tell them, and I want to hear it in English!"

He hesitated. I could almost hear him calculating his odds behind those lifeless eyes. In a low, determined voice, I said, "Reynaldo, I just killed three of your men with this same gun. I assure you I have no compunction about killing you."

He grinned slightly. "Very well," he called back to his men. "Lie down, all you, *ahora*!"

The football team reluctantly and collectively got down on their knees, then lay on their stomachs. I figured it was too much to tell them to throw their guns away. With that many guns waving around, somebody would start banging away. From my left pocket, I removed a plastic wire tie I brought from the boat. It wasn't as big as the ones cops use, but it would serve the purpose, "Now, turn around very carefully and put your hands behind your back."

I called to Ed, "Watch the joy boys, Ed." Reynaldo turned and put his hands behind his back. I stuck the Colt in my waist, then looped the tie around his wrists, pulled it tight, and retrieved my gun. "Get down on your knees."

With Reynaldo subdued on his knees, I knelt behind him and bent over to get the Narragansett flash drive. One of the bozos in back got up on one knee, drew his gun, and started firing. Ed shot back, then the others jumped up, and the place erupted in gunfire. Bullets hit in front of me, spraying shards of grit in my face. A slug whizzed past my ear. Every bird in the area took flight, screaming in protest. I knelt behind Reynaldo, tried to block out the noise, and fired, trying to make each shot count. Time turned into slow motion and the old training kicked in, each shot deliberate and aimed. Gradually, Reynaldo's men started to wither. Then the slide on my Colt locked back, the magazine empty. I heard Reynaldo grunt, then he fell against me. His body lying over me made it difficult to get to a fresh magazine. As I struggled to reload my pistol, several of the thugs now on their feet walked toward us shooting. Rounds hit all around us. Ed, out of ammo, went for the shotgun. He grunted, then stumbled.

Then the cavalry arrived,

BANG! BANG! BANG!—BANG! BANG! BANG!—BANG! BANG! BANG!

Liz opened up from our right with short bursts of withering automatic fire.

Then nothing. Silence.

It was over. Ed reloaded as he and I carefully walked over to what was left of Reynaldo's thugs. They were cut up pretty badly. My eight rounds, Ed's six rounds, twenty rounds from Liz's first magazine and most of a second had been fired into them. None survived. They hadn't been expecting an attack from their flank. Yeah, well that was the idea. Piss on them.

Elizabeth ran up with the rifle ready to do battle. "You, okay?" she asked.

"I'm fine," I said. I looked at Ed, "You, okay?"

"Peachy," he replied.

I took Liz's arm and turned her around, "Come on, you don't need to see this mess. How about you?"

"I'm okay. I was able to get to about a hundred yards, had a good place. I almost fell asleep, except for the flies. I didn't realize the selector was on full auto, but that close I figured it wouldn't matter, so I just kept firing." Looking back over her shoulder at the men on the ground, "I guess it worked. They shouldn't have clumped together. It was too easy."

"Glad they did. Let's get Reynaldo fixed up before he dies of a stroke."

Reynaldo was screaming and writhing on the ground. I told him to shut up, then lifted him out of the dirt, and leaned him against the landing gear. He looked as if he had a bullet wound in his right shoulder, a hit from one of his thugs. The wound was through and through, some tissue was torn, but no arteries or bones were damaged. Liz got a first-aid kit from the airplane, and we applied some antiseptic and gauze, then Liz tied her recently acquired apron around the area to put pressure on the wound. The bleeding looked like it had slowed to a trickle, so Reynaldo would probably be okay until we got him back to the States.

"Hey, bud, I need the flash drive."

I turned around. Ed was standing pointing a 9mm Beretta at my middle.

"Liz, stand over there." He pointed at a spot next to me.

She walked slowly to my right side looking at Ed, then at me, then back at Ed. The look on her face showed as much surprise as I should have felt. I guess somewhere in the recesses of my mind I suspected, but who wants to imagine betrayal by your best friend?

"Why, Ed?" I asked.

"Why? Why do you think? The money. Just give me the damn flash drive and do it carefully. Liz is too close for you to pull anything, and I don't want to hurt anybody, especially you, Liz."

I handed Ed the flash drive, then stood back, "So it's been you all along."

"No, not all of it. The State Department wants this guy. I just want his money. Now, sit next to Reynaldo and don't move." Reynaldo was whimpering about his arm. "Tell him to shut up or I'll shut him up."

I knelt next to Reynaldo and tried to get him to stay quiet without much success.

"You guys just sit there until my friends arrive."

"The money worth giving up your life?" I asked.

"Are you kidding? There are millions in this drive, probably hundreds of millions. What life do I have? With Caroline gone, I have nothing. It's a wonder I didn't shoot myself."

"What about Stacie?

"She'll be fine. I'll see to it."

"Ed, we've been friends for thirty years. I deserve some explanation."

Ed moved away from us, the Beretta unerringly pointed right at me. "You two are unbelievable. You guys some sort of secret agents or something?"

"We were just on vacation, Ed. If you remember, you're the one who got us into this mess. So, what's this about?"

"Okay, but any funny stuff and this is going to get very unpleasant, very fast, got it."

"Yeah, we got it."

He stepped farther back and knelt on the ground. I could see blood running down his left arm dripping in the dirt.

"Looks like you're hurt. Let Liz look at your wound," I said.

"I'm fine. You want to hear my sob story or not?"

"Okay, go ahead."

"When I was at Embry studying for my multiengine ticket, I met a kid whose father owned a bunch of produce farms in Brazil. The idea was to ship cantaloupes to the U.S. during late winter and early spring when U.S. production was nonexistent. He bought some old DC-3s and a DC-6s and asked us and a few other guys to fly them back and forth from Belem to Miami. We'd been at it for a while when a guy approached me, said he'd known my father, and asked if we would deliver some supplies on the return trips. He never told us his name but said he worked for the CIA and told me I would be doing a service for my country. He said he would pay for the fuel and give us a thousand dollars a trip. That was a lot of money to a kid. We were going back empty anyway, so we said sure. It didn't take long to figure out the supplies were surplus rifles, mostly M1 Garands, M1 Carbines, and a few 3.5 rocket launchers, you know, what the movies call 'Bazookas.'"

"I know what they are," I replied.

"Once, I even saw an old, water-cooled Browning. Anyway, we were flying this old World War II stuff all over the Caribbean, even flew into Cuba a couple of times. My Spanish is good, and one night I overheard someone call my business partner Dr. Pérez. He got angry and told the guy if he didn't shut his mouth, he'd kill him. Over about six or eight months I heard enough to figure out these people weren't CIA but DGI. I wasn't going to fly for the Cubans, so on my last trip to Miami I parked the plane and disappeared. I moved to New Jersey and stayed there for about a year, then I moved to Virginia, where I met you. You know the rest, except I left the FAA and went to work for the State Department.

"When Caroline died, I didn't give a shit about anything, I almost put in my papers for retirement, but on a trip to Fort Lauderdale to visit my mom, I saw him. There in the restaurant, sitting behind my mother, was the guy half the federal government was looking for—it was just dumb luck, but I found Pérez. I asked mom to take a cab home and followed Pérez to his house, actually his sister's house. The woman you bought the boat from was his sister. As far as I know, Pérez was never married. His sister was married to Estéban Morales and was with him when he was killed. That's one of the reasons Pérez was so angry with our buddy Reynaldo."

"That's why she made up the story about being married to Pérez. She couldn't tell us who her real husband was," I said.

"I guess. Anyway, I followed him around for days and discovered he spent a good bit of time on his boat, now your boat, the Pinafore. He even took it out a couple of times. Scared hell out of me, but he always came back. Finally, one night I confronted him on the dock and backed him into the boat. I forced him below, told him who I was. He said he didn't remember me but told me for old times' sake maybe we could make a deal. He offered me seven hundred fifty thousand dollars cash to walk, said he could get it right away. I told him we needed the records he took from Estéban Morales, and if he gave them to me, then we could deal. He said he would have to think about it, then he tried for my gun, we got into a struggle, the gun went off and he ended up dead.

"I took the boat out about twenty miles and dumped his body over the side. Believe me, it wasn't easy getting him up those steps or ladder or whatever you call them. By this time, I was sure I was going to sell the documents to the highest bidder. If they were worth seven hundred fifty thousand dollars to Pérez, they were probably worth twice that much to someone else. When we found the drive and learned it controlled access to bank accounts, I figured it was worth millions."

"So much for loyalty, patriotism, and saving the OPEC conference," I said.

"Fuck you, what do you know about it?"

"Nothing, I guess. What happened then?"

"I went to his sister's place, told her I was one of Alberto's associates, and needed the records he had been keeping for Estéban Morales. She was suspicious. Obviously, being married to Morales, she would have known his associates. She said she didn't know about any records and Pérez was away on business, and I should come back when he was home. Then I got called back to D.C. for a few weeks. While I was away, it occurred to me that Pérez wouldn't implicate or endanger his sister, so I figured the records were probably on the boat.

"When I got back to Fort Lauderdale, she had listed the boat for sale. I called the broker, then called you. I couldn't fucking believe my luck!"

"Lucky you," I said. "Then what?"

"Then nothing. I sent a few guys to Annapolis, but between you and the marina guys refitting the boat, my men could never get in and look around. That's when I called you to bum a ride."

"So, Fuentes worked for you?"

"No, he and his goons apparently worked for our friend here. Do you think I'm going to have people shoot at me? Reynaldo has his own agenda, which is to save his ass."

"But you would have them knock me over the head and kidnap Elizabeth."

"I told them to look in the boat. You surprised them, and they had to get away. I had nothing to do with the kidnapping. When I found out Reynaldo planned to take Liz, I told Adel to call and warn you."

"If you had nothing to do with it, how did you know about the kidnapping, and how did you get Adel to make the call?"

"Look, a lot is going on here that you don't know about, and I don't have the time or inclination to tell you."

The distant whine of what sounded like a Jeep interrupted our chat. Ed stood, never taking his eyes off us, and moved around to our right so he could watch the clearing and us. An old surplus Jeep drove around the two automobiles onto the end of the strip, stopping about thirty feet from the plane. The driver was dressed in tropical army fatigues, about forty. He had silvering hair and a black mustache. He addressed Ed with a toothy smile. "*Mi amigo*! You look good. You have some excitement, yes?"

"Hey, Carlos, how they hanging?"

"We ready to go *cuate*?"

"Yeah, ready to go."

Never moving the pistol from our direction, Ed crabbed around us and backed his way to the Jeep. "You guys are welcome to come with us –."

"*Cuate*, just shoot them and we go."

"Shut up, Carlos! If you two want to come with us, you're welcome. No questions, we just disappear."

"What about Reynaldo?" I said.

"Fuck him. He can drive one of his cars out of here or he can die where he sits. I don't care. You coming or not? Last chance."

"Thanks, we'll stay."

"Your funeral. Don't even think about flying out of here. The runway is too short. Hell, it would be almost impossible for me to fly the thing out of here, and I'm a great pilot. Better to take one of those cars, drive out, and try to get to a consulate. Of course, you might run into more of Reynaldo's goons." Ed got into the passenger's side of the Jeep, Carlos backed up, then they drove back down the road disappearing into the jungle, the noise from the Jeep faded to silence.

"Now what?" Liz asked.

"I guess we get out of here. Come on, help me get Reynaldo on the plane."

"On the plane? You heard Ed. we can't fly out of here, the runway is too short!"

"I don't see that we have much choice. If we don't get out now, we probably won't get out at all. Besides, I don't think Ed came into this strip with no chance of getting the plane out."

"Looks to me as if he wasn't planning to get out with the plane—he did just drive away with that guy and the Jeep. I think it was his plan the whole time."

"Maybe, but he spent a lot of time doing a preflight. As a matter of fact, he did it twice, maybe on the chance that Carlos didn't show. Ol' Carlos probably saved our lives just by showing up. And as I said, I don't think we have much choice. First, it's going to be dark soon; second, we have a good chance of running into the local *Federales* or whatever they're called down here, plus there may be more of Reynaldo's men out there. When Ed discovers he's carrying around a bunch of charts, he's going to come back here really pissed. So—"

"Okay, okay, I get the point. Jesus, this is like an old B movie. All we need is Tarzan to come swinging out of the jungle."

CHAPTER NINETEEN

Jungle Landing Strip, Nicaragua

We wrestled Reynaldo on board the airplane, then moved him to the back of the cabin, laid him down on the floor, and using tie wraps cuffed him to one of the D rings on the floor used for securing cargo. All we needed was Reynaldo running around the airplane during the flight.

I went back outside and walked around the plane to make sure the gunfire had not added any extra holes. I found one in the port well cover, but it looked superficial. In the distance, I could hear a truck. Actually, it sounded like several trucks, and they were getting closer.

I climbed back in the airplane and secured the door. Getting the plane off the ground, essentially by myself, was iffy at best, but we were out of choices. Praying I could remember the start sequence, I strapped into the left seat. Liz was already sitting in the right seat. "We got company coming fast. Are you ready for your trip to Disneyland?"

"So long as it's not to never, never land—company, what do you mean company? Who are they?"

"I don't know, too far away to see. I just heard them."

We did a cursory preflight, Liz calling out items on the checklist. I managed to start the engines. When the power was up and the gauges looked normal, I pushed forward on the left throttle with the right brake locked. The plane swung around until it was facing down the runway. My hope—make that my prayer—was that the cooler evening air and lighter fuel load would give us some advantage. At least there were only a few trees at the end of the runway. Wind was negligible, so no help or hindrance.

"Lizzy, when I say 'gear,' move that knob up until it stops. You should see three lights. They will go out when the wheels are in the wells."

"Okay."

"Also, I need you to call out the airspeed," pointing to the gauge.

"Got it."

"When I call for 'flaps,' move that lever to there," pointing to the lever in the console.

"Ready?" I asked.

"Ready," she replied.

Off to the left, I detected some movement on the road. Two trucks, a pickup, and an old, military duce and a half burst out of the jungle on the other side of the shacks heading directly for the plane. The deuce and a half had what looked like a .30 caliber machine gun mounted over the cab. The man standing behind had it aimed right at the airplane. No sense in telling Liz. She was worried enough.

I stood on the brakes, then moved the throttles to the stops and waited for the turbines to spool up. The trucks were getting closer, and I was sure any moment a burst from the machine gun would shatter the Plexiglas next to me. I came off the brakes and the plane started forward, moving faster, faster, and faster. Liz read off the airspeed, but we weren't fast enough and half the runway was gone. We zipped by the point of no return. I heard some *dings* as the plane took some hits. I've heard it before, and it's a sound you never forget. I held the plane on the ground, then at the last second, I pulled back on the yoke pointing the nose too high. We leaped off the runway.

"Gear up!"

"Gear up!" Liz said, over the engine noise.

The yoke started shaking, warning me of a stall. I left the flaps, praying the added lift

would outweigh the drag. At eight hundred feet I lowered the nose below the horizon to build up airspeed. We were still settling. The damn airplane was stalling. I dropped the nose more and tried to push the throttles farther forward. The airspeed perceptibly climbed, but the ground was coming up very fast.

"Flaps!" I yelled.

"Flaps!"

The airspeed climbed, and then suddenly the yoke stopped shaking. I pulled the nose back a little and waited for the airspeed to catch up with all my abuse. Passing through 3,000 feet, I set the throttles and trim for a normal rate of climb. *Holy shit, we were flying. We were actually flying!*

At 20,000 feet, I pulled the throttles to cruise, reset the trim, punched up the flight computer, and checked all the engine instruments. Everything seemed to be working. One of the turbine temperatures was a little high. Fuel was about 80 percent. We would be entering U.S. airspace soon. I entered Dulles IAD into the flight computer, which would take us to Dulles Airport in the Virginia suburbs, just outside Washington D.C.

Dulles airport has two, 11,000-foot runways and two others of about 10,000, so I could go in low and straight, giving me a chance at landing without killing us and some of the general population. We would be low on fuel, but the flight computer said we would be on the ground with some to spare. I asked Liz to check on Reynaldo.

"He's probably dead from fright." Liz slid her seat back and went into the cabin. She came back with two cups of coffee. "He's pale and clammy. Hell, I don't blame him. I'm pale and clammy."

I laughed and held the coffee while she got back into her seat.

"Looks like the bleeding has stopped. I think he's okay. What the hell happened with Ed?" Liz asked.

"I don't know. I've been thinking about it. Back in Martha's Vineyard, I kept having premonitions. Somehow, I knew something was wrong. It wasn't like Ed to throw us under the bus. The Ed I knew would have told his boss to pound sand up his ass before turning on a friend, let alone blackmailing one. It just didn't make sense."

"You two were best friends long before we were married, so I don't know him as well as you do, but as far as I'm concerned, he's as bad as Reynaldo and probably a traitor. So, what's the plan?"

"You mean after we land?" I asked.

"I certainly hope landing is part of the plan."

"After we land, we need to turn Reynaldo over to Silvers or the FBI along with the Narragansett Files. Then we go back to the boat."

"Boats are now my official favorite. No more airplanes."

"Ah, you're being unfair. Didn't this beauty extract you from the unknowable horrors of the deep dark jungle?"

"Not to mention the flies. Jeez, they were awful."

The left engine temperature was a little high, but other than landing, there wasn't much I could do about it. And landing before we got to Dulles would mean questions I wasn't prepared to answer. I needed to get closer to my golfing buddies. I wondered if Ed really called them, as he said he did. Too late now. I had enough to deal with without trying to work the radio to find them. I hated that I was now dependent on them. If the temperature got any higher, I would try pulling the throttle back. I wondered if the engine had taken a hit from the machine gun. What else was damaged? What if there were hydraulic problems and I couldn't get the gear down? I turned off the autopilot and moved the control surfaces a little. If there was damage, I couldn't detect any. So far, the cabin pressure was okay. Cabin pressure problems would come fast and at this altitude they probably were not survivable. I reengaged the autopilot and looked around for the oxygen bottles.

"Liz, I think the port engine took some hits during the firefight."
"Why, what's wrong?"

"The engine temp is too high, which means we may have to shut it down. The plane will supposedly fly on one engine, but as you know, I'm not really a pilot, a good one anyway."

"Great, I was just warming to air travel again. So, what are you telling me?"

"I'll do my best and I love you."

"Miami Center, this is Falcon November three, niner, two, two November requesting Flight Level 210 at zero, three, zero inbound to IAD."

"Falcon November three, niner, Miami Center, you are cleared at 030, maintain Flight Level 210, squawk 3750. Contact Jacksonville Center at 135.05."

Liz and I talked about anything but the last several hours. During intervals in the conversation, we sat quietly watching the remnants of the day turn into night. Below small towns and big cities lit like huge clusters of stars rolled under us as we flew north. The Atlantic Ocean was off the right wing. Occasionally, a small glint showed on the horizon, maybe a freighter.

"Washington Center, this is Falcon November three, niner, two, two November inbound to IAD."

"Falcon November three, niner, Washington Center, turn right to heading zero, zero, one, descend and maintain ten thousand, contact Potomac approach, 126.1."

The turbine temperature in the left engine was nearing the "oh shit" zone. The panel would be covered with warning lights soon.

"Potomac approach, this is Falcon November three, niner inbound IAD. We have a medical emergency and request straight-in approach, request the FBI be notified of our arrival."

"Falcon November three, niner, Potomac approach, descend and maintain five thousand. You are cleared for a straight-in approach to runway one right. Medical and authorities will be notified. Traffic at three o'clock at seven thousand. Contact Dulles Tower at 120.1."

I added some flaps and pulled back the throttles, applied some back pressure on the yoke, and trimmed. The nose lifted, and the airspeed dropped. I tried to retard the port throttle more, but the plane yawed, the left wing was already losing lift. If the wing stopped flying, we would flip over on our back and auger into the Virginia countryside. I pushed the throttle back. A red warning light started flashing telling me what I already knew: the compressor was overheating.

"Dulles tower this is Falcon November three, niner, declaring an aircraft emergency."

"Falcon, November three, niner, Dulles tower, state your emergency."

"Dulles tower, Falcon Novermber three, niner, we are experiencing excessive turbine temperature and concerned about engine failure."

"Falcon November three, niner, Dulles tower, ident 7700, you are cleared for straight-in approach to runway One Right, winds variable at ten, altimeter 313.

Not much help now, but I dialed the emergency number into the transponder, added flaps, and asked Liz to lower the gear. The gear *THUNKED* as it extended and showed green. Thank you, Lord, one less worry.

In emergencies, control towers crank up the lights to their heliarc setting. The runway could now be seen from the space station. Depth perception is an issue with night landings, especially for the inexperienced. I tried to focus on the big "R1" painted on the near end of the runway and kept repeating to myself, *watch the numbers, watch the numbers.*

As the numbers swept under the plane, I gently pulled the yoke back lifting the nose. I looked out the left window, concentrating on the runway, adjusting the yoke and throttles, trying to control the sink rate. The airplane stopped flying five feet off the ground and we hit the runway with a resounding thud, but nothing broke, and we stayed on the ground. Throttles at idle, I used the runway to bleed off speed, tapping the brakes slightly until the plane coasted to a stop. I shut down the port engine and using the starboard engine started taxiing.

"Dulles tower, Falcon November three, niner, taxi instructions to the ramp, please."

"Falcon November three, niner, remain stationary, shut off your engines. A tug will meet you. Contact Dulles ground at 121.62."

"Dulles tower, Falcon November Sierra, Roger, contacting Dulles ground at 121.62. Please have an ambulance waiting for us."

"Did we get shot down?" Liz asked.

"Very amusing. You know any landing you walk away from is a good one."

"I've heard that. Good job, sweetie, but find a parking lot so we can get out of this thing."

"Would you see how Reynaldo is doing?"

Liz came back in a minute, "He's looking better. I think he's happy to be on the ground. I know I am."

"That makes three of us."

A tug hauled us to the ramp. We were escorted by vehicles of various origins and descriptions flashing yellow, blue, and red lights. Two crash trucks flanked the plane ready to douse any flames with foam.

The medics hauled Reynaldo off the plane as I went through the checklist turning our sub-Mach jet into a pile of inert aluminum. When I finished with the checklist, I crawled out of the seat and made my way onto the apron. I was stiff, and my shirt and pants were soaked with sweat. I shivered from the wet clothes, the cool night air, and an overload of adrenaline. I walked around the plane looking for damage. I didn't see any to the engine or elsewhere, but it was dark. Anyway, now it was irrelevant. I started to walk away from the plane, then stopped and looked back. Ed was right, the Falcon was a great plane, hurt and poorly piloted, it got us home. I gave it a salute and walked away feeling akin to John Wayne in *The High and the Mighty*.

Liz was with the medics. I walked toward them and called out as they were about to insert Reynaldo into the ambulance, "Hold up for a minute, please!" Ducking some officious-looking characters, I made my way to the ambulance and stood next to Reynaldo, who seemed reasonably cognizant. Feigning concern, I spoke to him in a soothing tone as I slipped the Narraganset Files in his pocket. If he knew what I was doing, it didn't register. Then, nothing registered in those eyes.

"Thanks," I said to the flanking medics. "Can you hold on another minute?"

Liz and I turned to look for the FBI. Taking a chance, we walked to a black SUV just arriving. Four guys in dark suits stepped out. I walked up to the one getting out of the passenger side.

"You guys feds?"

"Yeah, who are you?"

"Can I see some identification?" I asked.

The dark suit showed me credentials identifying him as Tom Sawyer, Federal Bureau of Investigation.

"Cute name."

"Yeah, I've never heard that before. You can save the whitewash jokes, too."

"Don't have any whitewash jokes. I know one about a monkey in a bar."

"And you would be the smartass from Nicaragua?" he asked.

"My reputation precedes me. You guys talk to Richard Silvers?

"No, but our boss did. We're supposed to pick up some guy from you named Reynaldo Vicente."

"You'd better hurry. They're about ready to take him away in that ambulance," I said, pointing over my shoulder. "Oh and be sure to look in his pockets." Sawyer's partner rushed off toward Reynaldo and the ambulance.

"Wait!" I called to the partner. He stopped and turned to me, "At least two of you need to go over there and recover some evidence I'm pretty sure he has in his left pants pocket, and you should have those medics witness it, too. And at least one of you ought to accompany him to the hospital until your boss or Silvers arrives."

Sawyer nodded to two of the men and they jogged to the ambulance. "What happened to Silvers's special agent, Colombo? He's supposed to be with you," Sawyer said.

"We were in a firefight. He got hurt and was bleeding pretty bad, so we thought it best if we handed him off to the locals for medical treatment."

"He was worse than Vicente? You brought him back."

"Yeah, but I really didn't care if he croaked."

Sawyer's men came back. One held up the flash drive.

"Is this what we were supposed to find?"

"Yep, and if I were you guys, I would put an airtight, twenty-four-hour guard around that flash drive and Reynaldo. Do not tell anyone his location except your boss and Silvers. When Silvers shows up, hand him that flash drive, and tell him where you got it. You'll probably be the next directors of the FBI and Homeland Security."

"What's Narragansett?" asked one of the suits.

"Top secret code name," I replied.

"Yeah, sorry I asked," he replied.

"Guys, I'm not above pulling your leg, but I'm dead serious about keeping tabs on that guy, the flash drive, and keeping it quiet. Eight men that I know of have been killed for that thing, so don't lose it. But remember, the flash drive is no good without Vicente, and he is of no value without the flash drive. It has to be a package deal."

An airport police vehicle pulled up, and the airport police chief, mid-fifties, exited the passenger seat. A police sergeant, forties, exited from behind the wheel. The chief, followed by the sergeant, walked over to a few workers on the scene. The chief asked them a question. From a distance, I could see them point at me and Liz. The chief and sergeant turned and walked over to us. "Are you all okay?" the chief asked as he extended his hand to shake mine.

"Yes, sir. Pretty tired, but okay," I said.

"I got a few questions before you get out of here."

The police sergeant pulled out a notepad.

"Sure, but I doubt if I can tell you much."

"So—who owns the plane?"

"I found it."

The sergeant looked at me, then wrote in his notebook.

"Okay—where did you fly from?"

"Nicaragua."

"Did you file a flight plan?"

"No"

"Can you tell me, in detail, what you were carrying in the plane?"

"Nothing—sorta," I said as Liz, looking anxious, clasped my arm.

"Can I see your pilot's license?"

"I don't have one."

"You have a permit for the automatic firearm we found inside your bag? If not, we have a problem."

"Do you have a search warrant to look in my bag?"

"You just entered a federal property without—"

"If you will allow us to make a phone call, I think we can explain," Liz said.

The airport police chief motioned to the police sergeant. "Cuff him. Read both their rights and take them to the holding cell." The police sergeant reached for his handcuffs. Just as Liz and I were contemplating our sojourn to the federal lockup, Agent Sawyer intervened.

"Excuse me. These people are agents attached to the State Department."

"And who might you be?"

Sawyer removed his credential folder from his pocket and showed it to the chief. "Agent Sawyer, FBI. We were asked by State to pick up these two and their

passenger." Sawyer replaced his badge case and removed a paper. "This is an authorization letter from the undersecretary of state. He expected there might be a problem."

The chief took the letter from Sawyer and read it.

"They will be available for questioning anytime except now."

The chief handed Sawyer his letter. "Okay, take them, but they aren't leaving here with those weapons. I'll be calling ATF. For God's sake, one of them is an automatic rifle!"

"We have no problem with that, but I would appreciate it if you would do me one more favor and call my boss about the weapons." Agent Sawyer signaled to a black SUV and turned his focus on me and Liz. "Let's get out of here before he changes his mind. Silvers said to take you home. So, where is that?"

"Mount Vernon, in Alexandria."

"At the end of the George Washington Parkway, right?"

"Yes, please," Liz said.

Sawyer led Steele and Liz to the black SUV.

"Thanks for the backup," I said.

"No problem. Look—you got big ones waltzing around with that automatic rifle. If I were you two, I would lie low until Silvers can get everyone calmed down. From what I gather, this is his fiasco. Let him clean it up."

"No argument here."

"None here," Liz said.

The black SUV turned into a quiet suburban community. Streetlights barely revealed the comfortable colonial style homes and green lawns that lined both sides of the street. The SUV stopped in front of a two-story brick colonial. We thanked Agent Sawyer and the agent driver, got out of the SUV, and carried what luggage we had up the brick walk to a front door adorned with brass hardware and flanked by two flickering carriage lights.

"I feel like you should carry me over the threshold."

"I would, but I'm too tired."

"That's what you said after our honeymoon."

I grinned, "I was tired for a different reason."

"Well, there will be none of that tonight."

I unlocked the door and followed Liz into the house. Liz turned on some lights. Sable, a fluffy cat, ran up to Liz and started to purr and rub against her legs. "Hi, sweetie, did you miss us?" Liz picked up the cat and scratched her ears.

"Man, it feels good to be home." I said, giving Liz a passionate kiss.

Liz still holding Sable. "Hmmm, I may have to rethink my last comment."

CHAPTER TWENTY

Hunters Residence, Mount Vernon, Virginia

Liz and I spent the next several days at home. We slept a bunch, did some laundry, paid bills, and played with Sable. About noon our third day at home, I was catching up with the newspapers I forgot to cancel. Liz sat nearby working on her laptop.

"Honey, it's been a week, and we haven't heard from Silvers or Sawyer. I say we go back to the boat. This is supposed to be our vacation," I said.

"Okay, I'll see if I can get us a flight tomorrow morning." A cell phone sitting on a side table buzzed. Liz picked up the phone and looked at the number. "It's one of those restricted numbers."

"Answer it. Maybe we won the lottery."

"Hello.—This is she.—Yes.—Okay.—We would love to.—Thank you!" Liz hung up the phone. "I guess your tux is still on the boat?" She framed her statement as a question.

"Why?"
"We were just invited to the White House for a reception."
"What white house?"

Liz laughed, "What do you mean, 'What white house?' you big dummy? How many White Houses are there?"

"You mean the president just invited us to a cocktail party?"

"Well, the president didn't, but somebody at the White House did, and they're sending a car for us. It will be here at six tomorrow night. Moreover, it's not a cocktail party. It's a reception. Isn't that great?" she gushed.

"Yeah, my tux is on the boat. I'll have to wear a suit." I started reading the paper again.

"You get your ass out of that chair right now. We are going to Neiman Marcus, so I can get a dress and you can get a tux!"

"Come on, Liz, you have a hundred dresses, and I don't need another tux," I groaned.

"Move it, mister!"

"Okay, okay, I'm moving." And I did.

That evening, after spending all afternoon and the equivalent of two mortgage payments on a dress for Liz and a tuxedo for me, I was still trying to get through the newspapers. Liz was in our home office catching up on some work for her job. She walked into the den. "Look at this email I just got from Gery."

"Gery?"

"Yes, you remember Gery Peterson—at my office."

"Oh yeah, the South American desk Gery Peterson," I answered.

"Yes, and he just sent his analysis of the stuff on the Narragansett flash drive." She handed me some papers.

I was sick of the Narragansett Files. I should have called it Crooks Bay or maybe Crooked Bay. How about Thieves Bay? Yeah, I liked that, but I didn't have the chart. I glanced at the report without much enthusiasm, then started to read in earnest. About twenty minutes later, I looked up. Liz was still sitting on the chair opposite.

"Did you read this?" I asked.

"Yes."

"What do you think?"

"I think the president of Venezuela might be a murderer, a drug dealer, and a world-class crook, bordering on what some might call a financial terrorist, if there is such a thing."

"I agree, and I think this is what our golf buddies were really after."

"You were right. They are trying to topple the Venezuelan government," Liz said.

"But how did they know what was on the drive? In addition, why is this so important? There are lots of crooked governments. Is this about oil? Is it about getting their boss reelected? Or is it about something else entirely?"

"Maybe all of the above," Liz said.

Ten minutes before the appointed time, I was standing in our living room dressed in my new tuxedo and accessories. No gun this time. Liz walked down the stairs into the living room and did a pirouette "Ta-da! So, do you like it?"

"Jesus, Liz, you can't wear that to the White House!"

The dress was a truly stunning, black, floor-length, strapless gown with a low-cut neckline that showed more of my wife's cleavage than I would have preferred to be seen beyond our bedroom. It also had a slit almost to her waist. It showed a perfect leg, sheathed in a black stocking, finished with a black Louboutin, five-inch pump. Presumably, the other leg was in like finery.

"I thought you liked your woman in low-cut black gowns. 'I have *zee* room upstairs. Would *zee* big handsome man care to join me?'" She cooed in a passable Spanish accent.

"Perhaps you would like *zee* black wig if you no like blondes?" further hamming it up.

"Very funny. Believe me, I think it's a spectacular dress, just maybe not for the White House." I was treading on very thin ice here.

"Oh, relax. It comes with a jacket."

"It ought to come with an X rating," I mumbled.

"What was that?" she said, doing one of those eye-arch things that signals danger.

"I said the driver ought to be here by now. Did you know Louboutin was a high school dropout?"

"No, but a better question: How do you know Louboutin was a high school dropout?"

The doorbell rang. Never had "saved by the bell" been more appropriate. I almost ran to the front door to greet our driver.

Rush-hour traffic was going in the opposite direction, so the ride up the George Washington Parkway and across the Fourteenth Street Bridge took only about thirty minutes. Passing a cursory inspection, our black Lincoln was allowed through the gate to join a line of waiting cars and limos destined for the portico. When we arrived, a marine lance corporal in dress blues opened the car door. I said good evening to the lance corporal and admired his medals, including the Purple Heart. As I assisted Liz out of the car, I couldn't help noticing the slit in her dress was gone. We thanked the lance corporal for his service and entered the receiving line.

"What happened to the slit in your dress?" I whispered.

"It's adjustable. There is a small zipper. You can set it on demure or very sexy. I set it to scandalous for you," she giggled.

I smiled. More like *stroke,* I thought. "Well, after the party, will you please move it back to scandalous? You can lose the jacket, too. Then we will go to Ebbitt's and wow the crowd."

She held my arm tighter. "Only, if you're a good sailor boy," she said, giving me a bright smile.

I was out of the doghouse.

The east room of the White House reminded me a little of Rosecliff with the parquet floors and crystal chandeliers, this stunning room is dominated by the Gilbert Stuart portrait of George Washington, famous for being saved by Dolley Madison when she refused to abandon it to the British in August 1814.

The room was full of beautiful people, most of them politicians or hangers-on. None of the gowns were scandalous. Liz, sans scandalous mode, was soon the center of attention for half dozen or so seemingly unattached men dressed in military and civilian formal. I scouted the area for a Blanton's, but champagne appeared to be my only choice.

"Hello, how are you?" I turned on my heel to find Adel also with champagne. She was wearing a knockout green, full-length gown, but she wasn't scandalous either. Her hair was pinned up with an attractive Spanish fan-looking clip thing that matched her dress.

"Hi, Adel. I suppose I shouldn't be surprised to see you, but I am. Is Reynaldo with you?"

"No, as I think you know, he is—how should I say—indisposed. I am here with my husband. He is the cultural attaché for the Venezuelan embassy."

"I'll bet," I said. "Adel, excuse me if I'm not too gracious. Your brother tried to kill me at least twice, and he nearly succeeded in kidnapping my wife."

"Yes, it is a pity."

How did I know she was going to say that?

"Adel, you may want to work on your repertoire."

She just looked at me.

"I guess I owe you thanks for tipping me off to Elizabeth's pending trip to the Caribbean."

"You are welcome, but your friend insisted. He is a most unpleasant man, this Mr. Colombo. Is he with you tonight?"

"You mean Ed. No, he couldn't make it."

"Good." She walked off.

Happy to see her go, I was even more delighted with the view of her leaving in her form-fitting gown.

"I can't keep you away from that woman," Liz said, following my gaze. "She does have a cute figure."

"I was thanking her for saving your life."

"Uh-huh, well at least you didn't have your face down the front of her dress this time." Liz walked off.

Great, I was back in the doghouse.

"Good evening." Jonathan Collins was dressed in his best bib and tucker.

"Good evening. Where's your golfing partner?"

"Ah, he is, you could say, playing on another course. Did you know the flash drive Silvers found with Reynaldo did not contain what I believe you call the Narragansett Files?"

"Wow. Sounds like he lost his best caddy and didn't finish. It's a wonder he didn't end up fishing for balls, face down in the pond." I was running out of stupid golf metaphors. I thought about trying out my new word, *abaft*.

"I told those FBI agents to keep an eye on him. Tricky devil, that Reynaldo."

Collins did that disingenuous, sincere smile he does. "I don't suppose you know where the real flash drive is?"

"Collins, what are Elizabeth and I doing here?"

"The president wanted to thank you for your efforts, but she has to leave early and unfortunately, she probably won't have time to meet with you."

"My ass. She doesn't even know who Liz and I are, and you know it."

"Well, perhaps another time. I'm sure—"

"Good evening, gentlemen."

Collins and I turned to the owner of the voice, a tall, slim, very pretty African American woman dressed in a stunning purple gown. She seemed to exude power through a controlled smile and innate charm.

"Good evening, Madam President," we said simultaneously.

"I hope you gentlemen are enjoying the party. Johnny, you're looking very dashing this evening. Is Sylvia with you?"

"Yes, ma'am. I think she is in a huddle with your husband. I would be surprised if it didn't cost us a trip to Hawaii."

The president laughed good naturedly, then turned to me. I extended my hand, "My name is—"

"Yes, I know who you are," the president responded, with a 300-watt smile.

Lately, everyone was saying that. I made a mental note to check the post office for my picture.

"I just met your lovely wife. She was regaling me with an astonishing story of boats and airplanes, but with all the noise and interruptions I must admit to missing most of it. By the way, she said you have something important that you wanted to give to me. I see that you and Johnny are friends. Perhaps he could look at whatever it is."

"I would be happy to," Collins jumped in. "Madam President, we don't want to take up your valuable time. I was just saying perhaps we could schedule—"

THIS INFORMATION IS CLASSIFIED

Not for Duplication
File No: 6502849

These documents were analyzed for content and possible affiliation with each other (see instructions and specifications under separate cover). Most were written in Spanish. The rest were in English. All the financial documents, regardless of language, were audited and tabulated according to IIA standards in U.S. dollars. For clarity, the organizations herein were assumed to be structured as one foreign corporation, though there may have been as many as three separate companies. The documents do not seem to have been placed on the flash drive in any particular order. For clarity, the documents contained herein have been organized by the analyst into eight categories:
1. Organizational Structure
2. Bank Statements
3. Accounts Payable
4. Accounts Receivables
5. Suppliers with Contact Information
6. Vendors with Contact Information
7. Distribution Network
8. Notes and Comments

I pulled a folded sheaf of papers from my jacket pocket and handed them to the president. She looked at me for a moment and then took them. Collins looked as if he wanted to melt into the carpet, except there wasn't any carpet. The president unfolded the papers and started reading.

Organizational Structure
1. Analysis of the enclosed footnotes suggests that Victor Escudero is a substantial "stockholder" in all the corporations listed herein and is most likely the chief executive officer, if not officially, certainly *de facto*. Detailed information on President Escudero is available, but outside the scope of this analysis; however, it is relevant to note that Victor Escudero is the president of Venezuela.

"Madam President, I think you would be most interested in the section labeled Organizational Structure. Perhaps, if you would go right to that section . . ." I suggested. The president flipped over a page and continued to read.

The president looked up from reading the page. "Perhaps we should excuse ourselves from the party for a few minutes. Please follow me, gentlemen."

We walked across the parquet floor. The president stopped to say hello to guests that came forward, shook hands, exchanged a joke or two, then moved to a door in the far wall. Collins and I were sucked into the vortex left in the president's wake. A rigid marine corporal dressed in blues opened the door and we stepped into an adjacent room. Discounting the white trim, all the walls were covered with green silk fabric. No slouch on American history and folklore, I knew immediately this was the Green Room. It was also where the first declaration of war was signed, but I wasn't superstitious.

A graduate of Tulane and Harvard, and a product of the Louisiana political machine, President Harriet Jackson was a bright and tough politician. She was a former mayor of New Orleans and a former U.S. senator and a former army pilot with several combat tours. Her people like to publicize a story that her great-great-great-grandfather was a slave owned by Andrew Jackson, the former president and founder of the Democratic Party. Perhaps erroneously, President Harriet Jackson had the reputation for surrounding herself with people of lesser intellect. True or not, I was having no trouble believing Jonathan Collins lived down to the reputation. But I didn't play golf.

The president sat in a wing chair next to the fireplace and began reading the documents again. I stood and looked at a painting of a farm covered with snow, done by George Durrie. How terrific it would be if I could leave this mess and magically transport myself to that farm. Durrie painted it in 1858, so it was probably a shopping center now. These days you could find shopping centers anywhere, without transporting, so why bother? The president continued to read the analysis.

2. Analysis of the enclosed footnotes suggests that Estéban Morales was a substantial "stockholder" in all corporations listed herein and was most likely the chief operating officer, if not officially, certainly *de facto*. Detailed information on Morales is available, but outside the scope of this analysis.

3. Analysis of the enclosed footnotes suggests that Dr. Alberto Pérez was a substantial "stockholder" in all corporations listed herein and was most likely the chief financial officer. Detailed information on Pérez is available, but outside the scope of this analysis.

4. Analysis of the enclosed footnotes suggests that Reynaldo Vicente is a substantial "stockholder" in all corporations listed herein and currently the chief operating officer. Detailed information on Vicente is available, but outside the scope of this analysis, but it is relevant to note that Reynaldo Vicente is now director of the Venezuelan *Petróleos de Nacional,* and that Victor Escudero is Reynaldo Vicente's father.

<u>Financial Statements</u>
For brevity, financial statements will encompass Bank Statements, Accounts Payable, and Accounts Receivables. Though not to the usual and customary standards for corporate financial records, the transaction records have been recorded in remarkable detail with comments and footnotes throughout. The bank statements are of numbered accounts, but otherwise anonymous. According to these Financial Statements, large amounts of money were placed into the "corporate" accounts on a weekly basis (see enclosed reconciliation of accounts). The amounts ranged from $180,000 to $3,060,000. Substantial amounts of these funds were cash deposits, though it is interesting to note that some deposits were made by checks and wire transfers from Petróleos de Nacional (see footnotes for enclosed reconciliation of accounts). Reconciliation of these accounts indicated there is a total balance of $497,000,000 in five separate bank accounts (see enclosed list for banks and account numbers), not including $63,000,000 in accounts receivables (see attached list). The accounts are numbered and only accessible by password and authorization code(s). Examination of the anomaly within these authorization codes is crucial to understanding this analysis (see Notes and Comments). The authorization codes are not attached.

<u>Suppliers</u>
Suppliers of what is termed "raw material" are listed in the attached.

<u>Distribution Network</u>
For purposes herein, the analysis will encompass both Vendors and Distribution networks. Vendors of what is termed "finished product" are listed in the attached. A substantial number of vendors are in the U.S. Note there is a vendor labeled NE located in Newport, Rhode Island.
Distribution refers to protection, warehousing, and shipping sources. A substantial number are in Mexico (see attached).

2. Analysis of the enclosed footnotes suggests that Estéban Morales was a substantial "stockholder" in all corporations listed herein and was most likely the chief operating officer, if not officially, certainly *de facto*. Detailed information on Morales is available, but outside the scope of this analysis.

3. Analysis of the enclosed footnotes suggests that Dr. Alberto Pérez was a substantial "stockholder" in all corporations listed herein and was most likely the chief financial officer. Detailed information on Pérez is available, but outside the scope of this analysis.

4. Analysis of the enclosed footnotes suggests that Reynaldo Vicente is a substantial "stockholder" in all corporations listed herein and currently the chief operating officer. Detailed information on Vicente is available, but outside the scope of this analysis, but it is relevant to note that Reynaldo Vicente is now director of the Venezuelan *Petróleos de Nacional*, and that Victor Escudero is Reynaldo Vicente's father.

<u>Financial Statements</u>

For brevity, financial statements will encompass Bank Statements, Accounts Payable, and Accounts Receivables. Though not to the usual and customary standards for corporate financial records, the transaction records have been recorded in remarkable detail with comments and footnotes throughout. The bank statements are of numbered accounts, but otherwise anonymous. According to these Financial Statements, large amounts of money were placed into the "corporate" accounts on a weekly basis (see enclosed reconciliation of accounts). The amounts ranged from $180,000 to $3,060,000. Substantial amounts of these funds were cash deposits, though it is interesting to note that some deposits were made by checks and wire transfers from Petróleos de Nacional (see footnotes for enclosed reconciliation of accounts). Reconciliation of these accounts indicated there is a total balance of $497,000,000 in five separate bank accounts (see enclosed list for banks and account numbers), not including $63,000,000 in accounts receivables (see attached list). The accounts are numbered and only accessible by password and authorization code(s). Examination of the anomaly within these authorization codes is crucial to understanding this analysis (see Notes and Comments). The authorization codes are not attached.

<u>Suppliers</u>
Suppliers of what is termed "raw material" are listed in the attached.

<u>Distribution Network</u>
For purposes herein, the analysis will encompass both Vendors and Distribution networks. Vendors of what is termed "finished product" are listed in the attached. A substantial number of vendors are in the U.S. Note there is a vendor labeled NE located in Newport, Rhode Island.
Distribution refers to protection, warehousing, and shipping sources. A substantial number are in Mexico (see attached).

<u>Notes and Comments</u>
In addition to the footnotes for the above, one of the documents in the files was a journal written by Dr. Pérez. This journal contains daily notations on business activities from which some of the most significant information was obtained:
a) Notations in the journal (and substantiated in the financials) stated that Estéban Morales was the titular head of the corporation, but his compensation was some 50% less than Escudero's and 30% less than Vicente's. (Pérez and Morales received roughly the same compensation.)
b) The journal chronicles the resultant and ever-expanding rift between Morales and Escudero.
c) Pérez states that he overheard Escudero order the execution of Morales and names the participants, specifically naming Hector Guerro as the architect of the assassination (see enclosed).

d) The comments assert the assassination angered Pérez and made him fearful for his own life. For those reasons, he terminated his relationship with Victor Escudero.

Not a part of the journal but included in the Notes and Comments is an entry that states that the codes held by Pérez and the codes held by the others are different. The reason is unclear, however, in his notes. Pérez indicated that he held the "master" codes.

Conclusion

As mentioned above, the "corporation" is a loose collection of entities or operations formed partially by accident and partly by the need to control the substantial profits resulting from the corporation's enterprises.

Victor Escudero controls the "corporation" with the help of his son Reynaldo Vicente. Hector Guerro (see Notes and Comments) may also be in the hierarchy. These entities buy and sell illicit drugs (there is no indication of manufacturing) and launder money and assets from the wholesale embezzlement of money derived from the sale of crude oil, oil products, and fuels refined and sold by Petróleos de Nacional.

Alberto Pérez always deposited these profits until some ninety days ago.

The bank account codes held by Pérez and the account codes held by the others are different. The reason is unclear, however, in his notes. Pérez indicated that he held the "master" codes, which probably means they are unknown to the others and that Pérez therefore maintained absolute control of the bank accounts. Evidence within these documents suggests Pérez kept this matter concealed from the others by allowing their authorization codes to access "lockbox" or dummy accounts, which contained sufficient funds to forestall inquiry. Regardless, no one can access the primary numbered accounts, but Pérez.

There appear to be other assets, including a Bombardier Learjet 85 and at least six motor vehicles of various descriptions. The location of these assets is not evident or within the scope of this report. However, they could most likely be located through maintenance records within the accounts payables (see attached).

The assets described herein, including the major movables, the bank accounts, and account receivables, constitute the preponderance of the corporation's assets or approximately $560,000,000.

All these records were kept by Pérez. Curiously, according to the notes left by Pérez, other than Morales, none of the other corporate officers knew or for that matter knows the identity of Dr. Pérez.

As mentioned above, the assassination of Morales angered Pérez and put him in fear of his own life. Presumably, severance with Victor Escudero and Reynaldo Vicente, and appropriation of these records was to assure his safety and comfort. No record or evidence was found that would indicate that these documents have been duplicated. These records do not indicate Alberto Pérez's current location or evidence that he controls other assets.

Gery Peterson
Analyst

Enclosures
CC: File

CHAPTER TWENTY-ONE

The president put the papers down and looked at Collins, "Johnny, what the hell is this all about?"

"Well, ma'am, you remember we were going to try to neutralize President Escudero's hold on the OPEC conference—"

"Yes, I remember, you and Silvers were going to send Ed Colombo down to Florida—Fort Lauderdale, right?—he was going to try to find an old friend. Where is Ed, anyway? I haven't seen him in a couple of weeks. Jimmy, get Richard Silvers in here. He should be part of this."

I couldn't tell whether Jimmy was an assistant or a Secret Service agent, but he said, "Yes, ma'am," then went off to find Richard Silvers. This was going to be fun.

"Uuh, Madam President, Dick Silvers resigned a couple of days ago," Collins rasped.

"Resigned! How come I didn't know about this? Why in the hell did he resign?"

The president was human. When her temper heated, so did her vocabulary.

"Damn it, he works for me. I tell people when they get to resign!"

Jimmy came back into the room and reported that Richard Silvers was not at the reception.

"Yes, so I have just learned. Call Rick at home and get him in here."

"Yes, ma'am." Jimmy left to find a phone.

"Okay, Johnny, you were saying."

"Yes, ma'am. Aaah, well, we devised a plan—that is, Silvers devised a plan, and I concurred, for the most part—"

Already starting with the bob and weave and backsliding. I couldn't stand it anymore.

"Madam President, Ed Colombo, my wife, and I were integral to the plan. Perhaps we could all save some time if I told you what happened from the start, at least from when we first became involved."

"Are you and your wife federal agents?" the president asked.

"No, ma'am. I'm a real estate broker, and my wife owns a consulting firm, though she frequently does contract work for the government. She's a computer geek."

"Well, how in the hell did you get involved in this, and where did you get these papers?" She paused. "When your wife and I were speaking a few minutes ago, was she talking about these documents?"

"Yes, ma'am, I believe she was. If I could explain, ma'am?"

"Well, get on with it. Explain."

"Yes, ma'am. About five days ago—"

I told her everything, starting with buying the boat, the assault the first night in Newport, the attack off Block Island, the kidnapping, and the firefight on the coast of Nicaragua. I told her that we flew back with Reynaldo, even about the engine overheating. I paid particular attention and detail to the luncheon with the golfing twosome, Collins, and Silvers. It took about five minutes, but when I was done, except for music and laughter filtering through the door from the East Room, the Green Room was silent.

The president broke the silence, "Jesus, what did you do on your last vacation, invade Panama?"

"Barbados—"

"You invaded Barbados?"

"Ah, no, ma'am. We just sat on the beach."

"Right. Are you telling me that your wife out there killed four men with an automatic weapon?"

"Yes, ma'am, though I think from her view it was about keeping me from getting hurt. Given the right provocation, she can be pretty formidable."

"I'll bet you never stepped out on her."

"No, ma'am, not even a little."

We were interrupted by a commotion at the East Room door. A familiar voice penetrated the partially opened door.

"I don't care who's in there. If you don't let me in, I'm going to . . ."

"Jimmy, find out what all that commotion is about," the president sighed.

Jimmy hurried in the direction of the noise just as the door barged open. My wife, her expensive gown, and coiffure sailed into the room straight for me. She was clearly worried.

"Are you okay?"

"Yes, I'm fine. I was telling the president about our recent adventure."

Suddenly she realized who was in the room. Liz made a quick turn to where the president was seated without faltering, "Please excuse my intrusion, Madam President. My husband has a proclivity for getting himself involved with intractable situations that place him in a good deal of danger, especially where Mr. Collins is involved. I was worried that he was now in such a situation."

She looked at Collins with an all-too-familiar icy stare. Collins was the recipient, but I winced in a Pavlovian response.

"Elizabeth—may I call you Elizabeth?" the president asked.

"Certainly, Madam President. My friends call me Liz. It would honor me if you did so. Mr. Collins is your chief of staff, is he not, Madam President?"

"Yes," she replied, "but the day isn't over."

"Madam President, we were led to believe by Mr. Collins that this entire operation was, in his words, "at the behest of the White House," specifically you, Madam President. I have just had a conversation with Mr. Silvers, who led me to think this may not be the case. I assure you, we would not have considered getting involved in this scheme if you had not requested our help. Forgive me for waving the flag, but it was because of you and our devotion to country that we agreed to aid Mr. Collins and Mr. Silvers."

That put a fine point on it. Collins looked faint. I was betting even money he was wishing he had made Silvers disappear in Rock Creek Park.

"Ah, yes," she started slowly. The president was now the recipient of Liz's stare, but she quickly recouped and came in with a strong finish.

"Elizabeth, we appreciate your devotion to country, but I must admit being caught somewhat off guard by events," looking at Collins.

A marine lance corporal in dress blues opened the door from the corridor. Then what I assumed to be two Secret Service agents walked in the room with Richard Silvers in tow. Silvers was in blue jeans, a white dress shirt, and a blue blazer. He needed a shave and looked as if he had been in the liquor cabinet. Silvers walked to the president almost standing at attention.

"Madam President, please accept my apologies for my inappropriate appearance. I was only recently informed that you wished to see me."

"That's okay. You're the only one in the room that's comfortable. Incidentally, you are a political appointee, appointed by me, and you're not resigned until I say you're resigned."

Silvers glanced at Collins, "Yes, ma'am, thank you, Madam President."

"Save your thanks. As I mentioned to Johnny, the day isn't over, and we have a mess to fix."

"Yes, ma'am," Silvers said with considerably less enthusiasm.

The president started again, "Elizabeth, never apologize for waving the flag, at least not to me. Please have a seat, and let's see if I can figure out what happened. Then we'll work from there."

"Thank you, Madam President," Liz replied, sitting down.

"Madam President," I said, "may I make a suggestion or two?"

"Why not? You can't do any worse than these two, and I guess you earned a say."

"Madam President, I think Mr. Silvers's plan was workable. We were to acquire enough embarrassing information to forgive the term, blackmail President Escudero into siding with the United States and Saudi Arabia at the OPEC Conference, and in the process hopefully avert the threatened production cuts.

"What neither of these men told us," I looked over at both the men, "was the plan was also about capturing Pérez. Collins and Silvers realized that they needed a safety valve. If information about their operation was disclosed, deliberately or inadvertently, say through a leak to the press, more than likely President Escudero would be thrown out of office by his own people and we would be left with no way to advance our cause with OPEC. But with Pérez in the picture, the situation could still be controlled. If things started to go sideways for Escudero back home, they planned or plan to keep him in power by throwing Dr. Pérez to the wolves, blaming him for Escudero's transgressions or at least the ones that leaked to the press. In short, they could keep Escudero in power, but still keep a foot on his neck.

"Madam President, as proposed by Mr. Collins and Mr. Silvers, the plan does three things for you and the subsequent election. First, it makes you strong on energy because you saved the day at OPEC and, by default, you show strength on the economy. Second, it gives you a boost in the foreign policy arena. In one blow, you have successfully dealt with Latin America and the Middle East. Third, ferreting out and prosecuting the evil Dr. Pérez makes you strong on crime.

"The ensuing media attention and headlines before the election would certainly be very favorable and likely to help at the polls.

"Given a few more days, I think these gentlemen could have figured out how to include education and health care. Pérez *is* a dentist." I laughed at my joke.

Liz glared at me. The president snorted a laugh and squirmed in her chair. She knew more about this than she let on but at this point it didn't matter. Silvers, who had been standing, slumped into a chair.

Recovering from my fit of levity, I continued, "I was the bait to lure Pérez. Or, more precisely, my boat was the bait to lure Pérez out of hiding. Everyone, including Reynaldo, was sure the Estéban Morales records were on the boat and, of course, everyone was right. But what your guys didn't know or don't know," I looked at Collins and Silvers, "is that Dr. Pérez is dead."

"What!" Collins and Silvers yelped in unison.

"He was killed in Florida, then taken offshore, apparently in what is now our boat, and dropped over the side. This came to light during our trip to Nicaragua. It seems Reynaldo killed him about three months ago," I lied.

"He didn't tell us that," Collins exclaimed. "And why would he kill Pérez if he were the only one who knew the location of the files?"

"What did he tell you?" I asked.

"Well, nothing really," Collins said.

That's what I thought, "I don't think he lied to me. He had a gun stuck in my face at the time. He was bragging about it just before he planned to shoot me," I lied again. I avoided looking at Liz. "As for why, I think the interrogation got a little rough, and Pérez inadvertently died before Reynaldo got any information. Which is typical of Reynaldo's ineptitude. He's really not smart enough to be a crook."

Collins looked completely deflated.

"Anyway, I ended up with the files, and I plan to keep them until I'm sure Liz and I are safe from Escudero's bunch and, frankly, from these two," nodding at Collins and Silvers.

Both started sputtering about how absurd I was. *How I dare think either one would harm anyone . . .*

The president interrupted, "Sir, are you implying that a member of my administration would bring harm to you or your wife?"

"Madam President, someone broke into my boat and assaulted me. For several reasons, I'm certain it was not anyone from the Escudero Morales crowd."

Of course, I knew what they didn't know. Ed sent some of his guys who belonged to the State Department's SPEOPS to break into my boat. I had no idea who ran SPEOPS. Maybe Silvers, maybe the president. What the hell, in for a penny, in for a pound.

"I think they were men from an outfit called SPEOPS. Does anyone know what that is?"

I looked around the green room, make that *the* Green Room. Liz was sitting across from the president in a Duncan Phyfe side chair covered in red fabric. A Duncan Phyfe side chair was probably in the Red Room, covered with green fabric. Liz noticed my stare and gave me a slight smirk and a wink. Louisa Catherine Adams looked down on us. The former wife of a secretary of state and a president. I was wondering what she was thinking. She made a slight smirk, too, but didn't wink. All three had gone somewhat pale, which was a major deal for the president.

I continued, "Of course if the plan fell apart, Elizabeth and I were the fall guys. We have no association with the administration or the federal government. And God knows what Mr. Collins and Mr. Silvers here had in mind for that eventuality. Maybe SPEOPS would show up at our door some night and we would disappear."

I was being a bit melodramatic, okay very melodramatic, but it was fun to watch Collins and Silvers screw themselves into the ceiling. Through the din of denials and protestations, I continued.

"That's why I still have the Narragansett Files. I also have the money. As you know, the files are probably inconclusive without independent verification by witnesses or participants, which we will never have. However, if one has the money, which is the fruits of the crime, you have prima facie evidence of the drug dealing and the embezzlement. Reynaldo and his father could deny all of this, but who are the Venezuelans going to believe, Escudero or five hundred and sixty million dollars?"

Silvers and Collins started again, but the president spoke, raising her voice and holding up her hand to the other two.

"First, I want you to know that while SPEOPS technically works for the State Department under Mr. Silvers over there," nodding her head toward Silvers, "they work for me, and I assure you that they are not armed, that they only act in a diplomatic function to carry informal communication and gather information for my use. If, as you suggest, SPEOPS employees were detailed to perform an illegal act on your property and person, I assure you I will find and prosecute the people responsible."

I needed to calm everyone down. I said in a low tone, "Thank you, Madam President, there was no permanent damage. Elizabeth and I went into this with the full knowledge that we perhaps were to be the scapegoats. Other than ownership of the boat, these gentlemen would have had no other reason to involve us. Our reasons were altruistic and patriotic and, as Elizabeth said, 'a way to make a difference.' Was there some arm-twisting? Yes, but ultimately it was a voluntary undertaking. Now that we possess this information," I pointed to Liz's analysis still lying in the president's lap, "I suggest we try to work out a plan that will use it in the most beneficial manner, presumably as Mr. Silvers had originally intended, in the pursuit of United States interests at the OPEC conference."

"You said you had a suggestion," the president said.

"Yes, Madam President, at least the outline of one." It took about ten minutes to make my proposal. I answered some questions, then sat back and watched. The president was calmer now and had returned to what I assumed to be her normal demeanor. Having never been in her presence, this was conjecture. She had several more questions, then talked with Collins, Silvers, and some of her aides. When they finished huddling, the president turned in my direction and looked at me.

"What can I do for you.? Is your boat damaged? Do you need transportation back to Newport?"

"Well ma'am, the FAA is pretty annoyed with me. Perhaps you could speak to them. I don't think they will send me to jail, but I suspect there would be a substantial fine involved."

"What's the trouble with the FAA?"

"I was flying without a license or a copilot."

"Jimmy!" the president yelled.

Jimmy was right behind her, "Yes, ma'am."

"Oh, there you are. Go out and bring Kitty Davis in here. You know who she is?"

"Yes, ma'am. The FAA administrator."

"Right. Ask her if she would step in here for a moment."

Kitty Davis must have been standing just outside the door because she and Jimmy were back almost immediately.

"Kitty, this man needs a pilot's license. Can you take care of that for me?"

"Yes, ma'am." She looked at me dubiously, not that I blamed her. "Does he know how to fly?"

Fair question, I thought.

"He flew a dammed jet," she looked at me. "What kind of plane was it?"

"A Falcon 10, ma'am."

"He flew a Falcon 10 from Nicaragua to Dulles the other night," said the president, looking at me. "You said you lost the port engine?"

"Yes, ma'am. Fortunately, we just crossed the threshold, so I was able to shut it down immediately."

"So, I guess he can fly."

"He says you all are upset with him."

Kitty Davis, the FAA administrator, was not to be deterred. "Yes, ma'am, I remember hearing something about that. Does he have a medical?"

"He looks healthy enough to me, Katherine. Just take care of this, will you—as a favor to me, female pilot to female pilot. Did Bob come with you tonight?"

"Yes, ma'am."

"Okay, tell Bob not to leave. I'll be out in a few minutes. I need some of those golf tips of his, but take care of this for me, Kitty. Make this go away. Jimmy, get Mrs. Davis a copy of a driver's license or something so she knows who to license and where to send it."

Kitty replied, "Yes, ma'am. I'll take care of it personally." She then left to return to Bob, whom I assumed was her husband.

I handed my driver's license to Jimmy.

"Okay, is that it?" the president asked.

"Well ma'am, the FBI confiscated some of my property."

"What kind of property?"

"Ahh, some firearms, Madam President."

"You are talking about the ones you took to Nicaragua, right?"

"Yes, ma'am. And Madam President, well, they were pretty upset about the airplane, too. If Mr. Silvers hadn't interceded, they would have probably arrested me for stealing the thing."

"Who does it belong to?"

"An FBO in Miami, ma'am."

"An FBO?"

"Yes, Madam President, a fixed base operator, an airplane leasing company—"

"I know what an FBO is. You may have noticed the press take delight in my prowess as a pilot."

"Yes, ma'am. Reynaldo leased the airplane, and had it flown to Martha's Vineyard, where Ed and I commandeered it. We put the pilots in a hotel with the intention of returning to Martha's Vineyard and giving the plane back to the pilots, but Ed got hurt and with the engine problems, well, it didn't go as planned.

"Jimmy, ask Foster Douglas to come in here. He is probably foaming at the mouth, anyway, dying to know what we're doing in here. Thinks he's another damn J. Edgar Hoover, always has his nose in my business."

"Collins, have you found Ed Colombo yet?"

"No, ma'am, no luck. We are still looking."

They were not about to find Ed. I doubted they ever were going to find him. That's the one little detail I left out of my story. Liz looked over at me but didn't say anything.

The director of the FBI arrived in a cloud of cigar smoke, "Yes, ma'am, what may I do for you, Madam President?"

"For one thing, you can put out that damn cigar."

Foster Douglas's already florid face turned a darker shade of red, "Yes, ma'am, is that all?" He looked for an ashtray without success.

"No, that is not all. Your people confiscated some firearms from an airplane out at Dulles the other night. Do you know about that?

"Yes, ma'am. I am on top of everything the Bureau does."

"Fine, I want you to see that the property gets back to the owner, this man right here. Send the stuff to Newport, in care of his boat."

The president looked at me. "That okay?"

"Yes, ma'am," I nodded.

"Jimmy will give you the information."

Pointing at me with his cigar, Douglas boomed, "Ma'am, that man flew a foreign national and three or four weapons into this country in a stolen airplane without a flight plan and without permission to enter the country. Neither he nor the passengers had a passport or any other identification. Hell, I don't think he even has a pilot's license. We just opened a file on him for grand larceny, smuggling, and firearms violations."

"Foster don't fuck with me. If I have to get Homeland Security to take care of this, I will do it. Jimmy, if he is out there, ask Cox to come in here."

"Madam President, one of those weapons was an automatic rifle, not to mention he stole a million-dollar airplane!"

"I don't care if it was a damn bazooka. Give it back to him, clear? And send someone up to Martha's Vineyard to get those pilots, then take them to Dulles and give them back their airplane. Silvers over there will take care of any leasing fees. She looked at Silvers,

"Rick, I guess you should look into the engine situation, too."

The president looked at me, "Any bullet holes, or other things Silvers should know about?"

"Yes, ma'am, during the fight a round went through the port well cover. During takeoff, some people were shooting at us, and I think the plane was hit with some more rounds. Maybe that's what's wrong with the engine?"

Liz glared at me, "You didn't tell me somebody was shooting at us!"

The president looked at Douglas, "Okay, Foster, you got all that, or do I need to get Cox in here?"

Douglas glared at the president for a long moment, then said icily, "Yes, ma'am."

"Okay, that's all. Somebody get Jimmy and tell him to forget about Cox."

The smoldering cigar and the smoldering Foster Douglas, director of the FBI, left the room.

"I can't stand that guy. The arrogant prig smoking in a public building, not to mention it's my home, smoking in the fucking White House for Christ's sake. Johnny, remind me again why I appointed that SOB."

Well, ma'am, he's pretty good at his job," Collins replied.

"I guess." The president looked at me, "Anything else?"

I was pressing my luck, but what the hell, "There is one other thing, Madam President. Customs."

"What about them?"

"Ma'am, Director Douglas was right, I left and entered the country a couple of times and didn't check in with them."

"Oh, hell, I do it all the time. If they give you any trouble, tell them to call me."

CHAPTER TWENTY-TWO

1600 Pennsylvania Avenue, Washington, D.C.

Liz and I stood on the sidewalk bordering Pennsylvania Avenue looking through the wrought-iron fence at the White House. During the day, I saw it as the symbol of the most formidable, and in some ways probably the most terrible, power ever known by man. Unleashed, it could bring the world to its knees, never to recover. But at night, the lights bathed the White House in a majestic glow that for me conjured thoughts of peace, liberty, and hope. I wondered for a moment if there might be a message there, dark overcoming light instead of the other way around.

"Pretty, isn't it," I said.

"Yes, it is." Elizabeth took off her jacket and handed it to me. She wrapped her arm around mine, kissed me, and then we walked off toward Fifteenth Street.

Charles L'Enfant designed the nation's capital to be built in a series of non-concentric circles. Depending on which you believe, the design was inspired by the great cities of Europe, or it was for self-defense, presumably from the British.

Unhappily, when the British attacked, the battle took place in Bladensburg, Maryland. The Americans were soundly trounced and the British burned Washington, leaving only when a hurricane literally blew them out of town.

Nevertheless, Washington ranks as one of the most beautiful cities in the world, so long as you don't have to drive an automobile around one of its many circles.

"Do you think Ed will come back?" Liz asked.

I looked at Elizabeth, her bare shoulders were luminous in the soft artificial light reflected off the surrounding buildings. I tended to forget how lovely she was.

"I think so when he learns no one is looking for him other than a concerned employer. If I don't hear from him, I'll call Stacie. He'll keep in touch with her."

"Think he's mad that you gave him the dummy flash drive?"

"Furious, I should think, but he'll come to his senses. I'd like to think he'll be laughing about it soon. When he finds he still has a job, his daughter, and his friends he'll become his old self. When he lost Caroline, he just went, I don't know, stupid. They were high school sweethearts and married for thirty-some years. He never cared about money before. It was all about the job. He could have made a bundle in real estate, but he chucked it to join the FAA, then I guess he got into this other thing with the State Department. I just don't know, Lizzy, but I hope."

Arm in arm, we walked slowly. The evening breeze was cool, but the heat stored in the street and the buildings from a day's sunshine kept the temperature about eighty degrees or more. I looked at her again. In her five-inch heels, she and I were the same height.

"How are the feet holding out?"

"Oh, you know me, fashion first."

We turned right off Pennsylvania Avenue onto Fifteenth Street, walked past the Treasury building, then crossed the street to the Old Ebbitt Bar and Grill. Inside, the air was cooler, but the mass of people sitting at the two bars and three dining rooms were straining the air conditioner. We waited for a few minutes while the hostess found us a table. A few other revelers and diners were also in evening clothes, probably from the reception, but maybe the theater, though nobody dressed for the theater nowadays.

Ebbitt's, as the locals call the landmark, probably dates to the Buchanan administration. For me, it dated to my high school days. At eighteen, my friends and I were old enough to drink beer in the District, and Ebbitt's was our favorite watering hole. Until about thirty years ago, Ebbitt's was on F Street around the corner from where it now stands. It was long and narrow, only about thirty feet wide with the only stand-up bar I have ever seen. A leftover from the turn of the century, the bar stood at four and a half or five feet, no stools. The waiters were gracious black men dressed in white shirts, black bow ties, black pants, and red waist jackets. When the block was renovated, Ebbitt's moved to its current location, a former movie theater.

The movie poster cases still reside on either side of the entrance. No longer considered a watering hole, Ebbitt's has become one of the stylish places to be and be seen. The food is good, too.

The hostess showed us to our table, a booth midway down on the left side of the main aisle, a prime table. It must have been my new tux. Seated with our menus, I looked around the dining room, I nodded at a couple we had seen at the reception.

Liz glanced at her menu, "You think they will go for your plan?"

"I think so. I don't see too many alternatives. Do you?"

"No, but how come they couldn't figure it out? That's what they get paid for."

"Egos, for one, but I guess mostly politicos are so busy covering their asses there is little leftover for intelligent thought. When Collins discovered Reynaldo didn't have the real Narragansett file, I think his brain went into survival mode. It's hard to think clearly if all you're doing is trying to save your job."

"Jesus, it makes you wonder what else falls through the cracks."

"As somebody said, it's the worst form of government, except for whatever is second."

"It was Winston Churchill, and he said, 'Democracy is the worst form of government except for all the others.'"

"Well, as a country, we have it pretty good, and I guess we have to hope not too much falls through those cracks or 'We vote the bastards out.' Who said that?"

"Everyone," she said, putting her menu on the table.

The waiter, a fresh-faced kid with starched everything, including suspenders and bow tie, took our order. Liz ordered a Rueben with a glass of chardonnay, and I ordered the crab cakes with an iced tea.

When the waiter was gone, Liz asked, "When you had her attention, why didn't you ask the president to intercede with the police at Vineyard Haven? They may come looking for you with some tough questions."

"Let's assume the Massachusetts authorities charge me with a crime, God forbid, even murder. It's a capital offense, but it would be a local matter, not a federal crime. The president would have no right—or, perhaps putting it better, she would have no constitutional authority—to interfere. She could probably pardon me if it got that far. Anyway, I decided to wait and see. I don't know. Perhaps she could ask the Justice Department to intercede, take a personal interest, but I'd just as soon not play that card until I have to. She heard our story. I don't think she'll let me hang out to dry. Of course, if a new administration comes in, that could change everything."

We talked more about the extraordinary evening, but eventually the conversation turned to the more mundane. I was worried she wouldn't have enough vacation days to complete our sail. She was sure she could get a few more days. After all, she owned the company. I told her about a call from an old client asking for my help with some apartments he wanted to build in Louisiana. We finished eating and chatting, declined dessert, then paid the bill.

Our driver and car were waiting for us in front of Ebbitt's and after a pleasant, moon-lit drive along the Potomac, he dropped us at our home. I could get used to having a car and driver.

Liz went upstairs to get ready for bed while I checked for phone messages and made sure Sable had food and water. I checked all the doors, turned on the alarm, then followed Liz.

Posed with her left hand on her hip, Liz was leaning against the large doorway that led between the dressing room and our bedroom. She was wearing her Louboutin five-inch heels, her jewelry, and nothing else.

"Hi, sailor boy."

Always one for a snappy retort, I croaked, "Hi."

Like a runway model, carefully putting one foot in front of the other, she slowly walked over to me gently swaying her hips. The effect was tormenting. Reaching me, she pushed me over on the bed and slowly took off my clothes. When I was naked, she started kissing the inside of my knee slowly working up the inside of my leg. Gently and purposely, she moved her breasts, so her hardened nipples caressed me. Then, while kissing me on the mouth, she moved her hips over mine until she found the right position.

She said in a throaty whisper, "Don't help," and arched her back, slowly taking me inside.

CHAPTER TWENTY-THREE

Hunter Residence, Mount Vernon, Virginia

The following day was a bright, beautiful Sunday morning. We were in the dining room lingering over breakfast and the paper.

"That was fast," I said mostly to myself.

Liz looked up from the Sunday magazine, "What was fast?"

I handed her the paper, "Look at this."

WHITE HOUSE ANNOUNCES MEETING WITH VENEZUELA

WASHINGTON, D.C. — Today White House Press Secretary Brad Michael in a brief statement announced the president will meet with Venezuelan President Victor Escudero at 9:30 am Tuesday to discuss matters of mutual interests. The meeting will be held in the White House with respective staff members. However, it is expected the chief executives will lunch in private. Considerable speculation has been offered by administration insiders suggesting the president will use this meeting to address issues relating to the coming OPEC conference. Several OPEC members have made it known that they are angered by the United States' support of Israel and the bombing of Iran by the Israeli Air Force. Venezuela is a charter member of OPEC and the administration fears President Escudero, who is frequently at odds with United States policy, will use the OPEC conference to advance his political agenda. Should the Venezuelan and Arab members concur, sources say it is reasonable to expect sanctions against Israeli allies, including the United States, which could involve oil embargos and higher energy costs . . .

"So, it's on for Tuesday. That *was* fast. Are you ready?"

"I'm going to review the documents some. Do you think your South American desk can wring anything more out of the files?" I asked.

"I'll call Gery first thing in the morning. Better yet, I'll call him now at home just to be sure he'll be at work in the morning."

"Good idea, not a good time for him to go on vacation. Hey, when he does go on vacation, does he go to South America?"

"No, smarty pants, he goes to Martha's Vineyard."

"Oh, good that worked out well for us."

Monday came and went, but not before a FedEx arrived from the FAA. The package contained a second-class medical certificate and a commercial pilot certificate complete with instrument and multiengine ratings. Mrs. Davis also included a type rating for a Falcon 10. Type ratings are required for aircraft weighing more than 12,500 pounds. The Falcon's weight exceeds that by some 6,000 pounds.

Kitty included a note imploring me not to fly into the ground or anything else. I started to send her an email, then I regained my senses. Everyone can read an email. I scratched a quick note of thanks with assurances that the certificates would go into my safe for a few months and that when everything cooled off, I would return them to her unused. I put the note with other mail ready for the post office.

Aside from the almost crashing part, I had enjoyed flying again. Maybe I would go back and renew my "ticket" for real. Maybe not, it is expensive, and I had *Pinafore*.

Tuesday morning, the day of the big White House Conference, I was dressed in my best gray suit, which was my only gray suit. I never play golf, but I mostly wear golf shirts and khakis to work, usually, with boat shoes. I also mostly wear golf shirts and khakis to shoot and to sail and at home, except when I wear polo shirts. If it's really cold, I wear socks. Net result, there was very little time left over for wearing suits. My gray suit was accessorized with a maroon tie and a dapper matching handkerchief. I was wearing highly polished wingtip tassels or tasseled wingtips—I could never remember. The highly polished part was a skill and habit left over from the Marine Corps. I knew better than trying to leave the house in a suit without socks. She always checked.

Liz was not burdened with a dearth of suits. She was wearing a blue suit, of which she had several. Her selection was worn with some pearls I had given her last year for Christmas and conservative shoes, meaning they were three-inch as opposed to four- or five-inch heels.

We looked like bankers. Enterprise Rental Car agents look like bankers, too. I wondered why. Our car and driver arrived, so I didn't get to contemplate longer on the rental car agent thing. Probably unimportant.

The car and driver, again care of the White House, took us the same route, but this time in rush-hour traffic, so the ride up the George

Washington Parkway and across the Fourteenth Street Bridge took sixty-five minutes.

We went through the same scrutiny at the gate. At the portico, another young marine opened the car door for us, a decorated sergeant. I thanked him for his help and we each thanked him for his service.

A staff member who introduced herself as Olivia met us at the entrance. Olivia showed us to a desk where a uniformed Secret Service officer issued us temporary identification badges. Then Olivia walked us through the West Wing and into a large conference room known as the Roosevelt Room.

The Roosevelt Room was named for the two men who built the West Wing. They were fifth cousins and U.S. presidents of some note. Teddy Roosevelt was my grandmother's favorite president, and she frequently regaled me about the occasion when as a young girl she actually met President Theodore Roosevelt.

Olivia asked us to be seated and assured us someone would attend in a few minutes, then left in a determined flurry of clicking heels. The room contained a large conference table surrounded by leather-upholstered armchairs. A sofa sat against the far wall flanked on either side by two matching chairs. On the near wall was a butler's table with a pot of coffee and a selection of pastries artfully displayed over a silver tray. I poured coffee for each of us and sat at the big conference table next to Elizabeth. Several minutes later, Jonathan Collins entered the room. He was a bit starchy but spoke to us pleasantly enough, inquiring about our health, then asked if we required any additional refreshments. As we were not to be members of the meeting, but only observers, he politely asked us to sit on the sofa or the chairs that lined the wall. He also said the president would like to speak with us for a few minutes before the meeting. Then he left. I looked at my watch. The meeting was to start in about ten minutes. Liz and I moved to the side. She took a seat on the end of the cream-colored sofa. I sat in one of the similar colored chairs next to her. We waited and drank our coffee. Mindful of the surroundings, I took extra care not to slurp.

The president entered the Roosevelt Room trailed by Collins, Silvers, and two staffers I had never seen. We stood and said good morning.

"Please be seated. Thank you for coming. May we get you anything?"

I said, "No, ma'am, thank you."

The president pulled up a chair seated herself, then continued, "I wanted to thank the two of you again for your service and your courage. I was remiss not saying it before, but, as you could probably tell, I was a little ruffled. Presidents are not supposed to get ruffled, so I should have told you at the reception."

I couldn't figure where this was going, but for once I kept my mouth shut. Liz was holding my hand.

The president said, "From this point on and retroactive to the day of your arrival in Newport, you are contractual employees of and to the Federal Government. You will work for Silvers here," she nodded at Silvers, "under the SPEOPS program, but you will report to me." She motioned to Silvers, "The envelope Rick is handing each of you contains all the details, including salary, insurance, and other benefits. As I am sure you have no wish to become full-time employees of the government, no matter how exciting,"—we all chuckled dutifully—"you will be compensated for your time on an hourly basis and will be entitled to all the protections under prescribed law. I will occasionally call on your services, but as contractors, you are free to choose your assignments. Do you have any questions?"

I spoke first, "Madam President, does this have anything to do with the files and money we control through the Narragansett flash drive?"

"No. Anything else?"

"No, ma'am, I seem to be speechless."

"That's a first," Liz muttered. "Madam President, may I still work as before, I mean with my consulting company?"

"Certainly. As matter of fact, we may have a job for your people. Anything else?"

Liz and I looked at each other. She shook her head slightly, then I stole a glance at Collins and Silvers for signs of green but found none.

"No, ma'am, not at this time, other than to say we are honored you think that highly of us and our efforts."

"Good. Now I want you to listen carefully to what is said in this meeting. If either of you hear something that you don't like—no, that's not the correct word—make that, if you hear anything inconsistent with what you know to be true or with what you believe the objectives of this meeting are, let me know."

I asked, "Can you be a little more specific, Madam President?"

"No. All I can suggest is that you will probably know it when you hear it. Any more questions?"

"No, Madam President."

"Okay, let's get the good President Escudero in here." The president got up and walked out of the room, followed by her entourage.

I looked at Liz, "Well, that was a hell of a way to start our day."

"The day is young," she said wryly.

"Pessimist."

CHAPTER TWENTY-FOUR

The White House, Roosevelt Room

About five minutes later, the president entered the Roosevelt Room accompanied by a man I recognized from newspaper pictures as Victor Escudero, the president of Venezuela. Shorter than the American president, he was about sixty and had a full head of dark gray hair with matching mustache. He wore his expensive, dark gray, English-cut suit with a pale blue shirt, white collar, and white French cuffs clasped with large gold cuff links. Staff members accompanied both presidents. I recognized Jimmy from the reception and, of course, Collins and Silvers.

A minute or two later, Reynaldo entered the room with two large U.S. marshals. I could tell they were U.S. marshals because each wore a chocolate brown sport coat bedecked with a Deputy U.S. Marshal badge. Reynaldo was seated at the end of the table, next to one of Escudero's staff. In almost ornamental fashion, the marshals stood against the wall behind, and to either side of Reynaldo. He looked unimportant and worse for wear. He was pale and his hair was disheveled. Apparently, hair gel was in short supply at his current residence. Dressed in a blue suit and silver tie, his right arm was supported by a black sling suitable for business attire. I wondered what color sling he wore with his orange jumpsuit.

"Madam President," Escudero said in good but accented English, "I must protest the treatment of Mr. Vicente in this manner. He is a member of my executive council and the director of our *Petróleos de Nacional.*"

The president replied, "I'm sorry, Victor, there is no intent to upset you. As for Mr. Vicente," she looked down to the far end of the table at Reynaldo, "may I call you Reynaldo?" Not waiting for an answer, she continued, "As Reynaldo will be integral to our discussions, I thought it would be proper to have him in attendance."

Escudero persisted, "But he is treated like a common criminal. It is inexcusable that he should be brought here under guard."

The president looked at the marshals, "Gentlemen, please step outside, I'll call if we need you. Thank you."

The two Marshals left the room, closing the door behind them.

"Okay, good. Now," the president said, "shall we get started. Perhaps introductions are in order. Let's go around the table, shall we?"

Introductions were made. Liz and I were not included, which was okay with me. I didn't want anyone to know who we were. Reynaldo, now a close personal friend, avoided looking at us. Unless there was more than one cultural attaché attached to their Washington Embassy, I was pretty sure the Venezuelan sitting next to Reynaldo was Adel's husband. I also assumed cultural attaché meant he was an intelligence agent of some type. He glanced at me several times. I wondered whether Adel had mentioned our brief encounters and how he fit into the overall picture.

After the introductions, the president directed her remarks to President Escudero.

"Victor, is it your contention that Mr. Vicente works for you? He is also your son, correct?"

"*Si,* yes, as I said, he is an important member of my executive council, and he is responsible for the operation of Petróleos de Nacional, which I believe would be similar to your Department of Energy."

"So, much like Mr. Silvers here works for me, Mr. Vicente works for you. Is that correct? Except, unlike Mr. Silvers, Reynaldo reports directly to you?"

"Yes, he reports to me. I have said that." Escudero said, nodding his head.

The president turned her attention to the rest of the gathering, thanked everyone for attending, then said, "One item of business before starting with our meeting." She pointed at Liz and me, "I suspect the two people sitting over there are well known to several of you. You should also know that they are agents of the United States government and my representatives on many matters of importance to this administration. I hope my meaning is clear." The president paused and looked around the room, even lingering on Collins. Reynaldo turned red, and his father glowered darkly. Perhaps Escudero *did* know who we were.

"Okay, good. Now, Victor, let's come directly to the point. As we both know, you have a meeting pending with OPEC, and it is my hope we can come to some consensus on how you will conduct yourself at the meeting, at least as it pertains to the United States and oil production."

Victor glared. He must have practiced in front of a mirror because he was a skilled glarer. "Ma'am, how I conduct myself at the OPEC conference or any other meeting is not of your business, and I will not be dictated to as if I were a puppet state of *Estados Unidos*. I was told this was a meeting to discuss mutual interests, specifically as they relate to our refinery business and the gas stations the Bolivarian Republic of Venezuela now operates in these United States."

"True, Victor, but our mutual interests cannot be discussed without the inclusion of the OPEC conference. As an experienced public official and politician, I'm sure you are in full accord with the necessity of including oil production in any meaningful discussion of global economics. In turn, we, of course, cannot have significant discussions without including OPEC and the coming OPEC conference. Because Venezuela is an influential, founding member of OPEC, I thought it only right to discuss the complexities of these circumstances with you and perhaps glean, if you will, some astute recommendations."

Victor looked extremely uncomfortable. He sat for a moment, looked around the room, then said, "Well, of course, Madam President. I am happy to offer my assistance, but as you know, I cannot allow myself to be influenced in any way that would be detrimental to the interests of my country."

"President Escudero, I think what is good for your country can be good for my country, and I have no intention to ask you to act contrary to that ideal."

"Jimmy," the president said, "pass out those documents to everyone."

Jimmy, with Silvers's help, saw that everyone, including Liz and I, received a set of the documents. Conspicuous among the documents was a copy of Liz's analysis of the Narragansett Files.

The president said, "All right, as I started to say, let's get to the point. As you gentlemen—excuse me, *and ladies*—may know or may strongly suspect, we have recovered Dr. Pérez's files. What you have in front of you is an analysis of those files by one of our intelligence agencies. Included in the packet are copies of bank accounts and various other documents that support and supplement the analysis. No one other than members of my staff has yet seen this information, and I intend to keep it that way, which means no press and no federal or congressional investigations, at least for now."

Victor jumped up, "This is preposterous. These are lies. I will not sit here!" Victor's face turned red, and he was having trouble getting his breath.

"Sir, please sit down and try to control yourself. Let me finish, then you can speak."

Reading more of the analysis, President Escudero jumped up again, "This is outrageous, totally outrageous! We are leaving!" Victor yelled.

"I am warning you, sir. Sit down and be quiet! I will have a dozen armed marshals in here, and they will forcibly restrain you, if necessary!"

"You would not dare!" Escudero sputtered.

I looked around the room. To their credit, Collins and Silvers were ice cool. I was half-surprised to see Adel's husband had remained calm, too. Possibly, he was a good guy or, to paraphrase an overused metaphor, perhaps he was "looking at the writing on the wall" and planning his hasty retreat.

"Sir, you will sit there and be civil or, so help me, I will have you arrested and handcuffed!" The president said hotly.

Victor, a veteran of many a campaign, some of them in the military, was not given to meek surrender, "Arrested! For what?"

"Sir, Mr. Vicente has been arrested for first- and second-degree murder, kidnapping, intent to commit murder of a U.S. National in a foreign country, piracy, and drug trafficking.

He has also been classified under Title VIII of the Patriot Act as a terrorist. As you just admitted, he is an integral member of your executive council and the director of your *Petróleos de Nacional* operating under your direct orders. I doubt it would be a stretch to say you are guilty of the same crimes, so if you don't want to spend the next twenty years in Guantanamo Bay with your son, I am asking you for the last time to sit down and be quiet!"

I doubted that there was a chance in hell that Victor could be detained in the U.S., much less Gitmo. Nonetheless, there was something about the threat that seemed to connect with him because Victor returned to his chair. In a normal voice, he asked the president whether the man I knew as Adel's husband could leave the room as "he had pressing business elsewhere."

The president imperceptibly glanced at me. Subtly as possible, I shook my head. The president said, "No, we all remain in this room until we have concluded our business."

I wasn't sure which of my theories Victor's request confirmed. Was Adel's true love a patriot or an opportunist? I guessed it didn't make much difference. Either way could prove useful.

"Madam President," Victor implored, "even if what you say is true, there is such a thing as diplomatic immunity—"

"Stop there, Victor, Reynaldo doesn't qualify for immunity. We checked. As far as we are concerned, he is a drug dealer turned terrorist. As for any immunity you have, the sending state may waive immunity and you know it."

Victor tried another tack. "Madam President, I believe you know that to detain me in any manner could be considered by my countrymen as an act of war."

"Save the indignation and threats, Victor. You and I know that most of your revered countrymen would just as soon see you dropped in a dark hole."

That took Escudero back, but only for a moment, "We are all here men of the world. I appreciate that you have a difficult election before you and would like to show your fellow citizens that you have the leadership to continue as their president. But to think you can achieve this at the expense of my country, well, this is not possible. Perhaps—"

The president interrupted, "Jimmy, see those blue and green folders in front of Mr. Collins. Pass them out, please."

Jimmy and Jonathan Collins passed out the folders, then they sat back down.

"Victor, that blue folder contains a document declaring Venezuela a terrorist sponsor state—let me finish! The green one contains a document that allows the United States, under U.S. Code Section 1702, to seize Venezuelan oil refineries in Louisiana and Texas, and all appurtenant assets including the fourteen-thousand Venezuelan-owned service stations in the U.S. This includes the headquarters building and all other associated real estate and bank accounts. You will note they are signed by a federal judge. Our attorney general is sitting outside of this room. If you would like, I will ask him to step in so he can explain the finer details."

Adel's true love choked so bad a staffer gave him some water, but to his credit other than the gagging, he kept quiet.

Victor went apoplectic, loosening an effusive diatribe in which blackmail and extortion were the primary expletives. "This is blackmail! It is outrageous extortion! I will not tolerate such intrusion, we will not permit this, I will call out my armies, this will mean war! Your ambassador will be arrested, I will burn your embassy!"

This time, instead of trying to keep him quiet, the president sat and watched. Two U.S. Marshals and a Secret Service agent opened the door and hurriedly stepped in the room. The president looked at the three men, raised her hand. "Thank you, gentlemen, we'll be OK for now." The Marshals and Agent looked at Escudero for a moment and leave the room.

When Victor finally wound down, President Jackson spoke again. "President Escudero, after this meeting, you will hold a press conference. In that press conference, you will affirm that Venezuela and the United States have reached an accord or understanding regarding the international production of crude oil and as part of this agreement you will recommend to the OPEC members that they withhold any decision on sanctions or production cuts for twenty-four months—"

Victor jumped in, "But my word will not sway the members!"

"Perhaps not," said the president, "but it will send a signal to some members who will add their objections to production cuts. That should be the end to it, or at least until Israel bombs somebody else."

"Why should I do this? How will I—err, what is—how will this be of benefit to my country?"

"For a start, instead of behaving like a backwater rube, you can be a leader and sponsor of good economic policy, address international issues, and make a place for Venezuela on the world stage, where you belong, instead of being a foil for Third World thugs. For God's sake, Victor, Venezuela owns more oil than anyone in the world, but you act like some damn banana republic."

President Jackson paused and looked at President Escudero for several moments.

"Okay, I can see I'm wasting my breath. Let's be more succinct. Your son has a good chance of being executed for capital crimes. All Venezuelan assets in the United States are at risk of being seized and you are about to be exposed as a murderer, a drug trafficker, and an embezzler. The U.S. and Venezuela authorities will probably arrest you. But the real incentive—and you'll like this, Victor—we have all your money, we have the cash, the cars, the airplane, all your toys, all five hundred and sixty million dollars' worth."

"What!" Adel's husband had just been heard from for the first time. I guessed he hadn't read that far into the Narragansett Analysis.

Like a switch, with no outward signs of embarrassment or contriteness, Victor Escudero turned to his own interests.

"My money?" Victor said.

"Do you understand what I am saying? You will have no country, no power, and no money. If you get out of Venezuela alive, you'll be sweeping floors in a bodega in Havana," the president said.

"What about my money!"

"First, are we in agreement about the press conference?"

Escudero looked around the room for allies. He looked at Reynaldo, who nodded slightly, and then he looked at his staff again. None of them would look at him. He sighed, "Yes when I get back to Venezuela, I will hold such a conference. You may keep Reynaldo as guarantee."

Reynaldo jerked his head up, "*Poppie, por favor—*"

President Jackson held up her hand, "We will be detaining Reynaldo regardless, and you will hold the press conference this afternoon in the Rose Garden. Are we agreed?"

"Any meeting with the press will be held in my country—"

"Victor, no press conference, no money."

Escudero looked around the room again. He shrugged and sighed again. He looked physically ill. "*Si*, yes, I agree."

"Victor, if you pull a fast one and renege on our deal, I will release all those papers to the U.S. and Venezuelan press. Are we clear?"

"Yes, we are clear. What about my money?"

"Yes, the money, as you can see from the documents there, is five hundred and sixty million dollars, mostly in cash and negotiable assets—"

Adel's husband made a noise and drank some more water.

President Jackson smiled thinly, "If you live up to your end of the bargain, we will see that you receive ten million dollars from the funds in those accounts," pointing to the documents. "If you don't keep our bargain, you get nothing."

"Ten million dollars! This is an outrage! This is my money! You said yourself there is much more. What will happen to the rest of the money?" He allowed a slight sneer to form on his mouth. "Ahh, I see, perhaps it goes to your reelection campaign, yes."

"Thank you, Victor, for your timely suggestion, but, no, the rest of the money is going back where it came from. It pains me that I have to give you any of it, but short of killing you it's the only way I could think of to assure your, shall we say, participation."

"What do you mean give it back? It is my money!"

"I should have warned you our conversations, as most in this room, are recorded, so your admission of guilt will go into the transcript of this meeting. In answer to your question, the funds and assets will be transferred to a committee made of members of your government, the International Red Cross, and the United Nations. The assets and money will be disbursed to the people of Venezuela as determined by the committee."

"Victor, as my mother used to say, I can see the wheels turning," said the president, "which brings us to the last item on our agenda. You will be resigning next month as president of Venezuela. That announcement will also be made today at the press conference—"

Escudero lost it again. It took everyone in the room, including Reynaldo, to get him calmed and seated. The president, Liz, and I watched.

Finally, he wore out and with help staggered back to his chair, "I will never do such a thing, never, do you *hear* me, *never*!"

"Yes, you will. If you don't, you will never see any money, I will see you prosecuted for the capital crimes previously mentioned, and I will prosecute your son for capital crimes. You will each receive the maximum penalty, which in this case is execution. If for some reason, you avoid execution in this country, in addition to releasing unedited copies of those documents to the U.S. press, I will also send copies to the *Tribunal Supremo de Justicia*, the PNB, and the Venezuelan press. I don't know the penalty for murder in Venezuela, but I'll bet it's not pleasant. You also may want to think about your fellow citizens. They are already fed up with your administration. Are they going to welcome you with open arms after they learn you have murdered their fellow citizens and pilfered millions of dollars from their treasury? This will be the excuse they need to throw you out of office like so many of your predecessors. I don't think you'll make it to that bodega in Havana. You will be dead or in jail."

Victor slumped down, his head sunk between his shoulders.

The president had more, "Once you resign, you will relocate to somewhere in Europe or Africa, *not* Central or South America. When I determine you are settled, we will wire your ten million dollars. I suspect that Reynaldo's legal problems will be resolved by then, and he *may* be able to join you. Are we clear on that? If you return to the Americas, you will be hunted down and shot. I can't make it any plainer than that. Are we clear?"

Victor nodded his head.

"I want to hear you say it, Victor."

"*Si, si*, yes, I understand perfectly. We are clear."

"Okay, Jimmy, I think Mr. Silvers has more documents. Will you pass them to President Escudero."

Silvers handed some papers to Jimmy, who walked around the table placing them in front of Victor.

"Victor, in front of you is an agreement based on the discussion we just concluded. Sign all the copies, then pass them to your staff to sign as witnesses. Keep one for yourself and hand the remaining copies to Jimmy."

Victor signed the documents, barely glancing at them, and slid them across the table to his staff members. I was interested to see that Adel's husband volunteered to sign as one of the witnesses. Collins collected the copies and carried them out of the room.

Everyone but Victor rose as the president stood. She yelled through the door Collins had just opened, "Olivia!" Olivia quickly stuck her head through the door, "Yes, Madam President."

"Ask the marshals to come back in here, please."

"Yes, ma'am, right away."

The marshals briskly entered the room. "Yes, ma'am," one said.

The president pointed at Reynaldo, "Take that man out of here, put him in the basement or somewhere, and sit on him until I get back to you. You people had anything to eat? No, well, get some of your men over here so you can be relieved. What's your name, marshal?" Looking at the older man.

"Dillon, ma'am."

"Did you say Dillon?"

"Yes, ma'am."

"I'll bet you don't get razzed about that much," the president chuckled.

"No ma'am, no more than about a dozen times a day," Dillon grinned.

"Okay, Dillon, you're in charge. Mr. Reynaldo can have something to eat, but he is not to be out of your sight or the sight of someone you assign. Dillon, if you lose him your next assignment will be in American Samoa. Got it?"

Dillon grinned, "He'll be here when you need him, ma'am."

"Okay, good man. Now, let's all get out to the press conference."

CHAPTER TWENTY-FIVE

The White House, The Rose Garden

Except for Reynaldo, everyone started for the Rose Garden and the press conference. As the marshals were collecting Reynaldo, he looked at Liz and me but didn't say anything, then left with his escort. Liz and I had no idea where the Rose Garden was, so we followed the others walking past the Cabinet Room, then turning right through doors that lead out to the West Colonnade. The Rose Garden was on the right. I recognized it because it was full of members of the press and television cameras. I didn't see any roses. The president must have known a shortcut because she and Victor were already at the podium shaking hands for the cameras. A moment later, she stepped to the microphone.

"Good afternoon. I bring you some good news for the United States, Venezuela, and the citizens of our global community. Today President Escudero and I have reached an accord, which we believe will continue to bring stabilization of the world petroleum markets. As you know, Venezuela is one of the founding members of OPEC, and President Escudero has agreed to use this most prestigious position during the coming OPEC conference to seek from the other members of OPEC a rational and conciliatory approach to the escalating debate resulting from the divergence of opinions over recent events in the Middle East. President Escudero's leadership and diplomacy are well known in this arena, and we thank him in advance for his efforts at the impending conference.

"On a more somber note, I am sorry to inform you that President Escudero has just told me that for reasons of health, he will be leaving office on or at the end of this month. I know I speak for the citizens of the United States and the great country of Venezuela when I wish President Escudero the best in his retirement. Now President Escudero will have a few words. Victor, please."

Victor Escudero walked slowly to the podium and replaced the president at the microphone. He looked ill. "Good afternoon, ladies, and gentlemen.

Please forgive, as my English is not as good as I would like. First, I want to thank President Jackson for her gracious hospitality and to compliment her on her grasp of world economics. Our visit has been most remarkable. I wish only I could extend my trip to discuss other important matters of mutual interest.

"The president is quite correct when she says that Bolivarian Republic of Venezuela was one of the founding members of OPEC. As you may recall, the world-famous Venezuelan diplomat Juan Pablo Alfonso founded OPEC. *Coincidentemente*, he lived for some years in this beautiful city."

I leaned over and whispered in Liz's ear, "I wondered if he remembered the famous quote by Alfonso—'Oil will bring us ruin. Oil is the Devil's excrement.'"

She leaned into my ear, "That's a quotation you remember?"

I grinned at her, "Yeah, and he left out Alfonso's middle name, Pérez."

"How do you know this stuff?" she whispered.

"Your husband has an incomparable mind for historic detail."

"Yeah, that's why you can't quote Winston Churchill."

"Okay, I wrote a paper on Alfonso in college."

Victor droned on, "Less well known, Venezuela is also one of the founding members of the United Nations. During my years in office, I like to think I have continued this tradition of diplomacy and that , as a *diplomático*, I have honored Venezuelan citizens by carrying the *manto* left by Juan Pablo Alfonso. In honor of his memory and these legacies, I now call for my fellow members of OPEC to follow the Bolivarian Republic of Venezuela and increase oil production by twenty percent."

Among the press corps, the politicians, and staff behind the podium, there was some murmuring and applause, even from the cynical reporters. I looked over at President Jackson, but I couldn't see her well enough to gauge her expression. Victor had definitely gone off script, but at this point, I wasn't sure whether it was good or bad. A twenty percent increase in oil production sounded like a lot, particularly when the OPEC people wanted to decrease or stop production altogether.

Victor, pleased with the response, seemed to grow a bit in stature, and the color returned to his face. He pressed on with his speech. "I believe it is time for all countries to come together in peace, and what better way to start this new era than for the members at OPEC to show forgiveness to those who would transgress against them. In two weeks' time, I will personally take this, my message of peace and economic harmony, and place it before my fellow members of the OPEC conference."

More but less fervent applause filtered out from the onlookers.

"Thank you, gracias." Escudero, in full control now held up his hand, "Thank you. I must now make a most personal and distressing announcement. As President Jackson mentioned in her opening remarks, due to the rigorous mental and physical exertions of high office, I find my health has deteriorated to such a state that I must temporarily step away from my heavy responsibilities as president of the Bolivarian Republic of Venezuela. This saddest of days will be on the thirtieth day of this month."

President Jackson quickly stepped to the microphone, "Thank you, President Escudero, and thank you, ladies, and gentlemen. And God bless America."

Ignoring the flurry of questions from the assembled reporters, the president quickly stepped away and disappeared into the White House, holding Escudero by the arm.

I looked at Liz, "What do you think that twenty percent business was all about?"

"I don't know. Could be he really wanted to be remembered as a statesman. The problem is that the suggestion may have been so radical that the OPEC members could take it as a negative signal of some kind. More likely the twenty percent increase is so outrageous that they will ignore his comments altogether. In either case, our strategy will backfire. Did you catch the 'temporarily step away' comment?"

"Yeah, so did the president. Let's go back in and see what's happening. Victor is probably already in the Oval Office, staked out on an anthill."

CHAPTER TWENTY-SIX

The White House, West Wing

Liz and I walked back through the door from the West Corridor into the West Wing toward the Roosevelt Room. Even though the doors were closed, everyone in the building could hear the president dressing down Victor. No One privy to the preceding events could blame her. The time and effort put into the plan, all its incarnations and revisions, even before Liz and I became involved, not to mention the considerable personal risk—all of it was maybe now circling the drain. Reynaldo would be out of circulation, and it was doubtful that Victor would survive public scrutiny once the Narragansett Files were released, but would the president really release them? Fortunately, I didn't have to make that decision. I was already making plans to get back to the boat and finish our vacation.

I felt a tap on my shoulder and turned to find Adel's husband. He must have learned the technique from Adel. "Good afternoon," he said, "my name is Teodoro Sabas. I would like to speak with you if you could spare a few minutes."

"What can we do for you, Teodoro?" I asked as we shook hands.

"I assume your president is not pleased with President Escudero's performance."

"I think that would be an understatement. As you just heard, perhaps by error, President Escudero did not stick to the agreed-upon content for the press conference."

"President Escudero made no error. He is entirely corrupt. He is also very clever. Anything he said was calculated to do give him the most advantage. My American friends call me Teddy."

"Teddy, this is my wife, Elizabeth."

"Please call me Liz," Elizabeth said. "It was an exciting morning, was it not? We met your wife several times when we were in Newport. I hope she is well."

"Yes, thank you. She mentioned each of you with fondness. And, yes, it was an enlightening morning, which is the reason I wish to speak with you. May we speak candidly?"

I looked at Liz and impoliticly shrugged. "Sure," I said.

"My wife, Adel, and I are not exactly what we seem."

"How's that?" I asked.

"Adel and I are—are as you, we are also agents for our government. I am not actually a cultural attaché." He chuckled, "I am not sure what a cultural attaché does."

Liz and I laughed lightly at his joke, "Teddy, I'm not sure 'cultural attaché' is a real office in anyone's embassy. When I hear a title like that, it always conjures up a vision of James Bond–type characters. I suspected that you were more than a 'cultural attaché,' but are you saying Adel also works as an agent for your government?"

"Yes, Adel is, I think you say, under the covers."

I looked at Liz, who was trying to suppress a giggle, "Teddy, Liz and I are flying under false colors. We are not government agents or any other kind of agents. True, we have recently been appointed as part-time contractors, but the president made a point of our involvement this morning to protect us more than anything else. We are, well, we're just regular people."

"Of course," said Teddy clearly not convinced. "As you wish."

"You mentioned that Adel is not what she seems. She's not Reynaldo's sister?" I asked.

"Reynaldo is her half-brother, but she is no relation to President Escudero, Reynaldo's father. Reynaldo's mother left Escudero when Reynaldo was quite young. She remarried, and Reynaldo took the second husband's name. Adel is the offspring of the second marriage. You may have heard of their mother. She is famous pianist."

"Yes," Liz said, "I actually met her years ago at a concert."

"What did you want to talk about?" I asked.

Teddy looked around to be sure we were not being overheard, then answered, "For some time, factions inside our government and within influential members of our commerce and banking communities have been unhappy with the Escudero *administración*. To begin with, President Escudero does not come from a proper family. When the previous administration forcibly took power and General Juarez became president, Escudero was a major in the army with few prospects. By the time General Juarez died, Escudero was then a colonel and Juarez's chief of staff. He took control of the army with a series of directives allegedly issued by Juarez. Within a few days, Escudero had seized power, so the authenticity of the orders given to the army was immaterial, and Escudero became president. Aside from the proper lineage, a matter of importance in my country, we have long suspected Escudero of several crimes brought to light in this morning's meeting, but I must admit to being ignorant to most of what has taken place right before us."

"So, you don't work for Victor?"

"I work for the Bolivarian Republic of Venezuela or, yes, the Venezuelan government. I am assigned to our embassy in your delightful city because in the past I have been too vocal with my concerns about President Escudero and his practices. Had it not been for the influence of my family, I would have been sent to Moscow or worse."

"And Adel works for you?" Liz asked.

"She works for a group controlled by factions inside the government only known to a few and certainly unknown to President Escudero or his supporters. Her mission is to travel with Reynaldo to confirm Reynaldo's and therefore President Escudero's nefarious activities, if there are any to confirm. She is not acting alone in this task, but as she is related to Reynaldo, she was thought to be our best chance at uncovering such information."

"So that's why she knew who Liz and I were before we met at the Newport party."

"Yes, she was told of your arrival and given photographs to help identify you both. Mr. Colombo also gave us some background information."

"That was kind of him," I said dryly.

"By that time, it was thought Estéban Morales' associate Dr. Pérez had in his possession certain files that may have proved useful to us in removing President Escudero from office."

"It seems everyone was looking for those files, including Adel."

"Yes, Adel was trying to get them before Reynaldo found them. She loves her brother but hates Escudero and what he has done to Reynaldo and our country."

"And she warned me about the kidnapping."

"Si, we could not allow the kidnapping of Elizabeth without warning you."
"All along, I thought Ed Colombo had forced her to tell us."
"We found it useful to make you think that on the chance you were—er . . ."
"On the chance I was made to talk."
"Si, yes, Adel could not, I think as you say, to break cover."
"So, Ed, that is, Mr. Colombo, was working with you?" Liz asked.

Teddy replied, "No, Mr. Colombo works for your State Department, but he was working with us, I think, for his private motives. I do not think he liked Dr. Pérez. Moreover, as we know, your State Department had their reasons, too. Though, unknown to any of us, we were all of the same mind. We have not heard from Mr. Colombo since that day on Martha's Vineyard when he was supposed to have been with you on the airplane."

"He *was* with us, but he was injured in Nicaragua, and we were forced to leave him in the care of some locals."

"Oh, I am sorry to hear that," Teddy said.

"Do you know who hired the men to attack our boat?" I asked.

"I think it was Reynaldo. His father had some contacts in Cuba and told Reynaldo to use them to try to get the files, by force if necessary. These Cuban operativos are ruthless and afraid of very little. Reynaldo and his father were quite surprised at their failure. That is the reason Escudero told Reynaldo to kidnap Elizabeth and remove her to Nicaragua. He assumed you would be very willing to trade Elizabeth for the files. I am sure he was surprised you followed him to Nicaragua and captured his son."

Teddy, a little uncomfortable with his surroundings, looked around, "President Escudero's announcement about the twenty percent increase in oil production was an attempt to spoil your president's plans while appearing to stay with his bargain of this morning and, I believe the word is, *ingratiate* himself with the world press."

"I think we agree with you and judging from the yelling I heard coming from the Roosevelt Room, I think the president agrees with you as well."

"Perhaps it would be possible to sit down somewhere for a few minutes?" Teddy asked, "Away from so many ears."

I looked around, "I guess so, but we're guests here. Wait a minute, please." I saw Olivia standing at the other end of the corridor talking with another member of the staff. I walked down the corridor to her, "Excuse me, Olivia, is there a place the three of us," pointing to Liz and Teddy, "might conduct a short meeting?"

Olivia thought for a moment, turned, took a few steps into a small office, and looked around for a moment, "Well, we're pretty crowded, but yes, why don't you come in here."

I waved at Liz and Teddy to follow.

Olivia showed us into a well-furnished and equipped office, "The president uses this office sometimes. You can sit in here for a few minutes, but please don't touch anything, and you'll have to leave the door open." We thanked her and sat around a small coffee table, Liz, and Teddy on a small sofa, I on an upholstered chair.

Teddy began in a lowered voice, "What I am proposing would not have been possible until this morning." He leaned forward, "I can arrange to have President Escudero greeted by his doctors and an ambulance when he arrives in Venezuela. He will be placed in the ambulance and transported to a medical facility," Teddy grinned slightly, "where he can receive the medical treatment he needs for his exhaustion. I would not be surprised if his treatment should include a series of medications to hasten his recuperation in readiness for this retirement." Teddy went on to explain the rest of his plan, "Until President Escudero has 'recuperated,' the vice president, with the concurrence of the Asamblea Nacional, will take over the government as his office requires. I propose within the following week or ten days, he will meet with your president. After the meeting, the two will announce Venezuela's resolve to increase oil production as mandated by President Escudero and validate the twenty percent increase, but perhaps in increments. He will also accompany our delegates to the OPEC conference and deliver this message to the fellow members.

"There will then be no misunderstanding about Venezuela's intent. We may not be able to dissuade all the OPEC members from their current thinking, but as your president said, we will give some—I assume we were referring to Saudi Arabia—a platform from which to speak of opposition. In addition, as your president also said, Venezuela has the largest proven oil reserves in the world, including Saudi Arabia, so we bring legitimacy to the discussion. Barring further political discord in the area, I think we can persuade OPEC to table their proposed cuts, perhaps for an indefinite time."

"Teddy, this vice president, is he a good guy, and, more important, will he go along with your plan?" I asked.

"The vice president is the patriarch of one of the oldest families in Venezuela. He is a patriot. He has many friends in the business community and the *Asamblea Nacional*. He and

Escudero have been friends since their days in the army. Escudero appointed him vice president because of his influence among the old families and the *Asamblea Nacional*. However, the vice president has become disillusioned with President Escudero and his corrupt practices."

"He sounds like the right guy, but to outsiders like us he could just as easily be motivated by self-interest. I assume you are speaking to us because you want your idea in front of the president. Before Liz and I could agree to help you, we would have to be sure we are not replacing one tyrant with another. Are you sure of this man's motives?" I asked.

"And his willingness and ability to carry through with your plan," Liz added.

"The vice president is my father. I know him to be a man of *recusable* purpose and honesty. Once Escudero is out of the way, he will do what is necessary, and the rest of the government will follow. Father and I have talked many times of such things. As hard as it is to understand, Venezuela has found itself almost devoid of crucial industries. Agriculture, in particular. The country has been ravaged because of the many years of the expanding oil industry.

"This happened fifty years ago. Awash in petroleum, our industry, infrastructure, and social issues were ignored and decayed. The last time it took a national strike and several near revolutions to climb out of the chaos created by oil."

"Thus Alfonso's 'Oil is the Devil's excrement and will bring us ruin'—or words to that effect," I said.

"Precisely, and again we find ourselves close to ruin. A country with such a rich history and culture in agriculture that cannot feed its citizens is an abomination.

"If you can arrange such a meeting between my father and your president, Venezuela will reinforce its resolve to increase petroleum production—but with your country's help we also wish to announce a comprehensive program to rejuvenate Venezuela's agriculture. The profits from the increased production will be spent in the United States for farm and agriculture supplies and equipment. In addition, we will fund scholarship and exchange programs so our young people can attend universities in this country that specialize in agricultural studies and fund programs that will allow your scholars to teach agriculture in our universities.

"The funds will further support grants and loans to our farmers to revitalize their operations and allow them to pay better wages. Eventually, we will expand these programs to other industries such as manufacturing and transportation.

"With our new transparent government, we will invest our oil monies in growth industries and investments here in the United States. Returns from these investments and yes, petroleum revenues will be invested in our industries, reducing unemployment that will, in turn, begin the process of reducing the cost of our *bolívares* so Venezuelan goods will again be competitive in the world markets. True, this will be only the first of many steps to success, but such measures will help us be less dependent on oil. We can no longer be a country for only oil."

"Well, your plan, I assume by necessity, seems very complex, but I certainly applaud your motives," I said.

"I know it is an ambitious plan and will take much time, but it will be the start of a better future for Venezuela."

"I see a major problem, a political problem. The plan, as you outline, will give credence to the self-serving comments made by a criminal. Salvage your economy and you make Victor a hero. I can tell you with a degree of certainty that the president will not agree to help you unless you can convince her Victor Escudero will not survive politically."

"*Si*, yes, you are correct. That is why tomorrow or the day after, when he steps off the plane in Venezuela, he will have to be retired. Vice president

Sabas will take power immediately, and the Escudero administration will be finished."

I looked at Liz. We were both wondering what 'finished' implied, but neither of us said anything. I was starting to care less and less about Venezuela and its problems. I wanted to go sailing.

"Well, now all we have to do is get in front of the president. She's probably sick of the sight of us by now," Liz said.

CHAPTER TWENTY-SEVEN

Our discussions were interrupted by strident and animated conversations coming down the corridor. The president burst into the room along with Jonathan Collins.

The president looked at us, walked over, and sat behind her desk.

"Gentlemen, and lady, I'm going to have to ask you to excuse us. I'm several hours behind, and I still have to work out damage control. That smug SOB, I'll retire him permanently."

By this time, the three of us we were standing.

"Madam President, we may have a solution to that problem, if you will allow us a minute of your time."

She looked at us for a moment, then she leaned back in her chair, "Okay, let's hear it. What do you have for me? Johnny, take a seat."

"Madam President, we may be able to arrange for President Escudero to be met by some doctors and an ambulance when he arrives in Caracas tomorrow. Once he is in the care of these medical professionals, he will immediately be transported to a restful atmosphere where he can receive the attention and recuperation he requires."

"He's going to need medical attention to get my foot out of his ass!" the president offered.

"Yes, ma'am. Once President Escudero is recuperating from his various maladies, Vice President Sabas will step into office, and within days of taking over the responsibilities of governing, he would like to meet with you to discuss President Escudero's promises of increased oil production and representation at the OPEC conference."

The president held up her hand for me to stop talking, then looked at Teddy. "Sir, isn't your name Sabas?"

"Yes, ma'am, Teodoro Sabas, the vice president, is my father."

"That's what I thought. You and your father cook up this plan?"

"Madam President, I have had an opportunity to speak with my father, and the plan, as you call it, is held in the hearts of all Venezuelan patriots. It is an answered prayer."

"Uh-huh," the president looked at me, then at Collins, "Okay, go on."

"As Teddy, I mean Mr. Sabas, said, the vice president is his father, but I am told he is also a member of one of the oldest and most influential families in Venezuela—"

"I know who he is," interrupted the president.

"Then, ma'am, you also know he is not a fan of President Escudero and has immense support from the leading members of the Venezuelan political and business communities. Ma'am, according to Teddy, this could be the opportunity they have all been waiting for."

The president nodded, so I continued, "Venezuela's economy has become predominantly dominated by the petrochemical industry and, as a result, its other resources suffer from inflation. This has created a dependence on foreign suppliers for staples and has caused substantial unemployment—"

"Yes, it's known as Dutch disease, hyper interest in natural resources such as oil or minerals leads to a decline in other sectors of the economy. Go on."

"Yes, ma'am, Vice President Sabas wants to rectify this crisis by reintroducing agriculture, manufacturing, and other non-oil-related industries into the economy. And, ma'am, they see Escudero's capitulation as an opportunity to make this happen or at least to start to make it happen."

"Is there a *but* in there somewhere?" the president asked.

"Ma'am, for standing by President Escudero's proclamation of increased oil production and subsequent representation at OPEC to promote this decision and the U.S. position, Vice President Sabas would like your permission to announce a joint U.S.–Venezuelan resolution to rejuvenate Venezuela's agriculture."

The president said, "I just heard the sound of a cash register."

"Madam President, Vice President Sabas will announce that the, shall we say, *surplus oil production* will be shipped in U.S. registered bottoms to Venezuelan refineries in the United States, bringing dollars and employment into the states." This would be news to Teddy, but he didn't flinch.

The president interjected, "You mean if I don't seize the refineries."

"Yes, ma'am, if you don't seize them." I thought I saw a slight grin on the president's face.

The president jutted her chin at me. "Okay, go on."

"Madam President, the profits from the increased production or surplus will be invested and spent in the United States to help curb Venezuela's Dutch Disease in part by buying supplies, equipment, and services from U.S. companies to rejuvenate Venezuelan agriculture and related industries. These profits will also fund various scholarship and exchange programs with U.S. universities to further enhance Venezuela's agriculture. Perhaps later the program will be expanded to encompass other industries such as manufacturing and transportation.

"Ma'am, this plan will give credibility to President Escudero's comments. Instead of Escudero rolling us under the bus, the joke will be on him," I said.

"Mr. Sabas, one of the chief causes of Dutch Disease is greed. You understand that this is all a waste of time and money unless you guys create a government that looks out for the country's interest instead of lining each other's pockets."

"Yes, Madam President, my father looks forward to establishing a government open and transparent to the people. He and the Venezuelan Central Bank will develop monetary and investment policy and ensure that corruption is a thing of the past.

"Yeah, well, you have your work cut out for you. I wish you well, and we will help as we can, obviously. We would like Venezuela as a partner and an ally, but I don't want that SOB Escudero to get credit for this. You think about that?"

"Yes, ma'am, Teddy assures us that President Escudero will be retiring the moment he steps off the plane."

We discussed several details, then the president stared at us for a time and looked over at Collins, who nodded.

"Okay, let's do it!" the president said.

CHAPTER TWENTY-EIGHT

"Olivia!" the president yelled. A rapid clatter of heels from the hall, then Olivia stuck her head through the door. "Yes, ma'am?"

"Ask the chairman of the Joint Chiefs and the director of the CIA to call me on a secure phone."

"Right away, Madam President."

"Okay, here is what we are going to do. I want you three to get down to Simón Bolívar before President Escudero gets there," the president looked at Teddy. "Is that where he will land?"

"Yes, Madam President, I believe so, but he often lands at General Francisco de Miranda. It is a military airbase not far from Simón Bolívar," Teddy answered.

"Okay, I want you three to get there before he does and make sure all the wrinkles have been smoothed out of this before Escudero arrives."

"Wrinkles?" Teddy asked.

"In other words, make sure your father and his people are on board, and make sure the rest and recuperation place you spoke of is willing to accept Escudero and that they will agree to keep him under wraps until his term expires. Despite whom or what he is, Escudero is going to have some loyal followers, and I don't want them interfering with his retirement. I need you people down there to make sure everything goes as planned. What time do you think Escudero will arrive in Caracas?"

"He is scheduled to depart your Andrews Air Base at nine tomorrow morning, so he should arrive at Caracas about one in the afternoon," Teddy replied.

The president looked at me, "If in your judgment this thing is going sideways, you are to hightail it back here pronto. Got it?"

Me! I have no part in this. I'm going sailing. I don't have the first clue how to handle something like this. Stunned, I sat there trying to get my brain and mouth to work. *Please Lord, get me out of this!* I finally got my mouth to work, if not my brain. "Yes, ma'am, if you feel I am qualified to make that judgment," I said.

"It's your idea. Who else is qualified? Plus, you will have Teddy with you," the president said, looking at Teddy. "You will go with them, right?"

"Yes, ma'am, both Adel and I will go."

"Who's Adel?"

"She is my wife and also an agent for Bolivarian Republic of Venezuela."

"I see. Well, if you think it's—"

Liz broke in, "Madam President, we know Adel. She probably saved my life. From our perspective, she would be an asset to our trip."

"Okay, whatever you need. But as I was about to say, you're the one in the hot seat. If you need some guidance, call me. I'll leave instructions and your name with the operator."

Out of the corner of my eye, I saw Jonathan Collins squirm in his chair and give me a black look. I said, "Yes, ma'am, call if I need help."

"Otherwise, I want to stay out of it as much as possible," the president said.

Olivia poked her head through the door again, "Madam President, General Wallace Smith and Director Andrew Taylor are on the phone."

"Thank you, Olivia, please close the door." The president pushed two buttons on her phone, then pushed a third. "Wally, Andy, you are on the speaker with Johnny Collins and three others who will for now remain nameless. One is a foreign national, he is one of the good guys, but watch what you say."

The men replied in unison, "Good afternoon, Madam President."

"Gentlemen, I need something put together that's going to require help from both of you. Can you two play nice?"

Both assured the president that they could and would cooperate fully with each other.

"Good. Sorry to do this over the phone, but I don't have time to have you over here. Wally, I need an airplane at Andrews ready to go, wheels up, in about four hours. It has to look like a civilian airplane and have a range of about six thousand miles, fuel, and food for about a dozen and crew. Better, give me two crews. I also need some good communications on board, so you can't lease it. Can you do it?"

"Yes, ma'am, I think so. I'll need to make a call. May I ask where the plane is going?"

"No, but suffice it to say it's going foreign, and I want the crews to look like civilians, at least dressed like civilians. Wally, while you're at it, find out if we have any guys in South America, Seals, or special-ops types, that I can have real fast."

"Yes, ma'am, I'll get right back to you." With an electronic click, the general disconnected.

"Okay, Andy, I need some of your people equally fast. People I can use as protection and muscle for the team I'm sending on this mission. I want them to—" she looked at me. "We don't have time for any type of cover, any ideas?"

"I don't know, ma'am, an oil company," I thought for a moment. "No, not an oil company. They will be too well known. How about a supply company of some kind, or a manufacturer that supplies drilling or pumping equipment to the oil companies?"

The president nodded, "Andy, how about it, can you put something together?"

"Well, ma'am, on this short notice, I can have some business cards made, but I'll try to put together something more substantial."

"Tell you what, Andy. Find about eight people. I want them gray, dumpy, bald with lots of smiles, even if you have to pull some out of retirement and add a female or two. If need be, they can play tourist, but give them some briefcases and a couple of business cards and whatever weapons you think necessary. I want them to look like executives or tourists, not a bunch of assassins. They can use their own passports, if you like, or other identification if it doesn't say CIA. See if you can find some Spanish language skills, too, that would be a plus."

"Yes, ma'am, you want these people sent to Andrews, right?"

"Yeah, I'll have General Smith call you with the details. Oh, and Andy—"

"Yes, ma'am."

"If necessary, your people will need to be mean as snakes."

"Yes, ma'am. I just had a thought. I have the guy you want."

"Great. When Wally calls, make sure he tells you where your people are to meet my team, and tell him I'll have you two over for dinner next week and fill you in on what's going on."

"Thank you, ma'am. I believe I know the circumstances, but I look forward to dinner. Oh, ma'am, who should my folks report to?"

The president hesitated, then said, "For now, tell them to report to Sam Spade."

"Sam Spade, yes, ma'am." Director Taylor hung up.

"Sam Spade?" I said.

"Yeah, I know. It's all I could think of. Your name isn't too well thought of in some circles. Perhaps I should say you are an acquired taste. Anyway, I'd just as soon you stay in the background until you get on the plane."

"So, am I Effie Perine or Brigid O'Shaughnessy?" Liz said.

The president grinned, "I think you're more a Jo Ann Vallenari from *Tequila Sunrise*."

Liz laughed, "Thank you, ma'am, I've seen the movie."

Olivia came over the intercom, "Madam President, General Smith on the secure phone."

The president hit a button on her phone, "What do you have for me, Wally?"

"Ma'am, I found a C-37B, a military version of the G550. It belongs to the air force, but it has no livery. It's just plain white. Plus, it has some good com gear. It has about a seven-thousand-mile range and can max out about Mach point eight. I got you two crews and a commo guy. It will have room for thirteen or fourteen passengers. It's in Delaware now, but I just ordered it into Andrews, so it should be here in about forty-five minutes. I told them to go to the special-ops hangar. When it gets in, I have ordered a full load of fuel and food. Will you need a steward, ma'am?"

"No, they can make their own coffee. What time can the plane and crew be ready?"

"I should say no later than four o'clock, ma'am."

"Did you find some special-ops guys for me?"

"Yes, ma'am, we have some Delta Force guys in Panama doing some jungle warfare training. We can use some MH-53Js. They have terrain-following radar designed for low-level penetration, and we can refuel in the air."

"Wally, if I need them, they'll only get a few minutes' notice. It might be dark and will be in an urban area with lots of civilians. The distance from Panama to our target area is probably about nine hundred miles. I think that's going to be a problem."

"Ma'am, at nine hundred miles, that's going to be about five hours with refueling."

"No, five hours is too long. What else do you have?"

The general was quiet for a moment, then said, "Well, we could get some CV-22 Ospreys out of Tampa. They have some B versions that have about the same equipment as the 53Js. They could do the same trip in a little over two hours. They aren't very stealthy, though. We're about the only ones that have them, so if they're spotted the other guys will know who we are."

The president looked at me, "What do you think?"

I was caught mentally flat-footed again. *How the hell do I know? I'm a real estate developer.* "Ma'am, we probably won't need their help, but if we do, we will need it fast."

Teddy spoke up, "Madam President, the airport is on the coast, so if the aircraft could come in very close over the water they wouldn't be seen until they landed. By the time anyone noticed, they could be gone."

"Wally."

"Yes, Madam President."

"We have bases in Curaçao and Aruba, right?"

"Yes, ma'am, we have an airbase in Curaçao. But, ma'am, the Venezuelans have a fit every time we fly combat aircraft in there. That may not help with your mission."

The president laughed, "You didn't fall off the turnip truck yesterday, did you, Wally?"

"Well, ma'am, if I wasn't smart enough to figure out some of this stuff, you'd fire me."

"Get the Ospreys to Curaçao. For now, tell the crews it's a training mission and get some special operations forces or whatever you can spare in there, too. I guess you can bring both out of Tampa, but I'll leave that to you. Tampa or Panama makes no difference to me."

"Ma'am, what do you want me to tell the SOF people?"

"Tell them if they go in, it's to save American lives, but tell them not to start a war. I'd like them in place no later than ten o'clock tomorrow morning. Is that enough time?"

"It's going to be tight, but yes, ma'am, I think we can make it."

"If my guys need them, it will probably happen about one in the afternoon, so tell your men not to take a long lunch break."

"They are really capable people, ma'am. They will do a good job for you."

"Okay, their contact and control on the ground is Sam Spade. Call Andy Taylor and tell him I want his people in the Andrews hangar no later than five this afternoon. And, Wally, thanks, damn good job."

"Yes, ma'am, and thank you, ma'am." General Smith disconnected, then the president looked over at us. The president looked at me, "Okay, you'll have backup from special ops soon as you pick up the phone. Curaçao can't be more than fifteen minutes away from where you will land. I have no idea what else to tell you, so you will have to make it up as you go. So far, you've been pretty good at that. Just get the job done." The president directed her attention to Teddy, "Teddy, if Escudero wiggles loose from your dad, as sure as I'm sitting here, the first thing he's going to do is renege on his retirement plans, no matter what happens to Reynaldo. Moreover, if he finds out about this little operation, he'll probably retire you and your father permanently. Your father needs to get up to speed on this real fast."

"Yes, Madam President, my father has called an emergency meeting of the key members of the Asamblea Nacional. The meeting will take place tomorrow morning at nine o'clock. It's timed to take place while President Escudero is on his airplane, en route to Caracas."

The president sat back and squirmed in her seat, "Yeah, if he doesn't leave this afternoon or tonight."

"I don't think he will leave before tomorrow. There is a party at the Embassy in his honor, celebrating his contributions to Venezuela. I thought as cultural attaché I could do no less for my beloved *presidente*," Teddy replied with a wide grin.

The president chuckled, "Okay, you people get on your way. Call me if you need anything. If you can't get me, call Johnny."

"Teddy, there is communication equipment on the plane that will allow you to talk with your father or me or both, so use it if you need to. If your father wants to speak with me, I will be available anytime."

"Yes, ma'am. Thank you, Madam President."

The president looked at me, "Remember what I told General Smith. Don't start a war. And leave that damn machine gun of yours at home."

"Yes, ma'am," I replied.

The president turned to Collins, "Johnny, get some transportation for them, and see that they get anything they need."

Collins said, "Ma'am, if you like, I would be happy to go with them."

"Thanks, Johnny, I need you here to run things from this end."

Missed the bullet that time, I thought.

Each occupied with our own thoughts, Elizabeth, Teddy, and I walked out to the portico to wait for a car. I suspected Elizabeth was thinking the same thing I was, how in the hell did we get into this mess. I thought back to the sixth grade and Ms. Elinor's mandatory compositions on what we did on our summer vacations. She always suspected I made things up. She certainly wouldn't believe this. "Welcome to spies are us," I said.

Liz turned to me and said, "What are we doing? This is real espionage. We're not trained for this."

Teddy, still assuming we were real agents, and his and Adel's counterparts, gave us a puzzled look but didn't say anything.

"It's not really espionage. You're a businesswoman, right?"

"Yes, so?"

"Well, I'm a businessman. As businessmen or businesspeople, whatever, we are going on a business trip with some colleagues for a short overseas meeting. When we get there, we will just stand around and watch events, drink Piña coladas, enjoy some sun, then come home. How hard can that be?"

"Do you remember the last short, overseas meeting we attended?"

"Yeah, but this time we will be in a populated area and in one of the largest airports in South America."

"Yes, well, there are some Venezuelans that don't like you and me very much, and I had just as soon not find out what they do to people they don't care for, especially if we are actually in Venezuela," Liz answered.

"May I remind you that it was almost entirely your idea that we get involved in this little adventure," I said.

"That's when we were on our boat sailing around Newport and Block Island, not flying off to dangerous countries run by dangerous, lunatic drug smugglers!" Liz paused, "Sorry, Teddy, no offense."

"Elizabeth is correct. This could be perilous, especially if President Escudero lands at the General Francisco de Miranda Air Base. General Francisco is an old military airport, and if we are arrested, there it could be very bad," Teddy said.

"Well," I said, "let's make sure he lands at Simón Bolívar."

"And how are we going to do that?" Liz asked.

"I don't know, but we had better figure it out in the next twenty-four hours. You heard the president. We're good at making it up as we go."

CHAPTER TWENTY-NINE

Joint Base Andrews, Maryland

Liz and I were driven home, where I changed into some khaki slacks and a yellow golf shirt while Liz put on a pair of blue jeans and a blue striped T-shirt. We each wore boat shoes. As Liz packed a change of clothes and toothbrushes for us, I went to my safe, grabbed our passports and a Colt 1911A1 I kept in the safe. I didn't figure on any fireworks, but having the big Colt made me feel better than not having it.

Teddy decided against returning to the Embassy on the chance that he might be detained by business, so he sent word to Adel to meet him at Andrews. Collins assured Teddy that they would have access through the main gate then be escorted to the hangar where we would all meet.

Andrews Air Force Base is named for General Frank Andrews, one of the founders of the United States Army Air Forces, which later became the United States Air Force. He was also the first lieutenant general to die in the Second World War. Now home to the Air Force, Navy, and Marine units, it is called Joint Base Andrews. Known simply as Andrews to the locals, it is probably most identified as the home of the president's airplane, *Air Force One*.

Elizabeth and I arrived about four-thirty at what presumably was the special operations hangar, which looked large enough to house a Boeing 747, maybe two. The driver stopped the car beside a large business jet parked in front of the hangar. We unloaded our two bags and thanked the driver. The plane in front of us was a C-37B. As General Smith said, it was all white. The only identification was the tail number painted across the vertical stabilizer, which was capped by a pulsating strobe light.

A pleasantly mannered but rather stern-looking young man escorted us onto the plane. He was in his late twenties, early thirties with a ruddy, all-American, Midwest look. About five feet eight inches, he had short blond hair and was dressed in an unadorned, green jumpsuit common to military pilots. He introduced himself as Mr. Schultz.

Remembering just in time to use my temporary moniker and trying not to laugh, I introduced myself, "Mr. Schultz, I'm Sam Spade. This is my wife, Elizabeth."

"Yes, sir, we have been expecting you. The other two passengers are on board, and we are ready to take off whenever you are."

I looked around the aircraft. It was fitted with an assortment of comfortable-looking seats with a central aisle like all passenger planes, but the seats were divided, two to port, and one to starboard of the aisle, some with tables or desks. Two sections were arranged like small conference areas, the seats facing inboard. Some were in clusters, two sets of doubles facing each other so the occupants could converse with passengers sitting opposite. In the forward part of the cabin on the starboard side was a small console with various types of electronic equipment built into a console.

"Is this the comm setup?"

"Yes, sir, I'm the communications specialist."

"Is the crew on board?" I asked.

"The skipper and copilot are forward, sir. The relief crew is in the hangar, ahh, making a head call. That is, they are—"

"I know what a head call is, Mr. Schultz. Please tell the captain that we have additional people coming. It will be a few minutes before we can leave."

"Yes, sir." Schultz turned and walked forward to the front of the airplane.

Liz and I walked to the back of the plane, where Teddy and Adel stood as we walked up. Teddy was still in his business suit. Adel was dressed in cream linen slacks with a brown silk blouse and conservative cream-colored heels.

"Hello, Adel, you may remember my wife, Elizabeth. The two of you met at the gala in Newport."

"*Si*, yes, I remember you were most beautiful woman in all the party."

"Thank you, Adel, that's most kind. I believe I owe you for saving my life. I'm not sure how I can ever repay you."

"Your husband, he saves you. I just tell him where you are. Perhaps we can all enjoy dinner sometime and make joke of this."

"Yes, I would enjoy that very much," Liz said, meaning every word.

We heard some noise outside the plane. Through the small Plexiglas window, I saw the last of three black Suburban's drive up to the airplane. What I assumed to be our CIA escorts unloaded an assortment of bags from the SUVs and clambered aboard. I could not help but notice several golf bags strewn among the luggage. I wondered if these guys played golf with Silvers and Collins.

Director Taylor sent five men and three women, all in their fifties, most with gray hair. One of the men was bald, shaved bald, not natural. With one exception, none of them was flabby. Tanned and fit, they looked as if they just came off the back nine, or maybe the cast for a seniors-only resort commercial. The bald man walked to the back of the plane, where the four of us were seated. I stood and shook hands, introduced the others and myself.

He said, "Hi, I'm Jerry McGuire. I'm in charge of this op."

Jerry was about six feet tall, distinguished looking, and dressed in expensive slacks. He wore a polo shirt, probably because his neck wouldn't fit a collared shirt. Like the others, he was tan, but he was also muscular, the muscles you get when you work at it.

"The little guy up front said you were the president's aides and would brief me. Here's what we are going to do. Soon as the bird gets in the air, I'll get my people together, then you come down and make your presentation. Then I guess we can handle it from there."

"So, Jerry, you guys plan on playing a little golf?" I asked.

He turned to look at the golf bags at the front of the plane, then turned back to me.

"Yeah, we brought a couple .308 five irons."

Without another word, Jerry turned and walked back up the aisle, then apparently told Mr. Shultz to get underway. He sat down and fastened his seat belt.

Liz looked at me, "Should I ask him if he wants a hot towel? He seems to have had enough to drink."

"Let's get in the air first, then I'll take care of the chain of command."

"What does .308 five iron mean?" Adel asked.

"It means he has a couple of Remington Model 700 sniper rifles in those bags." The phone next to me buzzed. It startled me, but I recovered quickly and answered with my best authoritative, "Hello?"

"This is the pilot, at least the one that's driving. I know this is all very hush, hush, and everything, but before I take off, you mind telling me where we're going?"

"You don't know?"

"All I know is we have enough fuel to get to Paris, maybe Tokyo, so if you can't narrow it down some, I say we go to Paris. Supposed to be nice this time of year."

"Caracas, Venezuela."

"Any particular place, or you want I should put it down on the *Avenida Libertador*?"

"Simón Bolívar," I said, sheepishly.

"Okay, but Paris is better. Should be about four hours. I'll let you know more when we get to altitude." The phone went dead. I looked at it for a moment, then clipped it back into its cradle. I made a mental note to work on the authoritative in-command thing.

Liz had remembered to bring some magazines, as had Adel. The two women read, traded magazines, and gossiped about various miscreant movie stars. Teddy, in a major concession to comfort, loosened his tie, then went to sleep. I tried to relax and figure out how we were going to force President Escudero to land at Simón Bolívar if he really wanted to land at General Francisco de Miranda. The phone buzzed.

"Your friendly airplane driver again. We are at forty-eight thousand. Should be in Caracas in three hours sixteen minutes."

I said, "Thank you, captain." The phone was dead before I finished—man of few words.

I got to my feet, trying not to disturb the two women now sleeping, and walked forward to the communications console. Mr. Schultz was reading the *Washington Times*. I sat next to him with my back to the passengers. Without preamble, I said, "The captain can talk to me on that phone. Can I talk to him?"

"Yes, sir, just push button one. If you need the crew quarters, press number two. I'm three. The galley is four. And the head is five."

"Can I talk to the ground on it?"

"Yes, sir, but I have to arrange the call from here, then you press the green button and the red to terminate the call. We can transmit in the clear or scrambled, and we can use satellite or cell. Plus a few others I can't tell you about."

"That's okay. Can we get the White House operator?"

"The White House, sir? Ahh, yes, sure, we can get the White House."

"Okay, in a few minutes I'm going to buzz you, and I want you to get the president on the phone. Tell the White House operator it's Sam Spade. Can we put the call up on the PA system? The plane has a PA system, right?"

Mr. Shultz looked uncomfortable. Small beads of perspiration were forming on his forehead. He swallowed hard, "Yes, sir, the jet has a PA system."

"I'll call you back in a minute." I stood then walked back to my seat in the rear of the plane. Most of the CIA people were sleeping, but Jerry McGuire—*I assumed not his real name, but better than Sam Spade,* I thought—was having a lively conversation with his seatmate. He saw me and smiled, "We'll have that meeting in an hour or so." I smiled back but said nothing.

In my seat, I pushed button three. Schultz answered. "Mr. Schultz, put me through to the White House. Ask for the president. Tell her it's Sam Spade. And, Mr. Schultz, when she comes on, I want everyone on the plane to hear the conversation, including the crew."

"Yes, sir, I'll call you back." Mr. Schultz didn't sound very happy.

Five minutes later, the phone buzzed, "Sir, I have the president for you." The PA system crackled with some electronic noise.

"Go ahead, Madam President," Schultz said.

"This is Harriet Jackson. Sam, that you?"

"Yes, ma'am. Madam President, you are on speakerphone."

"Okay, no off-color jokes. What's up?"

"Ma'am, we took off about an hour ago and should be in Simón Bolívar in about two hours. Director Taylor's people look perfect for the part."

"Good, did General Smith fix you up okay?"

"Yes, ma'am, absolutely no complaints. The plane has no markings other than the tail number and, as you can tell, the communications equipment seems first-rate."

"All right, Sam do a good job for me, and give my best to Jo Ann."

The line went dead. The plane was quiet except for the engine noise. No one was sleeping. No one was talking. Liz looked at me, winked, then turned over and closed her eyes.

I punched the number three button on the phone, "Schultz, will you come back here, please?"

Schultz left his console and walked to the rear of the plane, swiveling from side to side, dodging tables, and seats.

"Yes, sir?"

I stood. Standing close to him, I asked in a subdued voice. "Are we going to have any problems with the aircrew? These CIA people I can handle, but I need to know that the crew is one hundred percent committed. If not, I'll pull the plug, and we can all go back to the barn."

Schultz pulled himself up straight until his head almost touched the overhead. His voice went hard, "Sir, we are Marines. We are all combat veterans, and we were ordered by the president to provide you with support. I assure you we will provide you with every assistance we can render."

"You guys are Marines?"

"Yes, sir. Except for Lieutenant Commander Vincent. He's Navy. I'm a warrant officer in the Marine Corps." His voice still had a steely edge.

I extended my hand to shake his, and with as big a grin as I could muster said, "Semper Fi, Marine."

His demeanor lightened, "You're a Marine, sir?"

"Former. And I was a sergeant, so you can drop the 'sir' stuff."

"Yes, sir."

"So, the crew is all Marine aviation?" I asked, "Except Vincent."

"Yes, sir, we all came from SOCOM out of MacDill in Tampa. Sir, all these men can fly the wings off this or any other airplane. Even the copilots are usually left-seat guys."

"Okay, but let's keep the wings on this one. Tell me about the captain."

"The skipper. That is, Colonel Barrett, the aircraft commander. He's flying now. He's tough as nails. He's had some grunt time, too. Had to bail out once and came down in the middle of what was left of a Marine rifle company. Anyway, they were chewed up pretty bad, lost their officers and NCOs. The colonel took command, and they held off the bad guys for three days with hardly any ammo and no food. When they ran out of ammo, he called an airstrike on their own position. The last night out, he had everyone throwing rocks trying to make the hajis think they were grenades. The colonel actually killed two of them with his K-Bar.

"Sir, these pilots are the best. When the chairman of the joint chiefs and the president ask for a crew, they get the best."

"How about you, warrant officer? Are you any good?"

CWO Shultz grinned slightly and said, "I can keep up, sir."

I smiled, "I'll bet you can. Back in my day, out of respect, we used to call warrant officers *gunners*. Do you mind if I call you gunner?"

"Sir, I'm a commo guy. But, no sir, I don't mind at all. Thank you." Schultz looked around, then lowered his voice, "Sir, you're the one who took out those guys in Nicaragua, aren't you?"

"Yeah, but Annie Oakley here did most of the shooting."

"I knew it was a Marine. Textbook L-shape ambush, and they were taken out by an M14. Sir, there was a report by the Coast Guard about someone hosing down a boat with an M14. I don't suppose that was you, too?"

"Probably not. That's all supposed to be pretty confidential. How did you know about it?"

"Sir, terrorist is what we do. Anything that smells like a terrorist act comes up on our radar. Plus, I'm a com guy, so I hear stuff." Schultz turned his attention to Liz, now wide awake, "Ma'am, is that true what Mr. Spade said about you taking out those bad guys?"

Liz looked at me, and I nodded.

"Yes, Mr. Schultz, unfortunately, it's true. The 'old sarge' here taught me a few tricks over the years, but I never dreamed I would have to use them for anything but punching holes in a piece of paper."

Adel and Teddy, now awake, looked at Elizabeth with a combination of disbelief and admiration.

"Gunner, I will need you to contact Venezuela every so often so Mr. Sabas here can speak with his father regularly, but I want to do it over the phone as opposed to using the radio. Can that be done?"

"Yes, sir. All I need is the telephone exchange, and we can get him through, no problem."

Teddy looked between CWO Schultz and me and said, "What is SOCOM?"

Then Liz said, "I know what SOCOM is, but what's a gunner?"

Schultz said, "SOCOM stands for United States Special Operations Command. It's a joint-service outfit that fights terrorism worldwide. We do other classified stuff, too. We're headquartered at MacDill Air Force Base in Tampa, Florida."

I continued, "A chief warrant officer with the specific job as a weapons officer holds a unique title of *Marine gunner,* with an insignia that looks like a bursting bomb. Over the years, as a term of respect, Marines started calling all warrant officers *gunner,* though it's actually incorrect. Warrant officers may also be called *mister.*"

Gunner Schultz stood from the chair arm he was leaning on, "Well, if you all will excuse me, I best get back to my console," then he walked back to the forward part of the plane.

"Okay, Teddy, why don't you go up to the communications console with Schultz and contact your father. For now, make sure we can get into the airport without trouble and ask that he be available, maybe by cell phone. We will need his counsel and help when we get organized. Please ask whether we can do anything for him that we aren't already doing."

"Okay, Mr. Sam Spade," he grinned as he stood and followed Schultz down the aisle.

CHAPTER THIRTY

The hum of the engines and the warm cabin made me drowsy, and I dozed lightly while trying to come up with a way to persuade Escudero to land at Simón Bolívar. I had to assume his communications were as good as ours. Perhaps not all the satellite stuff, but certainly good enough to talk to some of his followers in Venezuela. I also had to assume he would know about Sabas's surprise party. Hell, he could land at any of a half dozen airports, and there was nothing I could do about it.

I had to rely on his megalomaniac ego, which would not allow him to land anywhere but in the capital city. But he wasn't stupid. He would go for General Francisco de Miranda, where he and his loyalist could control the airport and surrounding area.

Best concentrate on the one airport I could do something about, General Miranda, and forget the others. The question was what? We could have their ATC tell them to land at Bolívar, but he could easily counter the order. Close General Miranda for maintenance. He could counter that, too.

Something was rolling around in my fog of sleep, something Mr. Schultz had said—then I remembered. Schultz told me, "These men could fly the wings off this or any other airplane."

I snapped awake and jumped up banging my head on the overhead, "That's it!"

Startled, Liz and Adel looked up from their magazines, "What's the matter?" Liz asked.

"I know how to do it," I exclaimed, then almost ran up the aisle to where Teddy and Schultz were sitting at the com console.

"You know how to do what?" Liz yelled after me.

"Gunner, do you have any aerial charts of Caracas?" Not waiting for an answer, "See if you can find some aerials of General Francisco de Miranda Air Base. You can probably get some off the internet, and while you're at it get some aerials of the Simón Bolívar airport."

"Yes, sir, I'll bring them back to you in a few minutes."

"Great, thanks."

Ignoring the stares from the other passengers, I went back and flopped down across from Liz.

"What is going on?" she asked.

I grinned, "I know how we're going to keep Escudero from landing at General Miranda."

"How?"

I gave Liz a smug look and said, "It's a secret."

"Okay, James Bond, just so it doesn't involve me lying down in a mosquito-infested rainforest." Sticking her face back in the magazine she said, "Call me when it's not a secret."

"How soon you forget who you're sleeping with. It's Sam Spade."

"You have your dreams, I have mine," Liz said, turning a page.

Gunner Schultz showed up carrying some papers, "Here are the charts. And I printed some aerials, several of each airport."

"Great, let's take a couple of minutes to look at them, then I think we'll get everyone together and go over the operation." I gathered all the material and moved midway down the fuselage to some seats equipped with a long table. The gunner followed.

"Gunner, can you use that internet map thing and get some street-level pictures of this area right here?" pointing to a place on the aerial.

"Better than that I can access a satellite."

"Great. When you finish, please give my compliments to Colonel Barrett, and ask him and any crewmen he can spare to join us. I'll need their advice on aircraft matters."

Everyone but Commander Vincent, who was flying the plane, gathered around the table, some standing, some sitting, all of them talking. Barrett and Major Huddleston, the second-in-command of the aircraft, joined the group. They were dressed in green flight suits sans insignia, but unlike the flight suit worn by Schultz, they were faded and stained from years of use. Barrett looked to be about forty-six, maybe forty-eight, trim, about six feet with a shaved head. I wondered if he and Jerry went to the same barber. Huddleston was two inches shorter and about ten years younger with short, dark hair; he was athletic with an impish grin. I started my presentation. "I suspect you have read in the paper or seen the news reports about the Venezuelan president stepping down due to reasons of health."

A collection of nodding and murmurs followed.

"I assure you it had nothing to do with his health. President Escudero is a narcotics trafficker and murderer. Besides killing many of his own citizens, he has embezzled as much as half a billion dollars from his country. He was, as they say, caught red-handed; however, the United States and Venezuela believe it to be in their best interests to let him retire and move on. Mr. and Mrs. Sabas here," I gestured to Teddy and Adel, "have placed their lives at risk to see that this jerk is removed from power, Mr. Sabas's father is the vice president of Venezuela and will run the country until there is a new election. President Jackson has vetted the principals and their motives in this transfer of power, so you can save any witty comments.

"President Escudero is a psychopath, and despite his recent assurances we think he has no intention of stepping down. Our objective is to help Vice President Sabas with President Escudero's retirement plan. We have no specific instructions other than to ensure President Escudero does not leave the airport by any means other than those prescribed by Vice President Sabas. Those instructions are to escort the very tired and ill President Escudero to a facility where he can rest and recuperate peacefully until his retirement at the end of the month. Sabas has control of the air force, and we think most of the army. The problem is Escudero was a career army officer and owes his presidency to his army connections, so he will still have many powerful friends inside its ranks.

"Our first problem is to make sure he lands at Simón Bolívar International and not at the General Francisco de Miranda Air Base, which is controlled by the army. The fun part will be to do this with just the people on this airplane."

Other than engine noise, the cabin was silent. Jerry McGuire was the first to speak, "So, did State or Langley give us an op plan?"

"As I said, we are to help Vice President Sabas. The only specifics come from the president and those were, and I quote, 'Don't start a war.'"

McGuire persisted, "I've seen your wife around some, but I've never run across you. You got the background for this, because I don't want my people involved in something that's going to blow up in our face."

"They're not your people, Jerry. They are my people, and if you can't play nice, I'll have the colonel here place you under arrest, cuff and gag you until I can throw you off the airplane. Are there any other comments or complaints?"

Other than the drone of the engines, the plane was silent.

"No? Well, Jerry is right in one respect. You agency people have years of experience doing this kind of stuff, so if you have constructive comments or suggestions, I want to hear them. Now, before I get into the 'op plan,' let's go over a couple of points. We do have an ace we can play if necessary. SOCOM is sending two maybe three CV-22s with a full complement of special op troops to Curaçao, which as you probably know is about fifteen minutes from Simón Bolívar. Colonel Barrett or Major Huddleston, I need you to appoint an air ops person who can handle the air and ground maneuvers, including staging our plane, President Escudero's plane, and should we need them, the CV-22s. All our arrivals and departures will have to be coordinated with the Simón Bolívar tower. I want the CV-22s' arrival as stealthy as possible. Any suggestions?"

Major Huddleston spoke up, "You had better let me do it. Last time the colonel here did anything like that, he called in ordnance on his own position. Most the guys think he did it for the medals, but I think he just can't read a map."

There was some laughter. The colonel glared at Huddleston, then looked at me, "You still haven't told us how you're going to keep Escudero out of General Miranda? The only way I know to control or close a hostile airport is to take over the airfield with troops or bomb the runway. Seeing as the president has discouraged us from starting a war, she will probably frown on both options. Plus, we have to do it just prior to the arrival of Escudero's plane so he is low on fuel and has to land at the next closest airport, Simón Bolívar. So, you got a plan?"

"Yep—we're going to crash a plane on the runway."

CHAPTER THIRTY- ONE

Air Force C-37B, in Flight over the Caribbean Sea

Jerry shouted over the din of laughter and crude appraisals of my intellect, "Are you serious?"

"Very serious," I said. "Now, if you all have finished with your votes of confidence and kind support, please settle down so we can discuss the details. If you have suggestions, please wait until I've finished."

Spreading the charts and aerial photographs on the table, I waited while the eight CIA retirees, three crewmembers, and the Sabase's gathered around the table. Liz pushed through the crowd and sat next to me. I began outlining my plan, confident it was as harebrained as it sounded. "Vice President Sabas will tell the air traffic control people to order Escudero's pilots to Simón Bolívar for the welcome-home reception and arrangements that will be at the east end of Simón Bolívar field. I'll tell you in a minute why the east end."

"Okay, but if Escudero wants to land at General Francisco, he's not going to give a damn about air controllers. How do you close the General Francisco runway?" Jerry asked again. "You can't just crash an airplane."

"That's both the easiest and the riskiest part of the plan," I said. You can see from the aerials," pointing to the papers on the desk, "the General Francisco de Miranda Air Base, fortunately, has only one runway. You will also notice a road that runs around the perimeter of the runway. And right here," pointing to the aerial, "the road comes within two-hundred feet of the runway—"

Jerry interrupted, "Yeah, so?"

"How about giving the man a chance to finish," Colonel Barrett said.

I continued, "We will rent an airplane with retractable gear and preferably one with a low wing. The retractable gear so we can make a gear-up landing, and the low wing to minimize damage to the cockpit and injury to the pilot."

"Jerry, when I come to a stop, one of your teams will be waiting in a car on the perimeter road next to the runway."

"What do you mean 'when I come to a stop'? You're not going to be on that plane. This damn airplane is full of pilots with a lot more experience than you have. Let one of them do it!" Liz snapped.

"True, but I'll bet I'm the only one who has a private pilot's license and a medical certificate. I'll tell the FBO that I am a tourist out for a pleasant ride around the countryside. Then as a stupid American tourist, I will become disoriented and land at the wrong airport without extending the gear."

One of the female CIA people said, "If this is a military airport, you're going to look pretty conspicuous. I've done some flying myself. The tower will be screaming at you long before you get over the threshold."

"Good point, but according to Teddy, the military use the airbase as their private flying club. It's common to see civilian aircraft fly in and out of the airport. I probably won't even be noticed."

Liz interjected, "Well, you're sure as hell going to be noticed after your spectacular landing. How do you propose to get out of there? Escudero and his thugs would love to get their hands on you, he being such a big fan and all. Not to mention he's probably a little annoyed that you got his kid shot and then killed half of his little private army!"

Everyone in the cabin looked at me, "My wife exaggerates—"

"The hell I do! You may remember I was there."

"—but her point is well taken and the reason I mentioned the perimeter road. We will rent two cars. Those of you who will be driving the cars should have the best cover stories because you will be the most likely to be exposed to the military or local police. One car will be waiting near this point," I pointed to the aerial. "Your job is to pick me up after I get out of the plane. If you look closely, you will see that there is a chain-link fence between the road and the runway. It looks old and in bad shape but bring something to cut the fence. When I come to a stop, I'll jump out of the airplane, climb into the waiting car, and we will return to Simón Bolívar. The trip should take about twenty minutes, depending on traffic. It will probably take five or six hours to remove the plane from the runway, and by that time we will be on our way back to Andrews, leaving President Escudero in the hands of his caregivers.

"One other detail. There is only one way on and off the perimeter road. The other car driven by two of our people will be waiting here," I said, pointing to the aerial again, "to block any military police that may try to intercept our getaway car."

"How are we going to do that?" someone from the back asked.

"I'll leave that up to you agency people, but probably something like a lost tourist, flat tire, engine trouble, I don't know. You just have to delay long enough so the getaway car can, well, get away. Three or four minutes, I would think. Jerry how about putting a team on it to work out the details, no more than four of you, I think a man and woman in each car will look less suspicious. I'll need the rest of you at Simón Bolívar."

Jerry grumbled some, but said, "Okay." I think he was happy to be doing something.

"A hotel is located almost at the end of the runway," I said, pointing at the aerial. "Once you rent the cars—there is a car rental at Simón Bolívar—drive over tonight and check into that hotel so you can be onsite first thing in the morning. Adel, you probably have the best command of the area and the language. How about you make the reservations for the cars and the hotel? Rent a room for yourself, too. Make sure it overlooks the runway. Take a radio or cell phone. I would like you to be our eyes. You, Jerry, and Schultz work together on the details."

Adel looked pleased to be involved, "Si, I can do this."

"I think it makes the most sense to use the airplane as our base or ops center. It's certainly mobile, and it has all the com gear we'll need. Which reminds me, Jerry, did you guys bring any mobile radios?"

"Yeah, we brought a bunch of them."

"Good, make sure you coordinate with Warrant Officer Schultz so he can talk to your people, particularly when they are at General Miranda. Fix me up with one, too."

The cabin got noisy again with side conversations.

"Everyone, please quiet down so I can finish. We will be landing in about an hour. When we land, we will park at the east end of the airport away from civil and general aviation. Most of that stuff is in the middle and on the west end of the airport. Some old general aviation planes are parked there, but for the most part the area is unused. We will use this gate here," I said, pointing at the aerial. "As you can see, it's close to where we will be setting up, and it doesn't appear to be manned. We will use it to get on and off the airport.

Plus, we can control access with one man. Jerry, when we land, ask one of your people to check for closed-circuit cameras at the gate and around the area in general. I don't want to be on candid camera. If you need it, I'm sure Mr. Schultz can help."

"Mike here is good at that stuff. He can take care of it," Jerry replied.

"Major Huddleston, I would like our aircraft staged here," I said, pointing once again to the aerial. "And as we discussed, set up our operation center here in the aircraft. Also, arrange a reception ceremony for Escudero, the fancier the better, not many people, but a bunch of flags, a band, that sort of thing. Coordinate with Teddy and Adel. They can get to the right people.

"Allow for the possibility that we may need the special ops guys to land. They will be in the CV-22s. I know zero about their flight characteristics, but I don't want to interfere with the airport operations. Vice President Sabas will give us some cover, but the last thing we want to do is draw any more attention to this than we have to."

"You mean no more attention than the president of Venezuela, our jet and three CV-22s with sixty-four heavily armed troops would normally bring," Major Huddleston said.

"Yeah, exactly. How hard can that be?" I replied.

That got a few chuckles, but this time I could sense less misgiving, even a little enthusiasm. Liz was furious.

"All right, now that we have President Escudero where we want him, what do we do with him? Fortunately, all we have to do is see he is safe aboard the ground transportation that Vice President Sabas will provide. Teddy, will you speak to that, please."

"*Si*, yes. First, on behalf of the people of Bolivarian Republic of Venezuela, my father, and my wife, I want to thank your President Jackson and most especially you people aboard this aircraft for your service to my country.

"Vice President Sabas with some members of the *Asamblea Nacional* and a contingent of Air Force officers will be the official welcoming committee. After a brief ceremony, President Escudero and the officials will board four Suburban automobiles and leave the airport grounds through the exit Mr. Spade has just shown you. The *escolta* and vehicles will accompany the president to a private clinic, where he will be cared for until he retires."

One of the CIA men seated in front asked, "What if he doesn't want to go, and how about his staff? Some loyal personnel are bound to be on the plane with him. Hell, probably all of them will be loyal to Escudero. Another thing, what about the press? They're going to be all over this, right?"

Teddy said, "You are quite right. The Air Force Honor Guard attending the ceremony will actually be heavily armed men from the Venezuelan Air Force Special Operations Squadron. They will attempt to discourage any problems, but should the need arise they will place these staff members under arrest, and President Escudero will be vigorously encouraged to board his Suburban automobile. The media, they will not be allowed on the airport and will be told to attend to *Palacio de Miraflores* at four o'clock. At that time, Vice President Sabas will give a press conference announcing the change of leadership."

Our plane landed at Simón Bolívar at nine-twenty. The late summer night had just fallen across the northern Venezuelan countryside. Runway lights, strobes from the parked and taxing aircraft, and the glowing main passenger terminal collectively created a surreal, edgy look that reminded me of a *Star Wars* set.

The airplane taxied to its parking place, and the engines shut down—silence. Gradually the cabin came to life with small conversations while the baggage was collected and sorted. One man walked around the cabin dropping coffee cups and other assorted trash into a plastic bag. A waft of muggy air scented with jet fuel flowed through the opened cabin door. We each walked forward, taking our turn to exit the plane.

Our end of the airport was especially dark. A few streetlights outside the perimeter fence made ineffectual stabs into the darkness. Some low clouds reflected light from the main terminal, but it was still dark. It was also hot and humid. Small groups of career agents and military talked quietly as they paced and stretched to work out the kinks earned during the four-hour trip.

I found Jerry and asked, "Is your name really Jerry McGuire?"

"Is your name really Sam Spade?"

"Touché," I said.

"What the hell are you doing mixed up in this? I know you're not a professional."

"Why, am I that inept?"

"No, you seem to have a quick mind, but you have no sense of political survival. That stunt you're planning at the airport could be a political disaster, and no career guy would chance it in a million years."

"Guess that's why the president sent me. Gives her what you guys call plausible deniability."

"You are a fast learner, but if this deal goes bad you and I will—"

"I know, we'll be, as they say, hung out to dry."

"An optimist, too. You're assuming we will ever be found to hang. Hell, no one will even look."

"Before I get any more depressed, how about asking your two teams to pick up the rental cars and drive over to the hotel. Make sure they have some cell phones or radios so we can talk. Tell them we will get to them when we have the details worked out. H-Hour will probably be about one tomorrow. Oh, don't forget to ask Mike to check for cameras."

"H-Hour? Who are you, Sterling Hayden?"

I laughed, "I always wanted to say 'H-Hour.' You know Sterling Hayden was a Marine and in the OSS? He was a sailor, too."

"Fascinating."

"Though, I don't think he ever said 'H-Hour.'"

"Okay, I'll get my people ready for H-hour," Jerry said, walking away, shaking his head.

CHAPTER THIRTY-TWO

Simon Bolivar Airport, Venezuela - Early Morning

Fitful intervals of sleep prefaced the morning's arrival. Several seats on the airplane converted to bunks, the remaining unfortunate slept sitting. A breakfast platter of ham and cheese sandwiches and coffee sat in the galley. I grabbed a handful of breakfast and started for the cabin door when a familiar figure caught my eye.

"Hey, Bob!" The man turned to face me. "I didn't know you were on this flight. Why didn't you say something?" I said.

"First, I wasn't sure it was you. Then, when you pulled that stunt with the president on the intercom, I knew it was you. Reminds me of the time—"

"I know, this time it was a dick measuring contest with McGuire or whatever his name is."

Bob laughed, "It was all I could do to keep from laughing out loud. Was that really the president?"

"Yep, that was her. How the hell are you? You and Amy doing okay?"

"She's great. Matter of fact, when the balloon went up for this thing, I was turning steaks in the backyard."

"You told me you retired. As a station chief. Bangkok, right?"

"You know us professional company types, we never really retire."

I laughed, "Liz and I were on vacation when we got roped into this cluster fuck. What's the deal with your buddy McGuire?"

"Never worked with him, so I only know him by reputation, but I hear he's the real deal. So, they did get you. Is your wife in the company? I've seen her around but never got a handle on who she works for."

"Liz has her own company. I guess she does some contract work for you stealthy types. As for me, it's just like I told you at the club, I said no to those guys. This is strictly a one-off deal. Listen, when this fiasco is over, if we're not dead or in jail, how about the four of us make another try at those steaks?"

"You got it. Let me know if I can help. It's been a long time since I was just muscle."

We shook hands, then I walked to the airstairs and ducked through the cabin door.

From my vantage atop the airstairs, I watched as small wisps of dirt and grit formed curlicues in the light air, twirling as they crossed the asphalt ramp. To the west, the airport runways disappeared into a ghostly mixture of watery heat mirages and morning mist. Our plane sat on a deserted corner at the southeast end of the airport once devoted to private aviation. An old DC-3 was parked on the ramp with other smaller dejected and nondescript aircraft. The airport and main runways ran east to west in a narrow valley wedged between two elongated hills. The higher of the two hills was at our back and continued off in each direction into the distance. To the front the smaller hill paralleled the runways partially obscuring the Caribbean Sea a mile or so further north. The hill sloped gently west to east terminating with the end of the main runway some four hundred yards distant and opposite our plane.

In the center of the airport, to our left, commercial airliners were already jockeying for gates at the main terminal. The smell of jet fuel coasting in on the slight breezes reminded me of my misspent youth. A youth misspent by others, in a war of no economic or political consequence other than the destruction of American lives. Thinking back to another War, I wondered if the events of this day, on this airfield would be President Jackson's Gulf of Tonkin? Too histrionic, maybe, but I kept asking myself the other question: why were we here? Are we helping save the United States and the world from a catastrophic oil crisis? Are we eradicating an illicit drug trade? Or are we ensuring President Jackson's reelection? I knew why Barrett, McGuire, and their devoted men and women were here. They were ordered to be here. Teddy and Adel wanted to rid their country of a despot. Good as any reason, probably better than most. But Elizabeth and I, why were we here?

"A centimo for your thoughts," Liz said, wrapping her arms around my waist.

"I was just wondering if we were about to start World War Three."

"Cheery thought," she said.

"Yeah, must have been the coffee. Hold me some more."

"Anytime," resting her cheek on my shoulder.

Colonel Barrett walked up behind us, "Good morning, Mr. Spade, ma'am." Liz and I turned and said good morning.

"Mr. Spade, I think you'd better let me take that flight into General Francisco."

"Why?"

"For all the obvious reasons. I'm a combat pilot, I have the experience, and I get paid to do this stuff. Besides, you're the brains of this outfit. If we lost you we would probably fail in our mission."

I could feel Liz squeezing my arm in a tactile plea to take Barrett's offer.

"Sir, as the senior pilot, I'm afraid I'm going to insist. Hudd and the guys can take care of anything here. They're all command-rated pilots."

"Colonel, I'm not sure you have the authority to insist—though the more I think about it, what you say makes sense. God knows I would be pretty good at crashing an airplane."

Barrett chuckled, "Yes, sir, wouldn't we all. The idea is to do a controlled crash, and I think I'm better qualified."

"Unless you brought credentials, how are you going to rent a plane?"

"I didn't, but you have yours. You rent the plane. We both get on board. We take it to the end of the strip or out of sight and then you get out."

Liz was cutting off the circulation in my arm.

"Okay, colonel, the trip is yours. Adel said the FBO is on the other side of the main terminal. Why don't we walk over there in about an hour and see what we can find?"

"You got it," he said and started to walk back into the plane.

"Colonel, if you have another moment."

"Sir?"

"What's the story on Schultz?

"Why, do you have a problem with him?"

"No, to the contrary. He has been extremely accommodating and resourceful. He seems to have an abiding affection for you, but the two of you are so different. My question is mere curiosity. I was in the Marine Corps, and he doesn't fit my definition of a warrant officer, at least as I knew them."

"I was in a recon bird that got shot up pretty bad and had to step over the side. I came down in the middle of some marine grunts having a bad time. Schultz was a corporal then and the company radioman. The bravest guy I ever saw. Probably saved all our lives. I called in an airstrike in front of our position. We were all hunkered down, but Schultz sat out in the open using his radio to direct traffic. After we got back, I offered him a job, got him some rank and the Silver Star. Anything else, you'll have to ask him."

"Thank you, colonel," I said.

Barrett nodded at Liz, "Ma'am," then walked back into the plane.

"Talk about giants among men," Liz said.

"Here's another quote for you," I said.

"What?'

"Alan Shepard, 1961, '*Lord, please don't let me fuck up.*'"

One of Jerry's senior citizens scouted around and found a Piper Cherokee sitting on the field. He gave the information to Adel, who called and reserved what was actually a newer version of the Cherokee, an Arrow, if you call 1969 newer. The Arrow has retractable gear and, like all Cherokees, it has a low wing, which means the main spar runs under the cabin, in theory providing a safer gear up landing.

Barrett was wearing civilian clothes, a green polo shirt, khaki slacks, and boat shoes. I was going to ask him if we shopped at the same store, but he didn't seem in a humorous mood.

The FBO contained a lounge with a small rectangular coffee table and some chairs. At the rear of the lounge, against the wall, was an ancient coffee maker residing on top of an old wooden desk. To the right of the front door was a counter, and behind the counter was an office with the usual desks, filing cabinets, and squeaky office chairs. A stout woman in her fifties was apparently in charge of the office. My astute observation was based on the absence of any others in the office.

We were standing at the counter when I remembered that my three years of high school Spanish left me with no command of the language. The woman squeaked her chair to the right and faced us. I was about to ask whether she *abla'ed* English when Colonel Barrett begin conversing in Spanish with an eloquence that elicited a wide grin from the office manager and an array of diverse squeaks from her chair. She dethroned and walked over to Barrett, ignoring me.

The Colonel turned to me, "Okay, break out your ticket and multi rating. We're going flying, but we have to fuel first."

I caught a slight glint in his eye. He didn't have to crash-land a plane with a full load of fuel.

"She says she doesn't have a check-pilot around yet, but we look honest, so she'll trust us if we say we can fly the thing."

I put the documents on the counter with my credit card. I couldn't wait to see my next bill. *Item: One Airplane—$60,000.* I fervently hoped the president won reelection. If not, I didn't see the next guy reimbursing me, especially if we started a war.

Colonel Barrett and the office manager *abla'ed* some more, then we left.

Our plan called for Barrett to come down on the runway about noon. We were assuming the lunch hour would mean fewer people around the airfield and a longer response time to the "accident." We also had to get Barrett off the field, so we wanted as few MPs around as possible. If we were really lucky, no one would be in the tower. The noon timing would also assure the runway would be fouled when Escudero's plane arrived over Caracas at about one in the afternoon.

Jerry's people had set up in the hotel next to the Francisco de Miranda Air Base directly at the end of the runway. As planned, both teams had a rental car. One would be the pickup car, and the other would act as the blocker for the pickup car. Teddy assured us that the base was accessible to civilians and tourists, but just in case, Vice President Sabas provided us with passes. Equipped with high-powered binoculars and a radio, Adel was in a hotel room overlooking the runway. From her perch, she would provide real-time observation and communications between the cars, Barrett's plane, and Gunner Schultz in the com center.

Barrett and I did the preflight. The fuel tanks were about a quarter full. At eleven o'clock, we fired up the engines and taxied out to the runway. Luck was with us. Planes were taking off to the west, so I got out of the Arrow in front of our jet and then watched Barrett as he took off. As the plane turned into a speck in the sky, I again asked myself why. I said a small prayer for Barrett and turned away.

About ten minutes after twelve, Adel called and said Colonel Barrett had landed wheels up at Francisco de Miranda. A small group of us gathered around the gunner and his console. Looking hopefully at each other, we sweated in the warm cabin and waited to hear more.

Adel called and said there was some smoke coming from the plane, but she didn't see any fire. The wing seemed "broken and twisted." She had not seen the pickup car yet. Nor had she seen Colonel Barrett.

We waited impatiently. I looked at my watch, three long minutes had passed since the last report. The radio crackled. It was Adel. The pickup car was at its assigned spot, but there was also a fire truck pulling up to Barrett's airplane—still no sign of Colonel Barrett.

"Gunner, tell those people they are not, under any circumstances, to talk or engage in any way with those firefighters. They are to get Colonel Barrett in the car and leave immediately."

Gunner keyed his mike and started to relay the message. I walked back and forth too nervous to stand or sit. For probably the hundredth time, I asked myself what in the hell I was doing playing special agent. Was I so naive or so arrogant as to believe I had the aptitude to get involved in this, this—I didn't even know what to call it—a job, a mission? Bullshit seemed the right—

Gunner called out, "Sir, we have a problem."

Fucking great! I ran to the com center, crashing into a table on the way. "What?"

"Sir, it's Colonel Barrett. They got him in the car, but he's hurt pretty bad. It's his leg. They said there is a lot of blood and want to know if they should take him to a hospital."

I snapped out of my self-pity-induced coma and focused, "No, absolutely not. Bring him here, but do not speed. Tell them not to take any risk that may expose them to arrest. Make sure they understand. Make them repeat the instructions."

"Yes, sir."

Liz looked at me but didn't say anything. She didn't have to. *If he's badly hurt, he could die.*

The answer to the unasked question was that he was a soldier, a Marine. This was what he signed up for. He said it that morning: 'I get paid to do this stuff.' That was a load of crap. It was all bravado. To die for something like this, for oil, for an election, for my stupid idea, for whatever, I would not let it happen. Yeah, right—more bullshit. Who was I, God?

"Liz, find Jerry and see if any of his people are medics. Then make one of those seats into a bed. Talk to the aircrew, find out where the first-aid stuff is stowed. Pull out everything you can find, especially if they have IV fluids and antibiotics."

"I'll take care of it."

"Gunner, what's the story?"

"They got off the base with no problem. The army is focused on the crash. The pickup car is en route with the blocking car close behind in case there are mechanical problems or something."

"Okay, have Adel take a last look. If there is nothing to report, have her come back here. And remind the drivers not to speed. No traffic violations. Make them repeat it."

"Yes, sir."

I called out to no one in particular, "Anyone seen Teddy?"

"I saw him on the apron a few minutes ago," someone replied.

I started down the airstairs, but Teddy was coming up. We both walked back into the plane.

"I was telling my father about the crash, but he already knew about it. He told the people at Francisco de Miranda they were not to worry about the pilot. It was most important to remove the airplane from the runway." Teddy grinned, "They assured my father that the plane would be removed no later than tomorrow noon."

"Well, at least some good news," I said. "Teddy, Colonel Barrett got hurt. Can you get us a doctor, someone that we can trust to keep quiet?"

"I am sorry to hear this." He thought for a moment. "Yes, I think my school chum lives close. He is a surgeon, a doctor. I will call him and ask him to help."

"Thanks, Teddy, I feel terrible about this, but I couldn't risk a hospital. Chances are he would be arrested, and if Escudero's people got a hold of him I'm afraid we would never see him again."

Teddy was back in a few minutes, "I found him, my friend. He said he will be here in twenty minutes. For now, he said to keep the patient lying down and calm. Apply pressure to the wound or, if needed, a torniquete. You know *torniquete*?"

"Yes, it's the same in English. Thanks, Teddy."

Ten minutes later, the CIA agents climbed aboard, carrying Barrett. His right leg was bleeding from an eight-inch gash. Liz and one of Jerry's people cleaned the wound and applied a compress.

As promised, the doctor arrived and stitched up the gash, bandaged the wound, started an IV, and gave Barrett a shot. When the doctor finished, he found me talking with gunner and said, "Your friend is going to be okay, but he needs to be in a hospital soon. He probably has some nerve damage. It's not extensive, and plastic surgery can usually repair such damage, but it needs to be done soon or he might lose some feeling and possibly movement in his foot. This would not be a good thing for a pilot."

"Thank you, doctor. I promise I'll have him in a hospital this evening. Will that be soon enough?"

"Yes, that should be fine."

He walked up the aisle to where Teddy was standing, exchanged some words, and left.

Events unfolded quickly. Teddy and Vice President Sabas arranged to have the reception area erected near our plane. A dozen civilian workers arrived in a catering truck, erected a canopy, laid a red carpet, and set up chairs and a refreshment table. A uniformed band arrived on a bus and milled around, trying to stay out of the sun. Two military trucks loaded with about twenty soldiers drove up to the ceremonial area and unloaded.

"Teddy, who in the hell are those men?"

Teddy smiled, "They are the good guys, the Air Force Honor Guard. They are here to honor the president's retirement. They work for my father's best friend, el Comandante of the air force."

Jerry scattered his people so they could watch our perimeter, keeping out the unwanted, especially the press. They also were subtly screening the arrival of dignitaries, though some of Sabas's staff was doing the heavy lifting. As requested, Jerry provided each of us with a small radio that we concealed or carried in a pocket.

Escudero's plane was due soon, and gunner was monitoring the tower frequency so he could tell us when the plane was on final.

"Teddy," I said over the radio, "everything okay out there?"

"Yes, we are very good out here, though one could wish for cooler weather."

Something else to worry about. With no engines and no auxiliary, it was getting hot in the plane. Soon it would be too hot. I looked over at Colonel Barrett, wondering how he was faring in the heat and otherwise. He was asleep.

Gunner yelled back to where I was standing, "Sir, Escudero's plane is on final. He should be on the ground in five. Probably take him another five or six minutes to taxi over here."

"Thanks, gunner."

I got on the radio, "Heads up, Escudero will be here in about ten or twelve minutes."

Jerry came up on the radio, "Spade, there are a bunch of cars driving through the gate. They don't look like ambassadors of goodwill if you get my drift."

"How many?"

"Four cars. Mercedes mostly. Looks like about eight to ten guys."

"Okay, we're here to keep something like this from fucking up the works. Keep an eye on them. Let me know if you see anything hinky."

"This whole train wreck is hinky."

"You all have your golf clubs with you?"

"Yep."

"You might want to break out a couple of five irons." *Geez, golf metaphors again.*

Jerry spoke into the radio, "Ready with the five irons. Betty and I will be behind the old truck and the shipping container. Just give us the word."

"Okay, and Jerry, I think that's good news, about the cars full of thugs. It means Escudero is coming to our reception. Despite the ego thing, I was concerned he would deplane at the main terminal and be out of our grasp."

"Whatever you say. You hook 'em, and I'll clean 'em." Jerry laughed, "Thought I'd change it up with a fishing metaphor."

"Not sure which is worse."

I watched as Escudero's plane landed, it was the Venezuelan version of *Air Force One*, but an Airbus A319CJ. It slowly taxied to the west side of the reception area, roughly perpendicular to our plane, which I hoped looked tied down and vacant. Air force ground crew guided the Airbus to a position where the occupants had to deplane directly onto the red carpet and in front of the awaiting dignitaries. The Airbus's two engines shut down, and the airstairs extended. Then nothing happened.

CHAPTER THIRTY-THREE

Simon Bolivar Airport - Afternoon

"Teddy, who is that guy standing to the left of the airstairs about six feet this side of your father?"

Teddy took the binoculars from the desk, looked through them for a moment, adjusting the focus. "That's Pérez's protégé, Hector Guerrero. I think he took over operations after Pérez disappeared. It has been rumored that he is the one who actually arranged to kill Estéban Morales on orders of Escudero. He and Pérez had a big argument the day before Pérez disappeared."

"I can confirm the rumor. His name came up in the Narragansett Files. I think he is Escudero's search-and-rescue team. He must have come in one of those cars Jerry warned us about."

"Major Huddleston, where are those SOCOM teams?"

"They're orbiting just over the horizon."

"Get them inbound and on the ramp. Tell them to forget the stealthy stuff, make it fast and noisy."

Huddleston said a few things over the com, then turned to me, "They will be on the ground in five, maybe six minutes!"

I turned to walk off the plane, "Come on, Teddy, you're with me!" Teddy and I walked toward the ceremonial area. I keyed my radio, "Jerry, your ambassadors of peace and light are confirmed as bad guys. Are your people in place?"

My earpiece crackled, "We're ready," Jerry replied.

I keyed the radio again, "Okay, listen up everyone. Remember our credo, 'Don't start a war.' If you have to use the golf clubs, make it a hole in one."

If I got out of this in one piece, I was going to write bad movie scripts. With lines like that, I could make a fortune.

Thirty feet later, Teddy and I were standing in the ceremonial area that measured twenty by fifty feet. Ceremonial flags twitched in the wispy, early afternoon air. The welcoming delegation looked bored and hot in the bright sun.

Escudero's plane was parked at the west end of the red carpet, the vehicles and escorts provided by Vice President Sabas were staged at the opposite, east end of the carpet. A small band and the military honor guard stood on the near side of the ceremonial area, flanking the longer side of the red carpet. The opposite side, the north side, was open to the main runway and the low hills. The Caribbean Sea could be seen in the distance. Vice President Sabas, three air force officers, and three senior members of the Asamblea Nacional were respectfully waiting at the bottom of the airstairs for President Escudero to deplane.

Teddy and I walked up to Hector Guerrero, also standing at the bottom of the airstairs, but to the side and away from the others. I stood in front of him.

"May my friend and I speak with you for a moment?"

He looked at me then at Teddy as if we were something he scraped off the bottom of his shoe. "I am busy. Go away," he said in passable English.

"I'm afraid we must insist," I replied.

"Do you know who I am? Get away from me or I'll have you thrown over the fence!"

Out of the corner of my eye, I saw one of Hector's goons open the back door of one of the Mercedes. I spoke into the radio, "Jerry, the guy in the pork pie hat, he's very interested in something in the backseat of the white Mercedes."

"I got him—personally," he replied.

Hector Guerrero looked at me and said in a menacing voice he probably practiced, "Who are you?"

I spoke in a low voice, very close to his face. He smelled of garlic, onions, and cigars. "Mr. Guerrero, I will not argue with you further. You will come with me. Please walk to the white aircraft behind me and do it now."

Guerrero's eyes widened. He looked at me and then over his shoulder to where his men were standing. He laughed, then sneered, "*Güero*, who the fuck do you think you are to give me orders? I am here at invitation of *Presidente* Escudero."

"You have been uninvited. You come with me, or I will kill you where you stand. It is your choice."

Our good-natured chat was interrupted by three CV-22Bs rumbling in from the sea over the ridgeline. The B version of the CV-22 looks like the main character in one of those nightmares you had when you were a kid. Painted almost black with various appendages, protrusions, and cankerous bulges, the aircraft has an evil, demonic look.

Flying in formation, they thundered over the main runway, landing in a line, west to east, front to back 200 feet from the ceremonial area. Dust, bits of trash, and debris whipped violently in the vortexes produced by the aerial ballet. I was so fascinated I almost forgot to keep an eye on Guerrero, who looked dumbfounded.

The aircraft immediately disgorged sixty special operations troops, who lined up three deep in formation in front of the Ospreys. They were dressed in helmets, dark green, camouflaged uniforms, and body armor festooned with pockets, knives, weapons, and ammunition. Each man carried an M-4 carbine at his front. It was difficult to say which was more frightening, the men or the machines. I spoke into the radio.

"Hudd, ask the special ops to send a medic or corpsman over here to look at Colonel Barrett."

"Will do"

"Now, Mr. Guerrero, as you can see, there is now a *güero* honor guard for President Escudero, and you are no longer needed. As I was saying, you have been uninvited to this ceremony, and you need to come with me."

Pork-Pie Hat leaned over and pulled an M-16 from the back of the Mercedes.

"Jerry, take him now," I said more calmly than I felt.

There followed a distinct *POP*!

Pork Pie sat down hard and then fell backward, his head making a *THUNK* as it hit the asphalt. Hector Guerrero turned in time to see his man die, then turned back to me in a rage.

Instantly there was a clatter like dozens of BBs falling on a metal roof as sixty special ops men chambered rounds in their M-4s. The ominous sound made the hair on the back of my neck stand up. I had heard the noise before, but a world away in time and distance.

I stuck my Colt in his solar plexus. "Hector," I said, nodding toward the fence, "you see all those rejects from a nursing home. They are all CIA assassins," I lied, "with instructions to kill you and every one of your men on my word. Now, unless you want to join your friend over there, I suggest you tell your men to drop all their weapons on the ground and go home. While you're at it, tell them to take Pork-Pie with them."

Hector looked at me and then at the sixty special ops men, then back at Jerry's 'rejects.' I suspected Hector had never heard of Falstaff, but he apparently decided that discretion was indeed the better part of valor. He turned and shouted something in Spanish to his men. I looked at Teddy, who nodded. Metallic clinks and clanks followed as weapons dropped to the pavement. The honor guard, band, and the rest of the entourage tried to look indifferent as two of Hector's men callously deposited Pork-Pie into the trunk of one of the vehicles. One by one, Hector's minions got back in their cars and filed off through the gate out into the city.

"Hudd, have two SOCOM men report to me," I said into the radio.

"On the way."

In the distance, I heard a command, then two of the troops broke ranks and ran to where Teddy, Hector, and I were standing.

"Good afternoon, gentlemen. I'm sorry to keep you guys standing in the heat, but it can't be helped."

One of the men grinned. "That's okay, sir, it's been a pretty easy day so far. What can we do for you?"

"This very unpleasant individual is Hector Guerrero. I would like you to take him into custody, be sure he is well searched for weapons, make sure he is securely cuffed, then transport him back to Florida, where he will be prosecuted for crimes too numerous to mention. If he gives you any trouble, you have my permission to kick him out of your bird en route."

I looked at Hector, who was no longer amused. "Hector, these men are some of the meanest creatures God ever put on Earth. I suggest you do not piss them off. If you give them the slightest provocation, they will toss you out of the airplane without the benefit of a parachute. Do you understand?"

"*Si,*" he muttered.

"Hector, those aircraft fly at twenty-thousand feet. Do I make myself clear?"

"*Si, si, comprende!*"

"Okay, guys, take him away. And thanks."

"No problem, sir." The two SOCOM men grabbed Hector by the arms and duck walked him across the apron disappearing into one of the CV-22Bs.

President Escudero stepped out of his plane, stopping at the top of the airstairs. He looked around the ceremonial area, glancing at the honor guard, then stared at the SOCOM troops. He then seemed to notice Vice President Sabas at the bottom of the airstairs and called down to him in Spanish. The two exchanged some dialogue. I looked at Teddy.

"He asked my father who the troops belonged to and the reason for their presence. My father said it was an honor guard sent by the United States in admiration for the President of Venezuela, for his long and honorable service and to wish him a healthy and pleasurable retirement."

"He buy it?"

"I don't think so. He asked for Guerrero. Father said Guerrero was in conference with the commander of the United States troops and is not available."

President Escudero looked around again, said something to one of his aides, and then walked back into the airplane.

Now what? The SOCOM men and machines couldn't stay much longer. In spite of Sabas' efforts, any moment a news cameraman or reporter was going to show up demanding to know why armed United States troops were sitting in the Venezuelan capital. I was sure Escudero would give them an ear full. Vice President Sabas must have been thinking the same thing. He was perspiring heavily, and I didn't think it was the heat.

Mentally, I started going over scenes from *Master and Commander*, trying to glean tips for boarding and taking a ship. I was about to ask Jerry if he had any boarding pikes in his golf bag when Escudero walked out of the plane. He paused, shot his cuffs, and then walked down the airstairs with a number of military and civilian staff following him.

The band started to play. The honor guard snapped to attention, the emissaries formed a reception line, and attendants pulled covers off the refreshments.

The SOCOM troops didn't move a muscle. They scared the crap out of me, and they were on my side.

At the bottom of the airstairs, Escudero and Sabas shook hands, then Escudero shook hands with the other dignitaries. Not wanting to be part of the festivities, I backed away and tried to blend into the background. The VIPs walked to a table laden with cold drinks and sandwiches, then sat in some folding chairs facing the podium, where Sabas was standing shuffling some papers. The band finished playing, and the honor guard was ordered to parade rest. Sabas began a long-winded speech, which I suspect was as spurious as the rest of the ceremony. I turned my head and spoke to the radio.

"Hudd, how's Colonel Barrett?"
"Not sure, the doc is still with him."
"Okay, let me know."

CHAPTER THIRTY-FOUR

Teddy hurried up to me and grabbed my arm, "Sam, we have a problem."

"What now?"

"They are sending some fighters after us. Escudero must have called them from his plane when he saw he was actually being retired."

"I thought you said your dad was keeping the air force on the ground?"

"He is, but these people work for the *Oficina Nacional Antidrogas*, our drug-enforcement bureau, and they work for Escudero."

"How appropriate. When you say fighters, you mean some of those Russian Sukhois you guys have?"

"No, not jets. These are AT-27 Tucano turboprops. They use them for drug interdiction, but they have machine guns, probably rockets. They are very fast."

"How many and when?"

"Two we know about. And maybe thirty minutes, maybe sooner. Father has just learned of them."

"Fucking great!" I triggered the radio, "Major Huddleston, do you know what an AT-27 is?"

Hudd was silent for a moment, "Yeah, they're trainers. Sometimes Third World guys use them as fighters—with the right packages they can be pretty nasty. Why?"

"There are two of them about thirty, maybe twenty, minutes out with orders to keep us on the ground. They are armed with machine guns and maybe some rockets. Any ideas?"

"Yeah, one. Get the hell out of here!"

"Okay, tell the SOCOM guys to warm up their birds, but keep the troops in place. Guess you should warm up our jet, too."

"Done and done."

Almost immediately, the turbines on the CV-22Bs started to turn over. Vice President Sabas looked over at me, and I gave him a "wind it up" sign with hand and forefinger. Over the radio, I called, "Jerry."

"Yeah, what's going on?"

"Our welcome has run out. All those goons off the facility?"

"Yeah, as far as I know. I didn't follow them off the airfield, but there are none close."

"Okay, we got to get this guy in a vehicle and out of here. Once he's off the airport, he's their problem. Tell your people it's happening now and watch these army guys. They are all carrying sidearms."

"How about the air force?"

"They're supposed to be on our side but watch them too. I'm bringing the SOCOM guys up to keep the peace, but if you see a gun come out, shoot first, then ask my permission. For God's sake, please do not hit the vice president. He's the guy we came to protect."

"Gotcha. Don't shoot the VP. I'll write it down."
'Hudd, tell the SOCOM troops to form a perimeter around this ceremony now."
"On it."

I heard the turbines on our C-37B spooling up. Standing among all the jets, it was getting noisy. I was praying it wouldn't get any noisier.

"Teddy, how much time do we have?"
"About twenty minutes, I think."

We had to shout to be heard over the jet engines now at full idle. "Okay, get Adel and Liz on board."

"Adel and I are staying here. Liz is on board."

I looked up. The SOCOM troops now enclosed two-thirds of the ceremonial area.

"Okay, Teddy, now!" I shouted above the din of the jet engines. We walked to the VIPs. They were no longer sitting but milling around, all looking perplexed, perhaps frightened. Teddy and I stood in front of Escudero.

"Mr. President, it is time to go!" I shouted over the noise.

"You!" he sputtered. "How dare you show your face in my country!" He turned to his staff, "I want this man arrested immediately!"

His staff looked uncomfortable and did nothing except step back a few feet. Escudero began one of his rants.

I looked at Teddy, "We don't have time for this. Can I put him in the car?"

"*Si*, yes!"

"Jerry," I yelled into the radio. "Give me a hand. I need to get this guy in a car and out of here now, and I don't want to use the SOCOM men." If a newspaper or television reporter sees U.S. troops manhandling their president, we would start a war.

"Be right there," Jerry yelled over the radio.

Three large men, two in aloha shirts and one in a polo shirt, stepped forward. None of them had a neck. The four of us lifted Escudero off his feet, carried him to a waiting Suburban, and tossed him in the backseat. Two air-force types followed under their own power. We closed the door, and the convoy of Suburban's drove off. I could hear Escudero screaming all the way through the gate.

CHAPTER THIRTY-FIVE

Air Force C-37B - Simon Bolivar Airport

Major Huddleston finished talking with Colonel Barrett, then turned to me, "Where to, sir?"

"Did the SOG aircraft get off?"

"Yes, sir, they're already over international waters."

"Not that we have a choice, but did the medic say the colonel was well enough to make the trip to Tampa?"

"Yes, sir," he said, nodding at the man in a green camouflage jumpsuit kneeling next to Barrett. "He stayed with us in case the colonel needs attention." The medic nodded at me.

"Okay, so let's head for MacDill, and let's do it fast."

"You got it. MacDill it is," the Major turned away and began walking hurriedly back to the cockpit. The plane was already moving. I walked forward to the com center.

"Gunner, any info on those fighters? Try not to give me any more bad news."

"Looks like we got eight, ten minutes, sir."

It would probably take us most of those eight or ten minutes to get to the far end of the runway for takeoff. I had a thought. I picked up the nearest phone and pushed number one. Major Huddleston answered, sounding a little tense.

"Yeah, what's up. I'm sort of busy?"

"Hudd, we could save some time if we took off from this end of the runway. Would the wind allow for that?"

"Maybe, but we'd be taking off in the direction of incoming flights, and this is a busy airport."

"I know, but I don't think we have enough time to taxi to the far end before those fighters get here. If they were jets, we would already be a cinder."

"You're the boss. The tower will go fucking nuts. Looks as if most of the traffic is coming in on 010, so I'll use 027."

He severed the connection, then came up on the PA system. "Okay, folks, belt up. The colonel doesn't let me drive very often, so I'm a little rusty."

The plane bumped and turned as we stored gear and rushed to get our belts fastened. I stumbled back to my seat, buckled in, then looked over at the colonel. He was in his bunk belted securely, IVs swinging from the overhead, still feeding him fluids. I must have looked worried because he gave me a weak smile and a wink. I smiled back, then he closed his eyes.

I turned to Liz, "Better tighten your belt and hold on."

"Jesus, not again. If I ever get on an airplane with another damn Marine, please, just shoot me."

Taxiing much too fast, the airplane now resembled an amusement park ride, jolting, thumping, and turning down the taxiway toward the wrong end of the runway. From the back of the airplane, looking forward, the tubular-shaped fuselage appeared to flex and twist. At the threshold, the major stopped briefly, then turned onto the 10,000-foot runway. The engines went from idle to a pulsating roar. He came on the PA once more. "Okay, boys and girls, hold on."

The Rolls-Royce engines wound up to a high-pitched scream as 30,000 pounds of thrust launched the C-37B down the runway. Gaining speed in multiples, the G forces pushed us back in our seats. In what was almost a simultaneous event, the nose abruptly pitched up, gear thumped into their bays, and the flaps retracted. As distinct from anything I had experienced in an airplane, it was how I imagined it would be to sit in a rocket. Just as I was getting used to the rapid ascent, the plane banked hard onto its right side, the wingtip pointing at the ground far below as Major Huddleston yanked the plane to the north, the G's making movement impossible. I looked across at the colonel, but he was sleeping. Liz looked as if she had just stuck her hand into an electrical socket. The plane rolled back to level, the nose still pitched up but less drastically, the engines still screaming at full power.

Minutes later, the major pulled back the power and the engine noise moderated.

The PA system crackled, "Sorry, folks, we were wearing out our welcome, and I wanted to get you home for dinner. We should be in beautiful Tampa in just under three hours."

My phone buzzed, "Sorry, sir, but I saw those AT-27s coming in from the south. They were in a shallow dive and really moving. They can't get much above twenty-eight thousand, so I wanted to get out and above where they can follow. We're at forty-two thousand now."

"That was an interesting ride. You come out of the astronaut program?"

"Yeah, I pushed the envelope a little—astronaut, no, when the colonel grabbed me, I was flying a F/A-18 Super Hornet off the Nimitz. Good thing Vinnie wasn't driving. He's flying copilot. He's navy, but we let him carry our bags. He's a former Blue Angel. Has this thing for barrel rolls, even barrel rolled an H-53."

"That's a helicopter."

"Damn, if it isn't. How's the colonel doing?"

"He's asleep. The medic is watching him."

"Yeah, he gets bored if he's not flying. Mr. Spade, the Venezuelans have a bunch of Russian Sukhois and some of our F-16s. This is a good bird, but it can't out fly those things, no matter how much I bend the wings."

"They're supposedly grounded by orders of the vice president, but you may want to keep an eye open."

"I'll keep both open. We'll call you when we're a few miles out." The phone went dead.

"Did I hear something about barrel rolls? I want off this thing if he's going to do barrel rolls," Liz said.

"No barrel rolls. Try to get some sleep."

I called the president to fill her in, mostly to assure her we hadn't started a war with Venezuela.

"Sam, I hope you're not calling from the local hoosegow."

"No, ma'am. We're on our way back. We have an injury, so we're going direct to MacDill. Probably a couple hours before we land."

"How bad? And who?"

"Colonel Barrett. He's the aircraft commander. He sustained a severe laceration during the mission."

"Is he going to be okay?"

"Yes, ma'am. I think he will be fine."

I was half asleep when Liz's phone rang.

"It's a FaceTime from Emily"

"Wonderful."

Liz plugged in one of her earbuds and handed the other to me as she answered, "Hello! Hi, sweetie."

"Mom, please, please, please, I need to borrow your car. We've been trying to FaceTime you—" Emily squinted into the phone. "Where are you?"

"I don't know why it wasn't working. Your dad always says it's atmospherics, so let's go with that." Liz hit mute and leaned over. "What do I tell her?"

I shrugged and turned over.

"You're a big help." Turning back to Emily, "We are on a plane." Liz said.

"I can see that. I thought you guys were sailing. That's all you talked about is going sailing. Now you're on some private jet. What's with that?"

"We went to Boston for dinner and a show, now we're flying back to the vineyard—Yep, stayed overnight. By the way, we'll be home for a couple of days to catch up on some business. Probably tomorrow, then back to the boat. Okay, thanks for checking in. Bye."

"No, mom wait, can I borrow your car? The oil light came on, and I had to put mine in the garage."

Sighing, "Emily, we have told you before: in that car, you have to check the oil every week. Yes, you may borrow the car—I love you, too." Elizabeth hung up.

"Our children are smart, too smart."

Yawning, "That's your fault." I rolled over and closed my eyes.

Steele, Liz, Emily, and Brad sat around the same low coffee table between the couch and the fireplace. Sable had regained her perch on the raised hearth.

"Mom, when we were talking the other day, it looked like you were on one of those big private jets."

"I told you we flew to Boston."

"So, mom, you holding out on us? Do you have a rich paramour?" asked Brad.

"Yeah, mom, do you have a rich paramour?" I asked.

Liz reached over and picked up Sable, holding her close and scratching her ears. "If I had a rich boyfriend, I would be playing Baccarat in Monte Carlo, not Scrabble with a furry-faced cat."

"Well, it looked like the plane was flying north. If you were coming from Boston, the airplane would be going south." Emily said.

Trying to bring the inquisition to an end, I said, "Are we playing Scrabble or not?"

"Dad, you're trying to change the subject."

"Then, dear, perhaps you should take the hint," Liz said.

Emily looked at her mother defiantly but said nothing more.

CHAPTER THIRTY-SIX

American Airlines Flight 4342

Economy class has its perks. No one is shooting at you, and you are generally not flying on your ear. A fortnight after our trip to the steamy jungles of Nicaragua, our White House debut, and our sojourn in sunny Venezuela, we were flying American Airlines back to Martha's Vineyard and the *Pinafore*.

I was puzzling out *fortnight*. It's a great way to say two weeks, but no one ever uses it except the Brits, but they say stuff like *car park*, *lift*, and *biscuits*. Whoever heard of a chocolate chip biscuit? I thought about introducing *fortnight* into the rest of my conversations. Maybe I could wait until another cocktail party and use it with *abaft*. I spent the rest of the flight trying to use abaft and fortnight in the same sentence.

We landed at Rhode Island International Airport, which used to be T. F. Green International Airport. To us old salts it's always been Providence, and pretty much the only way to get to Newport if you're flying. Lieutenant Gallagher was waiting for us at the gate.

"Should we be glad to see you?" I asked. "And how did you know we were on this flight?"

He grinned, "Thought I would give you good people a lift to Newport."

"That's very kind of you, but we have to get to our boat. It's on Martha's Vineyard," I replied.

"No, it's not."

"No, it's not what?" I asked.

"Your boat. I had a couple of my boys bring it back to Newport for you."

"How thoughtful," I could barely restrain my annoyance.

"Needn't bother to thank me. You know those guys mostly grew up on the water, but they enjoyed sailing a fancy yacht. So anyway, I thought I'd give you a lift in return for you telling me about Fuentes. We found him, you know. Came ashore at Crescent Beach."

"No kidding. He was dead?"

"Oh, yeah, took a round in the chest. Dead center, great shot. The coroner said it was a strange wound, very similar to the ones he saw when he was in the military. Said it looked as if the man was hit with an armor-piercing round."

"No kidding."

"Oh, and the Massachusetts State Police called and let me watch while they looked around an old shed at the Martha's Vineyard Airport."

I would have bet there was more to that story, but I wasn't going to ask.

"Found some dead guys there, too. Must have been a real shoot 'em up. They had all been killed with a .45 auto, except one who was killed with a .308—that's a 7.62 NATO round. I know that because whoever did the shooting didn't police his brass, so my guess is it probably wasn't a professional job. The guy with the .45 must have been a hell of a shooter. The dead guys were armed to the teeth, but they never fired a shot."

"No kidding," I said. Next time I was going to use "Really?"

"Kid you not. Do you two have any checked baggage?"

We made the short walk to Gallagher's unmarked and illegally parked cruiser. Liz got in back. I rode shotgun.

"The local sheriff was particularly annoyed."

"The sheriff was annoyed?"

"Oh yeah. His office is about three hundred yards away from the building where all the shooting took place, and nobody heard a thing. Pretty funny, really," he chuckled.

"Guess that would be annoying," I said quietly.

"Yeah, so I figured you should maybe avoid Martha's Vineyard for a while. That's why I asked my men to get your boat. You know— just in case you knew anything about the shootings.

"Another thing," Gallagher said. "When I was over at the airport, I was talking to the woman who runs the office. Nice lady. Anyway, she said some pilots were hanging around for a few days. She said they were really upset, said someone stole their airplane. You fly by any chance?"

"Uh, no, I don't have a pilot's license," I replied.

"Yeah, well the people who purloined—I like that word, never get to use it much—the people with this purloined airplane, filed a flight plan for Miami, but the plane never landed there."

"Really, well I don't have a pilot's license."

"Yeah, you mentioned that. By the way, one of my men found this in your sump filter." He reached in his shirt pocket and handed me a flash drive.

"My boys tried to use the shower, and the drain backed up, so, being the real handy types, they went poking around and found that," nodding toward the flash drive in my hand. "Nothing on it, though, other than some stuff about an apartment building and a blank real estate contract. Makes you wonder why someone would put a flash drive in a shower drain?" He eased the car into the southbound traffic on I-95. "Oh, and your air conditioner doesn't work," he said.

"Yeah, I know. It hasn't worked since I bought the boat. I don't care much for air-conditioning, at least on a boat, so I just forgot about it."

"Well, my men looked into that, too. Like I said, they're really handy. Guess why it didn't work?"

"Why?" I sighed.

"Seven hundred and fifty thousand dollars, all in one-hundred-dollar bills, were crammed into where the pump and condenser were supposed to be. What do you think about that?"

"How do you suppose that got there?" I said.

"So, you did know it was there. We thought we should put it in a safe place for you, so it's in the evidence room back at the station."

"We found it just before we left for Block island. I assumed it was the reason for the assault and break-ins. I didn't want to bother you." I said.

"Well, as far as we can tell from the serial numbers, it's clean, not even any sign of drug residue. Guess you know most circulated money has some traces of drugs, but this was clean, *laundered,* you might say."

We dropped south onto Route 4. No one said anything for a while. Eventually, I said, "Lieutenant, neither Elizabeth nor I knew that money was on the boat—"

"You got to wonder what all the fuss was about. To me, it doesn't seem like enough money to get all these people killed, but people have been killed for less. Maybe they were looking for something else, like maybe a flash drive,"

Gallagher said. "Anyway, I think you should pay my guys for the delivery and repairs."

I hadn't known Gallagher long or well, but he didn't strike me as a dishonest cop, and I had grown to respect him. But I had been wrong before. Perhaps he was part of the local mob. I had a momentary vision of ending up in an abandoned stone quarry, *under the quarry*, to be exact. Perhaps I had seen too much television.

"How much?" I asked.

"Oh, I don't know. I think a hundred fifty bucks would be fair."

"One hundred fifty dollars?"

"Yeah, that's fair. Unless you think it's too much?"

"No, no, I don't think it's too much," I stammered. "I don't have that much cash on me. Maybe Liz has some," I said, turning to her.

"Oh, I couldn't take cash. We don't want any hint of impropriety, do we? A check will be fine," he said.

"Ohhh, I get it."

"Thought you might," he grinned.

"Get what?" Liz asked.

I ignored her question for the moment, and said to Gallagher, "Problem is, I don't think our attorney would like me relinquishing any chance of a defense for an illegal search."

"Well, there is no law that says you can't keep money in your air conditioner. And there won't be any charges, even from the Massachusetts boys. Seems all those guys they found in the hangar had nasty criminal records. They figure it was a drug deal that went bad," he said. "Though, I would stay away from that sheriff for a while.

"You know there's been a good bit in the paper lately about Reynaldo Vicente. Actually, his dad mostly, President Escudero. You know, the president of Venezuela?"

"Yes, we heard."

"It seems he resigned, then disappeared. Said his disappearance had something to do with a large amount of misplaced government money, and maybe he was mixed up with drugs. Think Reynaldo was involved with that? Paper said Reynaldo was in prison awaiting trial for racketeering."

"Okay, lieutenant, if anyone has the need to know or at least the right to know, I guess it's you." I told Gallagher what had occurred during the last several weeks. Liz interjected with the details I overlooked or forgot. She expounded on my prowess as a pilot, dutifully forgetting to mention that I almost crashed on takeoff and our brush with incarceration in a federal jail.

I told him that Ed worked for the special committee inside the State Department called SPEOPS. I told him what little I knew about Dr. Pérez, the dentist who really worked for the DGI. I explained that Ed, thinking Pérez was with the CIA, ferried arms throughout the Caribbean for him.

"Pérez left Cuba in the 1986 power struggle, showing up in Miami for a while. In time, he went to work for Estéban Morales as his chief of security. Over the years, he eventually became Morales's second-in-command and bookkeeper." I explained to Gallagher how Pérez controlled all the bank accounts and operations and knew where all the skeletons were buried. He knew everything.

"When Estéban Morales was killed, supposedly in an auto accident, Pérez discovered the truth that it was an assassination ordered by President Escudero. Shortly after, Pérez disappeared with all the cartel records. Trained by the DGI, Pérez could be a nasty guy, and he was loyal to Morales. Escudero was scared to death that Pérez would show up on his doorstep one day and put a bullet in his head. Plus, Pérez had access to all the secret bank accounts, the only access to more than five-hundred million dollars."

"No wonder all of these guys were after you!" Gallagher said.

"Yeah, no wonder. Besides the money, the person who controlled the flash drive controlled the drug business, controlled President Escudero and, in turn, Venezuelan policy. Of course, Escudero and Reynaldo were trying to save the money *and* their collective asses.

"SPEOPS picked up some intel on the files and Pérez. The president's chief of staff and the undersecretary of state decided it was the perfect opportunity to get the administration out of a potential fiasco with OPEC. Because of his past connection, Ed was assigned by the State Department, actually SPEOPS, to find Pérez and the files. Ed had been tracking him for months with no luck until one night, by chance, he saw him in a Fort

Lauderdale restaurant. Ed followed him to what is now our boat, but Pérez disappeared again."

"So how did you get involved?" Gallagher asked.

"Pérez's wife or sister, we're not sure which, was living in Fort Lauderdale under the name of Vasquez. When Pérez disappeared, she wanted to sell the boat and leave the country. When Ed discovered the boat was for sale, he called me and talked me into looking at it. I liked it and bought the boat from Mrs. Vasquez, the same boat Pérez used as an office. Of course, I had no idea about the sorted history of the previous owner. Then for a lack of a better word, Ed conned his way into our vacation."

"Some guys have all the luck," said Gallagher.

"Yeah, he mentioned that. When I arrived in Newport, Ed sent some of his State Department guys, and Reynaldo sent his thugs, supervised by Fuentes, to the boat—"

Gallagher interrupted, "You mean they were working together?"

"No. Obviously, they were looking for the same thing but working separately."

"How did Reynaldo know about the boat?"

"I guess he had people looking for Pérez, too, but they didn't know Pérez by sight, so I think they were watching Ed. It wasn't a secret Ed was looking for Pérez. Anyway, they probably discovered the boat the same way Ed did. When I brought the boat here to Newport, Reynaldo sent his goons to find the records."

"So, everyone was trying to find the flash drive."

"They didn't know it was a flash drive."

"They didn't know the files were on a flash drive?" Gallagher asked.

"No, they weren't sure what they were looking for. They just assumed the records had to be on the boat. Coincidentally, Ed was the reason we found the drive. As you mentioned, the shower drain didn't work. When we opened the sump to clean the filter, we found the flash drive. I replaced it with one of mine, thinking if it were found, whoever discovered it would have to leave the boat to verify the contents. The operative words being 'leave the boat.'"

"What did you do with the real one?" Gallagher asked.

"I took one of the five or six flash drives I use to store my records and electronic charts. I removed the self-sticking label and stuck it on Pérez's flash drive, then threw it back in the navigation desk with the others. The label I used said Narragansett Bay."

"So, you hid it in plain sight. Very clever," Gallagher said.

"Yeah, me and Edgar Allan Poe. I always kept a blank flash drive in my pocket in case one of Reynaldo's goons showed up. Since Liz had a copy on her computer at work, I wasn't too worried if I had to destroy the original."

I told him how Silvers and Collins essentially threatened to impound *Pinafore* and detain us if we didn't help them trap Reynaldo so they could leverage his indiscretions into a seat at the OPEC conference.

"As it turned out, State got more than they hoped for."

"You mean President Escudero," said Gallagher.

"Yep, they were surprised President Escudero was as involved as he was. They had no idea he was running the operation. They thought it was Reynaldo. Escudero, by the way, is a real piece of work. As far as I can tell, he doesn't have scruple one."

The lieutenant listened patiently, asked a few more questions, and said, "When I saw that flash drive and my men told me where they found it, I knew it was the key to this mess."

Route 4 turned into U.S. 1, then we drove east on Route 138. We crossed the Jamestown Bridge, and, in a few minutes, we were on the Newport Bridge above Narragansett Bay. Out my window, I could see Newport Harbor and, in the distance, across Rhode Island Sound, almost on the horizon, I could detect the ghost of Block Island.

I remembered when I sailed into Narragansett Bay. I remembered the daydreams of *Pinafore* challenging the greatest of the great in sodden, windswept battles for the Auld Mug. I had my battle at sea, not against aquatic leviathans, but against avarice and evil, not with tools of grace and beauty, but with ugly tools of death. I was victorious. Was there a message in the reality versus the dream? Possibly, but there had always been greed and evil. If there was a message, it was too abstract for my brain to work out.

"By the way, a couple of FBI agents were looking for you."

"God, now what," I said more to myself than to Gallagher.
"They stopped by your boat looking for you, so Charlene sent them to me."
"Charlene?"

"Yeah, she's the assistant dock master, little blond girl. You must have seen her around."
"Sure, I know her. Nice girl, going to the University of Virginia. How did she know to send the FBI agents to you?"
"She's the chief's daughter. I'm her godfather," Gallagher said.
"She's the police chief's daughter?"
"Yeah, she and my kids grew up together. Newport is a small town once you take away the tourists. We pretty much look after each other. Looks as if Charlene took a fancy to you and told her dad about the problems you were having, so he asked me to keep an eye on you. I guess mostly you can take care of yourself."
"What about the FBI agents?"
"They were delivering a box at the particular request of FBI Director Douglas. I had to sign my life away before they would leave it."
"A box?"

"Yeah, my guess, it contains firearms."
"Oh, the president said she would try to take care . . ." I mumbled.
"Who?" Gallagher asked.
"Nothing. If it's okay, I'll pick up the box tomorrow."

I didn't want the Colt around for processing by the Vineyard Haven Sheriff's Department. Gallagher said I was in the clear. I fervently hoped he was right, but I was giving considerable thought to tossing the barrel into the ocean. A new barrel, extractor, and firing pin should take care of the ballistics issues.

"Brought it with me. It's in the trunk," Gallagher said.

Graciously declining our offer for an early dinner, Gallagher dropped us off at the wharf, and shortly we were back aboard *Pinafore*. Gallagher had somehow requisitioned our old slip, probably with Charlene's help. It was good to be home.

CHAPTER THIRTY-SEVEN

Newport, Rhode Island, aboard Pinafore

The next day, we deposited our windfall in the bank. We gave Gallagher a $150 check with the notation, "For boat delivery and repairs." We made donations to the Newport Police Relief Fund and the Coast Guard Foundation.

Liz and I spent the next several days on the waterfront walking, holding hands, dining, and last-minute shopping. During our last day in Newport, we resupplied the boat and checked gear and equipment in preparation for the sail back to Annapolis.

The air conditioner still didn't work.

Pinafore and I returned from a short jaunt to the fuel dock to top off the fuel and water tanks. We were just in time to help Liz with a load of groceries and goodies. She helped me tie up the boat, then I helped her get the packages on board and stored in preparation for the next day's voyage.

"Honey, I'm going to grab a shower before dinner."

I was sitting in the salon watching TV when Liz walked out of the shower, her hair wrapped in a towel. She sat next to me.

"You seem to be naked," I said.

"I know. I didn't feel like getting another towel wet." She crossed her legs and began to dry her hair.

At the bottom of the TV screen, a banner read *BREAKING NEWS* . . . *after Escudero stepped down and subsequently checked into a mental health facility, the new president of Venezuela met with President Jackson . . .*

"Looks like we made the news," Liz said.

"For the last time, I hope."

"You looking forward to the trip home?"

"I guess. I feel like we never had our vacation. Anyway, the weather is supposed to be good."

"Do you realize this will be the first time just the two of us have sailed Pinafore?"

I turned off the TV. "Well, remember the captain is always in charge." I walked over to my clothes locker. I pulled out a yellow polo shirt and some khakis and laid them on the bunk.

"That's what the captain thinks. Okay, I'm going to get ready. Where we going?"

"The Cooke House." I said.

"Yummy." She threw her towel in the hamper and walked into the master stateroom, then turned, "Should I wear underwear tonight?"

I smiled, then followed her.

Our last morning in Newport was one of activity and anticipation tinged with that small amount of apprehension that always comes with the foreknowledge of a blue water sail. Weather reports were forecasting ten to twenty knots from the northwest with a chance of some late afternoon thunderstorms. Overhead, there was nothing but bright blue skies and puffy clouds. The morning air was crisp with a slight hint of fall, which was just around the metaphorical corner.

Getting ready to leave or, as we salty types say, "making preparations to get underway," I was topside securing gear, removing the sail cover, and uncoiling the sheets. Liz was below, going through her preparations. I jumped from the boat to the dock and bent down to disconnect the shore power. The dock trembled, and I turned to see a man standing a few feet away watching me.

"Good morning," he said cheerfully.

"Good morning," I replied.

He was pleasant looking, even handsome, with a Mediterranean appearance, but with a pallor as if he was ill or had spent much of his time indoors. In his late sixties, perhaps older, he had a full head of gray hair, still black in places. He was well dressed in charcoal-gray slacks, a dark-blue or black knit golf shirt, and expensive black loafers. He spoke with a slight accent I couldn't place.

"I'm sorry to disturb you. I was admiring your beautiful boat," he said.

I thanked him, "Do you sail?" I asked.

He replied with some sadness, perhaps regret, "Yes, but it's been a long time." He paused, then brightening, "Your boat looks like a Passport topside, but it has the hull of an Alden or perhaps a Bristol."

"You are a sailor," I replied. "You're correct. She has features of all three. We have only owned her for about six months, so I'm afraid I don't know much about her pedigree, but she's fast and stiff. I've had her in some sixty-knot winds, though not intentionally," I chuckled. "Are you thinking about getting back into sailing?"

"Perhaps now that I have retired."

"Oh, what kind of business were you in?"

"Many things over the years, but I was an orthodontist for a time."

Liz came up from the cabin, looked over, and smiled, "I thought I heard some voices."

I stood and gestured my hand toward Liz, "This is my wife, Elizabeth. Liz, this gentleman is—I'm sorry, sir, I didn't get your name?"

The man smiled warmly, "Pérez. Dr. Alberto Pérez."

AUTHOR'S NOTE

Except for the wartime flashbacks, bits of history, most of the restaurants, geography, and some trivia, the novel is researched make-believe. All the flying, ship handling, rigging, sailing, equipment, and navigation is autobiographical, including the night landing at Dulles. The takeoff, as described at the airstrip in Nicaragua, was real, but in a different airplane. The firearms used in the book are real and the descriptions of their use are more than possible by a competent marksman. The aircraft and the military equipment are real, as are some of the military units.

The chief character and I share some traits and values. Unlike the hero, I rarely drink, Blanton's or otherwise, preferring iced tea and chocolate milk. I have an aptitude with firearms and think sailing is a gift from the Almighty.

The character Elizabeth is a tribute to my former wife. The two women are quite similar in their beauty, uncommon skills with firearms, languages, and proficiency with the violin. They also share a penchant for clothes and shoes and an oblivious disregard for hot water on a boat.

The character Ed is a composite of two of my oldest friends and their exploits. They are both from the Palm Beach area, about the same age, pilots, of Italian descent, and graduates from universities in D.C., yet they have never met.

Pinafore is also a composite based on two of my favorite sailboat designs. Emily, Brad, and Sable are based on their namesakes.

ACKNOWLEDGEMENTS

Those times when I thought this project was ill-advised or an unending chore, there were always family and friends who pushed me back in the right direction.

To Katherine Shemeld, for the endless hours of proofreading, your spelling and grammatical prowess, and your unceasing support in all things. Thanks, mom, you are the best!

To Elinor Shemeld, for suggesting and encouraging me to write my first novel. I hope you enjoy this second adventure.

To Ed Galasso and Sam Aurilio, for your forty-year friendships. You guys lived a life of fiction; the backstory for Ed Colombo is a composite of your adventures. Ed, thanks for teaching me to fly.

To Mayne Berke, for his encouragement, support, ideas, and editing skills. Mayne, you, sir, are a true gentleman.

To Carder Nastri and Daniel Macabuhay for their notes and ideas.

To my family and friends, for their support and encouragement.

ABOUT THE AUTHOR

Robert Shemeld is the author of the award-winning political thriller, *The Narraganset Files.* He has been published in a national magazine and has written numerous scripts for television dramas.

A former Marine and decorated combat veteran, he was a private investigator for fifteen years and a real estate broker, developer, and financial consultant for twenty years. An avid sailor, he favors New England, Chesapeake, and Caribbean waters. Robert is also an accomplished skeet and sporting clays shooter.

Mr. Shemeld used experiences from these and other vocations to give his writings its labyrinth of realistic narratives, persuasive conflict, and vivid images.

He makes no pretension to being a pilot, however; he has flown solo many times, and it is with some pride he alleges his landings equaled his takeoffs.

Mr. Shemeld is a native and resident of Northern Virginia. He attended American University in Washington, D.C. He is the proud father of three. His last nautical venture was a four week navigation of the Intracoastal Waterway.